Escape from Ephesus

Escape from Ephesus

A Novel of the
1st Century

by

Lance Webb

THOMAS NELSON PUBLISHERS
Nashville

Scripture quotations within the main text are the author's own paraphrase or free translation.

Scripture quotations set off from the main text are from *The New English Bible.* © The Delegates of the Oxford University Press and the Syndics of the Cambridge University Press 1961, 1970. Reprinted by permission.

Published in Nashville, Tennessee, by Thomas Nelson, Inc. and distributed in Canada by Lawson Falle, Ltd., Cambridge, Ontario.

Library of Congress Cataloging in Publication Data

Webb, Lance.
  Escape from Ephesus.

  1. Onesimus, Saint d. 109—Fiction.   I. Title.
PS3573.E195605   812'.54   80-21306
ISBN 0-8407-5742-5

Printed in the United States of America
1 2 3 4 5 6 7 — 96 95 94 93 92 91

To Elizabeth,
my joyful, loving companion
and partner in "The Way"

Contents

—Part One—
Slave of Philemon

*T*he spacious atrium of the elegant house of Aristarchus, treasurer of the province of Asia, was filled with the singing of birds. To Gaius, the only son of the family, their music sounded more like the chattering of so many feathered demons.

Gaius, his two younger sisters, his mother, Alcestia, and his father, Aristarchus, sat in stoic despair at breakfast. Their food was untouched. Gaius and his sisters waited in silence for their father to reveal what he and their mother had known since late the night before.

"Something terrible must have happened, Father!" Gaius exclaimed as he studied his father's face. Aristarchus's finely chiseled features were drawn with an inner pain, and his eyes were red and swollen.

"Yes, Gaius, something is very wrong." He spoke in a voice drained of emotion. "The blow I had expected has fallen. For weeks I have feared it. As your mother knows, I have sought in every way to prevent it."

Gaius looked at his mother and saw that she too was suffering. Her lovely face was whiter than usual. She held herself erect, and Gaius was moved to see the message of silent encouragement she emanated to his father as he revealed the appalling news.

Gaius and his father had spent many hours talking about the risks of his political position. Step by step Aristarchus had reported the clever ploys of the ambitious and unprincipled Vitellius Lucas and the long-term enemy, Lamachus. Now Gaius understood that they and their followers had at last won the confidence of the Emperor Claudius. The first nine years of his rule had been a respite after the brutal tyranny of Caligula. But during these years Lucas and his fellow conspirators were spreading lies against the governor of Asia as well as against Aristarchus and the other provincial officers loyal to him. With flattery and rich gifts they had succeeded in their foul plot.

"But . . . but what can they do to our great governor, Father?" Gaius asked. Gaius Flaccus had been his hero for as long as he could remember. Indeed, he had been named for this man who had ruled the province of Asia with skill and fairness for fifteen years.

"What can they do? My son, they can and have secured an imperial edict for Gaius and his fellow officers, including me, to be arrested and sent to Rome for execution as traitors to the Emperor." He continued in grief and resignation, "Under this edict they will see that all four of you, my dearest ones, are sold as slaves and that our beautiful home and my property are confiscated, with the proceeds going to build a palace for the new governor."

Gaius, mature for his seventeen years, gasped as he took in the full import of these terrible words. But taking the cue from his mother, he held his head erect and asked as bravely as he could, "Surely, Father, there must be some way for you to escape. Can't . . . can't something be done to save Mother and my sisters from becoming slaves?"

"How I wish there were, Gaius!" His father managed a smile at the unselfish bravery of his young son. "Immediately upon the announcement last night at a special session of the provincial assembly, Gaius Flaccus was seized and forcibly taken to his own guardhouse, while several of his officers and I slipped out of the room. Of course, we were spotted and followed by the legionnaires now at Vitellius Lucas's command. I rode my horse here as quickly as I could only to find our house already under guard. The centurion in charge stopped me at our gate and informed me I would be permitted to remain in my house overnight, an unexpected generosity not granted to our governor. The centurion was sympathetic to me, since I had been generous to him in the past, but he warned me against any attempt at escape. At my earnest request he promised to wait until the ninth hour this morning. In a few minutes they will be coming to take us away."

Alicia and Julia were crying softly, as their mother held them. *Her face is even more beautiful in the strength of her remarkable courage and love!* Gaius thought.

For a few moments he stood silently. Then with boyish abandon, he ran to his father's side. Stifling a sob, he said defiantly, "Father, I will do all I can to help Mother and the girls. But what a dreadful fate!"

"Gaius!" With affection his father grasped the strong young shoulders of his son. "Hold your head up, Gaius, and accept whatever comes."

The sound of horses' hooves on the road to the house broke into their tearful attempts to strengthen each other. Alcestia took the two girls in hand and brought them to her husband and son. Before the centurion knocked on the door, she had embraced each of them, and with an inner confidence amazing to Gaius, she promised, "We will live through this. And you, dear Aristarchus, will be bold and courageous." With a defiant gesture of pride she embraced him again. "I would rather be you than to be in the place of either of these perfidious villains who betrayed you."

Then turning to the weeping girls who clung to her, "Remember, Alicia and Julia, all your father and I have taught you. . ."

The doors to the atrium gave way, and the soldiers strode in to do their tasteless duty. Aristarchus was manacled and led out to mount his horse. As he rode away between two of Caesar's minions, his family waved and waited helplessly until they were loaded into an oxcart headed for the auction block in the Agora of Ephesus.

The three furlong journey from their home to the Agora seemed interminable to Gaius as they jolted along in the cart, escorted by three members of the Roman Legion on horseback. As the four held on to each other, Gaius and his mother tried to comfort the girls.

Though it was still early, the news had spread quickly, and some of their friends and neighbors came out on the streets to watch the sad caravan pass. A few spoke words of encourage-

ment. Most were silent with pity on their faces. As the cart
rumbled through the poorer sections of the city, there were
taunts and jeers for the family of the former treasurer of their
city, once rich and respected, now brought to the lowest state
possible. The humiliation Gaius felt was equaled only by his fear
for their fate.

At last the oxcart entered the Agora, a huge square encircled
with shops and stalls and a raised platform in the southeast
corner for the slave market. On this spot, for hundreds of years,
every morning and late afternoon an auction of the choicest
slaves in Asia had been held. At the rear of the platform were
booths where the slaves to be sold that day were prepared for
the market and confined until their time of sale approached.
The legionnaires and the driver of the cart stopped before the
largest of the booths, where they met the coarse slave trader,
Grannius. As a representative of Vitellius, the new governor of
Asia, he would be the person responsible for the sale of Aristarchus's family as well as the families of the other deposed officers
of the former regime. He was also auctioneer for most of the
sales being made that day.

"Here they are, Grannius, the family of Aristarchus! You
ought to get an excellent sum for each of them, especially this
young man." The praefectus accompanying them pointed to
Gaius. "He is not only well-formed physically, a handsome lad,
as you can see, but he has a brilliant mind. He has had the finest
of educations in philosophy."

"Yes, Lamachus told me all about them. The woman, Alcestia, is just in her prime. She ought also to sell for top price, with
her training and ability. And these two girls. . ." Grannius
lifted Alicia and Julia out of the cart. "Stop your sniveling!" he
ordered.

Then addressing these high born, well-dressed unfortunates,
he spoke gruffly, but not unkindly, "Your fate is a hard one, but
not unlike thousands of others over the empire. My advice to
you is to bear with this matter. No more tears, now, at least
while you are being presented for purchase. The more smiles
and the happier attitude you take, the more likely you are to get

a kind master. The life of a good-looking, well-educated slave is not such a hard one at that. Better fate than that of your father who goes to Rome to have his head chopped off!"

The girls burst into tears again. The rough slave driver, realizing he had said the wrong thing, sought to quiet them. "There, there . . . don't cry. Look at your mother and brother—try to be like them . . . and you'll come through well!"

Turning to his female helper, he commanded, "Here, Fannia. Take these girls and their mother to their booth and get them ready. I want to present them for sale this morning."

Then to Alicia and Julia, he spoke with a solicitude that surprised Gaius and his mother, "Now, don't you bother your pretty heads about anything. You are going to find a good home. So do your best to cooperate with Fannia—you are too lovely not to be loved!"

Before Gaius could say more than a crisp "Good-bye! May the gods go with you!" his mother and sisters were led into an adjoining booth. It was the last time he would ever see his sisters.

"Now, Son," Grannius turned to him, "let's go in here and have a good talk. I hate like the very *diabolus** the fate that has brought you and your family here. I have always highly respected your father, but it is not my job to change your destiny as a slave. It is my task to see that you are sold to as fine a master as may be ready to pay the best price for you within the next few hours."

They entered the main booth and sat down as Grannius drew from Gaius the story of his education, his years in the School of Phineas, the beloved philosopher-teacher.

"I am told that you were the most well-liked boy in your class, known for your nimble wit and amiable disposition. With your ability to write excellent Greek and to teach others, you should make a good candidate for some wealthy merchant who needs a

---

*Devil.

clerk, or who wants some intelligence in his household and business. Now, let's get ready."

Grannius insisted on stripping him of all his clothing—much to Gaius's embarrassment—without even a loincloth remaining.

"Come on, be sensible, young fellow. After all, any buyer of a slave needs to know his health and physical quality! You have the body of a Greek god, so let's show it. Now I want you to sit in this seat and pose as a thinker with your chin in your hand . . . that's it . . . Look as pleasant as you can . . . Hold it . . . That's fine!"

After reminding the youth in several ways that he must be sold to the best master on the basis of the use of his mind as well as his muscle, Grannius left him. Gaius tried to calm his tumultuous thoughts and prepare himself for the best showing he could make. He recalled Phineas's favorite saying, "Whom the gods would destroy they must first make mad."

"Well, I will not give them that opportunity. I will keep my sanity and find the wisest of masters and if possible persuade him to buy mother and my sisters also."

With this resolution the strong-willed youth waited until Grannius returned.

Gaius would never forget the burning shame of that hour, as he struck first one pose and then another to the vulgar words of Grannius. Shrewdly the merchant sought top price for the slave, not unaware of a larger share of the commission for himself. As auctioneer, he heralded not only the boy's strength, and classic profile, which he said "resembled the god Apollo," but dwelt long on his education under the well-known Ephesian philosopher Phineas.

As Gaius stood on the block, looking out over the customers assembled from all parts of the empire, he quickly discerned one man who stood out from all the rest. Tall, olive-skinned, with black hair and a high forehead, he seemed to Gaius to be the most intelligent in appearance and the most likely to be kindly in attitude. Silently, Gaius invoked the help of the gods to be sold to him.

The auction opened with a large bid by this very man. Gaius was encouraged as Grannius whispered to him, "His name is Philemon, a wealthy silk and woolen dyer and merchant of Colossae. He told me before we began the auction that he desired someone like you who could be trained to take the place of his aging clerk and who could teach his young daughter the best of the philosophers. I gave him a strong word for you. So, be alert."

Suddenly, to Gaius's consternation, Lamachus, already touting his new title as treasurer of Asia, put in a higher bid. Evidently he was finding great fun in bidding for the son of his old enemy. He and Aristarchus had been competitors as merchants and politicians in the city of Ephesus for many years. Gaius's father had stood for moderation and honesty in government, and the two had fought bitter political battles before the assembly. The spoils of possessing the handsome young son of his defeated enemy spurred Lamachus on to much higher bidding than he thought the young slave worth. The bidding was sharp. But after it passed six hundred denarii, Lamachus refused to raise the bid. Gaius held his breath until, with a sense of relief, Grannius gave him over to Philemon for six hundred and fifty denarii.

As Gaius descended from the block—Grannius handing him his clothes—Philemon met him and expressed his pleasure in owning him. As they left the slave market and walked to the stall where Philemon's silk and woolen wares were displayed, Philemon said frankly, "Young man, I believe you are the answer to my greatest need. I desire the best teacher possible for my daughter, Helen, who is just ten years old. I am impressed with your achievement as the finest student in the class of Phineas. He was my teacher also in my youth. I am glad to find you, because I believe you have the ability to be trained to take the place of old Polectus, yonder." He gestured to an aged slave who was counting money and keeping the records of the sales transactions.

"I regret the misfortune that has come to you and your family. I have been an admirer of the deposed governor and of your father. But since this tragedy has happened to your family, I am happy to be your master. I value my teaching under Phineas above money; it is fortunate that you will be able to give my daughter and other members of my familia the advantages of your training.

"I have decided to give you a new name. I know your father named you Gaius after the former governor. To keep that name, I think, would be too painful a reminder."

So Philemon named his new slave Onesimus (from the Greek word meaning "useful") and introduced him to Polectus and the other slaves helping with the marketing of the beautiful purple fabrics.

"Master, I have but one request," Onesimus pleaded anxiously. "You have been so kind in purchasing me and now in your welcome to your familia. I am grateful. Only one thing I ask, humbly and with all my heart: Please return to the slave auction and consider purchasing. . ." He choked with emotion as he realized the words he was using, "To purchase my mother."

Even as he spoke, he thought hopelessly, *Who could do that?* But regaining control of himself he pressed the issue further, "Surely, Master, there is no more beautiful and helpful person in Ephesus or all of Ionia than my mother, Alcestia. She would bring much skill and knowledge to your household. She could preside over the preparation and serving for your social occasions. And, Sir, she would be so helpful to me—with her presence, I know I could serve you far better. And if it is not asking too much, I have two sisters, also. What a joy if these of our family could be together!"

Philemon thought for a few moments.

"Onesimus, your mother could be a valuable addition to our household. But as for your sisters, that is not a practical possibility."

"Thank you, Sir," Onesimus said, bowing humbly. "I wish you success."

As Philemon returned to the slave auction, again the young new slave, Onesimus, prayed to the gods. Though sadly disappointed that Philemon would not consider his sisters, he was glad his mother might be coming with him.

The aging Polectus, wrinkled and gnarled with the years, put his hand on Onesimus's shoulder.

"My young friend," he spoke warmly, "I am happy to welcome you to our familia. You will find Philemon an unusually kind and considerate master. He owns a prosperous business dying silk and woolens with the purple for which Colossae is noted. There is a good spirit among most of the fifty-nine slaves who do the work in his business and household. Now while we wait, you might as well begin to be 'useful' to him."

Managing a smile, Onesimus sat down by Polectus and at his direction began to help count the money that had been paid for a large purchase of cloth.

Soon Philemon returned with Alcestia. Smiling even in her tears, she embraced her son. More tears were shed in that minute than through all the cruel hours preceding.

2

$\mathcal{O}$nesimus found his new life as Philemon's slave both galling and interesting. The merchant was an unusually good master as slave owners go. Holding the power of life and death over his slaves, able to use them or abuse them in any way he desired, he had never been the brutal, sadistic tyrant that many masters were. Polectus soon became Onesimus's counselor and friend and shared with him the confidence he had in their master.

"Only a very few times can I remember Philemon venting his wrath on a slave who crossed him or failed on the job. He always insists on hard work and punishes laziness or ineptness. He is fair. He attempts to treat us all justly according to the best principles of the philosophers. Since you are a philosopher," the old man said with a grin, "you will get along well with him, if you do what he asks. Better than most of us, who, to tell the truth, get a little tired of his quoting some of the favorite thinkers when he gives us a lecture!"

"That is my good fortune, Sir," Onesimus said. "As you know, he has asked me to take two or three hours every day to teach his daughter all that I can of the great Greek and Roman philosophers. I can see that he is no ordinary dyer and merchant. He tells me his father sent him as a youth to Pergamos, 'The Athens of Asia.' He was educated in the best gymnasium of the city. He says he took advantage of what I have heard is one of the best libraries in the world."

"I know nothing of that," Polectus said, shrugging his shoulders, "but I well remember him as a boy, who after coming home spouted the words of a dozen philosophers I had never heard of."

"I can tell you it is a great place to learn to think. I spent a year there myself when I was fourteen. Indeed, our Master and I both studied under Phineas, who is now very old but sharp as ever."

They were working together in the office where the records of Philemon's business were kept. Much of Onesimus's time was spent under Polectus's direction. But he enjoyed most the hours spent with Helen, a pretty little girl who reminded him of his sisters. She still played with dolls and at first found it hard to concentrate on learning to read the musty papyri in her father's library. It was Onesimus's first attempt to be a teacher, and he found it fascinating to watch her mind awaken and develop.

In spite of his bitterness over the brutal separation from his father and sisters, he found his new life stimulating and, with the counsel and companionship of his mother, bearable. He thanked the gods many times for the good fortune of sharing his humiliating servitude with her. In the evenings when the work was done, Philemon was gracious enough to permit them to be together.

As Onesimus had promised, Alcestia proved invaluable to Philemon and his wife, Apphia—a diminutive and quiet, but kind woman, whom all the familia respected. Helen also deeply appreciated Alcestia, who was teaching her the social amenities of her position in preparation for being mistress of her own family in a few years. All of the slaves admired Alcestia, with a minimum of jealousy, because of her strong character and accomplishments. She had been put in charge of the dinners and other social occasions which Philemon provided as a leading citizen of Colossae. With her kindness and wisdom she had naturally become friend and confidant to several of the female slaves as she directed the serving of food and the care of the linen and cutlery.

"You remember Plato's description of our souls which your father often talked about," she said one evening at dusk as the two shared together the cool of the *hortulus*, the small garden reserved for the use of the slaves.

Onesimus nodded. He recalled his father's quoting from Plato's *Phaedrus*, describing one of Socrates' dialogues.

"Socrates pictured our souls as being like two horses and a charioteer—the one horse white and good, with a lofty neck, needing no whip but only direction; the other 'a dark, crooked lumbering animal . . . filled with insolence and pride . . . hardly yielding to whip and spur!'

"Son, keep in mind that your soul must drive both of these horses, even in this our difficult time. There will be plenty of occasions when the proud horse will have to be held with a sharp rein. But if you are patient and persistent, the strong white horse of wisdom and prudence will enable you to control the other horse within the most creative ways possible. This is the real test both of us must face during these coming months and years."

"But, Mother!" Onesimus responded vehemently, "even if you are right, I cannot and will not force myself to accept my servitude gladly! But I will try to keep the dark horse of insolence from getting the upper hand. That would be both foolish and dangerous."

As the weeks and months passed, Onesimus found times when the dark horse of pride within him almost ran away with his soul-chariot; for he and his mother, in spite of their superior training and position in the familia, were treated much as the

other slaves. There were amenities, such as the *hortulus*, but
the complete separation of the slaves from Philemon's own
family continually galled the young aristocrat.

"I can spend hours with Helen poring over the philosophers,"
he complained to Alcestia, "but I cannot walk with her in the
garden or even speak to her any other time except in passing.
And Archippus, who is my own age and is being taught in
Pergamos just as I was, is as distant from me as if I spoke a
different language!"

Archippus, the only son of Philemon, had been home for
several days from his studies in Pergamos. He was tall and
lithe, with dark complexion and black hair like his father's. Only
once did he stop Onesimus to inquire about Helen's progress.
He spoke matter of factly, though not unkindly.

"Father tells me that Helen is enjoying your teaching, especially now that you have been reading Plato's *Phaedrus* and
talking about the meaning of true love."

"Yes, she is beginning to show some interest. In the beginning I thought I would never get her away from her dolls! But
Plato and his interpretation of Socrates' dialogue with Phaedrus did it."

"Well," Archippus responded with a hearty laugh, "I suppose
sooner or later a pretty girl like Helen is going to get interested
in *amor* and *eros*."

Onesimus was about to respond when Archippus turned
away and without a word strode on to the stables where his
horse was waiting for his morning ride.

"*Iste Diabolus!*" Onesimus exclaimed under his breath. "He
treats me as though I were a thing to be bought and sold and
used!"

But as he entered the library, where the little girl on her way
to becoming a young woman waited, he cooled his ire and
resumed her lesson on love. *I will have to tell her about the two
horses and the charioteer that are her soul*, he smiled to himself
as he sat across the table from Helen.

She was at the awkward age, but still possessed the charm
and great curiosity of a child that made his hours of teaching

enjoyable. She had dark brown hair like her mother's, with big hazel eyes and an infectious laugh that exploded when she found something funny, as she often did, in the philosopher's teachings.

Indeed, Onesimus mused, *she has made me dig deeply to understand some of the abstract and often obscure writings of our great old thinkers.*

Onesimus had good reason to hold the horse of pride and rebellion in check, for on a few occasions during the months that passed he saw Philemon angry. In spite of his philosophical mind, there were days when the master was depressed and irritated. Then his justice was heavy-handed indeed: Instead of the usual five lashes for impertinence, one might expect fifteen, and for the more serious offense of theft, a difference of one to ten days of solitary confinement in addition to the usual forty stripes. Onesimus was not tempted to steal. As yet he had not thought about to what lengths he might go in order to be free, but he did have great difficulty, as Alcestia had said he would, with his pride.

Several times it would have been so easy for him to have been even more insolent and impertinent than the poor slave he had witnessed receiving fifteen lashes. But he managed to hold his hot Phrygian temper in check. The months passed with outwardly good relations between him and his master.

3

*F*or nearly seven years, Onesimus spent two hours each day with Helen under the watchful eye of an old slave chaperon nearby. Onesimus watched Helen grow from an awkward little girl of ten into a remarkably beautiful, well-formed young woman. She was drawn to him as any young girl would be drawn to a personable Greek nobleman whose mind was as sharp as his body was supple and handsome. During their many hours together, he shared with her not only the thoughts of the philosophers, but also his own experiences. Her maidenly sense of justice and right was thoroughly aroused over the injustices to which he and his family had been subjected. Her warm sympathy mixed with adolescent admiration easily became a sure tonic for his often drooping spirits. Yet the intimate relationship thus begun was for Onesimus also a source of deep tension, frustrated desire, and bitterness.

During the fifth and sixth year of their teacher-pupil relationship, something more was added. Her large brown eyes filled not only with admiration, but with the same kind of longing he had for her. At last he felt so drawn to her that when she glanced into his eyes, he sometimes became embarrassed even as he tried to concentrate on Plato or Aristotle. Her charms grew with each lesson as he observed every graceful movement. He occasionally glimpsed the fair symmetry of her limbs through the white silk chiton worn so loosely that it revealed as well as concealed. Once as she stood near him pointing to the words of Aeschylus on the parchment he shared with her, he felt the touch of her breasts soft against his shoulder.

Did she share the tension mounting within him? He could not be sure. But from that day on, as he came away from each lesson, the touch of her moist hand, the movement of her delicate limbs, her wistful look filled him with a burning desire that only his condition as a slave prevented him from expressing. Her looks and warm gestures of thanks each time as he left the library always sent him into an ecstasy of yearning that made him hate his slavery and his master the more.

His feelings were complicated by the addition to Philemon's familia of Leslia, a curvaceous Nubian slave girl. She had been purchased at a slave auction in Ephesus together with her brother for their skills with the loom. However, it soon became obvious she had skills other than weaving. She often entertained the other slave girls by telling of her experiences not only with the more handsome male slaves, but even with her former master and his young sons.

"You had better watch her," Alcestia warned Onesimus affectionately, "she obviously has her eyes on you."

Indeed, from the moment she saw him, Leslia was drawn to him, and several times at meals she maneuvered her way to a seat in front of him. She used all her wiles to lure his attention from his food—and from the affection he was known to have for Helen. The relationship of Helen and her slave-philosopher had long been the object of much conversation among the other slaves.

"How can you stand it every day sitting so close to her?" his friend Pythius asked with a grimace. "I don't think I could endure it without exploding—such ripe fruit beside you and you can't even touch it."

"Be still!" Onesimus responded angrily and hastily left the room.

"Well, don't be so high and mighty," Pythius flung after him. "If Helen is out of reach, forget her—Leslia is following you around like a hungry bitch in heat. What's the matter with that?"

Though he was angry because Helen's name was used so irreverently, Onesimus began to ask himself the question constantly as he left the library after his study sessions with Helen. *Why? Why can I not break these bonds and be a man—free to love? Why can I not gather her into my arms and tell her how I feel?* It was all so hopeless and impossible!

Helen realized the dangers and hopelessness of their situation as well as he did. One day as they came into the library for their daily hour with the philosophers, they faced each other with full realization of their unspoken fear. At breakfast news had come to Philemon's familia concerning one of Helen's best friends, Aurelia, a young woman her age, who had been caught by her brother Horace in the arms of one of their father's most valued slaves. Helen listened to Archippus tell the horrifying story with much the same reaction as Onesimus, who had heard the story from the lips of several slaves including his mother.

"Horace was so angered," Archippus described the outcome, "that he exploded in fury and beat the slave into bloody unconsciousness. Aurelia has been banished to her room for an entire month."

The Philemon family expressed their shock as they listened. Helen burst into tears.

"I am sure it was but natural for Aurelia to be attracted to the young slave," Archippus said as he put his hand on hers, trying to bring her comfort. "He is indeed a handsome specimen, with blond hair, blue eyes, and fair skin. Doubtless his name Angell comes from his origin in Britain, where he was captured and sold by one of the conquering generals. Our friend Urbanus must have paid an unusually high price for him. He has been used to drive the carriage pulled by the two Arabian horses we all admire. I suppose everyone has marveled at Angell's adept way with the horses and his elegant appearance on the driver's seat. But it is too bad for him that his good looks and proximity to Aurelia brought him to such reckless folly."

"Yes," Helen said, still in tears, "Aurelia loves horses. I have visited her several times, and we watched Angell groom them at the stables. He taught her to ride, and once or twice I was present during one of her riding lessons. She is such a happy, active person! I wonder, was it at the stables where . . . where . . . they found them together?"

"That is right, young sister," Archippus answered affectionately.

"But what else did they do to Angell?" she asked with concern.

"He received forty stripes with a bull whip and his fair face was branded on both cheeks. His ear lobes were severed and, in addition, he is serving two months in solitary confinement with only bread and water."

"This may seem rather severe," Philemon observed, "but a presumptive slave taking liberties with the daughter of his master must be dealt with in severity and with immediacy, or none of our daughters will be safe!" As he spoke, he turned tenderly to his own daughter. "I am sure, Helen, that we have nothing to fear from Onesimus in this regard, for the punishment meted out to Angell will not be lost on our intelligent philosopher." He said it with a smile and walked over to put his hands on her shoulders. "At least if he were tempted, the fate of Angell should keep him within the bounds of his position."

Helen blushed but said nothing. Later when she met with Onesimus, she began to form in her own mind the nature of her feelings toward him and the dangers both of them faced. As they sat down for the lesson in philosophy, she could not help asking with flushed face, "Did you hear what happened to Angell and Aurelia?"

"Yes," Onesimus responded with bitterness. "What a fool he was not to recognize his bonds!" Then seeing her eyes fill with tears he added, "Don't worry your pretty head, my dear little pupil. I know my place, and I will keep it." He said it grimly. Both of them knew that any other relation between them would be foolhardy.

The moment the lesson ended, Onesimus strode to his favorite tree in the *hortulus*, his pent-up bitterness near to an explosion. After a few minutes of intense struggle in the solitude of the garden, the white horse within him emerged strong enough to take him on the road to prudence.

Yet the next morning he was even more bitter. As he left the atrium where, because of the heat, he had held his philosophy class with Helen, his love for her and his frustrations were at the boiling point. He almost stumbled over Leslia as she stood in the doorway leading to the outside garden. Her chiton was entirely open in the front, and the vision Onesimus saw as she smiled invitingly led him impulsively to smile back.

"How about a walk by the river?" he said without thinking.

"Why not, my gallant philosopher? You must be good at something more than those dull old thinkers whose words you teach our little mistress every day." She said it teasingly as she took hold of his hand and walked into the sun-drenched garden. Each step they took, he was more and more conscious of the closeness of her seductive dark skin and the gaiety of her dancing black eyes. He was too frustrated to answer her and too passionate to reject her. Why not? She was young and clean and sweet-smelling from the rose perfume she had used lavishly after a bath in the slave quarters.

Onesimus was glad. For the moment he would acknowledge the truth of Aristotle: "Argument about matters concerned with feelings and actions are less reliable than with fact." Wordless, they walked into the berry bushes and trees beside the river.

I know the facts of my situation, Onesimus thought. *I am a slave and I can't argue with that.* With his passion uppermost, his philosophy and thoughts subdued, he led her into the cool depths of the well-hidden spot under a huge myrtle tree where he had often gone to think. But now to feel and to act!

Scarcely a dozen words were said as their passions were expended. They lay back on the grass, looking up at the trees, hearing the song of the skylark. For the moment, Onesimus felt relaxed and at peace. It was a rare and good feeling.

As they returned to the slave quarters by the back way, Leslia chattered on about how much better it was to be in Philemon's familia than in the rigid and brutal place from which she and her brother had come. Onesimus listened with some dismay as she told how her former master had beaten her and decided to sell the two of them after she had seduced his youngest son. She told about her experiences with a laugh, as though the gods had rewarded her for her skillful exploits with the untouchable son of her hated master.

Onesimus was annoyed. Even as he admitted the pleasure of her warm body and the release of his tensions, he realized that not one word of love had been said. All had been accepted as a matter-of-course experience. Now the words of Heraclitus, Plato, and some of the Stoics came back to him. They agreed that the love which made life worth living was something more than passion. While he admired Leslia's luscious offering, he despised her for an empty mind that could think only of the pleasure of the body. The remembrance of his love for Helen returned, and he hurriedly told Leslia good-bye, his body satisfied, but his mind in a storm.

No wonder, he mused, *I thoroughly enjoy my time with Helen. What a contrast between the two girls! What a fine woman Helen has become. At sixteen, she is mature physically with all and more for my eyes and heart than Leslia. And mentally—she is far in advance of her years—more perceptive than any other woman I have ever known, unless it be Mother. I have always been able to sit and talk things out with her. She, too, knows the philosophers.*

As he thought of his mother he realized this was part of the reason he loved Helen so much. He admired and respected her keen mind and radiant spirit as well as her entrancing body.

"Helen is more intelligent and a better thinker than ninety-nine out of a hundred matrons in Ionia—and even the men!" Philemon boasted a few days later as he spoke with Onesimus concerning her progress. He gave a generous slap on the shoulder of his young teacher-slave.

"You have helped her develop her mind, and for this I am grateful."

Onesimus thought this was indeed an unusual thing—for a master to express gratitude to his slave. But Philemon was no usual master.

"She needs to know more thoroughly the truly great philosophers," Philemon said with fatherly concern. "I don't think she is quite ready to graduate from the school of Onesimus, and she has a lot more to learn before she enters the school of matrimony!" he finished with a wry smile.

Onesimus's response was visceral. His whole being was repelled by the knowledge. *Of course, Helen will marry not too long from now,* he thought, *but she is not for me.* He shuddered as he recalled Angell's fate and barely heard as Philemon continued.

"Alcestia also has been a good teacher. She has shared with Helen many of our manners and customs and, above all, the duties and privileges of an Ionian matron that will help her to make some man a very good wife."

Then his master said something that instantly alerted the

young slave's enthusiasm. "Onesimus, I want you to accompany us on our trip to the Agora in Ephesus for our spring market You need the experience with Polectus in conducting business transactions. Besides, Helen is going, too. Perhaps while we are on the journey you can help her better understand my favorite Ephesian philosopher, Heraclitus. He may have been critical of the ancient gods, but I like the gruff old thinker's honesty. What he says about the superstitions of their worship will be a good antidote for the excitement a sixteen-year-old girl might feel in the presence of Artemis and her lusty priestesses. But," and here he laid his hand on the arm of his young slave, "can you, riding on an ass, teach her the noble thoughts of Heraclitus?"

"Surely, Master," Onesimus answered with a trace of mockery, but caught himself just in time, "the back of an ass is the best place to learn patience and humility."

"I know nothing more desirable for a woman than patience and humility," Philemon responded, and they both laughed while Helen watched from the courtyard.

$\mathcal{T}$ he sunrise came clear and beautiful as Onesimus prepared to join the little caravan headed for Ephesus. He had told his mother the evening before some of the turmoil of the last few days and his mixed feelings as he thought of a return to Ephesus.

"Son," she laughed, "you must take the bad with the good. Life's joys are always mixed with sorrows and vexations. You must embrace the joy and learn to face the humiliation. Do not several of the great plays of Aeschylus teach us that we may learn more from our hours of humiliation than from the hours of easy success?"

So Onesimus put a few extra tunics in his leather bag and walked out to take his place on an ass. *How appropriate,* he thought, *an ass for a slave is even more fitting than walking.* He was surprised to see Helen also mounted on a donkey complete with cushioned saddle. *Safer than a horse,* he thought, his spirits rising. *After all, how could she learn philosophy riding a horse, with the teacher riding an ass?*

"Good morning, lovely pupil!" he said, returning her smile.

Onesimus surveyed her with delight as he thought of the hours they would ride together. He noticed how saucily she sat with her legs covered from the sun by a thin white silk chiton. Over the chiton, covering her shoulders, was a silk chalmys. Around her head was wrapped a tan-colored burnoose. She wore the chiton and chalmys loose with a bandeau beneath her breasts that held the garments in place. She was a flashing exhibit of the brilliant work of her father's weavers and dyers, all very safe and proper.

As they rode along the rich grassy banks of the Lycus River, fragrant with oleanders and fir, even the donkeys sensed the joy of the occasion. Onesimus would have given anything to have changed places with her donkey—but now he put all her radiant charm and his own passion out of mind as he said, "Are you ready to hear about an old philosopher's ideas on a beautiful morning like this?"

"Why not?" she answered coquettishly. "With you as interpreter, even Heraclitus might not be so bad!"

"Actually, this morning is a good illustration of his main point," said Onesimus, "which is, to paraphrase a little wildly, 'if you can stand the jolting of the donkey's jiggling, you will get to Ephesus by and by.' "

He explained to her how Heraclitus taught of the blessed unity that binds all things in the universe by a balance between the conflicting pull of opposite tensions.

"Life is good only through the wise acceptance of the conflict," he lectured as didactically as any teacher, "but when one manages to get rid of tensions, he finds nothing left but stagnation and death."

"Well, by the beauty of Venus, I don't want to die, so I had better make all the conflict I can," she challenged.

"I don't think that is what Heraclitus meant," he countered, "but I'll admit it sounds that way when he says, 'Strife is justice, and all things come into being and pass away through strife.'

"He even said that Homer was wrong in praying that strife might cease among gods and men. He said that Homer did not see that he was praying for the destruction of the universe; for if his prayer were heard, all things would pass away."

"That sounds to me as if he meant we should make all the strife we can if we would find a good life," she parried. "If so, the person most filled with conflicts is the most just." She laughed triumphantly as if she had cornered him.

"You're quite sharp this morning," he said affectionately, "but don't start any more trouble. You'll have enough as it is. Heraclitus did not mean that strife in itself is good, but what comes out of it is, if we use it rightly. We can die either way, by bitter conflict with the conflict or, worst of all, by just giving up. What Heraclitus meant, I'm sure, is that we must stay awake; for he said," and he smiled as he again assumed the role of lecturer, "and I want you to memorize these words, 'The waking share one world, but the sleeping turn aside each into a world of his own. To give up to injustice is to die indeed.' "

"Is this the way you stay so much alive, Onesimus? You haven't given up to the injustices that make you a slave, have you? And yet are you not fighting them so bitterly that you may die?"

Her frank words pierced him. How well she understood the problem, including his passion for her and its hopelessness. It was not Heraclitus with whom she was arguing, but Onesimus.

"I'm not dead yet," he answered stubbornly, as he tried to restrain his feelings. "I was born to be free; yet I am still a slave. I want revenge for the evils done my father, and here I am bound to a cloth and dyer merchant. I have as little chance of regaining my father's position as that rabbit does—" he said, pointing to a scared rabbit who bounded out of the bushes into which one of the dogs had stuck his nose. They both laughed.

"What are you going to do, Onesimus?"

"Well, I am not going to give up. Someday—someday—I shall be free." He said it quietly, deliberately, so the master traveling just ahead could not hear. "But, Miss Philosopher, we must get back to Heraclitus. He said, 'The sun is new every day. The sun will not overstep his measures; if he does, the Erinyes, the handmaids of justice, will find him out!'

"So I will try to act like the sun for a few more days."

That ended their conversation. He yearned to tell her of the biggest conflict of all; the tension of love unfulfilled, how he longed to hold her in his arms and tell her how beautiful and perfect she was. But he did not dare.

The caravan followed the path of the Lycus until it merged with the River Meander, and for the remainder of the day Helen and Onesimus dealt with other phases of Heraclitus's philosophy. While they rode alongside the winding flow of the river, Onesimus's desires were excluded at least from conscious consideration. But that night after the evening meal, while the twilight settled over the camp beneath the pines, Onesimus forgot his caution. With the freedom permitted a trusted member of the household, he said to Philemon, "Sir, your daughter and I need more conversation on one of Heraclitus's teachings that has baffled her—the idea that peace and well-being come only through a proper balance of the tensions of life."

Philemon laughed appreciatively. "That is one of the philosopher's most difficult points, my boy. If you can help her understand that, you will have done a good day's work, indeed."

"By your leave then, Sir, we will sit under that large tree by the river for a few minutes, and I will do what I can to make it clear." Philemon was glad to see his young slave so devoted to the art of teaching. He loved his daughter and wanted her to have the best in life. Unlike most of the men of his time, he believed an intelligent woman could profit greatly by learning the art of good living from the study of philosophy.

Teacher and pupil walked over to a grassy spot under a huge walnut tree by the dark waters of the river; meanwhile Philemon busied himself with arrangements for the camp. For a few minutes Helen and Onesimus were silent as they watched the water making faint ripples over a large rock in the riverbed.

"See that stone?" he asked her. "It does not prevent the river from going on its way. Soon that water will be free to join the sea. I trust all your conflicts produce no more strife than that rock does. But sometimes. . ." and here he spoke with bitter emphasis, "sometimes, there is no way to freedom."

She gave an understanding nod. Again there was silence. He knew this was no way to teach Heraclitus. But with the full moon rising just over the trees, this unexpected nearness to her made his head light. The fantasies of the past year were overtaking him. His hunger for her made him forget the facts and act his feelings. Before he knew what he was doing, his hand found hers. The touch sent the blood coursing even more wildly through his veins. But then it was too late.

Onesimus felt the angry hands of Philemon. Jerking him to his feet, the older man knocked him sprawling into unconsciousness. In a few minutes he came to, gasping for breath. He had been strangled almost by the water old Polectus, by Philemon's command, had poured over him. As his eyes began to focus, he saw Philemon towering over him, his face suffused with rage.

"Get up, you dog!" he commanded. "Who are you to take liberties with my daughter? I ought to kill you and be done with it . . . after all my kindness you take advantage of me." His breath was coming in short gasps. He roared, "I'll whip you until you learn your place. Bring me the lash!" And then, remembering Helen, he turned and commanded roughly, "Go to your tent! Have you forgotten that when a freewoman gives herself to a slave, she may be made a slave herself?"

"Forgive me, Father," Helen was weeping. "We meant nothing wrong, believe me. . ."

He snorted and motioned her away.

As Helen ran in terror to the tent, her father turned back to Onesimus. The muscular young man stood unsteadily, but the look of defiance in his eyes angered Philemon the more. Without waiting for the lash, the master struck another blow under the chin that sent the slave spinning against a tree. "I'll teach you your place, you dog! You cursed *diabolus!*"

This time, Onesimus fought to remain conscious. Philemon was irrational, but Onesimus would not beg for mercy.

"Sir, I know my place." He found his voice, weak but firm. "I meant no offense to your daughter or to you."

Onesimus would never forget the horror of that evening. His head ached, and hatred mingled with fear made him shake as he leaned against the tree, waiting for the punishment. Polectus stripped him of his tunic and tied him to the tree. Philemon said nothing, but took the lash. Five, ten, twenty, then forty times he applied it. His arms were strong, and each lash brought blood. With each blow the resolve mounted in Onesimus. He would get even! And he would be free, someday! At last it was over. Blinded with blood and gasping with pain, he crumpled to the ground as Polectus released him.

"Stand up, if you can," Philemon ordered with something of his normal kindness. He had worked off his anger, and his tone was calm, controlled.

Onesimus slowly pulled himself up on one knee and with the help of Polectus stood upright, his nerves and muscles still quivering from the beating.

"If I had not paid such a large sum for you . . . and if you had not been such an obedient and helpful servant and such an effective teacher for Helen, I would have killed you. But this is the first time you have been unfaithful. Let it happen again, and I will kill you with my own hands!"

Onesimus looked at Philemon's hands and believed him.

"I have planned for you a good life—better than any slave in Ionia. You are soon to become my chief clerk, with whom I trust my accounts. There are dozens of worthy slave girls from whom you may choose a mate, so put it out of your head that you may ever come near my daughter again. I understand Leslia is mad about you. Take her or whomever you want. Promise to keep your place and do your job as well as you have until tonight, and you will have a happy, comfortable life, the envy of most freemen."

Onesimus struggled with the hatred that called for defiance and the common sense that told him he could do no other than accept his lot. Philemon was offering him an enviable position for a slave.

"Sir, I understand my position," he found himself saying in subdued tones, "and I am grateful for all your kindness. I shall never forget how thankful I was that you outbid my father's old enemy and were kind enough to take my mother also. You have been a good master, and tonight I was not thinking rightly. Indeed I had stopped thinking, but I did not mean to be disloyal. Please believe me, I would never do anything to harm or discredit your daughter. It won't happen again."

"I believe you, Onesimus," Philemon said, "and I trust you will not forget this evening. But for now there will be no more lessons with Helen. Polectus, take care of his wounds." He turned and walked back to his tent.

Onesimus stood motionless, still stunned by all that had happened. The kindly old Polectus put his arm around him and led him away, saying quietly, "Take it easy, young fellow, you've got too much to lose by not keeping your place."

"My place, my place!" Onesimus could not help but growl. "What do you mean, 'my place'? Do you think I am going to be a slave forever?"

"What else can you be, my son?"

Onesimus ground his teeth in frustration as the old slave dressed his stripes and left him alone. Polectus's words remained in his mind for several hours as he tossed in his blanket on the hard ground. His bleeding back was sore and his mind was sour. "My place . . . my place . . . what else? What else?" It seemed to him that life was closing in on him.

As the first gray streaks of dawn appeared over the trees, the little caravan was well on its way west toward Ephesus. Helen was riding with her father; Onesimus and Archippus rode together. Archippus, whom Onesimus envied with all his heart, had just returned from a long visit to Rome. There he had found a dependable market to which purple cloth from his father's mill could be sent, with expectancy of larger profits than could be gained by depending entirely on the sales at Ephesus and Smyrna.

As they rode for several days together, the two young men found much in common. Archippus evidently agreed with his father that prudence as well as compassion should dictate a more lenient punishment for Onesimus than what Angell had received. Both Archippus and Onesimus loved the Stoic philosophers and disagreed heartily with the Epicureans. The Epicureans were too pessimistic, too hopeless to suit either of them. And yet, Onesimus found himself at times on the side of Epicurus.

"To gain happiness by ridding ourselves of hope is a foolish endeavor, indeed," Archippus said their first day together, "for no matter what the pleasures of the moment, unless there is hope for the future, there is no meaning to the present."

Onesimus agreed with a bitter grimace, and as they continued the discussion through that day and the seven days that followed, the talk led easily into his own conflicts. Archippus enjoyed a testing of wits and liked this intelligent young slave with whom he was becoming acquainted. With growing maturity, he abandoned his superior aloofness.

"How can I as a slave, with no hope for freedom, enjoy myself in the fine opportunities your father offers me, when the very things I want most are impossible?" Onesimus asked. "I suppose a slave could be a better Epicurean than a Stoic—live for the pleasure of the moment even if there is no hope for the future!"

"Never!" Archippus answered heatedly, "for Epicurus banishes all the gods and makes as if death and what comes afterward is of no importance. Do you want to be nothing more than a stone? That is all existence was to him—a human stone, drinking, eating, copulating and making merry, for today is all the time there is. No, if you have faith in the gods, you will be free, even though you are a slave."

"How can that be?" Onesimus snorted indignantly. "The gods are corrupt and cruel, like men. How can faith in jealous old Zeus, for instance, make any difference in my life? Or the lustful and lewd Artemis? How can faith in gods such as these make man any better?"

"If you are willing to be initiated into the Eleusian mysteries, as I have been, you will be sure of eternal life," Archippus said with a glow of pride. For an entire day they talked of this strange belief which was so popular among Greeks and Phrygians but about which Onesimus knew so little. To him it seemed just another way of temporarily escaping the injustices of life rather than doing something about them.

Archippus believed that there must be some god better than the ones they knew. "After all, how could my ideas of goodness be better than those of the gods? There must be an unknown god who is wiser and more dependable than the ones we have been taught. That is the reason I am so interested in the Eleusian mysteries. For there you may be cleansed of your evil and drink of the blood of this unknown god. Somehow you find the strength and courage to be unafraid in the face of all the evils and sufferings and death that come. Maybe it is this unknown god who gives courage."

Onesimus thought long about this conversation that evening, rolled up in his blanket under the stars. He wondered what this great Unknown might be, even as the same questions kept running over in his mind: *What is my place? What else is there for me? How can I live with hope for the future when I am a slave and the one person I love better than life is denied me forever? How can escape through a life of momentary pleasure be a substitute for the experiences which I can never know—the freedom to love and live with one whose mind and body were so clearly meant for me?*

He had seen Helen's face only twice since his flogging, and then her eyes were downcast, never seeing him. It made him furious . . . but then, what else . . . what else?

The fury was growing like a malignant tumor within him. As he saw the moon beginning to hide itself behind the trees along the river, the fury leapt inside him. Like one demon-possessed—maybe he was possessed by a demon, he would have to consider that possibility—he rose and shook his fist at this unknown God.

"What right do You have to permit such injustice?" he raged.

Exhausted, he fell into an uneasy sleep.

—————————————————————————————————*5*

Philemon's caravan moved slowly into the lush green plain where the Cayster River emptied its water and silt into the Aegean Sea. Located near the best harbor in all Asia, the marble columns and graceful buildings of Ephesus stood white and gleaming in the sunshine.

As a boy accompanied by his friends, Onesimus often had ridden along this road lined with mulberry and fig trees, the connecting highway between the Cayster and Meander River valleys.

What a difference then and now: riding into his beloved Ephesus as a hopeless slave on the back of a jogging donkey, with the knowledge of his hopeless passion and the memory of the unjust and degrading treatment meted out by an otherwise kind master. He recalled the freedom and happiness of his boyhood rides on the white Arabian horse his father had given him on his fifteenth birthday. Then he had looked with disdain on the dust-begrimed slaves who rode in similar trains from the four quarters of Asia. Once he had followed a caravan down the marble road into the Agora and watched them place their wares on display in one of the rented stalls. He recalled the distaste he had felt as he watched several young slaves, sweating and grim-faced, unloading merchandise. The master had

stood over them with whip and curses to direct the arrangement of huge piles of silk and woolen cloth—the same task he
and Philemon's other slaves would soon be undertaking.

As he passed each familiar landmark on this well-
remembered road, the events of his childhood and early youth
came up to taunt him: the gymnasium where he had spent his
early days in school, the leader of his class, liked by his
classmates and admired by his teachers for his nimble wit and
quick insights; the city hall where his father's office as treasurer
was now occupied by another; the majestic entrance to the
amphitheatre where he had enjoyed so many plays, presented
by the best actors and mimes in all the Roman Empire; the
brothel which he and his companions often passed, strongly
tempted but never quite getting up the courage to enter. He
smiled as he thought how innocent and carefree he had
been.

Now the caravan entered the Agora, a huge square encircled
with shops and stalls. There on a raised platform was the slave
market where he had suffered his first taste of humiliation and
mortification. This morning as he rode by the place of his
degradation, the auction had just ended, and the slaves with
their new owners were being tagged and some manacled to
prevent escape. A few were political captives, as he was, being
sold for the first time. Cries of sorrow over separation of
brothers, sisters, and parents rent the air. The scene brought
recollections too painful for Onesimus, even seven years later.
His pulse pounded wildly when he saw the very booth where he
had sat before the auction and the spot on the block where he
had been sold as a slave.

A wave of nausea came over him as he remembered all too
well the disgrace and ignominy of that hour—and now the
greater humiliation of an impossible love and the paradox of the
kindest, yet most cruel, master! He struggled to still his pulse
and hide his feelings from Archippus who rode beside him; he
measured the strange conflict of gratitude and rebellion that
made him hate so bitterly, even as he loved, the man who had
paid much more for him than a slave such as he would ordinarily

bring; the same man who had beaten him so unmercifully a few nights before.

Then he recalled how one of the first things Philemon had done after purchasing him was to give his new slave a new name. Onesimus smiled as he realized he had almost forgotten the name his father had given him.

I was and still am Gaius! he exclaimed to himself. *But the name 'useful' is one I have tried to live up to, as I promised. For Philemon's kindness and the fate from which he rescued me, I truly desire to be useful to him. And especially after he listened to my plea to purchase my mother. I could not have endured these years without her.*

A lump of gratitude filled his throat as he visualized the way Alcestia had borne the parting from her husband and two daughters with a calm bravery which would have made the best of the Stoics proud. When the legions of Vitellius Lucas took over the province on that bleak day, she was the guiding spirit that sustained her husband and wrought courage out of the despair in the hearts of her son and weeping daughters.

Yes, he had reason to be grateful to Philemon. Yet the past few days, the injustice of it all, had changed gratitude into unmitigated bitterness. As Philemon's caravan stopped in front of the stall where he was to display and sell his goods, it was all Onesimus could do to keep back the tears of hatred and frustration.

Since the caravan had camped just outside Ephesus the night before, it was only the last hour of the morning by the time their goods were prepared. Setting up shop was always exciting, and even Helen remained to help in arranging the displays. Grudgingly, Onesimus could not help but note the difference in Philemon's approach to the business and that of the cruel master he had watched as a boy. Philemon needed no whip, and there was little or no ill feeling visible among his slaves.

Buyers soon crowded around to feel and examine the merchandise and to haggle with Philemon and Archippus. Polectus sat at a table to count the money and make change. Onesimus had been assigned to help him in order "to learn the tricks of the trade." Within the first hour one of the largest buyers had picked out some of the choicest cloth and was making payment.

"You will be useful to me some day even as Polectus has been for so many years," Philemon said kindly. Then, with a warning gesture and stern voice, "Learn as much as you can, Son, help all you can, and you will make up for what happened a few days ago."

Onesimus's face turned crimson, but he held his tongue and put all his attention on the complicated business of trading with various coins, jewels, and foreign letters of credit which passed through the expert hands of Polectus. Onesimus helped to count and record. Here was much to learn, and although he was good in mathematics, he had to concentrate all his attention on the transactions.

Suddenly he and Polectus realized that the crowd of buyers had almost disappeared. The noise of their bargaining had ceased.

"What on earth has happened?" Onesimus asked.

Polectus smiled indulgently as though used to such distractions. "See that crowd surrounding the little Jew over there on the Agora rostrum? There are our customers, plus the customers of almost every other merchant in the Agora. Would you like to go listen to what the fellow, Paul, is saying? Our last customer told me that, though Paul is a Jew, he is quite upsetting to most of the other Jews—not only because their business is interrupted, but because he claims to be a follower of one whom he believes is their Messiah. This Messiah was a Galilean, Jesus of Nazareth, a poor ex-carpenter rabbi who was crucified by the Romans under Pontius Pilate at the insistence of the Jews only a few years ago. This Paul teaches daily in the lecture hall of Tyrannus, since the Jews have driven him out of their synagogue. Occasionally, he comes to the Agora to speak to all who will listen."

"It would be interesting," Onesimus responded, "but. . ."

"I'll stay and watch the money and the shop, if you want to go hear him," and with a broad smile he added, "You will be in good company, for I see that Philemon, Archippus, and Helen have all three succumbed to the wiles of this fiery little orator."

Onesimus approached the crowd with great curiosity. What did this man have to say that was so attractive to the hardened merchants from all over the world? He edged through the throng until he was close enough to get a good view. He certainly did not look impressive: about five feet and five inches tall, bushy-browed, baldheaded, bow-legged, with a face wrinkled and tanned as though he had been exposed to desert heat and mountain cold for many years. His eyes were diseased, but fiery. He was not an orator in the affected, grandiose manner Onesimus associated with the speakers he had heard charm crowds. His words were simple but eloquent, clear, and distinct, as though he had a most important message and wanted everyone to hear and understand. There was something arresting about his voice. He spoke with utter conviction: "I did not know Jesus as a man," he was saying as Onesimus first began to understand his words. "I believe He is the Christ—the Messiah—the one sent from God to reveal the mysteries hidden from the ages. I learned of His life story through His disciples who were with Him. They tell how He proclaimed the good news of the kingdom of God that has come very near to all of us. He revealed this kingdom in His loving acts of healing and help for the poor, the lame, the blind, and the discouraged. No man ever lived or spoke as He did. But it was not my privilege to know Him then. Neither did I see His crucifixion though I did witness Him in His glory after He arose from the dead—as upwards of five hundred of his disciples did."

At this point, several in the crowd began to whisper to each other. "The man is crazy," muttered a fat Cretan merchant standing near Onesimus. "No man ever rose from the dead."

Paul now spoke with such intensity of feeling that Onesimus was moved in spite of his own intellectual abhorrence of such a claim: "He made Himself known to me as one born out of due time. So I must make clear to you, my friends, that the good news I bear is no human invention. The story of what He did is

known to many who knew Him in the flesh—but the great
meaning of His life and death I did not take from any man: I
received it through a revelation of Jesus Christ Himself.

"Some of you have heard what my manner of life was when I
was still a practicing Jew; how savagely I persecuted the church
of God and tried to destroy it, and how, in the practice of our
national religion, I outstripped many of my Jewish contem-
poraries in my boundless devotion to the traditions of my
ancestors. But, then in His good pleasure, God, who had set me
apart from birth and called me through His grace, chose to
reveal His Son to me and through me, in order that I might
proclaim Him among the Gentiles."

Knowing glances were exchanged by some of the men around
Onesimus, but they were brought again to attention as Paul
stood at his full height and cried with great intensity of feeling:
"There is one thing I am sure—in Him all the fullness of the
Godhead dwells. He who created us, and in whom we live and
move and have our being, He has made Himself known in the
love and truth of His eternal Son—this man Jesus who loved us
so much that He was willing to die on the cross of shame and
share His good news with all men. In Him is freedom from fear
and guilt and evil. Death and the wickedness of the world are
conquered. He is alive from the dead! Peace and joy, freedom
and love are the gifts of His Holy Spirit given to all who believe.
I call on you to repent and believe in Him. And welcome to the
Hall of Tyrannus where I will speak more concerning His
Kingdom."

A strange stillness settled over the motley mass of traders
and artisans from all parts of the Roman world. Paul had spoken
in the common Greek language known to some extent by them
all. Onesimus was deeply interested in what he heard, but like
most of the others he rejected immediately the possibility of a
man's rising from the dead. As the crowd dispersed, Onesimus
saw to his amazement that Philemon, Helen, and a few others
followed Paul toward the lecture hall. Evidently they intended
to hear him further.

Archippus had been directed by his father to return to their shop. Seeing Onesimus, he motioned to him and they walked back together.

"What did you think of him?" Archippus asked quietly. He remembered that their talk along the Meander had dealt with the very same subjects Paul was considering with such assurance.

"From what he says about this Galilean carpenter's dying and rising again and about his being the Son of God, I think he is a fool!" Onesimus answered bluntly. "Of course, his talk about the way to freedom, peace, and love is intriguing, but as Epicurus would say it may be hurtful in raising false hopes."

"How do you know these promises are false?" Archippus flared. "The death and rising again of a god is a familiar story to those of us who have shared in the Eleusian mysteries. At least you will admit this man Paul is different from any philosopher you ever heard."

"Yes, he's different," Onesimus said with a laugh. Not wishing to anger his master's son, he said no more. Even to the sophisticated mind of Onesimus, the unpretentious little man held a strange fascination.

That afternoon when Philemon and Helen returned, they seemed excited as they shared with Archippus the things Paul had said and the questions they had asked. Onesimus was not near enough to hear anything but snatches of their conversation. When the market was closed for the day, the familia were assigned their quarters in one of the newest wonders of Ephesus—a large stone edifice with sections for rent to rich merchants and their retinue. Philemon ordered Onesimus to preside over the arrangements for dinner.

"Help Polectus purchase the food and arrange the table for three extra guests. Take Croto with you and get some of the best fruit of the valley and some good meat." Then, as an afterthought, "Only be sure it is not pork. Paul, the little preacher we heard today, and two of his friends are coming to dinner. Though he is a Christian, he is also a Jew, and I don't want to offend him. I will expect you to see that all goes well."

This new role for Onesimus added to his resentment—he was

a teacher, not a kitchen slave! But, since these guests would include Paul, he would be genuinely glad to hear the talk at the table in spite of his expressed disbelief in Paul's teaching. Then, too, he would be able to see Helen.

He soon lost himself in the sights and smells of the Ephesian food market. Croto, the cook, helped him choose fruits and vegetables, the best in Asia, and a tender leg of lamb that would roast nicely over the open fire already lighted in the huge kitchen of the rented rooms.

Onesimus supervised the preparation of the table. By the light of lamps, fine linens were laid out and fresh flowers brought the fragrance of roses and lilies into the room. Onesimus recalled how his mother had often prepared similar banquet tables, not only in their stately home in Ephesus but also as the slave in charge of Philemon's dining room in Colossae. Onesimus missed her very much during these days.

Paul arrived, accompanied by Tyrannus and Joanna, the benefactor in whose lecture hall his regular teaching sessions were held. Onesimus met them at the door.

"You are Paul. My master is delighted to share his dinner with you and your friends," he said in his best Greek.

Contrary to custom, and much to Onesimus's surprise, Paul acknowledged the greeting and then asked him his name.

"The name given me by Master Philemon is Onesimus."

"I am sure you are indeed most useful to all about you. You have much important work to do, young man. I am glad to meet you. This is Tyrannus and his wife Joanna. They have been your master's friends for years and are now mine also."

Onesimus bowed, slightly embarrassed by this attention so rarely given to slaves, but touched by the warm, personal interest this unusual man showed in him. *Archippus was right,* he mused, *this man is different from any philosopher I ever met.*

When the dinner was being served, Paul continued the same kindly interest in everyone at the table, including Polectus and the other slaves who served the meal. When he came to the juicy portion of lamb, he exclaimed in calm delight, "What a tasty meal. May I meet and thank the one who prepared it—especially this delicious meat?"

Croto was summoned and in painful self-consciousness came to the door, trying to hide his enormous bulk behind his cook's apron. Paul expressed his thanks. The fat little man soon lost his timidity and, in a mixture of Phrygian and Greek, mumbled something about how wonderful it was to cook for those who knew a good piece of lamb when they tasted it.

As they ate, Paul gathered information about Philemon and his familia, including their specialty of dying cloth with the precious purple for which Colossae was especially famous. When he talked, he seemed so alive and attractive in spirit that one soon forgot his bent stature and withered face. The conversation soon led to the morning's meeting in the Agora and the lecture hall. Tyrannus, one of Ephesus' leading merchants, had endowed the hall for the benefit of noted philosophers who often came to Ephesus.

"Of all the famous teachers and speakers since the hall was built," Tyrannus said with enthusiasm, "Paul has drawn the largest crowds and has done by far the most good." Tyrannus was a tall, dark-haired man with an intelligent face covered with a heavy beard. His eyes snapped and his voice was strong as he continued, "Indeed, I am proud to be called a Christian. These two years since Paul first came and baptized me have been the best of my life. But you should know that this, my friend and brother Paul, insists on continuing his trade as tentmaker, though I would be happy to provide all his expenses."

Paul nodded in response to say that he enjoyed working as a tentmaker.

Philemon interrupted with indignation, "Why should you make your own way when you devote your time to teaching? All the philosophers, with teachings not nearly so interesting as yours, are supported by rich patrons. Why not you? Of course, Tyrannus would be glad to sponsor you and so would I!"

"I am grateful for your confidence," Paul said simply, "but I am not primarily a philosopher, though I have read and studied

the best thinkers. By the grace of God, I am what I am, chief of
sinners, and yet one called to tell to all the world the good news
of Jesus Christ as Lord! For me to become a settled teacher
supported by rich men, even as noble as you, would hinder me
from telling this good news of the kingdom of God to the whole
world. Such hospitality as this," he said with a smile, "is more
than enough."

"Why are you so interested in risking your life and taking on
such costly responsibilities for the world?" Philemon persisted.
"Tyrannus and Joanna told me something this afternoon of the
wide travels you have made already—how often you have been
imprisoned and beaten because your own people or others stir
up trouble for you wherever you go. They tell me that many
times you have been face to face with death, three times
shipwrecked, once stoned and left for dead, constantly on the
road in all kinds of dangers from robbers, from extreme heat
and cold and false friends. They tell me how you have toiled at
your trade and gone without sleep in order to have time to
preach in the Agora and teach in Tyrannus Hall. I am glad you
paid the price to come to Ephesus, but why do you do it?"

"I do it in the name of God our Father, whose kingdom has
been revealed to us and is reserved in heaven in the great age to
come, when Christ will reign and all things will be under His
feet. It is in His name and at His will that I am an apostle."

Onesimus watched the wonderment and fascination on the
faces of the little group surrounding Paul, as Philemon broke
the silence.

"When you spoke this afternoon of the 'kingdom of heaven,' I
wondered what you meant. Is it some far-off place where this
God revealed in Christ is supposed to reign?"

"By no means," Paul answered eagerly, "the kingdom of
heaven is here, within us, about us, around us, though it is not
recognized and accepted by most men; and this is the reason for
their conflicts and misery—so Jesus taught His disciples. The
rule of the mighty Creator, Father of our Lord Jesus Christ,
includes all the cosmos, as well as the earth. The Holy Spirit,
sent by Christ, is teaching us to understand and to know the

width and length, the depth and height of the great love of the Father, that we were chosen before the world was founded. We are men and women, full of love, accepted as His children through Jesus Christ, that all in heaven and earth might be brought into a unity in Christ."

"By the gods, what a conception," Philemon exclaimed. "This kind of phenomenon far surpasses Empedocles' ideas of unity when love at last conquers strife. Empedocles gets no further than love as the top of an endless cycle, with four transitional stages in which love and strife fight for supremacy. But you sound as if love is the ruler now and will someday conquer all."

Onesimus was fascinated by this conversation. Empedocles and his disciples, Anaxagoras and later Aristotle, were among his favorite philosophers. He knew that both Anaxagoras and Aristotle believed there is only one world and that there is a unity to it. But Onesimus could never see how this unity would be maintained, for how could Empedocles's love and strife ever really be united? The arguments were running through his mind when Philemon turned and asked him to see that the slaves cleared the tables and brought fresh wine. With disappointment Onesimus obeyed, for he wanted to see if Paul had the answer to his riddle. This Paul, whom this afternoon he had called a fool, was a tremendous thinker. And yet, something was wrong. The incongruity of a man crucified in ignominious shame and suffering being the one who represents the Creator who unites all things? This was too much. The whole idea was completely baffling to his logical mind.

He returned in a few minutes to hear another statement from Paul that increased his puzzlement, because what Paul said was so enticingly beautiful and desirable. Onesimus's mind was captivated by it; it related to his deepest longings.

Archippus had just asked the meaning of Paul's words when he spoke of becoming "a new creation in Christ."

". . . the old nature of ruthless greed, lust, and idolatry is put off and the new nature is put on, being constantly renewed in the image of the Creator and brought to know God. There is no question here of Greek and Jew, circumcised and uncircumcised, barbarian, Scythian, freeman, slave; but Christ is all and in all. In regeneration you put on the garments that suit God's chosen people, His own, His beloved: compassion, kindness, humility, gentleness, patience. You are to be forebearing with one another and forgiving. To crown it all, you are able to love with a love that is not self-centered and destructive, but that binds all together and completes the whole. Then Christ's peace is the arbiter in your hearts . . . and you are filled with gratitude. It is because of this great gift that we as Christians are always singing thankfully in our hearts to our great and loving Father God, doing everything in the name of the Lord."

As Paul finished these words, the room was filled with a quiet hush. His grizzled face seemed transformed by an inner light. Then Philemon rose and dismissed the slaves.

Onesimus's mind staggered at the grandeur of these promises of Paul. As he returned to his sleeping quarters with Polectus, he asked himself, *Can men truly live like that in an evil and selfish world like this? If so, there would be an end to slavery, brutality, injustice, and greedy self-aggrandizement—sooner or later these would be done away!* Dazed with the possibilities of Paul's picture of "the new creation in Christ," Onesimus was even more amazed when another slave came to say that Paul wanted to speak to him before he left.

What kind of man is this who cares even for a slave? Onesimus asked himself as he hurried back to the dining room. "Perhaps there *is* such a thing as a new creation in which all are free and no one is enslaved." He found Paul at the entrance, bidding Philemon, Archippus, and Helen good night. Then Paul, seeing Onesimus enter, advanced to put his hands on his shoulders and said with such deep sincerity that the youth was deeply moved: "Onesimus, you have been useful indeed to all of us tonight. Your preparation of this delicious dinner was well done. Thanks be to you and your fellow workers. I will be happy to talk with you or any of Philemon's familia; but remember," and here those black eyes seemed to penetrate Onesimus's very being, "whatever happens, remember you, too, are chosen for a mighty work. You have much for which to be thankful now and in the days to come."

A stammered word of thanks was all Onesimus could manage, while he looked furtively at his master. How would he take this treatment of one of his slaves as equal? But Philemon was in what seemed a state of sustained ecstasy.

When Paul left, Philemon came to Onesimus, put his hand on Onesimus's arm, and thanked him for his good work, concluding with words Onesimus never thought he would hear him say: "In the Spirit of this Christ I forgive you, Onesimus, for what you did on the way, and I want you to forgive me. I know not whether Christ is the Lord of the universe, but this Paul has given me more hope and peace of mind than I ever thought possible. So go and rest. Tomorrow we will learn more from this great man of God."

When Onesimus responded hesitatingly, but gratefully, Philemon turned and left, and the young slave returned to his room in a flush of new hope.

"You have much important work to do . . . much for which to be thankful in the years to come!" Onesimus saw nothing to look forward to in his future. But if what Paul said was true . . . if Philemon believed it . . . if he had become a "new man" in Christ—whatever that was—perhaps . . . perhaps . . . And Helen? It was too much for Onesimus. He lay down and dreamed the wildest dreams of freedom and joy that had come to him yet.

Next morning, however, the world looked and felt the same: gray with a touch of black. The business in silk and woolens was brisk. Philemon was still the master. Onesimus was still the slave. At the eleventh hour in the forenoon, Philemon, Archippus, and Helen left the business to Onesimus and Polectus and walked eagerly to the Hall of Tyrannus to hear Paul again. Onesimus would have given anything to accompany them, but he was still a slave. The words of the night before were like a dream too good to be true. The work of the day was the rude awakening to reality.

Epicurus was right: It is wrong to hope. Hope is a traitor.

Better enjoy yourself in living for the moment. If the circumstances are hard, then be a Stoic. Confront the situation, and in courageous fortitude accept the facts, however unpalatable. Here is the only peace possible to man. Human nature and institutions cannot be changed.

—————————————————————— *6*

Philemon's sales were good. The money and jewels poured in to be changed, evaluated, and counted. The bookkeeping was now assigned to Onesimus, and he did his best to follow Polectus's instructions. Onesimus put Paul and freedom out of his mind, until Philemon returned from the Hall of Tyrannus with an obvious sense of well-being, a lightheartedness his slaves had not seen before. What had happened? What more had he learned? Philemon did not say. The afternoon wore on. Onesimus was exhausted with the intensity of the inner battle and the demands made by his complicated tasks. Once he made a bad mistake and Polectus, discovering it after several minutes of checking before the books were balanced, rebuked him—something the kind man rarely did.

"Come on, wake up, young fellow. You are too bright to make that kind of error!"

Stung by his words, Onesimus put all his attention on the accounts.

That night there was no formal dinner. Philemon and his immediate family had accepted the invitation of Tyrannus and Joanna to join Paul and some other Christians at their house.

Onesimus found himself at a loss; he was too restless to stay in the slave quarters. He walked out into the streets, filled now with the pleasure-seekers of Ephesus: visiting merchants, sailors, adventurers, thieves, prostitutes. All seemed to be walking in the same direction—toward the Temple of Artemis, or Diana, as the Romans called the ugly, many-breasted goddess who sat on the throne in the most gorgeous temple anywhere outside of Rome. Onesimus's ears were filled with the din of revellers already half-drunk. He recalled the words of Apollonius of Tyana quoted by Philemon as he described the people they would see in Ephesus: "They are devoted to dancers and taken up with pantomimes, and the whole city is full of pipers and full of effeminate rascals and full of noise."

There were plenty of pipers and noise all right. At every corner, it seemed, along the marble road leading to the Temple, there were pipers galore. They played their accompaniment to the writhing of male and female dancers who displayed their bodily charms, enticing the lustful hunger of the visitors from around the world. Onesimus found his own passions stirred as he walked and watched.

Part of Ephesus' popularity was its notoriety as the "fun capital" of the empire. Here anything that was pleasurable was permissible, blessed by the goddess Diana herself. She represented not only fecundity, but also uninhibited pleasure. Both were equally sanctioned by the divinity supposedly reigning on the golden throne, where for fifteen centuries she had been worshiped under various names: Cybele, Artemis, and now Diana.

Onesimus made his way slowly up the Sacred Way, fascinated by the pipers and dancers. Several times his youthful beauty attracted the dancers, who surrounded him with their suggestive rhythms and invited him to choose one of them for an evening's pleasure. But much as he was attracted by them, Onesimus politely shook them off and walked up the street. He had never seen the Temple and Diana, its Queen. As a boy, his parents had thought him too young for such an experience. Now, at least, this was one freedom a slave such as he could enjoy when his work was done. Though the words of Heraclitus making sport of the emptiness and debauchery of the religion came to his mind, he was human and wanted to see it all for himself. As he passed the huge colonnaded entrance of the amphitheatre, hundreds of people were purchasing tickets and entering to participate in the celebration of a new play in which a star actor and pantomime were featured. *This would be fun,* he thought, *but first, the Temple.*

As he approached, he could hear the songs of the several Temple choruses mounted on the platforms on each side. Around them were the Temple prostitutes, young women dedicated to the goddess. They were completely naked except for the long hair which flowed over their shoulders. It was their privilege and responsibility to dance to the music of the pipers and singers in front of the throngs gathered on the steps and to choose young men from the audience to be their partners in the world-famed fertility rites. The erotic stimulation such visible intercourse produced was part of the encouragement of fecundity to which their goddess was dedicated. The scene was one of orgiastic abandonment and wild participation in sexual pleasures. While only a few actually took part physically, the remainder of the crowd participated as voyeurs, and Onesimus, still needing to escape his own frustrations, joined the latter group.

Watching for a while, Onesimus felt himself drawn by his aroused passions to accept the invitation of one of the sacred prostitutes. Halfway up the steps, he suddenly stopped. He could justify his adventures with Leslia—the pleasure was good; but he knew he could not lend his body to such things as this. The words of Heraclitus, who laughed at the goddess and her temple of lust, came to him; and then the words of Paul from the night before: "He has chosen us to be accepted as His children, to be dedicated people full of love."

This might not be true, he reasoned, but it was better than this display. There was no real love here at all, only people using each other's bodies in a public spectacle. With growing revulsion, he passed the platforms with their lewd actors and made his way to the center of the shrine where Diana sat, a golden spectacle before whom hundreds bowed in awe, wives and husbands praying for sons, mothers praying for children.

Seated on a golden throne, the statue of the Mother-Virgin and Protector of Fertility looked to him like a huge, ugly overgrown woman with a dozen large breasts protruding from her bosom. There was little trace of the womanhood he had come to cherish in his own mother and loved in the graceful beauty and dignity of Helen. If Diana represents the highest reality, he thought, there is nothing to life but a few scattered orgasms of physical pleasure in the midst of pain and suffering, old age, and death. Why reproduce such fertility for another generation to endure, since the pain and trouble, the sorrow and woe of human life far exceed the pleasures?

The goddess of fertility had done him a good service that night. He wondered even in his few sexual experiences if passion is truly good unless accompanied by responsible love, such as his mother and father had shared. He did not know and would have to find out. But for that evening, his keen mind and the insights of his teachers—plus the influence of this Paul— kept him from trying it. He walked back over the Sacred Way to the amphitheatre; but he was too tired and confused now to enjoy a play. There would be other nights. He went back to his room and, to the accompaniment of Polectus's loud snoring, undressed and tried to go to sleep. He struggled both with his aroused passions and the deeper longing for the kind of love Paul had described. He wanted Helen as his lover and wife, but this was still as impossible as it had been by the River Meander. At last he fell asleep from exhaustion. He dreamed of sharing in the Temple orgies and nature's release came as he slept.

The next few days were much the same. The sales continued to mount, and Onesimus was frustrated as he saw the Philemon family go and come from Paul's teaching. What would he not have given to have been with them or, most of all, to have been able to talk with Helen. But Philemon, though kinder than usual, had never once suggested that Onesimus might go with them to hear Paul, nor did he say anything about a changed relationship which would have made conversation with Helen possible. He was still the master and Onesimus the slave who must stay in his place.

On several evenings Onesimus tried to forget his bitterness by attending the plays in the amphitheatre with Patroculus, another young slave who was in charge of keeping the stock of fabrics in good order. The two had little in common except youth and a desire to be free, but it was better than being alone. As a boy Onesimus had thoroughly enjoyed a good play, especially the classics, and one of Euripides's was showing one night. However, the old joy in the theatre that once had united him in empathy with the actors was gone. He felt detached and distant from the brilliant pantomimes which brought roars of approval from the audience. He simply could not overcome his disappointment over the gap between Philemon's words the night when Paul had come to dinner and his lack of action in carrying them out.

On two other occasions, the apostle was invited again to dinner at their quarters. Both times Onesimus presided over the preparations and stood at the left behind his master, able to overhear much of what was said. But now the eager words of the family and the animated responses of Paul sounded foreign and abstract. The more Paul talked about the love of the eternal Father and the responsibility of all who knew God to love their fellows even as Christ loved all men, the more confused and bitter Onesimus became.

One night, nearing the time of their departure for Colossae, Philemon commanded Onesimus to summon every slave into the dining hall. Half in hope that Philemon would begin to act on this "brother-love talk" and half in fear that he wouldn't, Onesimus found his heart pounding as he stood with the other nine slaves awaiting their master's word. The others also had great expectation in their faces. What would their master do now? For days, the talk had been concerning this new religion Philemon and his family seemed ready to accept. Some of the slaves had slipped into the lecture hall or had listened to Paul in the Agora. All had heard enough to know that Paul taught the love of one God, Creator of all mankind, Father of this Lord Jesus Christ, whose "family" included everyone, whether Jew or Greek, slave or free, male or female. All were brothers and sisters, and love for each other was "the first great law." It was a beautiful ideal. Though none were so deeply involved emotionally as Onesimus, they had speculated in their conversations about the difference it would make. All came with unformed hopes that somehow this new faith of their master's would make things better for them: namely, that it would bring some measure of freedom.

With Paul at his side Philemon arose and said a few words of appreciation to his slaves for their services during the market. This was unusual. When had their master been in the habit of thanking them for the work they had no choice but to do?

"Tomorrow we will begin our preparations to return home," he said with a voice filled with emotion. "Tonight I want to tell you, my familia—who according to my brother Paul are also to be treated as my brothers and sisters as well as my slaves—of the greatest gift ever given to me and to my son and my daughter. I trust in due time it may also belong to each of you."

He paused to get better control of himself as he uttered the words many of them had come to expect. "I am now by the grace of God ready to be a follower of His Son, Jesus Christ, who was crucified for me and for all the world. Unworthy as I am, I will be baptized into Him and His church—which Brother Paul speaks of as the body of Christ. I want to be a Christian." He spoke with deep sincerity, so that even Onesimus could feel the strength of his commitment. "Now I will let my son and daughter speak for themselves."

Archippus stood and in his deep voice declared his intention also to follow Christ. Then, looking toward Onesimus, he said, "I have found in Him and His way, through the teachings of Brother Paul, the fulfillment of all the finest truths of the philosophers whom I have most admired. What Heraclitus, Socrates, and Plato taught in the abstract has come to life for me in Jesus. He is the Word made flesh, revealing the knowledge of God which we all may share. The depths of His love alone can conquer strife and all the evils and woes that threaten us—even death itself!

"Onesimus, He is the 'unknown god' you and I were discussing on the way here. His name is Love, His nature is compassion, and in His will is our perfect freedom."

Onesimus was beginning to be moved by the same kind of hope he had felt that first night when Paul spoke of freedom in love.

"I am glad," he murmured. And he said no more.

Then Helen stood, pulling the veil away from her face, looking more beautiful than Onesimus had ever seen her. Her eyes were alight and her voice was strong and clear as she declared her intention of becoming a Christian. And then she in turn looked to Onesimus as he stood flushed with feeling, "Onesimus, you have been a good teacher. You prepared me for what the apostle Paul has told me—that Jesus Christ alone can bring the proper balance between the tensions of life, as Heraclitus described it. The peace of Christ is the most blessed peace any of us can know. I have found that peace," she said simply, her eyes filled with tears. "Onesimus, I hope you will find it, too."

Embarrassed and shaken, he could only murmur, "Thank you." But he dared not look at her—or anyone. His mind was unclear. This seemed to be a "new world," in some strange way, "a new creation," as Paul had described it: These three people who controlled his destiny *were* different. They were sincere.

Paul stood and said with a smile that lighted every wrinkle of his weatherbeaten face, "My brothers and sisters, let us find all joy in the work of Christ in our hearts. I regret that most of you have been so busy at the market that you have not had time to learn of the Way as your master and his family have. I wish it were possible for me to teach each of you personally, but I have spent many hours with Philemon and Helen and even more with Archippus. They will be able to teach you all you need to know in order to come with us. Join with me when these three are to be baptized, along with others."

"I would like you to come," Philemon interjected. "You are welcome, but none is to feel he or she must be present. I want you each to become a Christian if you sincerely believe as I do that Jesus Christ is Lord and if you love the Father who has called us by His grace." Turning to Paul, Philemon asked him to bless all in their household in the days ahead.

As Paul began to pray in simple words, as if speaking to One who stood in their very presence, Onesimus's hopes rose to their highest peak. For Paul was praying that the familia of Philemon might live together truly as a family, loving one another even as Christ loved them, forbearing with one another, and when one did wrong, forgiving even as God for Christ's sake forgave them. Then he pronounced what was to become to them a familiar benediction, "The grace of the Lord Jesus Christ be with you all."

Onesimus ran to his room where he buried his face in his arms and wept as only a grown man can weep. If freedom did not come now, it would never come. Had not Paul said that in Christ there is neither slave nor free? Yet nothing had been said about giving any of them their physical freedom. And what of Helen?

He slept a troubled sleep. He dreamed of the door to heaven through which an angel bade him look—and it slammed shut. Awakened with a start, Onesimus saw that the door to the "kingdom of heaven," as Paul called it, had been shut on him by the very man who claimed so boldly and with seeming sincerity that he was entering it by faith. If Philemon was determined to live in "the kingdom of heaven," he had certainly slammed the door to its glories and joys on Onesimus!

Being a Christian is good policy for his business and home, Onesimus thought cynically, *but there is still no hint of freedom.*

Oh, yes, it is all very sacred and good, Onesimus thought, *but it has nothing to do with setting me free. It is kindness without justice, the worst cruelty of all.*

On their last evening in Ephesus, all of Philemon's familia were invited to the home of Tyrannus, where the first Christian worship service Onesimus ever witnessed was held. It was a simple affair, beginning with the singing of a hymn of praise to Christ. Paul offered a prayer of thanksgiving for these new friends who had obeyed the gospel, followed by a prayer of confession, in which he spoke words strange to Onesimus's ears—words of sorrow and contrition over sin, the pride and selfishness that so often separated people from each other and from their Lord. He then gave thanks with many joyful words for God's forgiveness through Jesus Christ incarnate, crucified, and risen. He prayed for perseverance in each of their lives, ending, as was customary, with his benediction.

Onesimus joined as fully as he was able in this prayer, hoping that now Philemon would see that as a member of the family of God, he could keep no man as his slave. To hold the power of life and death over another was not the attitude of one brother to another! *Let him repent of that,* he thought.

But Paul was speaking again, telling once more the story of the love of the man, Jesus, His brutal death and how on the cross He had prayed, "Father, forgive them for they know not what they do." The teaching was deeply moving to Onesimus. As he considered these last words of the dying carpenter-teacher, he felt how appropriate they would be should Philemon fail to free him and his mother. But Onesimus was sure he could not say such forgiving words.

The catechumens, those being prepared for baptism into Christ, were asked to stand as Paul explained, "We are baptized in the name of the Father, the Son, and the Holy Spirit for the remission of our sins, that we may receive the gift of the Holy Spirit. For thus our union with Christ is established. Indeed, as our Master taught, we are born of the water and of the Spirit."

He explained further that they were to receive this baptism early in the morning. Tonight, he said, was their preparation and acceptance by the church, and he urged each one to spend the time in prayer and meditation so that the sacrament would be a high moment of entrance into the new life.

Onesimus was not present for the early morning rite, but he would never forget the expectant joy he saw as Paul spoke, especially the transfigured beauty of Helen at that moment, her upturned face filled with assurance and peace.

"They are hopeful but mistaken!" Onesimus murmured the next morning as they rode back up the road by the River Meander. *It is all a delightful but dangerous hoax—a vain superstition,* he mused. *For if Christ is alive as they claim, if they are truly new creations of this great and wondrous God of love, they certainly have not acted on their faith in Him. Yes, they are all kinder. It will be easier to live and work in Philemon's familia. But it is obviously a sham, for still there is the distance—the injustice—the inequity!*

Much of the time he rode alone on the way back to Colossae, one conviction growing in strength with every hour that passed: This Christian love and devotion to a God who rules in love is a beautiful but false dream!

Hypocrites! was the word most often in his thoughts. *Sincere?* Well, yes, he granted that, *but saying one thing and doing another is hypocrisy, whether sincere or not!* The more he pondered it, the more angry he became. As he rode into the lovely estate of Philemon, the now "Christian" master, he did not know how long he could endure it.

Part Two

Escape to Freedom

The little city of Colossae lay silent beneath the full moon of a perfect spring night. Only the sleepless eyes of the young Phrygian slave, Onesimus, noted the gleaming travertine of the natural bridge spanning the turbulent Lycus River. A lone nightingale piped its fluted song on the quiet air.

Onesimus was annoyed even by the bird. More than two years had passed since his painful trip to the market in Ephesus—years filled with a hope deferred which left him emotionally and mentally depressed.

Sitting on the edge of the bridge, he watched the foaming spray of two waterfalls that emptied the contents of two underground streams into the river a short space east of the bridge. One stream issued from the rugged Cadmus Mountains nearby which formed a majestic backdrop to the south of Colossae. These waters were cold and clear. The other stream came from mountains farther away to the north, where he remembered the grumbling, hissing noises of hot springs as the pent-up water and steam, heated by Vulcan's fires, burst its bonds and found its way down the mountainside. As it left its prison, the water covered everything over which it passed with a white chalky deposit so that the hillsides shone as if snow-covered.

Onesimus calculated the speed of the river. At this rate, in a little over two days—four at the most—the once imprisoned water would be free to join the Aegean Sea. The thought exhilarated him. But then he remembered the water still locked within the mountain.

"How long can I take it?" he asked bitterly. "I hate the frown on Philemon's face as he and Helen walk by me in the courtyard. I only look at Helen, and clearly he warns me to keep my place. I was not born to be a slave!"

Jumping up almost with a shout, he cried, "I *shall* be free!"

He caught himself and lowered his voice with a shiver of fear, as he repeated the magic words over and over. He looked around, almost expecting to see the bridge covered with *sparteoli*, or bucket-men, as the police were called. But there were no witnesses of his desperate decision, except the bird who continued to cry mockingly.

He left the bridge and walked rapidly back to the house, where Philemon lay asleep in his comfortable bed. At the thought of him, Onesimus burned. But his decision to escape helped release him from the frustration that had raged within him during the past two years.

For a few minutes he sat under the acacia tree in the *hortulus*, his place of reflection so many times. He went over again the justification for his critical decision.

"I have witnessed countless gatherings for worship during these months that have passed. The letters from Paul have been read and good words spoken. But at no time has Philemon even mentioned that 'there is neither Jew nor Greek, slave nor free, but Christ is all and in all!'

"Of all the lying hypocrisies of which the human spirit is capable," he whispered with vehemence, "this is the most insidious, the most damnable!" He stood up with his fists clenched.

"The idea of a kingdom of heaven where there is no slavery is an illusion. It is a dirty trick to keep the slaves in a place of subjection. I will have nothing to do with this execrable sham!" He said it aloud, his voice hardened and clear. "I am at peace! Whatever it takes, I shall be free."

The matter settled in his heart, he arose and walked quietly back to the side door that led to his room. As he took off his tunic, washed his feet, and stretched himself wearily on his pallet, his mind was made up. At the earliest possible moment, he would escape . . . whatever the cost. He would do whatever he had to do. He would not stand this bondage another hour longer than necessary.

He knew things could be far worse as the slave of some other man. If caught, he knew the penalty: branding his face, cutting off his ears, other indescribable torture or even death. But to be so near and yet so far from freedom, from Helen—this denial was more than he could take.

"Yes . . . yes . . . I will steal . . . I hope I do not have to kill . . . but whatever it takes I will do it in order to be free," he told himself. "All that remains is to plan and take the best opportunity in the wisest, safest way possible!"

He slept better that night than he had in years.

-- *8*

&mpatiently, Onesimus waited for an opportunity to escape. Though his decision to run away remained unaltered, there were hours of regret and depression. He was leaving his only home and his mother with her wise counsel and encouragement; he was risking life and limb; and he was betraying those who had been kind to him under the universally accepted institution of slavery. Worst of all, he would be leaving Helen. But being near yet separate from her was intolerable. With every day his resolution to be a free man became stronger.

Weeks passed into months, and a full year went by as Onesimus sought his escape. The Philemon family and home had become the center for a church in Colossae. Every first day of the week, the growing number of Christians gathered in the large patio or sunroom where Philemon, Archippus, or one of the other more advanced Christians led in the simple worship. The familia, the catechumens, as new "seekers" were called, and other interested visitors were permitted to remain for the first part of the worship, the *synaxis* or "meeting." This was very similar to the Jewish synagogue worship, but besides selections from the Law, the Prophets, and the Psalms being read, there were letters from Paul to the Christians in Galatia and to the church at Corinth, and communications from other apostles. Stories of the life and teachings of Jesus were told and retold. Joyful hymns of praise to Christ and prayers of confession, intercession, and petition were always offered as though the risen Christ were actually present.

Onesimus attended most of these worship gatherings, lest he be conspicuous by his absence. He appreciated much of the beauty and wisdom of the Christian faith and teachings. He was especially fond of the readings of Paul's letter to the church at Corinth, which had been written to this very human and imperfect group of Christians while Paul was in Ephesus. He liked particularly the portion that contained a beautiful poem or hymn to love. But each time he heard it, the inconsistency and failure of his master and son to act upon the obvious implications of their faith entrenched his anger further.

Onesimus was always glad when all but the baptized Christians were dismissed with a blessing, after which the little church celebrated the Holy Eucharist, "the Thanksgiving." Alcestia, his mother, had been asked by Philemon to provide the bread and wine that were used at this joyful meal of remembrance in which Christ was present. In this sacred moment, Christ was said to commune with those who obeyed His command to eat the bread as His flesh and drink the wine as His blood.

A few of the slaves had become catechumens and were now baptized Christians. Among them were Patroculus and Croto, whose intellectual capacity and interest Onesimus looked on with great contempt.

Leslia had been unmoved by it all, as if she lived in a different world. *Her mind is on other things,* he laughed to himself, *that is, what mind she has!* But then he rebuked himself for being unfair. He admitted that she was very shrewd in getting the practical things she wanted. It had required his utmost skill to avoid another confrontation with her as she continued to entice him, often in the most disturbing ways. He knew he would have succumbed to her allures, which were still as tempting as ever, were it not for his present frame of mind. His whole mind and heart were consumed with plans for his escape from this absurd, demeaning situation. Fortunately, in his new task of learning the intricacies of bookkeeping and purchasing of supplies from the aged Polectus, who had fallen gravely ill, he was able to work in a separate room and had little time to mingle with the other slaves.

As for his teaching the philosophers to Helen, Philemon had never asked him to resume his work—a rebuff which increased Onesimus's bitterness whenever he thought about it.

What disturbed Onesimus more than all else during these seemingly interminable weeks was the fact that his own mother became interested in the new faith of Philemon, his wife, Apphia, and the others. Alcestia's enthusiasm for the new faith was a disappointment to Onesimus. Some of the most intense conversations they had ever shared arose over the contradiction Onesimus saw in the words and deeds of the followers of Jesus Christ. He could not understand how she could be so blind.

"Don't forget," she warned him, "Philemon's whole way of life, his livelihood, and his standing in the community would be threatened if he began to set his slaves free. You see the difference in his life and attitude; can't you be satisfied with these fruits of the Spirit, as Paul's letter to the Galatians describes them: love, joy, peace, long-suffering, gentleness, patience, self-control? I think a miracle has taken place in him and all of his family!"

"But, Mother, don't you see," Onesimus remonstrated, "the very first fruit, love, is denied when people are held beneath the grinding limitations and inequalities of slavery. How can they be sincere and true to their 'Lord Christ,' claiming such love and then doing nothing about those of us who have the desire for freedom? Remember, Mother, Paul's words to the church at Galatia, 'For freedom Christ freed us; be firm, then, and do not submit to a yoke of slavery.' How can one be free when he is still a slave?" His question was one of exasperation, asked a hundred times. Her answer was always the same, with variations.

"There is a worse slavery than physical bonds, my son. Someday you will understand that freedom is not dependent on outer circumstances."

"What foolishness," he cried in anger. "This Christian love is but a new kind of opium, cheaper than the drug imported from the East, but just as effective in lulling to sleep and acquiescence those who are trampled upon."

Then seeing the hurt expression in her eyes, he would always hasten to ask her forgiveness. The scene was repeated in different words every time they discussed the faith. After a time, he decided not to talk of it with her again. For she had now chosen to be a catechumen, and within a few weeks of training joyously accepted baptism at the hands of the one who was not only her master but also her "brother in Christ."

Deep down Onesimus was glad for her, as he was for Helen. Helen's lovely spirit grew even more beautiful as she found solace and comfort in what she spoke of as "the presence of Christ"; and now his mother also could eat the sacred food and drink "the priceless cup of His life that had been given for her and for all humankind." A harmless superstition perhaps, but good for them.

The morning after her baptism, his mother embraced Onesimus and joined his tears of frustration with her tears of joy. "Mother, I am happy for you. May this new experience be the doorway to whatever the kingdom of heaven is for you. Forgive me, that in my desire for freedom, I cannot share your faith; but I am glad you have it."

Onesimus's time and attention were now consumed almost entirely with learning the details of Philemon's business, for Polectus who had befriended him so often was increasingly weak and incoherent. With barely enough strength to spend an hour a day with Onesimus, he taught the young slave all he knew of the task as chief clerk and business manager. It was a difficult undertaking even for one with such a quick and retentive mind, but he had mastered most of it and was ready to take over completely when the old man became too ill for further work.

It was late the next winter that Polectus fell into a coma and died. Having also become a Christian—with the same kind of resistance to Onesimus's reasoning as his mother had given— he fell asleep with a quiet peace and dignity that Onesimus grudgingly recognized as a strong witness to Christ. A Christian burial service was held in the atrium at sunrise on a brisk, frosty morning.

Onesimus was struck by the difference in the approach to death made by the Christians. While some of the slaves who had been closest to Polectus were unrestrained in their grief, there was no bitter wailing and despair so common at the funeral of non-Christians. Sorrow there was, as he saw in Polectus's aged wife, but a noble, even joyful note of praise and thanksgiving took the place of the doleful commitment of the departed to the life after death, which at its best was for most Greeks and Romans a place of shadows and disembodied spirits.

"This is reality," he admitted reluctantly to his mother, "if their faith is real; but for me, I will go along with Aristotle and Epicurus and accept as certain only those things that can be tested by the senses. This is the only dependable fact of human life."

His mother shook her head and said gently, "My son, remember Paul's words, 'Eye has not seen, nor ear heard, neither can man imagine what God has prepared for those who love Him.' "

I am glad Mother has embraced this comforting faith, Onesimus said to himself. *It will make it easier for her when I leave.*

One morning in early summer, Philemon, as he went over the day's work with Onesimus, stopped to say: "Next month I want you and Archippus to make the journey to Ephesus for our annual market. I am unable to go because of this illness in my bones that makes riding a misery. With your knowledge of the business and your experience in Ephesus from before, I believe the two of you can do as well without me."

And here the master laid his hand on the knee of his slave.

"Onesimus, I am pleased with the way you have taken the place of Polectus. He was so capable and honest, it takes a faithful man to fill his shoes. You are proving trustworthy, and I am thankful. My sadness is that you have not seen fit to join with your mother and the others of our familia in the church of God."

Onesimus was embarrassed. He could not reveal all of his true feelings, but he managed to say as forthrightly as possible, "Thank you, Master, for your kind words. But I cannot accept a religion based on the horrible crucifixion and suffering of one man, no matter how good He may have been. I simply cannot believe that this man is the highest revelation of the reality that unites and controls all things. I think Empedocles is nearer right when he says that life is in constant transition between strife and love. I am not sure there is any ruler over all. But I am thankful for your ability to conquer strife and to live in love."

Then, for the first time, Onesimus hinted at his real frustration. "I must be honest, Sir. I cannot see how one who believes in the love you describe in Christ who is the ruler of all could accept so readily the evil systems of the world without attempting to change them."

Philemon looked puzzled. "I am not quite sure I understand, Onesimus. What do you mean?"

Onesimus drew back, immediately regretting that he had spoken. "I'm sorry, Master. Some day I hope to be able to talk with you about it, but there is too much to do now to get ready for the journey." With that he turned the conversation to some pressing questions about a shipment of silk that had not arrived, probably because of bandits that might have waylaid the caravan from the East in one of the narrow mountain passes.

During the month following, Onesimus had a double preparation to make. Not only did he preside over the arrangements for the journey to Ephesus with the counsel and direction of Philemon and Archippus; but he also spent much time in planning his escape. Since becoming chief clerk, every time he went to purchase provisions for the household or for the journey to Ephesus, he kept back a small portion; but he knew this was not nearly enough for a runaway slave going to Rome, and Rome was by far the easiest place for a runaway slave to escape detection.

The morning came for the caravan's departure. The good-byes were tearful on his mother's part, and, to Onesimus's surprise, Helen came to him as he sat in the clerk's room making a final check on the goods being loaded. They had enjoyed only a few brief conversations during all the time since their costly episode by the river. These had been casual, except for one conversation in which she also had expressed her regret that he chose to stand apart from Christ.

Talking more freely to her, as his old pupil, he had asked teasingly, "Remember the quote from Heraclitus? The one about 'the waking who share one world, but the sleeping turn aside into a world of his own.' "

Helen finished the quotation, "To give up to injustice is to die indeed."

"What a good memory you have! You were a good student. I'm sorry we had to stop our lessons with the philosophers. But those words of Heraclitus mean more to me now than the words of your Christ about loving one another and being at peace. I cannot give up to injustice, or I will die."

"Oh, but love is justice, the strong wise love of Jesus Christ our Lord," she remonstrated.

"I haven't seen much of justice for my lot," he said indignantly, and then regretted that he had said it.

"But Onesimus! Haven't we been kind to you? Hasn't my father treated you well and trusted you fully?"

"Indeed, he has. But I am still a slave. Remember that!" he said grimly. "If anything ever happens, remember that I do not want to be any man's slave."

She had left him with ill-concealed tears, and he had gone back to work with the old passion aroused—but with utter disgust he had quenched it.

Now she came to tell him good-bye and quietly but feelingly warned, "Onesimus, please don't do anything rash. Sometimes to do so creates even more injustice. I trust you and so do my father and my brother. Remember, I will pray to the Lord for you every day!"

She turned and walked away. After a few steps, she broke into tears and ran back to the house.

Onesimus hesitated, then resolutely plunged into the last hurried details for the journey. Did Helen suspect what he was going to do? He had talked quite freely with her. He was risking all; he knew that. And for a moment he thought once more of her and his mother. But he knew his chances for release by staying were small indeed. Kissing his mother good-bye and waving to Philemon and the familia, he and Archippus set off on their journey.

_9_

$\mathcal{A}$s they rode their horses at the head of the camel train, Onesimus thought with a grin, *At least I have graduated from a donkey to a horse!* Scarcely had they left the bustling city of Colossae for the quiet, fragrant trail along the Lycus River, when Archippus broke the silence. "Onesimus, since you and I are going to spend several days together, how about declaring peace between us? Let us talk as frankly and profitably as we did when going to Ephesus together the first time. You are technically our slave, but I also consider you my friend."

"Well, 'friend' Archippus—if a mere slave may dare to call his master's son his friend! We do not need to declare peace, for I am not fighting you; but if there is to be any communication it must begin with honesty on my part as well as yours." Archippus nodded with a quizzical smile, as Onesimus added, "You are right in feeling that a wall has been between us, ever since you professed your faith and were baptized."

"Yes, I have felt it, and frankly it has hurt me because I like you, Onesimus. If we are to be honest, I must say I like you very much. The toughness of your intellect and the quality of your spirit I admire, but you have never told me what it is that has separated us."

"As you asked, Sir, I'll tell you." And Onesimus grimaced so noticeably that Archippus looked at him in amazement.

"You and your father are hypocrites! And you don't recognize it." Then, realizing he was out of step for a slave, he said hastily, "Forgive me. But when you tell me I am your slave, but you consider me more your friend, I don't believe a word of it."

Seeing that Archippus was more wounded than angry, he dared go on. "You profess to belong to God, the Father of One whom you call your Lord, Jesus Christ. You also profess to believe that my mother and I, indeed every one of your slaves, are your equals and that we are all loved by God. Is that not right?"

"Yes, and you have said it very well. For as Paul teaches, there is no such thing as Jew and Greek, slave and freeman, male and female: for you are all one in Christ Jesus. . . You are no longer a slave but a son, and if a son, then also by God's own act an heir."

"Ha! And still you don't see why I think you are hypocrites? A son and not a slave, an heir! What in God's name do you think I am heir to? Nothing but the privilege of obeying every nod and gesture of your father, Master Philemon. And now that you are taking his place, I suppose I am heir to being your slave and doing your bidding! How in the name of Zeus or Satan or your own Jesus do you balance that with all the lofty words of Paul? There has not been one word—or the slightest indication that you are truly concerned about me, your 'equal.' " He repeated the word almost as an epithet. "Your *equal!* What do you care about *my* freedom?"

The explosion left Archippus wordless for at least a full minute. So this was what had made Onesimus coldly aloof from the life of the Christian *koinonia,** which had been like a new

---

*Greek word for church fellowship.

world for Archippus and his family. He could understand now. He recalled parts of the conversation they had shared on the way to Ephesus, and Onesimus's bitterness. He recalled the story of the treachery that overthrew the former governor of Asia and that led to the execution of Onesimus's father and the enslavement of himself and his family.

"But, Onesimus." Archippus searched for words to make his defense as strong as possible. "The apostle Paul never meant freeing the slaves *physically* any more than he meant men were to be no longer men nor Greeks no longer Greeks. It is a *spiritual* freedom to which we are all called. . ."

"Spiritual—by Jupiter!" Now thoroughly aroused with pent-up resentment, Onesimus countered: "What is that but spiritual opium for your slaves? It keeps us all docile so that you will get better service out of us. What good is spiritual freedom when I am not given the dignity of *being* a man, free to choose my way in life?" As though arguing a point of philosophy, but still with heat, he asked, "Do you recall Plato's description of the dialogue between Callicles and Socrates, in which Callicles accused the great teacher of double-talk? Socrates, said Callicles, confused the law of nature with man-made conventions and argued from first one viewpoint and then the other, when as a matter of fact the two are in contradiction. Let me see if I can remember the gist of what he said:

> The rule of nature declares that to suffer injustice is the greater evil than to do unjustly; while the artificial law of human custom and convention says it is better to suffer injustice than to do it to another.

We invent this artificial law, Callicles reminded Socrates, and impose it on our fellows, of whom we take the best and strongest from their youth upwards, and tame them like young lions. We charm them, saying that with equality they must be content, and that the equal is the honorable and the just (no matter how unjust it is to you).

"That is what your civilized conventions and laws have done to me and thousands like me." The words poured out of him, hot and fast, "Even your Paul, as he gave those empty principles to you, had some words not only to wives and husbands and children, but for slaves. You remember how he said, "Slaves, give entire obedience to your earthly masters, not merely with an outward show of service, to curry favor with men, but with singlemindedness, as if you were doing it for the Lord and not for men."

"Oh, but wait a minute, Onesimus. . ."

"Wait? I have waited for years! Callicles, not Paul, is right. All this teaching of love and obedience is but a useful sedative to prevent 'natural justice' from taking over. As Callicles put it to Socrates,

> If there were a man who had sufficient force, he would shake off and break through, and escape from all of this; he would trample under foot all our formulas and spells and charms and laws which are against nature; and the slave would rise in rebellion.

But now in your civilized laws, as Pindar says so well, 'Law is king . . . and makes might to be right, doing violence in the highest hand.' I take it that this Christian love of which Paul speaks so eloquently is nothing more than this, and therefore I heartily reject it."

Archippus, astonished, did not know how to answer this brilliant argument. He was honest enough to admit as much to the young rebel riding by his side.

"Yes, slaves are taught by many that obedience and submissiveness are great virtues," he said, "and it is thus as well as by fear that the vast majority of people in the Roman world are kept enslaved. But Onesimus, I believe, indeed I *know*, that Christian love is much more than a sly way of preserving injustice and wrong. I know, because Christ's love was born in the willingness to be crucified in order to be a sacrifice, an offering, for sin. This is God's way which all men may live in true freedom, each one finding joy and life in serving the other as belonging to God's household. Perhaps this kind of love is an ideal too great for our small hearts, though Brother Paul has assured us so often that God's grace is sufficient for all our needs. 'In Christ we are able.' I can see that Father and I have not applied our faith as directly as we ought."

Archippus made the admission Onesimus had hoped for but really had not expected.

"We simply have never thought about the contradictions you have pointed out."

"Hmpf . . . I think it is time you Christians begin to relate your belief to your lives," Onesimus responded tenaciously but with less heat, for Archippus's honest admission had calmed him considerably. "After all, if you do not do this in relation to slavery you are not even as far along in your understanding as Aristotle. He asked the question, Is anyone intended by nature to be a slave? He recognized that others affirm the rule of a master over slaves to be contrary to nature. The distinction between slave and free man exists in law only and not by nature, and being an interference with nature is, therefore, unjust. Though he himself believed that some by nature are inferior and better off under the rule of a just master, he questioned the justice of making slaves from political captives taken in war whose natures are thus violated. My whole nature and life have been defamed! If there is a God who is the loving Father of all, he would be as wrathful as I over the defamation of the life of one of His sons."

Archippus was deeply moved by his companion's words. "I recognize the truth in what you are saying, my friend, and I ask our Lord to forgive us for being so blind. Of course, there is no justice in your slavery. The accident of your being the son of a high officer in the Roman government who was deposed—this does not justify us in keeping you subjected. But my father paid a high price for you, and you *are* useful to him in many ways, indeed invaluable!"

"Ha!" Onesimus snorted once again. "So money is of more value than a person, and I am your father's property. I am kept a slave because I am useful to him. What reasoning!"

"No, I did not mean it that way," lamented Archippus. "I simply meant that we are all caught up in a world filled with injustice. And I agree, if we are to continue to profess our faith in the Father as Jesus reveals Him, we cannot abuse His sons without cause. We must talk this over with Father when we return. I will try to help him realize what we have been doing that is so wrong and to decide how to be just under the circumstances, to do what is right and best."

"Archippus, you truly are my friend! I am greatly surprised at your understanding of my plea. But I cannot expect as much of your father. You have an open mind, but we are all caught up in a system that is too deeply entrenched. It will never be broken, not in our lifetime. Your father is an older man who is set in his ways. It is very unlikely he will set his slaves free, even that he would set me free. And it would be unjust if it were only me. He has had four years to consider this. He has done nothing."

"Give us time, Onesimus," pleaded Archippus. "The evils of generations cannot be corrected overnight. I cannot guarantee that Father will see things the way I do. But he genuinely does believe in the love of Christ, the ruler of all, and he wants to act according to his belief."

The conversation continued until they stopped in the heat of the day for lunch and rest under a grove of cypress trees by the river.

Onesimus was still disturbed. His decision to run away was once more under question. Could it be that Archippus might have enough influence on his father that he would be set free? But he remembered his mother's warning: Philemon's whole way of life depended on his slaves. Indeed, the entire economy and society of the Roman Empire was built on the system of slavery.

Archippus is young and idealistic, he thought. *Philemon is old and realistic. I'll never have a chance at freedom if I miss this opportunity.*

At the slow pace of the camels the caravan continued down the Lycus and by mid-afternoon reached the Meander. Both young men were reflecting on the morning's conversation, and little more was said.

That night they camped at the very spot where Onesimus had
been beaten by Philemon. As he looked at the tree where he had
been tied, he relived each stripe vividly. A hardening of his
spirit closed the door to any further consideration of his decision.

"Enough is enough," he muttered as he went to sleep. "If
there is a God who cares, He will have to show Himself more in
His creatures. I will not wait to see."

As day broke, he was awakened by the unearthly noise of
camels fighting! Two males obviously were struggling over the
one young female who had come into heat during the night. The
whole party awoke and began the difficult process of stopping
the fight. It was a rare sight, one Onesimus had never seen. The
huge animals, generally calm and placid, were biting and kicking each other with savage success, punctuating their efforts
with grunts and groans. Both of them were bleeding and
bruised. One of the camel drivers explained to Archippus and
Onesimus that when such a fight occurred, unless there was
some outside interference, the two would continue to fight until
one or the other was either incapacitated or dead. Then, while
the victor took his satisfaction with the female camel, she would
lick his wounds, his mate from that time on. The fight was
stopped before either animal was wounded seriously, and the
caravan proceeded toward Ephesus.

The two young men spent the morning comparing the natures of animals and men, and both agreed there was a certain
similarity. "You must admit, though," said Onesimus sardonically, "no camel ever enslaved another!"

"Nor did ever a camel revolt at being a camel and try to
change himself into a horse," responded Archippus. Onesimus
had an apt response—but he knew the argument could have
gone on interminably. He chose to be silent.

The caravan entered Ephesus, and the slaves unloaded the
merchandise. Under the guidance of Archippus and Onesimus,
the shop was ready by mid-morning. This time Archippus was
the only salesman and Onesimus the only moneychanger and

bookkeeper; but their work went well, and by nightfall a good day's sales were in the books and the money in the safety box which Archippus kept by his side at all times.

That evening, Archippus sought out the Ephesian Christians and invited Onesimus to accompany him. Firm in his resolve to escape, Onesimus refused. He did not want to be disturbed any more by those who were part of such a costly superstition.

Archippus went first to the home of Tyrannus and Joanna. He found them well but saddened by news just received of Paul's imprisonment in Rome. They related how after Paul had been arrested in Jerusalem, he had appealed to Caesar as a Roman citizen. He was sent first to Caesarea where he remained in prison for two years. After several trials before the governors of Caesarea he was put on a ship bound for Rome.

After shipwreck and much trouble, in which Paul was of great aid to the ship's officers and crew and won their respect, they arrived in Rome. Here, the ship's captain and others of influence on board had turned him over to the Emperor Nero's praetorian guard with the finest recommendations. Also, a few rich and influential Roman Christians had interceded for him. As a result, Paul, though still a prisoner, was permitted to rent a house where he was chained night and day to one of the guards. But he was given much more freedom than the usual prisoner.

Archippus was deeply distressed by the news and shared it with Onesimus. But Onesimus was too preoccupied with his plans to care.

_____ *10*

*T*he next few days were so busy there was little time for conversation. In the evenings Archippus sought the Christian community, but Onesimus steadily refused to go with him. His choice instead was the amphitheatre or the Sacred Way, the wide marble street that retained such a fascination for him.

The great Ephesian library was kept open till late in the evening. Here, by the light of burning torches, a group of philosophers and their pupils were examining the manuscripts that were so precious to Onesimus, as they were to anyone who sought to think through the meaning of life. Onesimus spent much time looking for his favorite philosophers' writings. He dipped into several of Plato's works so familiar to him and was disappointed to find him speaking more of the need for inner understanding and wisdom than of the injustice of slavery as such. Aristotle similarly spoke of the kind treatment which should be given slaves, but none of them spoke as Paul had spoken of the family of God the Father, in which all men are brothers and "there is neither slave nor free." What did this mean if it didn't mean that those who believed in Christ should work for physical as well as spiritual freedom of their brothers? Someday, he sighed, he would dearly love to ask Paul that question.

Thus, the days passed. During a lull in sales late one afternoon, Onesimus slipped away to finalize his plans for escape. First, he went down to the harbor and inquired of the sailings of the several ships that regularly left the crowded harbor of Ephesus for all parts of the world. To his surprise, he found that one Phoenician ship bound for Rome would leave about the same time he and Archippus with their caravan were to return to Colossae. The exact day and hour were carefully noted as he talked with one of the sailors.

Next he went into an apothecary's shop and, introducing himself as the son of a rich merchant, ordered "Prepare for me a good sleeping potion that would not be harmful to my father. He has been unable to sleep well recently and needs something to give him a few nights of sound rest."

The merchant responded matter-of-factly and prepared the powder, telling the young man just how much to use for medium sleep and how much for heavy sleep. "The mixture is not harmful, if he does not take too much," he said.

Onesimus took the powdered preparation and paid for it with money he had been given to buy provisions for the return trip to Colossae.

Because most of the goods they had brought were sold, he suggested to Archippus that they plan to return home in two days. "This will give us enough time, will it not, to complete our business?"

Archippus agreed, and Onesimus felt everything was working out well. On the night before the day set for their departure, *The Phoenix* was set to sail at daybreak, about the fifth hour after midnight.

Finally the critical night arrived. The booth was already closed. The books were balanced, and the money and jewels were both stowed away safely in the money box which Archippus kept hidden in his room. Onesimus knew its contents— much more than enough to buy his passage to Rome, with plenty left over for several months' living if he were careful. He would leave enough, of course, to keep his master's caravan supplied on the way home—most of the supplies were already paid for—and enough in addition to buy at least a beginning of the raw silks and woolens Philemon would need for the next year's business. This was fair, Onesimus reasoned. He was stealing the major part of the profits for an entire year's work, but his master had other resources. No one would be hurt, and he would be free!

"Free!"

In his elation, the very word slipped out of his mouth as he waited for Croto to bring in the food for their last dinner together. Archippus had not yet entered the room. Onesimus went carefully over his plan. Though Archippus had invited him to join in his meals, Onesimus insisted on getting the wine and seeing that Archippus's cup was always full. They enjoyed their meal—at least Archippus did. Onesimus found the food hard to swallow. After a few moments of eating and of superficial conversation, Onesimus said, "Come, let's have an extra drink tonight since we have had such a successful market. Your father will be proud of you."

He reached for the tall pitcher of wine and said apologetically, "What carelessness—I failed to refill the pitcher. Perhaps I'm not such a good slave after all," he joked as he left the room. Outside he found the cruse of wine and poured just enough for one cup. Hastily he took one of the sleeping powders and sprinkled it in the pitcher, swirling the liquid as he returned to the room. Pouring it into Archippus's cup, he cried, "Let us drink to our success as merchants. To a safe journey home for you and your caravan!"

He lifted his cup which he had left purposefully nearly full. The two drank, then sat for a few moments in silence.

"I have some last minute checking to do before I retire," Onesimus said casually, "so good night to you, 'Friend' Archippus."

"Good night, my brother Onesimus. I will retire early and be ready for the morrow."

Onesimus went to his room, which was adjacent to Archippus's with a connecting door. He had tried the door earlier in the afternoon and knew it was unlocked. He flinched as he realized this was an indication of the trust Archippus placed in him. After packing his belongings in a rough leather traveling bag he had purchased that day, he sat down by the light of a candle to write his good-bye message to one who had become truly like a brother as well as a friend. It was the most difficult task he had ever undertaken. How could he betray such a friend? It was only through a rehearsal of his grievances and the chain of rationalization that had led him thus far that he found the courage to write briefly:

> Forgive me, "Brother" Archippus, for taking my freedom in this manner. If you were my master, I could trust you for my freedom; but it is your father who "owns me," as a piece of his property. You have been more like a friend and brother to me than the son of my master, but since he and the people called Christians preach one thing and practice another, I have no choice but to reject your Christ

and seek for life on my own. I want to own myself and will be owned by no other. In spite of Paul's teaching on love, if I am captured, your father would likely have me killed or maimed. . . . This risk I must take. I wish you joy and happiness in all your future and, if there is anything to your faith, I trust you will act on it and test it. To me it is a dangerous superstition. Farewell!

Your "brother" Onesimus

As he finished, tears came unbidden to his eyes. Brushing them away, he arose resolutely.

It was midnight and the sleeping powder should have done its work. Covering the candle, he opened the door and listened to the deep breathing of his friend. Then, in his bare feet, he walked to the side of the bed, picked up the money box, and returned to his room. He knew that Archippus kept some money on his person, but the gems and the bulk of gold and silver used for trading were in the box. Having experimented several times before, he easily picked the lock and, counting out the amount he had planned to take, placed the money in a special pouch tied securely to his body. Carefully he locked the box, placed the note on top, and returned it to its place by the side of the sleeping Archippus.

"Good-bye, my 'brother,' " he whispered as he shut the door, "I hope you understand my desperation and forgive me. Someday I trust whatever God there is to bring us back together again!"

In the darkness lighted only by a half-moon he slipped through the narrow streets to the wide road leading down to the harbor. There were still a few drunken sailors and other visitors to Ephesus coming out of the brothels he passed, and several merchants with their wares carried by porters or slaves made their way toward the ships that were to leave at daybreak. Onesimus hurried down the road, his forebodings and sadness soon obliterated by hopeful expectation as he began the new life of freedom.

At the dock he watched as several deckhands on *The Phoenix* loaded a number of bales of cloth on board. Tapping the shoulder of one deckhand, Onesimus inquired where he would find the ship's officer who could sell him a passage to Rome. Pointing to a burly man with a heavy beard and a booming voice, the deckhand went back to his work, warning, "He's a tough'un, young man. Take care how you address him."

With this warning, Onesimus took out the papers he had prepared with a letter signed by himself with the name of Gaius Julius, merchant of Pergamos, assuring any to whom the letter might be presented that the bearer, his son Gaius Julius III, was on a business trip to Rome and requested their kindness and aid.

Thus reinforced, he approached the big man who was over-seeing the loading of final provisions for the long voyage. Bowing to him, Onesimus said in clear Greek, "Good morning, Sir. I am Gaius Julius from Pergamos, desiring a passage to Rome. Here is a letter from my father, a merchant from Pergamos, and the necessary identification papers."

The man whom Onesimus came to know as Martius Publius, the captain's mate, grunted indifferently as he routinely read the papers in the flickering light of the nearest torch. Looking into the handsome but soft face of Onesimus, he said brusquely, "It's a long, tough voyage, young man; but if you can take it we'll be glad to have you on board. There is one bunk left, just below the deck. That will be six hundred fifty denarii." As Onesimus counted out the gold Roman coins, he remembered it was for six hundred fifty denarii he had been sold to Philemon.

On board the ship, he found his way to the passengers' quarters. All but the very rich were stationed in bunks or hammocks arranged in rows in a room large enough for some twenty men, if they did not mind some over-crowding. The steward received the wooden ticket with the number assigned to Onesimus and without a word led him down a series of steps to the sleeping quarters. He showed him his bunk—the very top one on the last row. Hoping to be treated well, Onesimus gave him a coin no doubt larger than he usually received. The steward, a rough Phoenician with a limp, changed his sour expression and smiled broadly in thanks. Onesimus stowed his bag on one end of the bunk and looking around noted that his fellow passengers were mostly hardy traders and adventurers of various sizes and shapes. No one paid any special attention to him, so he climbed back up the steps and stood out on the deck of the ship, watching quietly the final loading of supplies and the coming aboard of a few late passengers.

Just as dawn was breaking, the command from the captain on the brig to cast off was given. The ship moved from its mooring out into the harbor.

Onesimus stood at the rail looking at the sleeping city of Ephesus and the coast of Ionia as it faded in the distance.

As the familiar scenes receded and the ship sailed out to sea with a good wind to carry it forward, Onesimus surrendered to his feeling of elation. He lifted his arms and breathed deeply.

"Free! Free! At last I am free!" he almost shouted in the wind. But seeing a few others standing near, he withheld his outward expressions. "This is the hour and the morning I have waited for so long! No man will ever again tell *me* what to do. My life is my own, and I will live it fully," he exulted as the sun had fully risen and the blue waves of the Aegean Sea sparkled and danced.

Onesimus thought back to what must be happening in the apartment in Ephesus. By this time Archippus would have read the note and realized the betrayal. What would he do? Tell the *sparteoli?* Report to the commissioner charged with the capture of runaway slaves? He did not know. Onesimus could imagine his friend kneeling by his bed, praying for forgiveness for the slave who had betrayed them. Perhaps Archippus would pray the very words of Jesus on the cross, "Father, forgive him, he does not know what he is doing."

Did he *really* know what he was doing? Again and again, he rehearsed the scenes of the past months and especially the past few days. Archippus had understood and accepted his rebellion at being held a slave, then had promised to talk with his father and had been so kind and trusting. Onesimus had robbed and betrayed his only real friend! Philemon had been kind also in his way. He simply had not connected his Christian love with keeping slaves. How would he take this betrayal of one so valuable to him? Onesimus did not know.

A burden of guilt and then fear swept over Onesimus. No matter what good thing came in the future, he could never erase this betrayal. And what if he were traced and caught? He felt justified in seizing his freedom even at such cost of perfidity; but *is it really better to do unjustly than it is to suffer injustice?* Was Callicles right? Or Socrates? And what about the idealistic words of Jesus and Paul, "Love your enemies . . . blessed are you when you are persecuted for the sake of the right." It sounded like folly to him, but Paul believed this kind of love is the way God loves . . . who sends the rain on the just and the unjust.

Onesimus was overwhelmed with his doubts and guilt, his spirits dampened and his heart sick. As if this were not enough, his stomach was churning. He had heard of seasickness and had hoped he would not suffer from it, but now this too was added to the burden that weighed on his heart like a mountain of oppression.

His first day of freedom, and he was bound hand and foot by his fear, his guilt, his human frailty—and his loneliness!

"What freedom?" he moaned as he made his way down to his bunk and tried to go to sleep. With the rolling and pitching of the ship, he found the semi-darkness in the room and the darkness of his own feelings too much for him. He got up and went out on the deck. Leaning over the rail he retched until there was nothing left within him.

The limping old steward to whom he had given the handsome tip came over and sought to help him by leading him away from the rail and bathing his face in cold water.

"Take a little of this dry bread," he said kindly. "It will help more than anything." Onesimus munched on the bread and felt a little better. Helped by the steward, he made his way back to the bunk and fell into a troubled sleep.

— Part Three —
Free but Enslaved

ive weeks had passed and with them countless hours of seasickness and depression for Onesimus. At last the ship was made secure at the dock, and he found himself on unsteady feet walking off *The Phoenix*. She had brought him through two storms and many tears to the harbor of Ostia. As he felt beneath him the firm earth that led to Rome and freedom, he sensed the first elation since departure from Ephesus and slavery.

It had been a difficult and painful voyage. He was more often nauseated than not, fighting off waves of guilt and remorse, lonely and afraid of the future. He had made friends with only a few of the passengers and his faithful steward, whom he had encouraged with a few more coins. He did, however, dare to pass the day by visits with Martius Publius, who took a genuine interest in the handsome young "merchant's son."

He was afraid to talk with the merchants on board. One of them, especially, resembled a silk buyer whose payment he had received in the Agora a few days before the voyage. Sitting across the table at dinner one night, he had frightened Onesimus by asking, "Didn't I see you in the shop of Philemon of Colossae back in Ephesus?"

"I suppose there are many people who resemble each other," Onesimus had answered, trying to look calm. "No, I am not from Colossae. I am Gaius Julius III, and my father is a merchant from Pergamos who is sending me on business to Rome."

This seemed to satisfy the buyer. Nevertheless, Onesimus continued to be terrified at the thought of being recognized. He avoided conversations and close proximity with the passengers. His sleep was often interrupted with nightmares in which he was being discovered and tortured in various ways.

Onesimus remembered the stories of the terrible kinds of treatment to which runaway slaves were subjected when found and turned over to the magistrates. They were seen as a threat to the entire Empire. Sometimes, the owners themselves took the responsibility of punishment, especially if they were the kind to enjoy it. To make an example before others who might be tempted, fugitives who were caught were often beaten and branded. Many wore a *furca*, a wooden yoke painfully borne around the neck. Or they were thrust into the stocks for days at a time or sent to work in the mines or the galleys. Some were even left to die chained to each other in a stinking hole called an *ergastulum*, from which there was no escape. Onesimus shuddered as he thought of such a fate. He hoped that Philemon being a Christian and an unusually kind master would treat him more leniently if he were found. But he knew that Philemon still might think it his duty to turn him over to the authorities. Such fears were worse by far than seasickness.

Now, with solid land beneath him and his future before him, his hopes returned. With his leather bag thrown over his shoulder, he walked jauntily along the dock into the street which had been pointed out to him as the one leading to the Appian Way. Stopping in a small inn, he bought a meal and some extra bread and cheese for the long walk ahead. Fed and strengthened, he began his walk toward Rome, whistling an old song he had known since boyhood.

The Appian Way, the historic road into Rome over which countless conquering Roman commanders had led captured enemies in triumph behind their chariots, rekindled old feelings. *My father walked this very road*, Onesimus thought with a new wave of hatred as he saw the picture in his imagination of the family enemy, Vitellius Lucas, in his chariot, taunting Gaius Flaccus and the bedraggled former officers of Ephesus. He could see his father being pulled behind the chariot, and it was enough to make him curse under his breath and walk faster.

Today there was a mixed crowd on the famous old road: merchants with their bales of goods on the backs of donkeys or in carts pulled by oxen; adventurers; shady, ill-smelling characters; and a few wealthy travelers returning from business for themselves or the State. These traveled in carriages pulled by horses or were carried by their servants on comfortable litters with luxurious cushions and curtains to keep out the sun. Onesimus enjoyed being part of this diverse procession, all going the same way toward the capital of the world.

In the distance he heard the sound of many horses approaching, their hooves pounding on the cobblestones. A legion of Roman soldiers came up the road from the harbor. Everyone scattered. Even the carriages and the servants carrying their litters moved to the side of the road to let the legion pass.

Onesimus was thoroughly frightened as these symbols of the State appeared—the State whose laws he had broken, whose system of slavery his rebellion defied. It was too dangerous, he decided, to enter Rome in daylight along this public way. The merchant from the ship who had questioned him about being in Philemon's shop just might be on this road. And if they met anywhere near the soldiers, the man might risk reporting Onesimus in the hope of the customary reward from his master. Onesimus was not sure that his forged papers showing himself as the son of Gaius Julius, merchant of Pergamos, would stand up under examination of the practiced eyes of one familiar with such documents. There had been no difficulty with the port officer in Ostia. He was a congenial man, content to look at the papers only casually after receiving the generous gold piece Onesimus had slipped into his hand.

Deciding the road itself was too risky, Onesimus walked into the bushes away from the busy highway. Here he found a lush growth of berry plants, ripe for picking and eating and dense enough to hide him safely.

All day long he sat, plucking some of the ripe fruit and munching on his bread and cheese. Some of the courage and good feeling had left him. At dusk he set out along the edge of the road so as to attract as little attention as possible. When travelers with torches passed by, he took to the bushes again. At last, after midnight, the city of Rome could be seen up ahead. Only a few lights outlined its darkened buildings. Since the walls of the city were too high for him to climb without help, he decided to chance it through the main gate of the Appian Way. The fat gatekeeper was nodding sleepily as he approached, since travelers entering Rome at this late hour were few. He awakened with a start as Onesimus presented his credentials, and with the help of another gold coin, barely looked at the handsome youth as he nodded permission for him to enter.

Onesimus walked down the wide street until he was out of sight of the gatekeeper, then turned quickly into a side street. By the pale light of the moon, he made his way toward the northeast section of the city, carefully avoiding parties of carousing citizens returning from their nocturnal celebrations.

From the talk of several of the adventurers on board *The Phoenix*, he had learned something about the Subura, a rough, noisy district northeast of the Forum between the Esquiline and the Quirinal. Here lived the underground characters, who made their livelihood by preying on the vice and cupidity of the rich, especially the debauched scions of wealthy senators and businessmen. Here the *sparteoli* did not dare to come. There were only a few city policemen hired by the Emperor to protect the homes and businesses of Roman citizens. They were poorly paid and could not possibly police the poorer section of Rome. Onesimus had been told that one took his life in his hands to enter the Subura, especially if he looked prosperous and well dressed.

Onesimus looked at his tunic. It was not the dress of a slave, for Archippus had given him several of his own garments so that "you will look more like one in authority as you receive payment from our customers." Onesimus smiled as he realized that though these handsome tunics had stood him in good stead on board the ship, they were now a handicap. He must exchange one or more of them for some cheaper garments; but it was the middle of the night and no shops were open.

He would wait until morning. Meanwhile, he chose the shelter of a bridge where he would be concealed from passersby. In the shadow of the bridge braces, he pulled out a small blanket, the only one he had with him. Wrapping it around his body, he curled up and fell into a sleep of exhaustion.

———————————————————————*12*

*O*nesimus made his way the next morning to the Velabrium, where mussels and fish were bawled for sale and where many other kinds of shops were doing their early morning business. The odor of fresh fish and recently pulled onions and garlic besieged his nostrils. Then he saw a pawnshop. Entering it, he offered to buy several coarse garments he had chosen from a rack. The Greek shop-owner was quick to sense fear in the eyes of the tall, lithe, dark-eyed young man. Suspecting as he always did with most who came into his shop that there was more to be learned, the fat little Greek started to ask him a question. But he was stopped by the magic influence of a silver denarius in his palm.

"Perhaps you would like to change here?" he smiled knowingly, and motioned to a small room in the back. Onesimus quickly took off the lovely tunic given him by Archippus, and donned the simpler rough tunic he had exchanged for it. Feeling that the pawnshopkeeper understood his situation and would be no threat to his security, Onesimus asked the way to the Subura.

It was not to be easy. Leaving the marketplace, he also left the well-paved and drained principal streets of Rome, which were unusual in their cleanliness, at least when compared to the undrained stench of most of the other city streets anywhere in the world. He found himself in the crowded, stinking alleys of the Subura. On each side were ill-kept apartments, taverns, brothels, and gambling halls, filled with the dregs of all nations—"the sewer of Rome," as it was called. It was indeed like a sewer, with putrid garbage and the stench of horse and human dung covering the streets. The people moving through the dirty streets jostled each other in resentment or indifference. He noticed some were as young as he, but few were without the marks of dissipation. If he must stay here for a few weeks until the search for him was ended, he knew that he must live by his wits like those all around him.

"It is better to do injustice than to suffer unjustly," he repeated to himself. Callicles's philosophy did not really appeal to him, but, for the moment, he might have to be an Epicurean rather than a Stoic, and certainly not a Christian. Yes, if it came to his freedom, he too could be a bit tricky and unscrupulous along with these others, many of whom he guessed were runaway slaves like himself.

Surely there are some in this river of vice and self-indulgence whom I may trust, he thought. His natural optimism returned. He stopped in the best-appearing tavern he could find and sat down at a table near a very attractive young woman with the dark hair and eyes of an Ionian. Her lips were painted red and her olive skin was touched with pink cosmetics. The blue chiton she wore was cleaner than that of most of the women. Her hair was long and loose over her shoulders, reminding him of Leslia's, but with several small curls around her forehead. Obviously her sitting alone in a public tavern meant she was a prostitute; neither Greek nor Roman women would venture into such places even with their husbands or friends. He was not looking for a prostitute, but he needed a friend. This woman might be the answer. He sat down at the table next to hers and placed his order.

"Will you join me for a cup of wine?" he invited.

She smiled and nodded. On his entrance she had immediately been drawn to him. His suntanned face, clean-cut features, large brown eyes, black hair and tall, athletic form were most attractive to her. *Here is a newcomer,* she reasoned. *He may be good for several denarii.*

She rose and joined him with her warmest smile.

"What are you doing here, young Adonis?" she asked flatteringly.

"Just what you are doing, lovely Venus," he answered back with a show of bravado.

"Well," she said, "I am looking for a man, some fun, and a little money to keep me in food, clothes, and jewelry."

This was more honest than he had expected.

"I'm a man, and I like to have fun, and I have very little money." He added the latter cautiously. "I am also looking for a friend and a place to live. I, too, need to make some money in order to keep on living."

"That makes us even," she said as she lifted her cup. "Here's to our discovery of each other, and to the success and fortune that belongs to each of us."

He drank with her, then warned, "Let's not be so sure that our fortune is good. Remember, 'hope is a traitor,' as our old friend Epicurus would say. It's the moment that counts. By the way," he looked at her with renewed interest, "your accent tells me you are a Phrygian. I, too, come from Phrygia, though I was not born there. But I have lived for seven years in Colossae."

"I knew there was something about you beyond your good looks that appealed to me. Here we are, two ex-Phrygians sitting in the Subura in Rome drinking a toast to each other!"

"But why are you here?" he asked curiously, with obvious concern. "A lovely lady like you should not have to make her living in a place like this."

"It's much better, believe me, than being a slave back in Phrygia. As a slave I was prostituted not only with my body but with my soul. And *that* I will not take!" she countered as her black eyes flashed.

"A fellow philosopher," he exclaimed. "By the gods, you and I will be good friends." Throwing caution to the winds, he confessed, "I, too, am an ex-slave, a runaway, if you please. I agree, it's better to be here and free than a slave back in Phrygia—or in anyplace else!"

Over the wine, they found mutual sympathy and a natural attraction for each other.

Her name was Marcia. She was living in a "dingy place with three rooms," as she described it, with her twin brother, Nicia. They had been in the Subura for almost a year after escaping from their owner in Hierapolis. Their story was more pitiful than Onesimus's tale. The man who owned them was a lecherous glutton who used and abused them with only an occasional show of kindness. He had taken them with him on a pleasure trip to Ephesus "to get away from his wife and family." On the way and in the city he had used Nicia as his valet and he had brought Marcia along for his own satisfaction.

"He was cruel, uncouth, and a very devil," she said with deep hatred. "One night he was drunker than usual, and it was a simple matter for Nicia to knock him out with a blow on the head and rob him of all his money. I had made friends with a pawnshop dealer and managed with the little money I had taken from time to time to pay for some clothes that would not betray us as runaway slaves. Like you, we found a ship bound for Rome. And so here we are—companions in crime and freedom!" She was elated at their triumph.

Frankly, she told Onesimus, the best way they had found to live was through practicing the age-old trade of prostitution. Nicia had joined a company of personable young men making quite a success of their relationships with some of the dissolute patricians and even an occasional senator or member of Nero's court.

"With Nicia's help I have been able to work independently of any brothel, counting on an occasional 'pick-up' on my own, as I thought you might be," she smiled piquantly, "and trusting to Nicia and his friends to bring the lucrative clients to our place."

"I think it must be a rather hard life," Onesimus sympathetically remarked. He was thinking how this occupation, especially that of Nicia, was completely repugnant to him. He had read the moralizing of too many Stoics and had listened too long to his own mother and to the Christian teachings on the use of the human body to feel comfortable in this kind of situation.

"It isn't like having a respectable home with a husband and children," she answered honestly—and here Onesimus thought he saw a tear in her lovely dark eyes. Pulling herself up she said, "But it is so much better than living with that beast back in Hierapolis; it seems like paradise in comparison."

"Yes," replied Onesimus with empathy, "I can understand. But isn't there any other way to make a good living than this?"

"Well, we tried several things. But until it is safe to leave the Subura permanently, there isn't anything half as profitable. Someday we hope to save enough to purchase a shop of our own and then," she said softly, "maybe even a home. But enough of this. Onesimus, my friend, what are you going to do?"

"I don't know," he answered. "I have a good education given me by my father. I would make a good *amenuensis*,* for I am a fine, clear writer, or I could teach some wealthy man's son." He told her of his six years as Helen's tutor.

She looked at him admiringly. "You won't have any trouble once you have escaped the threat of being caught," she said. "But that will take some time."

After a moment's hesitation, a half-formed idea came into her mind. "Why don't you come home with me and Nicia? Perhaps he will have some ideas. After all, as ex-slaves we owe something to each other. You can be our friend and not our client." She touched his hand kindly as she said it, but Onesimus felt more than friendliness in her looks, as he did in his own feelings.

"You are most kind." He gripped her hand in his. "I promise you I won't be a burden. I have some money and will certainly make it worth your while. I confess our meeting here is like the smile of what old Plato spoke of as 'providentia.' "

He paid for the wine and the two left the tavern—he with a lighter heart than he had known in months.

They made their way the few blocks to a six-story dwelling. It seemed better kept than the other buildings, though it was obviously no palace. Her quarters were plain and clean, furnished with several lovely mosaics and pictures that made Onesimus exclaim in pleasure, "To think this is in the Subura!"

"Well," she replied, "when two work as hard as Nicia and I have and save scrupulously, we do get along better than most of these poor devils."

She showed him a bedroom where he might stay that night

---

*Secretary.

until some more definite arrangements were made. Nicia would be in shortly, and they could talk.

"Whatever you would have made by using that room tonight," he offered, "I'll be glad to pay you."

He said it with a blush and, with a woman's intuition, she recognized his inexperience and decided not to push him. That would come in time, she was sure; but he was too attractive and interesting for anything he might think crude. Besides, his hint had left her sure that he did have more money than he first indicated. She liked him and would wait and see how Nicia felt.

"Would you like to rest?" she suggested graciously. "You look exhausted after all you have been through. Here is a basin of water and a towel."

Gratefully he accepted, washed himself, shaved well for the first time in weeks, stretched out on the couch and slept heavily.

He was awakened later in the day by voices in the next room. Rising, he combed his hair and opened the door.

"Well, our young Adonis has had his beauty sleep!" Marcia cried. "Onesimus, this is my brother, Nicia."

"Welcome, fellow freedom-seeker," he exclaimed with a hearty, resonant voice. "Marcia and I have been talking about your situation. Both of us are happy to welcome you to partake of our humble quarters for a while, at least until you can find something more lucrative than taking strange women for a cup of wine in a tavern!"

Nicia was tall and well-formed, with darker complexion than Onesimus. His hands bore the marks of one who knew the meaning of hard labor.

"Thank you from my heart," Onesimus replied. "But you must admit that buying a lovely, black-eyed beauty a cup of wine was richly repaid."

"Marcia tells me that you think little of our profession. After you have been here a while, you will find that it is less repulsive. It pays higher dividends and is much safer than most any other job open to a runaway slave. Besides, this is preferable to belonging to the *lazzaroni** who crowd the streets with nothing to live on but the *sportula*† supplied by the Emperor and wealthy princes who want to curry their favor and buy peace. And there is danger of being discovered, for the officers in charge of locating runaway slaves are always present when the *sportula* is handed out. No, friend Onesimus, there are worse ways of making a living than this, such as housebreaking, thievery in the markets, or just plain gambling. We don't really have much choice. When you are ready, I will be glad to show you how to get started."

Then appraising the young beginner with a cool eye, he said, "You'll make it with some top prices. How would fifty denarii for one evening sound to you for a starter?"

"I . . . I'm not sure I could do that," Onesimus stuttered in embarrassment.

"Of course you could. But I'll not press you. Now, let's have something to eat and then we'll go out and meet some of our partners. By the way, tomorrow is the gladiatorial combat in the Coliseum. Marcia and I and several of our friends plan to go. You come along, too."

Onesimus was delighted. He had heard much of the famed gladiators of Rome. Though some of the philosophers had spoken against the bloody cruelty of the games as cheap amusement fit only for a bloodthirsty *vulgus*,‡ he was curious and decided to see all he could.

That night their evening meal was simple—bread and cheese and some hot peppery sausage Marcia assured him was a Roman specialty. The best thing of all was that Onesimus felt himself among friends, accepted as an equal. It was a good feeling.

After dinner they left for a tavern on the edge of the Subura, where they met a half dozen of Nicia's sporting partners seated around a large table. Introductions were made, and the five

---

*Paupers.
†Dole, i.e., free handouts of food.
‡Mob.

young men looked admiringly at Nicia and Marcia's new discovery. They exclaimed their delight. "So the Phrygians get together! Not too bad when you have the physique of a Greek god," one of them cried.

Onesimus flushed and felt uncomfortable although he was pleased with the compliment.

"Here's to Onesimus," another exclaimed as he lifted his cup. They all joined in the toast. "May he be useful to himself and to his friends as he once was to his hard-hearted master!"

"Philemon really was not cruel to me," Onesimus tried to say. But they were talking and laughing so loudly they did not hear him. He remained quiet.

Already his conscience was beginning to hurt. He knew he had to be a part of this new world, but he was not sure how far he could go. He did his best to enter into their bantering fun, all the time trying to justify himself by recalling how Lucretius had sung the praises of Epicurus, who had destroyed belief in the gods and liberated man from oppressive and unnatural morality. In his essay "On the Nature of Things," Lucretius rejoiced in the new liberty to enjoy the tastes and pleasures of good food and uninhibited passion, regretting that too often men had been "abasing their spirits through fear of the gods."

For the time being, Onesimus decided to be "liberated" not only from chattel slavery, but from slavery to his old-fashioned moral prudery. He would live for the day and enjoy it. Thus, his brilliant wit, enlivened by the wine, finally enabled him to take part and to charm his companions. He parroted several comforting quotations from Lucretius and Epicurus that pleased all of them immensely. The freedom of pleasure for pleasure's sake was celebrated with great elation.

Then, one of the group called the others' attention back to the work of the evening. Each of them had engagements, including Nicia. Marcia and Onesimus were left to return to their quarters. As they walked the dark streets together, the touch of Marcia's hand and the feeling of her warm body brushing his aroused his desires fully. When they reached the dwelling, he followed her without a word into her room.

$\mathcal{H}$e awakened suddenly. It was dawn. Silently he slipped out of Marcia's bed and tiptoed to the room assigned to him, which in his "new liberation" he had chosen not to use. Yes, he was choosing his path. He recalled every step of the rationalization that had led him to the oblivion and self-abandonment of the preceding hours. For a few hours he had forgotten all as he surrendered to the pleasure of bodily fulfillment. In the gray hours of the dawn, he did not care if love included respect and admiration.

The simple truth is, I used Marcia to meet my need, he admitted to himself. *And she used me. Why not?* He knew a good answer, though a hundred arguments to the contrary sought to stifle it. From what Phineas had taught him, he knew that the overwhelming forgetfulness of the River of Sexual Lethe did not last. Aristotle, who made more sense to Onesimus than most of the Stoics, had warned against *amor** or even *amicitia*† when based purely on utility or pleasure rather than upon mutual respect and shared concern for each other. *Amor* and *amicitia* as the Greeks called them, were good only when used with moderation toward the highest love, or what the Latins called *caritas*‡ and the Greeks *agape*.

He lay back on his bed and watched the sun rise outside his window over the stinking streets of the Subura. He somehow remembered the beautiful lines of Paul's hymn that had so well expressed his vision of Helen: "Love [*agape, caritas*] is patient and kind. It envies no one. Love is never boastful nor conceited nor rude; never selfish, nor quick to take offense. Love keeps no

---

*Romantic love.
†Friendship.
‡Self-sacrificial love.

score of wrongs. . . delights in the truth. There is nothing love
cannot face; there is no limit to its faith, its hope and its
endurance."

This was the love he desired above all else. He had
memorized the words as he heard them read many times over in
the Christian worship in Colossae. He remembered them not
only because they spoke his deepest desire, but because he
knew Helen had expressly requested they be read.

"Will I ever know this kind of love?" he questioned himself.
"With Helen perhaps I might," he sighed deeply. "With Marcia,
not likely." He had tried to talk to her about *caritas*, but she had
laughed at him. "*Caritas* is all right for the wealthy and
favored," she had said, "but for you and me, friend, we had
better stick to *amor*. We cannot afford *caritas*—it would cost us
our freedom if not our lives. Besides, I'm sleepy. Who wants to
talk philosophy at a time like this?"

"Marcia was right," he muttered. "That hour was no time for
philosophy, and Marcia was no philosopher." As usual, he had
been trying to think through his situation as he had been taught
to do.

That moment his reverie was disturbed as he heard Nicia
shouting to Marcia to get up and prepare some breakfast.
Onesimus rose and washed his face. *She has been kind,* he
mused. *Maybe she knows more of* caritas *than I expect.*

But as he came into the combination living room, bedroom,
and kitchen where Nicia had slept, he missed what he sought so
eagerly in her eyes. The fire was gone. She was very matter-
of-fact and business-like.

After breakfast, as if she had been thinking principally of
money in those hours preceding, she frankly asked him for the
fulfillment of his promise the day before.

"You mean the money for the room," he flushed. Digging into
his money pouch he came up with a much larger gold coin than
she had anticipated, for when she saw it her eyes brightened.
She took the coin and, without a word of thanks, turned to the
fun of the day. She had quickly regained her old smile.

"Let's hurry and get to the Colosseum before all Rome's *lazzaroni* have filled the good seats," she cried with enthusiasm.

Nicia was tired and uncommunicative but agreed it well to start soon.

"You have no idea what a *turba** of smelly humanity will be there," he explained to Onesimus. Nothing had been said about the night before; for this Onesimus was grateful. The proceedings were taken for granted by both brother and sister.

This is the professional way to look at their business, thought Onesimus, *but it is not for me.*

Onesimus looked forward to the gladiatorial fights. He had heard so much of these magnificent spectacles. "But how can we afford to risk the danger of being caught in such a public place?" he asked them. This worry gnawed at his mind. He had already found that a fugitive slave could not go many places safely.

"That's simple," Nicia answered. "A gladiatorial combat is *the* one great spectacle of Rome society. From the poorest *lazzaroni* to the Emperor—all will be there, including the officers whose job it is to recover fugitives such as we. But it is a holiday, and even the officers are primarily interested in the fights and the fun. The entrances are large, and we can melt into the crowd. There is very little chance of being discovered."

It was a gala day. They were joined at the tavern by Nicia's friends, and soon they were swept along in the throng. Merrily and banteringly they pushed on by the Forum, the Temples to Jupiter, Mars, Dionysius, Diana, and other Greek and Roman gods until finally they entered the wide gates of the magnificent Colosseum.

It was a heady day for Onesimus. He was seeing his first glimpse of the historic and world-renowned monuments of which he had heard so much, and the excitement of the throng was contagious. The little band stayed together by linking arms. Onesimus, next to Marcia, again felt the stirrings of

---

*Crowd.

pleasure as they jostled each other in the press. It was a good day, and he was going to enjoy it.

The huge Colosseum was filling quickly with the exception of the reserved seats for which rich merchants, princes, and others without political influence paid a pretty price. And, of course, the center section of choicest seats was for the Emperor and his court, the senators and their families, surrounded by members of all the praetorian guard on duty. Nicia and his band found good seats not too far from the reserved section, close enough to see the pages who guarded the royal booths where the Emperor would recline. Nicia and Marcia pointed out the interesting spots within the huge oval as Onesimus, sitting between them, eagerly devoured the colorful scene.

"Nero is as bloodthirsty and cruel as Caligula ever thought of being," Marcia whispered. "It is common knowledge that he poisoned his mother, Aggripina, as she poisoned her husband, Emperor Claudius, in order to gain power for her son!"

"She had already poisoned her husband Crispus Passeus, the wealthy orator." Nicia joined in on the lurid story of their Emperor's background.

"The irony of it—or maybe it is Nemesis, if there is such a goddess—instead of Mother Aggripina ruling Rome through her son Nero, as she expected, he murdered her and has become a tyrant. They say he is soon to do the same to his brother-in-law, the handsome young Britanicus, who is the son of the former Emperor Claudius. Now everyone in high position is afraid for his head."

"In spite of the spectacular entertainment such as this Nero provides," Marcia explained, "what makes us hate him, as do most of the Romans we know, is the way he treats the beautiful and virtuous Queen Octavia, Britanicus's sister. You will see that she is not with him today. Very likely the treacherous Poppae, wife of Otho, one of his courtiers, has taken over as the object of his fickle affections. To think that only four years ago, Nero was a timid, well-behaved boy, caring more for art and amusement and taught by the renowned philosopher Seneca! After such good training he completely changed his character under such apt tutors in vice as Otho and Tullius Senecio, 'the Gilded Youth' as all in Rome call them. Nero has surpassed the viciousness and depravity of his teachers."

"But what about Seneca?" Onesimus asked, puzzled. "Has he not had influence on his star pupil? They say Seneca is one of the ablest teachers of morality among the Stoics."

"Seneca is a big joke," laughed Nicia. "With all his high-sounding talk about virtue, he is so afraid of offending Nero that he has gone along with him. They even say he prepared Nero's speeches for him at times when the Emperor tried to justify himself before the Senate in such murders as that of his mother and others who were in his way. Oh, Nero never admits it. But his arguments are cleverly written and specious indeed—only a Seneca could have thought of them. So Seneca has lost the confidence of the truer Stoics, they say, such as Lucan, his brilliant nephew, and Cornutus, the one Stoic most highly respected."

"How do you know all this?" Onesimus asked with fascination.

"One of our clients is a friend of Lucan—who continually admonished him about his particular vice that enriches my pocket. But he is a good Stoic and virtuous, as they call it, in many other ways. Lucan's friend says Seneca has good intentions but is afraid of losing his own head. Back in the early days when he could have held a tight rein on his young pupil, he made one concession after another until it was too late. Without the reins of moral conscience or anyone in authority over him, he discovered he could do exactly as he liked. Now that he has come to regard himself as a god whose wishes are the laws for all mankind, there is nothing too low, too evil, too devilish for him to do if it gives him pleasure. He spends his time in one bacchanalian orgy after another, with the most vicious men and women of Rome. They say he is also a sadist, enjoying the blood and suffering of those he tortures."

"I'm surprised to hear you talk like this," Onesimus started to say. But at that moment a loud roar of applause came from the crowd as one of the favorite patrons of the poor entered. His *sportula* alone had kept large numbers of them from going hungry.

The crowd was becoming even noisier, for every minute or so another well-known prince or senator entered. Onesimus was interested in the splendor of the scene; but his mind reverted again and again to the description of Nero and Seneca and the contradictions of Nicia and Marcia's condemnation of Nero against their own lack of principle. Or did they have principles in other areas? His mind began to wander in the din of the crowd. What makes a thing right and wrong? The question had bothered him during the time he had been planning to rob his master and escape. It disturbed him more now, as he faced the prospect of accepting or rejecting Nicia's invitation to join in an ignoble profession that could give him an easy living but which revolted all his deepest instincts and convictions about right and wrong.

"Where does God—or the gods—come in?" he asked himself. "If Epicurus is right and if there is no god higher than I, then I must make up my own moral codes, and isn't that exactly what Nicia and Marcia as well as Nero are doing? What's the difference except in degree? If it is convenient and necessary to save my skin, to give me pleasure, it is good; if it gets in the way of my pleasure or safety it is bad."

His deeper self rejected such meaninglessness and lack of worthy purpose. Again, one of the apostle's phrases rang through his mind, "I may give all I possess to feed the poor or even my body to be burned, but if I have no love, I am nothing." He shook his head. He could not understand—what is love and virtue?

With a start, he was brought back to the Colosseum. Marcia was pointing excitedly as a hundred trumpets sounded shrilly through the air announcing the grand entrance of the Emperor and his court.

"There he comes, the cruel *diabolus!*" she exclaimed.

Nero was carried in on a litter with gold-lined curtains by six of the brawniest slaves Onesimus had ever seen, surrounded by his most brilliantly dressed courtiers. He was reclining with his fat jowls hanging loosely from his face, giving an impression of boredom which even the distance that separated them could not prevent Onesimus from observing. When Nero arrived at his cushioned seat, he stood to recognize the applause of the mob. Time and again, they shouted and stomped their feet. Though many hated and feared him, never had there been such free and thrilling entertainment as his gladiatorial combats provided. Several times he arose and, holding his hand over his heart, acknowledged their applause.

"How well he knows," Nicia said with bitter irony. "The mob is his master just as it is his slave. He knows as well as Tiberius knew that he is 'holding a wolf by the ears.' "

At last Pedanius, the master of the show, rose to throw down the scarlet napkin announcing that the show was to begin.

The first thirty minutes were more like the circuses Onesimus had seen in the amphitheatre in Ephesus: a trained bear dancing to the tune of pipers, a tiger led by his keeper with a chain of flowers, monkeys and their trainers playing games on the back of elephants.

Then the wild beasts were released to fight each other till the sand of the arena was blood-spattered. Bears, lions, tigers, and leopards were baited by armed *bestiari*.* Often enough, to feed the crowd's taste for blood, one *bestiarus* and then another would be felled by a lion's paw and his breast torn open by the beast's hungry jaws.

Onesimus was sickened by the scene, especially when a group of twenty criminals, including several political prisoners (so Nicia described them), whose only crime was a few words spoken in the wrong place about Nero or one of his favorites, were forced out into the arena. Several wild bears were joined by tigers and lions in making their midday meal from the defenseless victims. These poor wretches stood with stupefaction as the snarling beasts approached, fighting a losing battle with only their bare hands. The *venationus*† was received with

---

*Wild beast fighters.
†Wild beast show.

savage appreciation by the crowd. Onesimus turned to look at Marcia and then at Nicia and their companions. Each of them was enjoying the butchery thoroughly, especially when one of the victims made an unusual fight against unequal odds and wrestled with a lion or a tiger until the animal's teeth found the mark. They shouted their approval with the mob.

How could one who cares for human life take pleasure over the death of anyone? Onesimus asked himself. This was human nature at its worst, and he was to see more of it that day than he cared to believe existed. Marcia and Nicia both were in a state of nearly hysterical ecstasy. *But how could they?* Onesimus asked himself over and over. They hated Nero for his evil ways, but enjoyed his brutal entertainment. The contradiction did not make sense.

The sun shone so hot that curtains were pulled over the Emperor and his court and the other wealthy spectators. For the mob, huge sprays of cold water were released to refresh them, followed by sprays of perfume that filled the Colosseum. Then, to the delight of the *lazzaroni* and the plebians who were included in the Emperor's huge party, baskets of fruit were passed and each one helped himself to a delicious lunch, making them all the more ready for the real sport of the day: the gladiatorial combats.

While they were eating the fruit, Nicia and Marcia stayed busy pointing out to Onesimus various important personages. He was especially interested to see Seneca, an old man with a tired but an intelligent, even noble face. *Too bad,* thought Onesimus, *Seneca has good moral principles, but he lacks the power to fulfill them. A tragedy! But maybe he is like I am and all other men—forced to do what he knows is wrong in order to obtain just due for himself. But is it better to do injustice to others than to suffer it yourself?* The old question remained unanswered still.

The sandy surface of the arena was scraped to remove the gore. Bloody flesh and bones of animals and men were thrown into carts and hauled off to be dumped into the Tiber or to be buried outside the city.

The great event was now at hand. Pedanius dropped the scarlet cloth, and the gates were opened. To the music of the trumpeteers, the gladiators marched around the arena—twenty-four of them clad in glittering armor, four on white horses—until they stood before the Emperor. As one man they saluted and chanted the greeting: "Hail, Caesar! We, who are about to die, salute you!"

Once more at the signal from Pedanius, the gladiators put on an exhibition with blunt swords, as Marcia and Nicia pointed out their favorites whose skill and strength had enabled them to survive other occasions such as this. These were the heroes, the darlings of the populace. If they remained alive long enough, they were often rewarded with their freedom, plus rich estates and many precious gifts.

At another drop of the scarlet cloth, Pedanius signaled for the battle to begin. First came the four mounted gladiators on white horses. Pairing off, they fought each other, knowing that for all but one this would be the last battle. With loud shouts they charged, swords and spears clashing on helmets, until at last the spear of one pierced through the joint of the armor of the first victim, and he fell bleeding to the ground. The crowd bellowed *"Habet"** and when he lay still they shouted again, *"Peractum est!"*†

To Onesimus's horror, Marcia, Nicia, and all five of their companions were joining in this cruel ritual with all their hearts.

A second rider bled and fell, then a third. Now the fourth reined his sweating, panting horse in front of the Emperor and saluted. The Emperor arose and gave the sign of victory.

"He will be given a great villa and one hundred thousand denarii," Nicia cried with admiration. "What a man!"

Onesimus was stunned by the scene. *To the victor belongs the spoils? Yes*, he thought, *in this world he who does injustice because he is strongest is better than one who suffers injustice,*

---

*Let it be.
†There's an end to him!

no matter how good he is. The words were bitter in his mouth as he watched a slave enter the arena with a heavy blunt instrument and crush in the skulls of the three fallen gladiators to be sure they were not still alive.

Then came the main event: Twelve Sammites and Murmillos were matched against as many net throwers and chasers. The difference between those with nets and those without them was the lack of armor, so that every cut and gash could be clearly seen in the flesh of the net-throwers and enjoyed by the throng. The Sammites and Murmillos were equipped with British and Gallic armor respectively, including helmets; but their armor was often their ruin as the more agile and unencumbered net-throwers succeeded in entangling them in their nets and piercing them with their swords.

For thirty minutes the fight raged from one side of the arena to the other. One after another of the Sammites and Murmillos were caught in the nets, and the net-throwers were gashed with the spears of their antagonists. One after another the victors stood over the vanquished, waiting for a sign from the crowd or the Emperor to deliver the fatal blow. That day all but one received the sign from the crowd and were immediately killed by their adversaries. At last, four of the Sammites and three of the Murmillos remained alive; the remaining seventeen gladiators died in agony. The seven victors lined up again before the Emperor, who stood to salute them for their bravery. Pedanius summoned them to the platform where they were presented with costly gifts and medals for their courage. The mob went wild in its enthusiasm.

It had been the most horror-filled day of Onesimus's life. While his companions shouted and waved their handkerchiefs, he stood like one in shock. *Could this be the greatest sport of the mighty Rome, the city he had admired since boyhood—the Rome of Augustus Caesar, of Cicero and Virgil, of Lucas and Seneca? And were these his friends made of a different order of things than he?*

As they stood to leave the Colosseum, Marcia began to notice for the first time how Onesimus felt.

"What's the matter, are you *timidus**?" she laughed as she saw his somber expression and white face. "Can't you take the sight of a little blood? Look," she called to the others, "our Phrygian friend has lost his nerve."

As they waited for the huge throng to pour out through the gates, the little band joined together in a circle around him. Onesimus was on the spot, but his indignation could not be hidden.

"I was never so ashamed of my fellow humans as today," he cried with flashing eyes. "How could you join with this mob of inhuman beings, gloating and feeding on the blood and agony of others, some of whom were more worthy and virtuous than any of us? We who have fought for justice and freedom for ourselves, how could we watch any such spectacle with glee?"

For the moment, his denunciation of the combats and of the hearty participation of his fellow-spectators caught them by surprise. Then Nicia spoke with stinging ridicule, "Who is this virtuous man to lecture his friends—this man who drugged his master and stole his money and is now ready to practice whatever thievery and vice he thinks is necessary for a good life? Who is he to condemn the greatest sport of the empire?"

He put his arm around Onesimus, "Come down off Mount Olympus, my young god-friend. Such a spectacle is enjoyable to us because we are not in it! It makes us better enjoy our own freedom for the day, for tomorrow we may not be able to enjoy it. You will have to admit, that's the Epicurean way you admire. The poor devils who lost their lives out there would have been killed anyway. Why not give the other poor wretches of Rome, whether in the Subura or on Capitoline Hill, the sadistic joy of watching them struggle against hopeless odds even though they lose? 'To the strong go the spoils.' Think of the glory and honor those seven heroes will receive!"

Onesimus was silenced by his own guilt. Who was he to lecture them on morals? What did he know or care about right and wrong? Was he not a rebel at law and virtuous customs?

---

*Chicken-hearted.

"Obviously, my actions agree with you," he answered. "All of us here *act* upon the assumption that it is better to do injustice to others than to have it done to ourselves. So why not make a holiday out of watching others receive unjust agony and death, rejoicing, as you say, that we are still safe and secure and, by the gods, intend to remain so."

"That's a man," shouted Venturus, the loudest and coarsest of Nicia's partners. "Now you're getting down to earth! Compassion and mercy are luxuries which we in the Subura, or anywhere else, cannot afford. Safety first, self-preservation and joy for the hour—that is the only real way to live."

The others joined in the congratulations, assuming Onesimus was fully with them. They walked down the now half-emptied aisles and onto the street leading back to safety in the Subura. Only Marcia saw that Onesimus was not converted to this hedonistic, selfish existence. She could see the fires underneath his outer acquiescence, and she hated him for his superiority, as most human beings hate another who makes them feel morally uncomfortable. She, too, had fought a battle with the question of justice, but she had had so much injustice done to her that she was hardened in the belief that it would take a lifetime to even things up. Onesimus's ideals disgusted her. He was too soft for her liking.

He soon discovered her true feelings as they entered the tavern and gathered around the table to celebrate the holiday. Onesimus was sickened and wanted nothing more than to get away from this crowd to whom he could not make himself belong. He had to think things out. But they were not to give him time.

After consuming huge portions of a large and luscious pork roast Nicia had ordered prepared the morning before, they drank and talked about their work for the night. Onesimus was completely unprepared when Nicia turned to him with the question he most dreaded to hear. "All right, Mr. Adonis, when do you begin to cash in on your good looks and put away a few more coins for the gilded future you are planning as a freeman? I am willing to supply your first customers for one-fourth the take until you get established."

Onesimus did not know how to answer. He knew he could never join the profession in which Nicia, Marcia, Venturus, and the other five were so much at home. But he had to say something. And his answer, he realized, would pronounce his doomed relations with all seven of these erstwhile friends.

He caught a sidelong glance of amusement that Marcia and Nicia exchanged as he began to speak. "Whether or not there is any right and wrong, good or evil in the nature of things, I am still free to choose to live by at least a few remaining principles. One of them is that I will not sell my body for anyone's pleasure. Why give up one kind of slavery for another? No, Nicia. Thanks for your offer, but count me out. I will have to find another means of making my way."

"Well, if that's your decision, *habet*, as they say in the arena. Let it be," Nicia responded in icy disdain.

As the meaning of Onesimus's decision became clear, the others looked at each other knowingly. Without a word, Nicia arose and beckoned to the five partners. They joined him in the corner of the room where they conversed for a few minutes. Onesimus could not hear what they were saying. Baffled and hurt, he turned to Marcia and found her looking at him in utter contempt.

"You may be handsome, Onesimus, but you are stupid. Or else you are too good to live in this hard old world. I am disappointed in you. We could have made a great team and had a wonderful time together."

Seeing his crestfallen face, she showed a moment of pity, "What will you do? What can you do that will not endanger your life?" He thought of what he had told her the day before about finding some work as a scribe, but before he could remind her, the six friends returned.

"Come, let's drink up," cried Ventura. "Here's to some soft easy job for our friend, Onesimus! He ought to be useful for something." In the meantime, Nicia had brought a fresh jug of wine, and all the cups were passed to him for refilling.

Self-conscious and embarrassed, Onesimus received his cup and raised it with the others. "Thanks, Venturus, that at least we may be friends. I hope to see you all many times."

Though no one responded to his overture, he joined them as they drained their cups, still trying to discern their actions. Only then did Onesimus realize what was happening. Nicia had put something in his wine. His tongue became so thick he was not even able to accuse them of their betrayal. The last thing he remembered was Marcia's mocking repetition of his own words in a sing-song voice, *"Tis better to do unjustly to others than to be treated unjustly!"*

————————————————————————— *14*

 everal hours later, he awoke as the tavern keeper jabbed him. "Hey, fellow, you've slept long enough. Time to close up." He had seen what happened and had been rewarded for his silence. Now he splashed cold water on Onesimus's face, helped him to his feet, and led him out the door.

Unsteadily, Onesimus stayed on his feet long enough to lean against the wall. What had happened? Then he remembered the conversation of Nicia and his friends and the last drink together. He felt for his money pouch, and his heart stopped as he realized it was gone. He felt for his money belt which he carried around his waist. Only the empty belt remained where once the rich stake he had brought from Ephesus had been carried—ten thousand denarii and all his precious gems gone! He was without a farthing.

In the darkness of the street he stomped his feet, beat his head with his fist, and shouted curses at Nicia and his companions, at his fate and at whatever gods there might be. Nemesis had caught up with him through professed friends. He was desperate as he started walking down the street deeper into the Subura. His first thought was to call the *sparteoli*, but there were no police in the Subura. Then he remembered. He was a runaway slave. He dared not risk being found out. Perhaps he had it coming to him. His whole frame shook with anger as he thought of Nicia and Marcia. "By the gods, they shall pay for this!" He started in the direction of their quarters. What would he do? In his blind fury he did not think nor did he care.

At long last he arrived at the building and climbed, panting, up the stairs. Without knocking he tried the door. It was locked. He backed away a few feet and threw his body against it; the door burst open. He met Nicia standing with his hands clasped matter of factly behind his back, looking at him with disdain.

"Give me back my money, you thieves! You traitors! You devils!" Onesimus shouted. "You have no right to. . ."

"No right to what, you soft-headed fool!" Nicia replied coolly. "I have as much right to this money as you do. Remember where you got it? Now you get out of here and don't come back, or I will kill you."

Infuriated, Onesimus charged toward him. Blinded both by the drug and by his own bitterness, he did not see the club Nicia had in his hand until one blow from it caught him between the eyes and sent him reeling backwards through the door. Nicia followed him into the entryway and struck him again on the back of his neck. Then he kicked him down the staircase where Onesimus landed in a heap at the bottom.

At this moment, Marcia appeared at the door, her face suffused with anger. Onesimus, looking up through the blood that obscured his vision, could barely see her or hear her bitter words: "Who do you think you are, Jupiter or Zeus, that you can live so superior to the rest of us?" she accused. "You are too soft to live in this world. We will use the money you stole from your master to buy that shop. It is not our business what happens to you."

With that they slammed the door. Marcia's words cut like a knife. Onesimus's anger and bitterness were at their peak, but his common sense told him there was nothing he could do. The hurt was much worse than just that of the blows on his head and neck, though these were bleeding profusely.

That night, with head bandaged from a piece of his tunic, he slept by the side of a wall with the beggars. Though it was summer, the night was cold; he shivered both from the chilly air and from the fear brought by his sudden disaster. The pain of his wounds seemed to heighten as morning approached. He knew only a fitful sleep.

In the early dawn, he saw the poor wretches all around him, covered with stinking rags and sores, still asleep. Their faces were hard, unshaved; their bodies were lank with hunger, for the *sportula* of Nero and the rich barely kept them alive. He got up and walked in the direction of the River Tiber. His head throbbed with pain but walking helped his circulation. He hoped the river would enable him to think better. It always had back in Colossae. What would he do? He had no money, no food, no friends. He felt rejected, not only by man but by God. If there were a God or gods, they must be making sport of him.

At last he reached the river and found a grassy spot along the bank. As the sun was rising, he sat down to think.

So, this is freedom! he exclaimed to himself. *Freedom to be alone, unloved, unwanted, hungry, cold, lost in contradiction and confusion. But maybe I have been a fool! Why should I not be "prosperous" and "happy," "well fed" and "merry" as are these my former companions? Why must I be so inconsistent—surrendering my principles in order to escape slavery and then sticking by other principles that prevent me from enjoying the warmth, safety, and companionship of others?* But even as he asked the question, he knew the answer. Whether it meant the life of a beggar or death, he simply would not, could not be another Nicia. He would not surrender mercy, compassion, kindness, tenderness, and the other gifts of the Spirit, as Paul called them. Maybe he was a fool, but it was the way he was.

He stood up and, swinging his arms, he knew there was no answer to his questions—at least not that he could see. In the meantime, he was hungry; but as a runaway slave he could not go to the feeding trough where the human pigs were to receive their daily dole of black bread and fruit. He suddenly realized he was wearing the colorful yellow tunic of Archippus.

"Blessed Archippus, how could I have betrayed you?" he cried. "By Jupiter, I wish I were back . . . no," and he clenched his fists in disgust, "I can't go back. I am *free!*" He said it mockingly.

He started walking toward the market place where he had exchanged one tunic for the rough clothes that were now with his other garments in the bag in Marcia and Nicia's apartment. He would trade this yellow tunic, now stained with blood and the mud of the night's stay by the wall, for another cheaper tunic and, perhaps, enough money for his breakfast.

When he entered the store, the little shopkeeper acted as though he had never seen him before. Without questions or even words, he exchanged the yellow garment for a coarse one and two sesterces. *Not much,* Onesimus thought, *but enough for two scant meals.*

Fortified by a piece of bread and some fruit, he walked back to his thinking-place by the river Tiber. He sat down for an hour or two under the shade of the trees watching the small boats and rafts pass by on the muddy little stream. But his philosophy was all idle meandering in spite of his attempt to recall from Plato or Aristotle or Heraclitus words that might give him guidance.

He began to walk the streets, anxiously looking for someone with whom he might share his need and gain some help. All the faces that passed him by were faces of indifference, uncaring, hardened by the world's injustice and by their own rebellion, dissipation, and despair.

He was discouraged, hungry, and afraid; nevertheless, Onesimus would not admit defeat. He would find a job—any kind of a job—and a place to stay somewhere in this wretched hole until it was safe to seek for a position more suited to his abilities, such as a tutor or a secretary for some rich family.

First, he tried the pawnbroker who had made the change of clothing for him. He had seemed kind enough, but when Onesimus asked him for a job the old man cursed him roundly. "What do you think I am, young fellow, an ass to be burdened with your troubles? How many other runaway slaves have asked for a job just because I have traded some clothing for some of their stolen property! I don't need the services of the likes of you. The first time an armed squad of legionnaires looking for runaway slaves entered this place, you would be caught and I would be a dead rabbit. How else could I explain the presence of a good-looking cuss like you working in a pawnshop?"

"But I have some identification papers to show that I am the son of a Pergamos merchant."

"How long do you think that forgery would last? The son of a rich merchant from Pergamos working in a pawnshop. Now get out of here and stay out!"

With less confidence, Onesimus tried a tavern. The hardened barkeeper put it straight, "Harboring fugitive slaves is the quickest way to get thrown in the *ergastulum** myself! 'For he who harbors a runaway slave suffers the same punishment as the slave when he is caught.' "

Onesimus soon discovered that the only persons who could work openly at even the most menial jobs in the Subura were freemen. Marcia and Nicia were right in this, at least. The only way to make a living in this doomed place was to join the ranks of the other criminals, prostitutes, and thieves.

"Too bad, Sonny, this is no place for the proud," one old beggar told him. "I'm not proud, just lazy. So if you are too cowardly or too proud to do these things, then join us this afternoon as the *sportula* is handed out. It isn't much, but it does hold body and soul together. Let the rich feed you."

The old man is right, Onesimus thought to himself. *I am proud, too proud to make my living by becoming a professional prostitute or thief, but I am not lazy. How can I ever lower myself to join this flea-bitten, cowardly, lazy crowd who lets someone else care for them?"*

For several days, he continued to walk the streets. He grew gaunt from hunger and sick and weak from exposure and diarrhea. Soon he came to the place where he accepted the old

---

*Prison.

man's invitation, put mud on his face and tunic, and accompanied him to the "feeding trough" where the human cattle of Rome accepted their dole—little baskets of food handed out to the ungrateful who had lost all pride and self-respect in their hunger. Many were lazy; some were at their row's end like him.

He took the basket, fearfully hiding his face from the government employees who gave it. Shaking off the garrulous old pauper, he walked back to his spot by the Tiber. Several dogs accompanied him, barking and clamoring at his heels. Without thinking, he broke off a few small pieces of his bread and fed it to them, then took a stick and drove them away.

Weary in body and mind, he ate the fruit and the remaining pieces of bread. "This is it," he said to himself, "either I find someone I can trust and some way to use this freedom bought at such a price, or I throw myself into the Tiber."

And then the thought came to him. . . . There was one man in Rome whom he knew he could trust. It was Paul, the man who said he was "the chief of sinners" and called himself "a slave of Christ." Onesimus was baffled by such talk from this man from whose face and life had shone only goodness and compassion—genuine *agape* love. That was the answer. *Paul was in Rome!* The thought electrified Onesimus. He recalled the story Archippus had heard from Tyrannus and the Christians in Ephesus. Somewhere in this city was the bent and scarred little man named Paul with the big heart and the great mind and the wide soul.

Onesimus stood with fists upraised in his excitement. "That's it," he told the birds and the trees. "I'll find Paul. At least he will not let me starve. And perhaps he has enough of the *agape* he talks about to help me get a job." Then a shaft of fear pierced him. "He could send me back to Colossae. I'll have to take that chance. Going to this man who at least seemed kind when I knew him back in Ephesus is better than dying here of starvation—or existing as a rogue, making my way by beastly acts."

Onesimus felt a sense of relief. "This is reason enough. No one in all of Rome cares what happens to me unless it could be

Paul. Maybe he will care enough to help me." Lying back on the grass he dwelt long on that thought. *"Caritas*—what a beautiful word—meaning the same as the Greek *agape*, but it sounds sweeter somehow." As he lay there, he remembered one of the unusual stories of Jesus that Paul had told them in Ephesus— the story of the Good Shepherd who left his ninety-nine sheep safe and well fed and went out into the cold and darkness to find the one sheep that was lost. He sat up.

"I hope this is a wiser decision than the one made by the River Lycus," he reflected. Then he shook his head. "No, it was the only choice I had. I am not sorry I made it."

—Part Four—
Enslaved but Free

15

*A*rchippus had told Onesimus of the universal sign by which Christians recognized one another. He began in neighborhoods near the city, looking beneath the lintel of every dwelling he passed for the carved sign of a fish. Many of Jesus' original disciples were fishermen; evidently the Christians preferred this simple symbol to represent them above any other. The Greek letters for "fish" also made an acrostic standing for "Jesus Christ, Son of God, Savior."

The morning was cool and sunny. Even with an aching body there was fresh hope in his heart. For quite some time he walked the streets, and then there it was. He saw the sign of a fish carved in wood on the door of an unpretentious house. With only a moment's hesitation, he walked up and knocked on the door. When it opened, a kindly-faced woman with her hair tied in a knot on the top of her head greeted him. A look of fear came over her after seeing his shabby tunic and dirty, bearded face. She almost closed the door, but Onesimus stopped her by raising his hand and making the sign of the cross. He repeated softly the passwords of a Christian, "Jesus Christ is Lord."

With a smile, she opened the door and invited him in, offering him a seat in the simple patio where a few flowers grew.

"Thank you for your trust," he said quietly. "I can understand how my appearance would frighten you, but I have undergone several days of suffering and hunger. My name is Gaius Julius. I am from Corinth where I have barely escaped with my life. A new persecution has broken out in our city after Brother Paul, the apostle of our Lord, left. My family and I were among the Christians who met in the rented hall. We were driven out by the mob stirred up by angry merchants whose sale of the images of Diana was hurt by Paul's teaching. Several of the Christians were killed, including my father and mother. I could not bear to stay in Corinth. I managed to get enough money from what my parents had left to buy passage to Rome, but not enough to get food or clothing."

"May the Lord bless you," the woman murmured. "Forgive me for doubting. Let me go and get you some food. My name is Junia and my husband, Nereus, would want me to share with you our humble home. I will warm some water and you may use one of my husband's clean tunics until this one can be washed. Stay with us until you are refreshed, and when Nereus returns I am sure he will help you."

With that she left Onesimus in the patio garden, musing on the immediate acceptance those magic words had provided. He felt guilty for telling such a lie, especially by pretending to be a believer. This was, he hoped, the summit of his perfidy. But he *had* to find Paul and some way to the freedom for which he had already paid so dearly.

Soon she returned with some bread and cheese, an apple and a pear. As he ate ravenously, she talked with quiet excitement about the little Christian community that had begun to grow in numbers and strength even before Paul had arrived. Some traveling merchants from Galatia had first planted the seed, then others came from various parts of the Mediterranean, where already the good news of Christ had spread.

"What about Brother Paul?" Onesimus asked in the middle of her story of the Roman Christians and their life together.

"What a joy his coming has brought!" she exclaimed, but added sadly, "He is still imprisoned and chained to a praetorian guard. But he is permitted the unusual privilege for such a prisoner of living in a dwelling which we have helped him rent." She added the latter proudly, then went on in a lowered voice, "We do not know when the charges against him will be heard. He hopes to be set free, but knowing Nero," and here she barely whispered looking furtively around, "we are all afraid for the worst."

"Is this place where Paul is prisoner near?" Onesimus asked.

"Further along this very same street," Junia answered. "Now you will want to rest until Nereus comes. He will give you some good suggestions. I hope you have had enough to eat?" she asked solicitously as she led him into an adjoining room. After bringing him the warm water and a tunic and giving him again her blessing, she closed the door and left him to the delightful experience of getting clean and shaved again.

Soon he was stretched out on a pallet, and a sense of well-being and security came upon him.

There is something wonderful about these Christians, he mused. *They may be fools, but I admire their courage and, above all, their kindness.* With that he went to sleep.

He awakened only as he heard the voice of Nereus conversing with Junia on the patio. Rising, he put on the clean tunic, brushed his hair with the brush Junia had provided, and walked out to meet them.

"Greetings, Brother Gaius!" The deep voice of Nereus welcomed him, and his strong arms embraced him. "We are delighted that you have come to share your story of the courageous Christians in Corinth. Your presence with us is indeed our good fortune. Junia has told me of the sad news from your home city and of the death of your mother and father. I congratulate them and you over the joyful crowns they have won in the presence of our Lord. But we share in your sorrow and loss. How can I help you?"

Nereus was an artisan by trade and one of the leaders of the Christians in Rome. He was superbly gifted in the casting of the bronze and gold goblets and plates and works of art that adorned the palaces of the wealthy. His hair was gray, but his face was still ruddy and tough with years of hard work and temperate living. His eyes were warm and generous as he offered whatever help Onesimus might need.

"Dear Nereus, you and your good wife are kind indeed. I am grateful for your hospitality. The food, the bath, and this clean tunic have restored me to life. In response to your generous offer, there are just two things I want more than anything else right now: first, to see the apostle Paul, whom I heard back in Corinth when I was younger. I would cherish the privilege of meeting with him and listening to him again. The second need I have is to join in your *koinonia* and to find some way to make my living."

"Your first request can be fulfilled easily," Nereus answered with a broad smile. "Nothing would do the apostle Paul more good than to meet with you and give you his encouragement, but," here he stopped for a moment, "it will take a little more time to find you work and a place to live, though you are welcome to our humble quarters until you find something. Christians are beginning to be suspect by the Roman leaders. After we have had our evening meal, I will take you to Paul."

"Thank you for your goodness," Onesimus responded as he took a place at the table with his kindly host and hostess. Nereus, after he had given thanks, began to tell Onesimus of the rapid growth of the church in Rome.

"There are believers even in Caesar's household," said Nereus, "beginning with a number in the praetorian guard, some of whom are assigned to Paul. What a thing for any man to endure—to be continually chained, waking or sleeping, to the arm of a hard-bitten Roman soldier. And those who are made members of Caesar's select praetorian guard, believe me, are the toughest in the empire! But what an amazing man Paul is! He says his chains are for the good, for they have enabled the gospel to reach farther, even into the palace of Caesar. It has been a moving experience to see several of these rough soldiers touched by Christ's Spirit through Paul's teaching, to see them receive baptism, and to observe the change in their behavior."

"Paul's influence has not stopped here, for he has reached the noblewoman Pompania, who has influence with many of the leading citizens of Rome, including the family of Nero. She is the widow of a former Roman senator who, by his character and leadership, became too popular with the people and the other senators. He was beheaded by the Emperor Claudius, who considered him a prime threat to his own position. But by Pompania's personal character and influence even before she became a Christian, she was trusted by Nero's mother, Aggripina, and is said to have considerable influence still on Nero.

She is one of the wealthiest widows in Rome, but uses her wealth unselfishly. She had been guided toward our Christian faith even before Paul's coming and helped secure for him a more privileged position as a prisoner of the Emperor than he otherwise would have had. She was taught and baptized by Paul, whom she loves devotedly. She is part of our *koinonia* along with a large number of her household, and is of great encouragement to Paul and every one of us. A beautiful character not only physically but with the fruits of the Spirit that mark her from among the vain, dissipated women of the court . . . I tell you, Gaius, there is indeed a marvelous reality in our faith. The living Christ is with us. Nothing can defeat Him or His great purpose."

Onesimus looked with awe into the animated face of his new friend. *He really believes in his "good news,"* Onesimus said to himself. Nereus's assurance made Onesimus hopeful—and uncomfortable.

When the meal was over, Onesimus thanked his two benefactors again and went out with Nereus to walk to the building where Paul was imprisoned. Along the way Onesimus found his heart beating faster, his whole person strangely excited as he approached the great man who held his future in his hands. Would Paul know him? He hoped not; but if he did, would he denounce him for his deceit to Nereus and Junia and his costly betrayal of Philemon and Archippus? Or would Paul show the *agape* he talked about so much, accept him, and understand his desperate need for freedom?

They walked up to a house much like all the others on the street, except for a tall, helmeted soldier who stood on guard. Recognizing Nereus, who greeted him with a warm smile, the guard admitted them without hesitation.

The courtyard Nereus and Onesimus entered was suffused with a warm glow and the scent of flowers. Paul was sitting at the east end looking toward the golden evening sky. By his side stood another guard, and Onesimus could see that only a short piece of chain about three double hand breadths long separated the soldier from his prisoner. As Onesimus approached, he saw that Paul had aged considerably since the days in Ephesus. His hair and beard were gray, his face more wrinkled, his cheeks sunken. But his eyes—in spite of the disease which had given him trouble—were as piercing and yet as kind as when Onesimus had last bade him good-bye.

The apostle rose, looking at him steadily, reached out both of his hands and took Onesimus's right hand without saying a word. Nereus stood by ready to tell how he and Junia had ministered to the young man. But he sensed that something unusual was about to happen and became silent. Onesimus was trembling, as he waited for what seemed an interminable period of time. Then Paul spoke, his voice warm and friendly:

"My friend Onesimus, slave of Philemon from Colossae!"

With his hand in Paul's at that moment, all Onesimus's pent-up bitterness burst loose in a flood.

"Yes," he shouted, "I am Onesimus, but I am not Philemon's slave. I am no man's slave. I am free!"

He could continue his deceit no longer, but he was not prepared for Paul's response. Paul's eyes were filled with tears as he put his hands on Onesimus's shoulders:

"My son, you are no slave except to yourself. You are still a slave to the distorted human way of looking at things. You have run away from the kindest master any slave could have. No doubt you have your reasons. We will talk about that later. But you do not understand the freedom with which Christ has come to set us all free."

Paul spoke with loving-kindness, as he continued. "I, too, was once a slave to the old self and its corruption. Saul of Tarsus, full of pride and demanding his own rights, proving his superiority over others in every way he knew how—principally by the rigid observance of the Jewish Law. I was as you are trying to be, subject to no one. Even when I kept the strict letter of the law I did it to prove how righteous I was. I wanted to be preeminent among all my people. The humility of serving others through Christ Jesus angered me—this was the last thing I wanted to do. I would force even God to recognize my greatness!

"But everything I did seemed to result in the opposite from my intentions. I did not do what I wanted to do, and I did often what I did not want to do. In my zeal I helped to stone a man—a new Christian. In the loving courage of the dying young Stephen—never had I seen such character, such excellence, such love! He was free even though we were killing him with the stones that cut his head and his face. And when he died, asking that our Lord lay not this sin against us, I knew that I was the one enslaved. It was after this that Christ captured me and set me free to be His bondslave."

Onesimus and the guard, Janus, and Nereus listened in silent awe as this unusual man unveiled his innermost secret. The apostle gripped Onesimus's shoulder more tightly and said, "Son Onesimus, let me help you turn to Christ the Light."

The floodgate of the young man's tears opened and he wept like a child, his face in his hands. Nereus was weeping too, and the guard's eyes were filled. Nereus had never seen a proud praetorian shed tears.

Paul stood straight and lifted up his hands in blessing. "The Lord Jesus Christ give you the grace for repentance and all else you need to do, Onesimus. May He fill you with all joy and hope in the Holy Spirit."

By this time Onesimus recovered himself sufficiently to realize that he had been overcome for the moment by the loving spirit of this most persuasive person, but the cold realities of his situation were still unsolved. He was sure of Paul's acceptance—but would his guards turn him over to those responsible for dealing with runaway slaves?

"Sir, your words and love have moved me to shed more tears than I ever have except the night Philemon beat me with forty stripes on the way to Ephesus four years ago. I must tell you my whole story. I cannot accept the contradictions between what I have heard and seen you and the other Christians back at Colossae say and do and the fact that I am denied the very freedom which you promised that first night I listened to you around Philemon's table. I admit readily to the deep conviction and faith you possess, but I have yet to see them acted upon. Oh yes, up to a certain point . . . Philemon became a much kinder master. He called us his brothers and sisters as well as his slaves and, as his slaves, we worked harder; but the separation is still there! For four years I waited and expected that he would do something to act on some words you said that I have never forgotten."

"I know," Paul broke in, as he smiled sympathetically. It was now dusk and Nereus asked one of the Christians whose turn it was to serve Paul to bring a lamp. "I know the words you mean, and I believe them: 'In Christ there is neither slave nor free, Greek nor Jew, male nor female, but all are members of one family, children of God, and not slaves.' Is that not what you are thinking of?"

Onesimus nodded. As the light of the lamp revealed the understanding face of the diminutive teacher, he dared to make his accusations even clearer.

"Philemon. . . " and then he hesitated.

"Go on, Onesimus, tell me truly how you feel."

Onesimus went back to the beginning, relating the story of his life as son of Aristarchus, treasurer of Ephesus, until the tragic change when his father was executed and his family sold as slaves. He described briefly his tutoring of Helen and his growing love for her, the humiliating scene by the River Meander, the beating and suffering of soul as well as body, their experience in Ephesus which Paul had shared.

"Your consideration for me as a slave, dear friend Paul, and your words about there being no slavery or other unjust distinctions in the family of God gave me false hopes. For when they were not made a reality, I began to believe again with Epicurus that hope is indeed a traitor and with Callicles that it is better to treat others unjustly than to continue to suffer such galling and bitter injustice. I confess, I would like to believe your words written to the church at Corinth, which I heard read so often in the meetings in Philemon's house. You wrote, 'Love never fails.'"

"Yes, I believe it—I know it is true!" Paul exclaimed. "*Agape* does not fail!"

"Well the love of your disciples in Colossae failed me," Onesimus retorted bitterly, "and I must confess that I reacted by betraying and robbing my dearest friend, Archippus. He had understood my feelings and had promised to speak to his father to see if our relations as slave and master might be altered. But I had had too much! I was in despair, because I believed that Archippus was only an idealist. I knew the lash of Philemon—before he became a Christian. I had seen him become kinder, but I had not seen any sign of a love for justice. He will never free his slaves! If your Lord is truly the king and ruler of all things as you say, and He knows my heart, then He understands the rebellion I feel. And He feels this contradiction as much as I do."

Paul responded with passion. "He who knew no sin was made sin for us. He suffers with us and much more than we can ever know. 'He was wounded for our transgressions and bruised for our wickedness and, by His stripes, we are healed.' He was made perfect by obedience even in His suffering on the cross for the guilty and with the guilty."

"Does that not prove what a crowd of hypocrites you Christians are?" Onesimus burst out. Then apologetically, with his head bowed, he spoke more quietly, "Forgive me, Sir. But if the galling pain of slavery hurt the great Christ who makes us to be God's sons, and if you who profess to be His followers do nothing about it, what is that but hypocrisy and the worst of contradictions?"

"I understand, Son, go ahead and say it. It will take some time for us to talk this through. Say what you believe."

Onesimus had expected a hot argument at least, but Paul seemed to be encouraging him.

"All right, I will," Onesimus continued in a subdued voice. "If your Lord understands and suffers with me and the millions of slaves who are hurt and mistreated and even killed all over the empire, why doesn't He do something about it? Why don't you do something about it? Or is there no such Lord and Ruler, no *agape* love? Is your Lord Christ loving and kind, but powerless, no king at all? Do you only jest and say 'Jesus Christ is Lord'?"

He had said it—the ultimate blasphemy, no doubt, to one who risked his life daily and suffered so much for his Lord Christ— but Paul had asked him to be honest. Now he watched Paul as he sat for a moment with bowed head and closed eyes. He was sorry if he had wounded him, this dear man who called himself a "prisoner for Christ's sake."

"Son Onesimus, you are en route to *your* Damascus. I understand because I had to walk that road, too. I said everything you are saying. As I watched them stone Stephen, I was encouraging them and holding their clothes while they did the deed. Up to that time, the cross was a stumbling block for me as it was a scandal to the Gentiles. You ask if our Lord suffers when the children of the eternal Father suffer unjustly, and why doesn't He do something about it? I answer, He has! What more could the eternal Son of God do than humble Himself and take human flesh so as to take our sufferings upon Himself? He became a slave for *you*, Onesimus. Our Christ and His cross are both the wisdom of God and the power of God. The agape love you speak of does not fail."

"Bu. . . but . . . Sir," Onesimus stuttered. "You still have not answered my deepest question." He dared not look at Paul. "Why have *you* done nothing to bear the sufferings of millions of slaves such as I? Pardon me, I know you have suffered much— but how could you let my master Philemon and many other Christians such as Pompania, whom Nereus and Junia described, continue keeping their slaves under subjection? It is simply wrong!" And he began to weep bitterly.

Paul arose, came over to his side and put his hand on his shoulder. "Christ is victor. His love does conquer all. But not as some men measure conquest. God's way of righting wrongs is not our way. It was this fatal error that led Judas to betray the Lord, thinking to force His hand. He was disappointed because Jesus did not by force of arms or by the mighty power of the angelic hosts, immediately mold this evil scheme of things into a world where there would be no more injustice and evil."

Onesimus could not help but break in, "Why does our Lord

not free every slave and command that we his followers do so immediately, waiting on nothing?"

Paul answered with words which Onesimus would always remember, though he did not understand them at the time. "Because to do so would be to take away our freedom, to force goodness and love and brotherhood upon us. This one thing remember: *There is no justice but in agape love; and there is no agape love but in justice.*

"In the kingdom of God there is now a new relationship in which slaves and their masters are partners with Christ, even though externally they are still slaves and masters. One thing is sure, Onesimus. No one is helped by being set free from one master if he is going to be enslaved by a dozen other more cruel masters. The only true freedom is in Christ and the only true justice is in the freedom to love even as Christ loved. Otherwise our justice becomes unjust."

Janus the guard had listened as Nereus had, with every bit of his mind, for he was one from Caesar's household who had recently professed Christ and been baptized. Now he spoke.

"Brother Paul, I who am your guard and you who are my prisoner are both partners in the kingdom. It is not in my power to set you free, nor to declare Christ to all of Rome, as much as I desire to do so. But you, Brother Paul, are the freest man I have ever met. I pray our Lord to give me some small measure of your freedom." Turning to Onesimus, he continued, "Though I break Caesar's law, there is a higher law to which I bow. Christ is now my King. I cannot turn you in. Since Paul accepts you, I do also. May you find his freedom."

Onesimus listened in amazement. This was a reversal of all he had ever thought or known. A proud member of Caesar's private guard swearing allegiance to Christ, obeying the authority of this little Jew who was chained to his arm!

The hour was late. Paul rose and embraced Onesimus, saying, "Will you stay with me, Onesimus, at least for a while? I am sure Nereus and Junia would be glad to keep you; but you will be useful to me, as I hope I can be to you. You are skilled in the use of words, in writing, and I very much need someone who can write letters for me to some of the churches where counsel and encouragement are badly needed."

Onesimus blushed with pleasure. "There is nothing, Sir, that could give me more satisfaction than to know I could help you even in some small way. I will be happy to be your *amenuensis* or do anything else needed."

Nereus was standing near, deeply moved by the evening's experience. Onesimus turned to him with a gesture of regret, "Dear Nereus, how can you ever forgive me for the lies I told you about coming from Corinth? I have no excuse but my desperation to find Paul."

"My friend Onesimus, whom I first called Gaius," Nereus broke in, "you do not need to beg my forgiveness. It was given the very moment I realized you were deceiving me. Junia and I will expect you to visit us for a meal once in a while, and you shall always be dear to me. Your true name, Onesimus, will be even more meaningful here in the service of our Lord as you minister to our beloved Paul." With this, he embraced Onesimus, then Paul, and lastly the guard Janus, for whom he now had an even greater admiration.

"Tomorrow, you will meet four valuable partners of mine," Paul said. "Doctor Luke, who has traveled with me for several years, a great and good physician; Timothy, my son in the gospel, whose mother Eunice and grandmother Lois were among the first disciples in Philippi; Tychicus, who became a follower of the Way when I was with him first in Crete; and Epaphras, one of the Christians from your own city of Colossae." At the mention of Colossae a sudden look of fear came over Onesimus's face, and Paul quickly reassured him.

"You have nothing to fear from Epaphras. He is one with us in the freedom of Christ."

Onesimus had felt again the tremors of the old terror, and now he realized he still did not know for sure his fate.

"But, Sir," he spoke with shaking voice, "You still have not told me whether you will send me back to Colossae. Remember,

I am still Philemon's slave, and he has the power of life and death over me."

"Have you forgotten so soon, my son, what I said a few minutes ago? Love does not force its will on others. I hope the time will come when you go back to Colossae and to Philemon, but for now I am more interested in your finding inner freedom. Once you find that, you will be free to do what our Lord wills for you. So go now to your bed and rest with the assurance that the love of Christ never fails and that together, working through His Spirit, we will find the way for your life to be more useful than you have imagined in your fondest dreams."

This was too much for Onesimus. Again he broke down in tears. Once more he took the hand of Paul, who embraced him. Wordless, Onesimus accepted the outstretched hand of Janus and turned to climb the stairs.

16

*O*nesimus had much to think through—and much for which to be thankful. He knew he was safe here in Paul's house. He trusted even the Roman guard, Janus, but he was deeply puzzled. It was all too good to be true. One thing he knew, he would no more deceive—or would he? If the conditions changed, if his own life were in the balance? He did not know. A wave of shame and guilt swept over him as he lay in bed and looked through the window at the stars. *There is no justice except in love and no love except in justice.* The words were strange, but comforting. *What good is it to be delivered from slavery to one master, only to become slave of several more cruel masters?* For an hour he lay awake, and then he slept until the morning light streaming through the window awakened him.

"Greetings, my son. Onesimus, I want you to meet my dearly loved friend and physician, Doctor Luke," Paul said as they gathered for breakfast.

Onesimus shook hands with the distinguished-looking doctor. He was dressed in a blue Roman toga, and had a carefully trimmed beard on his chin and eyes that were brown like his skin, warm and amiable. Onesimus immediately knew him as a tender-hearted man capable of deep compassion and sympathy with the sick and suffering.

"Paul has been describing your journey," Luke said. "It is good to have you join us. I am sure your knowledge as a philosopher and your skill with words as a writer and thinker will be of great value to us all. Welcome!"

Paul then introduced Timothy, a fair-haired, blue-eyed younger man, who smiled and greeted Onesimus cordially: "We are glad you are with us, Onesimus. Like you, I have been a student of the Greek philosophers. We must talk together about the wisdom of God who spoke through the prophets and now is the Word made flesh."

With this, the four sat down, but not before Paul had also introduced him to his new guard, Plutonius, who, to Onesimus's surprise, also greeted him warmly. Onesimus watched curiously during the meal to see how Paul and the guard ate. Paul's right arm was chained to Plutonius's left, so that Paul could eat with his right only when the guard let his arm rest on the table. This he did the entire meal, leaving Paul free with both hands, while the guard used only his right hand. Onesimus marveled at the respect and affection for Paul shown by Plutonius and Janus. The former was stockier with dark bushy eyebrows and longer beard, but his face was filled with the same kindness one would rarely, if ever, assign to the tough praetorians who so prided themselves on their cruelty.

The breakfast was good—eggs, bread, and milk.

"The food is brought in by one or another of our fellow Christians," Timothy explained. "Several own small farms on the outside of Rome, and they keep us well supplied. I am sure we fare better than most of the populace of Rome."

"You think it is strange that some people should share their wealth or forsake family affections in order to follow our Lord?" Paul asked as if reading Onesimus's thoughts. "Our Lord sets us free from many false masters, one of which is indeed the very wealth and plenty which makes the rich greedy and the poor bitter."

"Yes," responded Doctor Luke, his voice clear and resonant. "As Jesus said, 'No man can serve two masters. He will love the one and hate the other, for we cannot serve both God and material things.' This does not mean that material things are bad in themselves, but they are not to be our master. Only one is Lord and Master!"

"But should we be content to let the poor continue poor and hungry?" Onesimus ventured to ask.

"Of course not," answered Doctor Luke, and he told another beautiful story the apostle Matthew had told him from his memory of Jesus' teachings. It pictured a king on his throne before whom all peoples are gathered to be judged. Some would be sent away into the outer darkness. "Because," said the king, "I was hungry and you gave me no meat, sick and in prison and you did not visit me, naked and you did not clothe me."

"But when did we see you hungry and not feed you, in prison and not visit you, naked and did not clothe you?" the king's subjects asked.

And the king answered, "Every time you failed to do it unto one of the least of these, my brothers, you did it not unto me."

"What an illustration of the compassion of our eternal Father," exclaimed Paul after Luke had shared the story. "He sent His Son Jesus to be our light and truth! Praise to our Lord!"

"Amen!" all around the table cried; their joy was infectious. Onesimus had never felt so much at home, so close to any group of his fellows as he did now at the table of Paul. The Roman guard Plutonius, the handsome young philosopher-Christian, Timothy, the skilled Doctor Luke, the apostle Paul, and now Onesimus, the slave who would be free. *It is a miracle,* he thought. *I could never have imagined it possible.*

When they had finished eating, Paul beckoned to Onesimus, who followed him out into the small courtyard around which the house was built. He learned later that this was an unusually good living arrangement, generally available only to those who were able to pay a rather high rent. Paul had first lived on the third floor of a six-story *insula* or apartment building; but one of the newly professed Christians owned this house and offered it at half the usual rent.

Luke followed them, carrying in his hands some papyri with pen and ink. They sat on stone benches, enjoying the early morning fragrance of the garden.

"We might as well start our work together, Onesimus," Paul observed. "Luke has brought sad news of more persecutions at Lystra, where the small, struggling church is having difficulty surviving."

"It was there that I met my first stoning," Paul said pensively. "What I had first seen done to Stephen was done to me, only I was not killed. They threw me out of the city half dead and, but for some of the faithful who rescued me, I would not be here. Now they are again having trouble. Several have been imprisoned; one has suffered martyrdom. I want to write them a brief letter of hope and encouragement that will help them hold to their faith."

Onesimus received the papyri and the reed pen with a bottle of ink and sat at the table near Paul and Plutonius, ready to write.

As Paul began to dictate, his chin rested on his free hand and his eyes looked as though he were seeing things far away. Onesimus found the dictation fascinating. *What a master of words Paul is, what capacity to inspire*, he thought. And then he lost himself in transcribing the message to the church in Lystra.

The brief letter contained more of the same kind of assurances Paul had been sharing in his conversations with Onesimus. He concluded with greetings from the Christian leaders known to the people at Lystra and the usual benediction: "The grace of the Lord Jesus Christ, and the love of God, and the fellowship of the Holy Spirit, be with you all."

As Onesimus wrote these last words, he was struck by their beauty and sincerity. Paul spoke them almost caressingly, with the ecstatic look in his eyes that had moved Onesimus so often before. Yet even as he admired the beauty of spirit shining in Paul's appearance, Onesimus was skeptical. These words were describing some kind of mystical presence of a once-crucified carpenter and mixing it all up with what Paul called "The grace of our Lord Jesus Christ, the love of God, and the fellowship of the Holy Spirit." It was all built on an assumption that Onesimus could not make and certainly did not understand.

"Friend Paul, forgive me," Onesimus broke in on the old man's reverie. "I have written exactly what you said. It is beautiful, but mystifying. I congratulate you on having the courage to go back to Lystra and for your encouragement of the little band who may have to endure more stonings; but I cannot understand what you mean by living by the power of God. Jesus died in weakness on the cross. I heard you back in Ephesus describe how this Jesus, once crucified, is now risen and exalted and at the right hand of God. You call him 'Jesus Christ our Lord'! What do you mean?"

Paul looked at him with kindness and answered patiently, but with deep conviction. "I mean nothing more nor less than that this man Jesus, who lived and died and whom the disciples and upwards of five hundred experienced alive again—this man is the Chosen One of God sent to reveal the unearned, undeserved, self-giving love, which I call the grace of the eternal Father, who is now, always has been, and always will be. Continually, He provides for our salvation. Therefore, in Jesus' life and death and resurrection, we see revealed before our very eyes the purpose hidden by God the creator of the universe for long ages. This hidden purpose, now revealed by the risen Christ in the Church, is so wonderful, so utterly beyond our highest imagination, that we are willing to die, if need be, to share this great secret with others."

"But what do you mean by the 'fellowship of the Holy Spirit'?" Onesimus asked. "It is difficult enough to believe that Jesus was actually raised from the dead. My whole intelligence rebels against this, this unverified claim, as Aristotle would put it. But even more, this mysterious belief that what you call 'the Holy Spirit' is with us in this very moment."

"Son, you are now just as I once was. Remember I said last night you are still on your road to Damascus; that is, you have seen the fruits of the Spirit in the lives of these brave Christians around you. But you have not yet faced up to who the Spirit is who calls you to Christ and to the Father. What happened to me on the way to Damascus was the sudden realization that, in persecuting men like Stephen, I was persecuting the Lord of heaven and earth. 'Who are you? Are you the Lord?' I asked as I fell in the blinding light before the risen Christ.

"The answer was clear, 'I am Jesus whom you are persecuting.' "

"So, my doubting friend, you too are faced, by the Holy Spirit, with the presence of Christ that shines like the brightest sun in the lives of Nereus, Julia, Plutonius and Janus, in the faith of those at Lystra, and, I trust, in some way even in my unworthy life. You cannot escape Him any more than I could."

"But how do I know? How can I be sure?" Onesimus asked with intense feeling.

"That, my son, is the key question. It took me a long time to find the answer. Like you I did a great deal of harm as I fought to resist the truth of it. You can know only by faith, which relies on the mercy of God. You can be sure only as you surrender yourself—as I did—to the highest answer my intelligence could ask, 'What would you have me do?'

"It was then I was directed to Damascus, to see a man named Ananaias in a house on the street called Straight. Here I found love from the very man whom a few hours before I would have helped to kill. My sight returned. My faith was very small at that hour. I believed one thing and one thing only—that the Spirit I had seen in Stephen as he died with forgiving love in his heart and on his lips was the same Spirit that had spoken through Jesus of Nazareth, and this same Spirit was calling me to live by faith in Jesus supremely. I had met the Lord of all the Universe.

"I will admit I did not fully understand, nor was it easy to accept. For three years in the desert of Arabia I fought my doubts and sought to understand with my intelligent reason all it meant. I, too, was a proud mind, Onesimus, trained as a strict Pharisee to believe that God had revealed Himself only in the Torah and in the prophets; but over these three years I came to experience the presence of the risen Christ. It is His presence I invoke when I say the beautiful words, 'The fellowship of the Holy Spirit be with you.' His fellowship is the presence of the One who walked and taught and loved in the Man of Galilee, the presence of the Father Creator of the universe, whose loving grace is now given to me, as one born out of due time. He is the Immanuel, 'God with us,' of whom Isaiah wrote."

He looked at Onesimus with loving intensity, which Onesimus could feel even as the night before he had felt Paul's warm and comforting embrace.

"I do not know how long it will take you to acknowledge Jesus Christ as Lord and by faith be brought into union with Him by water and the Spirit. It may take you three years, as it did me. It could take three months or three days. These humble Roman guards have accepted Him with the faith of little children. So did Nereus and Junia, but it took several weeks for Pompania to lay aside her pride of intellect and believe. Christ nailed to the cross and yet alive and ruling this universe is indeed a stumbling block to the Jews and folly to the Greeks; yet for those who have heard and accepted His call by faith, Jews and Greeks alike, He is the power of God and the wisdom of God!"

Onesimus was overwhelmed by these words spoken out of the white-heat of the experience of this remarkable little man, whose mind was certainly every bit a match for his own. He heard the words, but the acceptance by faith was, if ever, still to come. He realized that he had made some progress, as he thanked Paul for his frankness and help and went to his room. He began to understand, at least intellectually, why Paul always coupled "the grace of the Lord Jesus Christ" with "the love of God and the fellowship of the Holy Spirit." Obviously, they could not be separated. As he sat on his bed and looked out of the window at the people walking in the streets outside, he realized that he too must do battle with this thing Paul called his "pride," "the old man," the intellectual fortress he had built around himself to protect him from believing. He had done this back in Colossae in order to justify his running away and stealing from his best friend. It would take a lot of trust and grace to tear down the fortress. He smiled as he realized how right Paul was in saying that he was indeed on his own "Damascus road."

-- *17*

*T*ychicus and Epaphras, two more of Paul's "partners in the Gospel," entered the courtyard. Tychicus was a small, dark-skinned Cretan while Epaphras was taller and lighter-skinned, but both bore marks of suffering and deprivation on their faces.

Timothy arose to introduce them to Onesimus. Obviously, Paul had already talked with Epaphras about Onesimus. It was a happy surprise, therefore, when Epaphras came over and took the arm of his fellow Colossian.

"Onesimus, I am glad to see you. I bring you word concerning your mother and Philemon's familia. They are all worried about you but are praying for your safe return. As for Philemon, he was very angry when Archippus came back from Ephesus without you and the money you had stolen. I hear that he reported your escape, though Archippus is said to have begged him to wait. This means that you are among the wanted list of runaway slaves. I can not predict what his reaction would be if you were to return, but I have confidence that he is trying to conform his attitudes and actions to the spirit of love which is in Christ."

"Thank you, Sir, for your understanding," Onesimus said with some hesitation. He had listened with the old terror rising in his throat. He was thankful that Epaphras was forgiving, but he could understand Philemon's feelings and knew that, even should his runaway slave become a Christian and return home, he still would be running the risk of being punished severely, perhaps even to the point of death.

The next few weeks were filled with opportunities for Onesimus to observe firsthand the words and acts and the beautiful Spirit in the lives of the Christians in Rome. Paul's house was a magnet that drew them all, one by one or in groups, to visit with the man they loved and respected so highly. Thanks to the kindly encouragement of the praetorian guard, the comings and goings of the Christians were no problem— even on the first day of the week, when so many gathered for worship that they filled the atrium and the dining room. They always came early in the morning while the remainder of the city was sleeping.

The worship was similar to what Onesimus had experienced in Philemon's house, except that with Paul's prayers and preaching there was a depth and meaning to this good news of Christ which he had never known before. When the time came for the Eucharist and the catechumens and visitors were dismissed, for the first time Onesimus found himself reluctant to leave. Perhaps the taking of the bread and the cup would help him have faith; but this help was denied him now, and he went to his room to meditate as the great service of thanksgiving was celebrated. He could hear snatches of song, voices raised in joyful praise, and then the quiet hush as the sacred bread and wine were passed. It was an *anamnesis*, or recalling of the sacrifice of Jesus as the Lamb of God whose blood was shed and whose body was broken for sinners. In this act, His risen presence was said to become more real than ever. Onesimus hungered for "the bread of life" he had heard Paul describe; but though starving for life's meaning, he was not yet ready to eat.

Onesimus was delighted to see Plutonius, Janus, and other members of the guard, even when not on duty, stand humbly with the other believers for the joyous singing and sincere prayers with which the worship was begun. He was intrigued especially with the Lady Pompania. She possessed such a winsome, gentle look in her strong face that Onesimus was drawn to her.

One morning after the worship service, she remained to talk with Paul. Onesimus was invited by Paul to go with them to the garden where they sat for several hours. Onesimus listened as she drew from Paul stories of his relationships with several former residents of Rome who had become Christians. She asked about a Jew named Aquila and his wife Priscilla who had been forced to leave Rome after the edict by Emperor Claudius, which stated that all Jews should vacate their homes and business in Italy. These, her two Jewish friends, had become Christians and had befriended Paul during his stay in Corinth.

"It was my privilege to make my home with them, since Aquila and I are both tentmakers," Paul explained. "They were both very apt in learning the meaning of our gospel, and were articulate in bringing it to others. We were so close to each other, they chose to go with me when I left Corinth for Cenchrae."

"How did it happen?" Onesimus asked. He was always stirred by Doctor Luke's accounts of Paul's hardships and narrow escapes.

"It was at Cenchrae, where I found much opposition from the Jewish leaders of the community. Due to the influence of the Saduccees in Corinth they had been warned of my coming and set out to inflame a crowd of people who had gathered in the Agora to hear me. Stories were told slandering me as a dealer in black magic and accusing Christians of killing babies for blood to use in our worship—a terrible lie that has since been told here in Rome. The crowd was unruly even as I began to speak, and having heard these lies they soon began to mock me and threaten me. I am sure I would have been killed but for Priscilla and Aquila, by whose quick thinking I was spared. Both of them stood up on the platform with me. Being of striking appearance and articulate speech, they interrupted my address to tell the crowd that I was only a tentmaker and had come with them recently from Corinth. They spoke so forthrightly, challenging the stories told about the Christians, that the mob quieted; and miraculously I was able to step down from the platform and leave with them from the Agora before the mob knew what had happened. We left Cenchrae immediately and went to Ephesus, where I parted with them. They had received word of Nero's new edict permitting the Jews to return to Rome."

"Where are these two now?" Onesimus asked.

"They have returned to Corinth," Lady Pompania answered. "They found in their enforced leave from Rome that Corinth better suited the needs of their business, and the church in Corinth with its many divisions very much needed their influence."

Paul continued to talk about Corinth and other cities where his mission for Christ had taken him. Obviously, Pompania was fascinated by his account as much as Onesimus was. For her, it was evidence of the reality of her faith. For him, it was further confusing evidence of the remarkable spirit of Paul, adding more questions as to what it all meant.

Before leaving, Pompania asked Onesimus to tell her something of his background and how he came to be in Rome. Paul, realizing the interest that Onesimus had shown in this vibrant Christian, left the two alone to talk.

"It was a happy day for the church when you believed in Christ and were baptized, Pompania," Paul said sincerely as he bid them farewell. "You are such a great help to us all. No doubt, your influence is one of the reasons Christians are let alone by this man who rules the visible world. This shows that the grace of God is at work in every heart, even in the most depraved, working for a way to open it to the Holy Spirit. To the world, Nero is the hopeless, debauched beast they see. To our Lord, he is still a precious soul who is like the prodigal son in a very, very far country."

Amazed by this declaration, it took Onesimus several minutes to pull his own thoughts together. But then for the next two hours Onesimus poured out to Pompania the story of his childhood and youth, his sale into slavery, his experiences in Ephesus with Philemon and his family, his perfidious betrayal of the trust of Philemon and his son Archippus, and his dismaying experiences in the Subura. Pompania's genuine, intelligent interest, so like his mother's, encouraged him to share his feelings unabashedly.

"The story that you told of your early boyhood and the tragedy that separated the family reminds me of the day when your father, Aristarchus, and the former governor, Gaius Flaccus, were brought before Emperor Claudius, though I do not recall the charges against them," she said when he had concluded. "I knew that they, as so many other good men, were sacrificed to the greed for power and wealth by those who curried favor with the Emperor. But it would seem to me, friend Onesimus, that you have been greatly blessed with the *providentia* of our Lord! You certainly are in the right place to learn the meaning of true freedom. I hope you have seen plenty of this in the lives of Paul and Luke and these wonderful Christians who, like you, belong to God's own family, His chosen and beloved."

Onesimus was embarrassed as she included him in their *koinonia*, but answered simply, "Yes, Lady Pompania, I am thankful beyond words for the love and kindness of all you who care, even as you say the Lord cares. The apostle Paul has taught me so many things; but one thing he told me that I still cannot understand." He spoke frankly now, with some passion in his voice. "How can I ever believe with the faith that you and Paul and these other Christians have, when my reason tells me the resurrection of Christ is something unproven by any sensible evidence? How do we know that Christ is alive? And that His Father and the Holy Spirit with Him created and rule this universe, with all of the suffering and pain and evil in it? Paul says we know it by faith! What is faith?"

"My son, you have a first class mind," Pompania commended him. "But sometimes the 'wisdom of men' is utterly foolish compared to what Paul calls 'the foolishness of God' . . . which is the only wisdom. This is a paradox, of course. Paul was saying to us, you remember, that there is no place for human pride in the presence of God. Jesus Himself said, as Doctor Luke quotes the blessed memory of His disciples, 'Except we become like a little child, we shall not see the kingdom of heaven.' Through God's own action in His Son, Jesus Christ, He has made Himself and His love known to us. Paul puts it this way: 'In Him all the fullness of the Godhead dwells.' "

"You mean it is this action of God in Christ that we are to take by faith? But most of us, even Paul, did not know the human Jesus."

"Very true. Paul readily admits he never knew Jesus in the flesh. But we have the Holy Spirit who makes known to us the living Christ; the very same Spirit that empowered Jesus and brought Him back from the dead has quickened us. We cannot see Him with our physical eyes or prove Him by our reason or feelings; but when we yield ourselves completely to Him, He makes Himself known to us—just as He did to Paul during his three years in Arabia."

As she spoke her eyes were shining. "Just as He has revealed Himself to me during these blessed weeks since I abandoned my proud demands for proof and recognized Christ in the lives of Paul and his partners in the gospel."

"Then it is not by reason or feeling that I shall know Him, but by the abandonment of all these so-called 'proud demands for proof' of any sort? Is that what you and Paul mean by faith?" Onesimus asked in bewilderment. "This means the abandonment of my intelligence. How can I do that and keep my integrity?"

"Not at all," Pompania came back with deep feeling. "You are not called to abandon your intelligence. Faith means lifting your intelligence to a new level of consciousness in which you know God even as you are known. You will need your intelligence, friend Onesimus, for we are to love God with all our *minds* as well as our hearts and strength! It means for me the complete abandonment of 'the old man'—or the 'old woman.' "

She continued, "It means saying 'yes' with everything within me, an 'amen' to the great 'amen' God is saying to us in bearing witness to His Son. And this means liberty—the only freedom there is; freedom to love even as He did; freedom from fear and hate and selfishness, freedom from death. Oh, Onesimus, this is good news indeed! If only all humankind might know it!"

Pompania had poured out her deepest feelings and thoughts. Now she took his hands in hers and blessed him.

As she left, Onesimus felt a sense of hope and expectation he had not had before. He pondered all that had been said. *If she, with all her sufferings and loss and all the evils she knows of Nero and Rome, can "abandon the old woman," as she put it, and become the wondrous "new woman" whom I so much admire, surely there is hope for me. But to abandon myself—to say "yes" and trust myself to the eternal Father, the Son, the Holy Spirit—how does one do that?*

18

The next morning Paul told his household at breakfast that he had a very important letter to write to the church at Philippi, and that it might take most of the day. Accordingly, they all went immediately to the court garden, Onesimus with his papyrus, pen, and ink.

Timothy sat closest to Paul and his guard Plutonius. The young Christian had arrived in Rome only a day or two before Onesimus joined the household and had been encouraging Paul with reports of the rapid growth of the believers—not only in numbers but also in spirit—in Philippi, Athens, and even Corinth, where Paul had had such difficulty in healing divisions in the church. Now Timothy was to return to Greece as Paul's emissary, and Paul wanted to send with him a letter to the

Philippians giving thanks for their growth in faith and the spread of the good news to so many new disciples.

"Timothy," Paul said to his young assistant, "I have had more joy over the church in Philippi than any of the other churches which I planted. I remember so well, as I want to remind them now, that in the early days of my mission in Greece as I came over from Macedonia, the Philippian believers were the only ones who entered into partnership with me in giving and receiving. Now with the coming of Epaphroditus, they have given even more generously in supplying my needs and providing for our living expenses. Their giving is not just from a sense of duty, but is out of the abundance of their love. Will you join me in this letter to them? Whatever the Lord speaks to you as I dictate to Onesimus, please say it."

Paul settled back in a large comfortable chair, a present of the Lady Pompania, and closed his eyes for prayer. Then he began to speak with animation as Onesimus wrote:

From Paul and Timothy, servants of Christ Jesus, to all those of God's people, incorporate in Christ Jesus, who live at Philippi, including their bishops and deacons.

Grace to you and peace from God our Father and the Lord Jesus Christ.

As Onesimus wrote this apostolic blessing from the lips of Paul, his eyes were misty. *This grace is the gift Paul has given to me—a greater freedom than I have ever known,* he thought, *and yet I still am not free of guilt and fear.* It suddenly came over him that an even greater gift was waiting for him. He continued to write Paul's expression of thanks, filled with more joy than any other words Onesimus had penned for him.

My prayers are always joyful, because of the part you have taken in the work of the Gospel from the first day until now. Of one thing I am certain: the One who started the good work in you will bring it to completion by the Day of Christ Jesus.

What a wonderful assurance Paul has, Onesimus thought.

He remembered that Paul had this same kind of expectancy for him.

Paul continued with his eyes closed and head uplifted:

> This is my prayer, that your love may grow ever richer and richer in knowledge and insight of every kind, and may thus bring you the gift of true discrimination. Then on the Day of Christ you will be flawless and without blame, reaping the full harvest of righteousness that comes through Jesus Christ, to the glory and praise of God.

As Onesimus wrote, he felt the prayer included him also: to be free from guilt and blame, to be able to choose with true discrimination, and to love as these about him loved.

> Friends, I want you to understand that the work of the Gospel has been helped on, rather than hindered, by this business of mine. My imprisonment in Christ's cause has become common knowledge to all at headquarters here, and indeed among the public at large; and it has given confidence to most of our fellow-Christians to speak the word of God fearlessly and with extraordinary courage.

What a miraculous fact this is, Onesimus thought. The chains by which Paul was connected to his guards had indeed been a channel through which his faith and love flowed. He thought of Plutonius and Janus and several of the other believing guards, including Burrhus, the captain of this select group of Roman soldiers. He thought of their families and many others, who came not only from Caesar's palace but from the homes of plebians such as Nereus and Junia.

Paul rested for a moment, then began to speak again. This time he spoke of the inconstancy and jealousy of some of the Christians, especially a few leaders who felt Paul had taken away something of their importance. It was difficult for Onesimus to see how anyone could be jealous of Paul, but then he realized the 'old man' still might not be dead in many who call themselves Christians.

> The others, moved by personal rivalry, present Christ from mixed motives, meaning to stir up fresh trouble for me as I lie in prison.

What does it matter? One way or another, in pretense or sincerity, Christ is set forth, and for that I rejoice. Yes, and rejoice I will, knowing well that the issue of it all will be my deliverance. . . .

Onesimus wrote these words with something like exaltation. To see and hear and feel the mighty freedom that pulsed in this little man's life. Freedom to love these petty persons who tried to hurt him even in his imprisonment because of their jealousy! How could Paul do it? His next thoughts gave the answer:

. . . because you are praying for me and the Spirit of Jesus Christ is given me for support. For, as I passionately hope, I shall have no cause to be ashamed, but shall speak so boldly that now as always the greatness of Christ will shine out clearly in my person, whether through my life or through my death. For to me life is Christ and death gain.

Onesimus swallowed hard and blinked the tears from his eyes: Here was no egomaniac trying to conquer the world for his own ideology and glory. For him, life indeed is Christ—the reality of his experience of the present risen Lord was without question. Here was the great evidence Onesimus could see in Paul just as Paul had seen it in Stephen. Paul spoke about his confidence that, whether he lived or died, he would be free; but how thankful that he could live and speak his good news! Though he yearned to be with Christ in a fuller way, his love still was uppermost:

This, indeed, I know for certain: I shall stay, and stand by you all to help you forward and to add joy to your faith.

This includes me, Onesimus thought. *What an exalted privilege to know Paul. How much greater when I come to know Christ.* He had thought it! Onesimus began to realize the significance of what was happening within him. Through Paul and these other Christ-like spirits he was coming to know the living Christ. By faith? Yes, mediated through his experience during these priceless days. And then Paul continued:

Only, let your conduct be worthy of the gospel of Christ, so that whether I come and see you for myself or hear about you from a distance, I may know that you are standing firm, one in spirit, one in mind, contending as one man for the gospel faith, meeting your opponents without so much as a tremor . . . for you have been granted the privilege not only of believing in Christ but also of suffering for him. . . .

Thus, you will be my pride on the Day of Christ. . . .Rejoice . . . and let us share our joy.

Here Paul stopped dictating as he caught a glimpse of Onesimus's face. Flushed with profound feeling and inspired by the remarkable words he had just copied, Onesimus put down his pen and laid his head on his hands. In the quietness that followed, Paul and Timothy nodded to each other and remained silent as they lifted their prayers for this man who had come to his hour of conversion. They knew that something more than emotion was surging through the young philosopher's mind and heart. It was a struggle to the death of the old egoistic pride he had fought so long.

Onesimus, oblivious to their presence, saw with a clarity he had never experienced before. *I have sacrificed everything to escape slavery, even betraying those who loved me. The harder I tried to escape, the faster I ran, the more enslaved I became.*

The conflict was over. Onesimus saw but one course before him. With the best thought his intelligence could summon he knew that what he had seen and heard these weeks was the highest good, the most desirable life, the most triumphant victory he could imagine.

The conclusion came rapidly: *If this is the result of a falsehood, the fruit of a vain superstition, then there is nothing in life that makes sense; for the falsehood, if falsehood it is, has produced for humanity more good than all the concepts ever described by philosophers and poets. If so, life has no meaning, and all is useless and vain. But life such as Paul's, love such as revealed in Christ, His life and His cross and His victory over death, do have meaning. In Him is the highest and most*

intelligent Word ever spoken. I accept the Word by faith—the
life that is the light of the world. I cannot prove it by logic, or
physical evidence; but I will live it, even though it costs me as
much as it has Paul.

He lifted his head. There were no tears. He was perfectly calm as he looked into the faces of Paul and Timothy and said, "I will live by faith in your Christ, for he is my Lord. I know for the first time that the only way to freedom is His way."

Then, with his eyes uplifted, Onesimus shared his first spoken prayer, expressing the new-found faith in the *koinonia* with Paul and Timothy:

"Thank you, O Divine Master, for the gift of faith," he prayed simply and with quiet joy. "Forgive me that I tried to *make* myself have faith and sought for proofs that would not be faith. I was afraid to take your gift without being a *victim* of wishful thinking. Now I am a *victor* able to think clearly in Your presence."

Paul and Timothy listened with awe as they shared the victory of their young friend.

"Lord, whom I cannot see or feel or prove, whom my mind cannot encompass nor words define, You are the Lord of life and death and eternal life whom I accept by faith. You created all this vast universe, yet You emptied Yourself. You assumed the nature of a slave. You were obedient even unto death, and now You are exalted above all things, the Lord of all creation. I accept Your call to share with these my brothers and friends in the partnership of Your gospel. I do it for Your glory and not mine and for the sake of all others who are enslaved both within and without. Amen."

Onesimus stood up. Paul and Timothy came to him and the three embraced, shedding tears of joy and thanksgiving. Then Paul said, "Son Onesimus, your greatest struggle is over, though life will continue to be filled with struggles; and your faith, which now is so clear and strong, will at times be covered with clouds of doubt. This is the human lot. But you have been given faith, a living confidence in the grace of God. It came as a gift, but only as the soil was prepared and the seed sown. This hour we have seen the tender plant thrust its head up to greet the sun. What joy indeed is ours this day. Whatever comes in the future, trial and pain and temptation, you will overcome just as you have today. Remember that, Onesimus. The rule of the Lord is 'a yoke that is easy and a burden that is light.' "

The noon hour had arrived. They went together to the table to eat and drink strength not only to their bodies but to their spirits. A new life in Christ has begun. They would celebrate.

After lunch, they returned to the letter to the Philippians. Every word that Paul dictated took on new meaning for Onesimus. Paul told the Philippians of his own experience— Onesimus was sure he was doing it for his sake as well—how he had in his pride once put his confidence on things external. He had been "circumcised on my eighth day, a Hebrew born and bred, a strict Pharisee in attitude toward the law, in pious zeal a persecutor of the church." As to the law, he considered himself faultless.

> But all such assets I have written off because of Christ. I would say more: I count everything sheer loss, because all is far outweighed by the gain of knowing Christ Jesus my Lord, for whose sake I did in fact lose everything. I count it so much garbage. . . . All I care for is to know Christ, to experience the power of his resurrection, and to share his sufferings. . . .

Every word described accurately Onesimus's new-found faith. He, too, had lost almost everything for the sake of knowing Christ. What of wealth, position, pleasure, power—all that he had ever dreamed of possessing—all now so much garbage! He could accept the good that came and enjoy it, but he did not *have to have it*. Paul gave him even more encouragement as he continued:

> I have not yet reached perfection . . . All I can say is this: forgetting what is behind me, and reaching out for that which lies ahead, I press towards the goal to win the prize which is God's call to the life above, in Christ Jesus.

"That is beautiful!" Onesimus exclaimed aloud. He looked at

Timothy to see him nodding his head with glowing eyes. Then came phrases which in the use of the word "joy" surpassed any piece of prose or poetry Onesimus had ever seen:

> Therefore, my friends, beloved friends whom I long for, my joy, my crown, stand thus firm in the Lord, my beloved! . . . Farewell; I wish you all joy in the Lord. I will say it again: all joy be yours!

Onesimus wrote this last exclamation boldly and underlined it.

> The Lord is near; have no anxiety, but in everything make your requests known to God in prayer and petition with thanksgiving. Then the peace of God which is beyond our utmost understanding, will keep guard over your hearts and your thoughts in Christ Jesus.

> And now, my friends, all that is true, all that is noble, all that is just and pure, all that is lovable and gracious, whatever is excellent and admirable—fill all your thoughts with these things. . . . and the God of peace will be with you.

The climax of the letter Onesimus would carry with him the remainder of his days, as Paul thanked the Philippians for their care which reached him even in Rome.

> Not that I am alluding to want, for I have learned to find resources in myself whatever my circumstances. I know what it is to be brought low, and I know what it is to have plenty. I have been very thoroughly initiated into the human lot with all its ups and downs—fullness and hunger, plenty and want. I have strength for anything through him who gives me power. . . . And my God will supply all your wants out of the magnificence of his riches in Christ Jesus.

How infinitely superior this is even to the highest in Stoic philosophy, Onesimus thought, *for there one must bear whatever comes in his own strength.* But Paul was describing a new way of life, a partnership with Jesus Christ that cannot fail. Onesimus was ecstatic and yet peaceful in his new-found faith. "I, too, can do all things through Christ who will give me the power."

After the letter was concluded, Onesimus again embraced

Paul and Timothy, and they parted to rest before dinner. In his room, Onesimus knelt by his bed and lifted his mind in humble thanks. He lay down to rest, his mind racing as he reviewed what had happened.

Now I am free! There is no load of guilt on my shoulders. I am free now not to do just as I please: that is the false freedom from which I have escaped. I am free to do what I was meant to do. I am free to love as I never was before, even to bear a cross for others, if need be. He thought of Marcia and Nicia, marveling that his old bitterness was gone, replaced by a desire to find them again and help set them truly free.

Suddenly he remembered Helen and his almost forgotten love—and the fire leaped within. He sat up in bed, put his feet on the floor, and spoke directly to himself, "All right, Onesimus, this is your first test. Are you ready to face the trial? Are you willing and unafraid to return to Colossae, to ask forgiveness of Philemon, Archippus, and Helen though in so doing you are risking your life?"

He knew the answer immediately. Strangely, this was no longer a problem. *Of course* he would return to Colossae, just as soon as Paul directed. He would accept Paul's offer of a letter to Philemon, but other than this and the armor of the Spirit he would take nothing else to defend himself. He almost shouted it, "This is enough: To be free in Christ is to be free in all the ways that truly count."

That night at dinner, Onesimus quietly thanked his brethren for their patience and their part in his new faith. "As much as Paul has done for me, without the *koinonia* of which you are all a part, I am sure Paul knows I might never have been able to accept the gift of faith."

Paul nodded and said simply the words Onesimus had written that day, " 'If then our common life yields anything to stir the heart, any loving consolation, any sharing of the Spirit, any warmth of affection or compassion, fill up my cup of happiness by thinking and feeling alike.' You, my dear Onesimus, have filled my cup of happiness to the full. It is overflowing. Thank God for the church, the body of Christ, in whose *koinonia* we all find ourselves strengthened, encouraged, and able to believe!"

"Brother Paul," Onesimus broke the silence that followed these happy words, "I must tell you now that your prayer is answered in another way, as you predicted. I would like to return to Colossae, make full confession and restitution to Philemon, and yield myself to his mercy. If you will write the letter you promised, I will be thankful; with your blessing, I desire to go back home." His voice was exultant.

Paul knew he had passed the first test of freedom in Christ and said quietly, "Thank you, Lord." Before they left the table it was agreed that early in the morning the Christian *communitas** would be invited to Paul's dwelling for Onesimus's baptism. As soon as Paul wrote a letter to the Colossians and the letter to Philemon, Tychicus and Onesimus would take ship for Ephesus and together deliver the two letters. That night Onesimus slept as he had not slept in months, with the perfect peace that Paul called "beyond all understanding."

When the dawn came, Onesimus found himself surrounded by the little community of Christians who gathered in the atrium of Paul's house to celebrate his entrance by baptism into union with Christ through His body the church. He was wearing the simple white tunic provided for him by Junia. Paul greeted him with words that now overflowed with meaning, "Grace and peace to you, Onesimus, from God our Father and the Lord Jesus Christ." Then he gave the invitation: "Let us join in singing a hymn of praise to Christ as the light of life."

Onesimus had heard this song in services of Christian worship both in the house of Philemon and in Paul's house as he had witnessed Christian baptism. As he heard it now, he was thankful to open his life to the light of Christ.

> Awake, sleeper.
> Rise from the dead,
> and Christ will shine upon you.

---

*Composed of those who are allowed to participate in the Eucharist.

"Brother Onesimus," Paul addressed him, "the baptism which you are now to receive is an outward sign of your new life in Jesus Christ. Through this, God declares that He has adopted you as His son, making you a fellow heir to His riches in Christ. Your baptism assures you that you are no longer a stranger and foreigner to His kingdom, but a fellow citizen with the saints and a member of His household, the foundation of which is the apostles and prophets with Christ Himself as the chief cornerstone. Are you ready to accept this amazing gift of God's grace in Christ, and do you respond with your willingness to be faithful in all to which you are called by His Spirit in fearless witness and loving service?"

Onesimus's eyes were fixed on the light that shone from the apostle's face as he answered simply, "Unworthy as I am, I do accept this gift of the grace of God in Christ who forgives my sin and by His Holy Spirit will enable me to be faithful to the end."

"Do you, Brother Onesimus, accept Jesus as Lord, not only of the universe, but of your own life?"

"With glad heart and mind, I do!"

The apostle then took Onesimus's arm and led him from the atrium to the pool in the garden. As he waded into the water, he noticed for the first time that Paul for this occasion had been unchained from his guard, Janus, who stood joyfully with the others by the side of the pool.

Paul asked Onesimus to kneel in the pool. He took a pitcher of water from the hands of Doctor Luke, poured the water over the head and shoulders of his young friend, and spoke the words of holy baptism with a strong voice: "Onesimus, I baptize you in the name of the Father and of the Son and of the Holy Spirit."

As Onesimus continued to kneel, Paul lifted his voice in a prayer of thanksgiving and dedication, thanking God that "as this young man is buried into death with Christ in the waters of baptism, so may he rise from the dead with Christ by the glory of the Father. May he walk in newness of life from this day forward!"

The Christians joined in a fervent, "Amen."

Then Paul lifted Onesimus to his feet and they all began to sing the hymn known as the "Doxology":

> Praise God from whom all blessings flow,
> Praise Him all creatures here below,
> Praise Him above, ye heavenly hosts,
> Praise Father, Son, and Holy Ghost.

Paul embraced the new disciple and gave him the kiss of peace. As he came up out of the pool, one by one the Christians also embraced him, their newest brother in the faith.

The next two days were spent in hard but joyful work as Paul dictated the letter to the Colossians, using extraordinarily beautiful passages to describe the harmony and kindness made possible by the love of Christ. Onesimus thought the entire letter a matchless gem, sparkling with the light of Christian love. He determined to memorize every word of it before they landed and to copy it on a separate parchment so there would always be a copy available for any of the churches in Ionia or elsewhere that he might go. He especially loved the lines in which Paul prayed,

> May he strengthen you, in his glorious might, with ample power to meet whatever comes with fortitude, patience and joy; and to give thanks to the Father who has made you fit to share the heritage of God's people in the realm of light.

Onesimus knew how much he would need this prayer in the days to come. He also relished the tremendous admonition later on in the letter:

> Put on the garments that suit God's chosen people, his own, his beloved: compassion, kindness, humility, gentleness, patience. Be forbearing with one another, and forgiving, where any of you has cause for complaint: you must forgive as the Lord forgave you. To crown all, there must be love, to bind all together and complete the whole. Let Christ's peace be the arbiter in your hearts; to this peace you were called as members of a single body.

How magnificent the truth of these words. I have already experienced the power of forgiveness toward Marcia and Nicia, Onesimus thought. *Will Philemon be able to forgive me?* The question lay unanswered. He hoped so, believed so; but he could not know until that hour for which he waited, not with anxiety, but with confident peace.

He had one more discussion with Paul about the system of slavery as Paul dictated several paragraphs admonishing the slaves to give their entire obedience to their earthly masters, "with diligence, out of reverence for the Lord and not merely to receive favor from them."

"I can see now, Brother Paul. If one is a slave externally and cannot do anything about it, if what he does is for the Lord and not for men, the sting is taken out."

"Precisely," commended Paul. "Write this also, for these words make plain what I mean:

There is a Master who will give you your heritage as a reward for your service. Christ is the Master whose slaves you must be. . . . Masters, be just and fair to your slaves, knowing that you too have a Master in heaven.

The letter to the church at Colossae was finished, including some personal greetings indicating that Tychicus would bring them Paul's own message of love and announcing that Onesimus would be coming with him. Onesimus was moved as Paul dictated the words describing Onesimus as "our trustworthy and dear brother, who is one of yourselves."

Onesimus also appreciated the closing paragraph which included a special word to Archippus, "Attend to your duty in the Lord's service and discharge it to the full." Onesimus knew this meant in part that Paul was depending on Archippus to help soften the heart of his father Philemon, and Onesimus knew this charge would be fulfilled. He fully trusted Archippus.

"Onesimus, I am going to end this letter in my own hand, so there will be no question but that I wrote it. I don't want any misunderstandings in regard to your coming and what I trust will be your forgiveness by your master Philemon." Taking the pen, Paul wrote his name following the words Onesimus had written. "This greeting is in my own hand," the great apostle wrote in large letters, "PAUL."

"Now add the words, 'Remember I am in prison. God's grace be with you.' "

Part Five
Free Within and Without

19

*T*he ship bound for Ephesus was pulling away from the docks at Ostia with a good wind filling its sails. Onesimus and Tychicus stood on the deck waving a last farewell to the little band of Christians who now, with tears in their eyes, were praying for a safe voyage and successful conclusion to this mission. The entire *communitas* in Rome had come to know and love Onesimus; and with the trust they shared, his situation was clearly understood. There were Junia and Nereus, Doctor Luke, Epaphras, and other leaders of the church in Rome whom Onesimus had come to know: Ampliatus, Linus, Urban, Apelles, Persis, Rufus, and Olympas; even Pompania with several of her household.

Doctor Luke was often quoting from the new manuscript he was writing containing the accounts of Jesus' teachings and deeds which he wanted the entire church to read. As he had embraced Onesimus in farewell he had said, with the words attributed to Jesus Himself, " 'By faith all things are possible. If your faith is small even as a mustard seed, you can remove mountains.' My prayer for you, Onesimus, is that your faith will grow into a mighty tree. May not only this event ahead, which seems to you as large as a mountain, but many other obstacles be removed. I am confident you will have a good and effective ministry in the service of the Lord."

As the coast of Italy faded in the distance, Onesimus and Tychicus felt a mutual sense of sadness and yet of victory. "Nothing is more blessed than our *koinonia*," Tychicus observed. "It is like being a member of a closely knit family where everyone is loved and trusted alike."

Onesimus agreed heartily. "I owe my freedom and life to it," he confessed, "not only to Paul and Doctor Luke and Pompania, but to all of the *communitas. Koinonia* is a beautiful way to describe the church at its best."

The weather was perfect; the sea calm. They settled back in the chairs the steward had provided and Tychicus went to sleep. But Onesimus's mind was crowded with thoughts. With an overflowing cup of thankfulness he pulled out the letter to Philemon and read it again, as he had a dozen times since Paul had finished it. *This letter could have been written by no one but Paul himself,* he mused. He read it aloud softly.

> From Paul, a prisoner of Christ Jesus, and our colleague Timothy, to Philemon our dear friend and fellow-worker, and Apphia our sister, and Archippus our comrade-in-arms, and to the congregation at your house. Grace to you and peace from God our Father and the Lord Jesus Christ. . . .
>
> I thank my God always when I mention you in my prayers, for I hear of your love and faith towards the Lord Jesus and towards all God's people.

"What a master of human understanding Paul is." Onesimus exclaimed aloud as he stopped to think of how these words would be welcomed by Philemon. His generous works and sincere longing to be of use in the service of the Lord even Onesimus could appreciate. It was this very contradiction that had irked him so much: his goodness and generosity in all things, but his blindness in seeing what a galling burden slavery is to anyone of spirit. He continued to read.

> Accordingly, although in Christ I might make bold to point out your duty, yet, because of that same love, I would rather appeal to you.

This is so like Paul's attitude toward me and all others—though he possesses the apostolic authority, he chooses instead not to force anyone nor take undue advantage of a relationship, Onesimus observed.

> Yes, I, Paul, ambassador as I am of Christ Jesus—and now his

prisoner—appeal to you about my child, whose father I have become in this prison.

Onesimus stopped reading as a surge of thankfulness went through him. What a privilege to be called by Paul "my child" and to think of Paul as his father.

With a deep joy, Onesimus continued to read,

> I mean Onesimus, once so little use to you, but now useful indeed, both to you and to me. I am sending him back to you, and in doing so I am sending a part of myself. I should have liked to keep him with me, to look after me as you would wish, here in prison for the Gospel. But I would rather do nothing without your consent, so that your kindness may be a matter not of compulsion, but of your own free will.

These lines reflect the true greatness of Paul, Onesimus mused. *He believes supremely in the power of the love of Christ and his matchless influence on those who truly know and love him.* 'Agape *never fails!'* "

Onesimus recalled the stories Luke had told of Jesus' rejection of the devil's temptations in the wilderness and in the Garden of Gethsemane before His crucifixion. *He refused to force even the good upon God's people by calling for a legion of angels. His force was moral and spiritual, the power of caring, self-sacrificing love. From our Lord, Paul learned to respect the freedom of the human will. No wonder he believed that sending a runaway slave back in love, as a part of himself, would be more effective than demanding my release under his authority as the apostle to whom Philemon owes his 'very life!'*

A complete reversal of the world's values! Onesimus thought. *He is saying to Philemon that I am "no longer a slave, but more than a slave . . . a dear brother."*

He was filled with awe anew as he thought of the power of the love of Christ. He went back to read the conclusion of the letter:

> If then, you count me partner in the faith, welcome him as you would welcome me. And if he has done you any wrong or is in your debt, put

that down to my account. Here is my signature, PAUL [Onesimus remembered Paul had written his name right at this place in the letter—for here was the one place where he wanted to be sure Philemon *knew* it was Paul himself writing]; I undertake to repay—not to mention that you owe your very self to me as well. Now brother, as a Christian, be generous with me, and relieve my anxiety; we are both in Christ!

I write to you confident that you will meet my wishes; I know that you will in fact do better than I ask.

Onesimus lay back in his chair, his eyes closed. *It will take a very hard-hearted master indeed to reject such a plea,* Onesimus reasoned. *Philemon is not hard-hearted. But he is a very astute businessman, and he might feel setting me free would establish a precedent that would ruin his business and make him suspect as a Christian. But I will risk it! Whatever comes, I had rather be Philemon's slave and free in Christ than to be a runaway freeman, a slave to myself. Whatever comes, Lord, You have Your way with me! Thank You, Father, for the freedom with which I have been set free. Forbid that I should ever again be entangled in the yoke of bondage!*

After two months the ship pulled into the harbor of Ephesus with sails trimmed and passengers lining the deck. The load was largely cargo, but as usual some fifty persons had been voyagers together with Tychicus and Onesimus. With the shouts of the captain and mate and the returning cries of the crew, the ship was tied to the dock and the gangplank put in place. The two Christians found themselves walking up the cobblestone road into the city. Onesimus thought with thankfulness of the difference between now and the last time he had walked it nearly a year before.

Onesimus knew Ephesus better than Tychicus did and easily led the way to the home of Tyrannus. Here they were received with undisguised joy. Any Christians from Rome, especially direct emissaries from Paul, were always given an enthusiastic welcome. At lunch in the beautiful garden, Tyrannus and Joanna drank in eagerly every word Tychicus and Onesimus told them of Paul's good health and glowing spirit, the remarkable growth and influence of the young church in Rome, and of their plans for the coming weeks.

"You will surely meet with our congregation," Tyrannus insisted. "Tomorrow is the first day of the week, and it will be a happy privilege to have both of you present. All in our *communitas* will want to hear all they can from Paul, for he is our father in the gospel, beloved as no other person in the world. Perhaps you will even be so kind as to read the letter Paul has written to the church at Colossae, for I am sure what he says can be applied to us as well."

The two from Rome agreed. Onesimus had been recognized by Tyrannus only after they entered the garden—and then because Onesimus reminded him of their past experiences with Paul and the family of Philemon. Onesimus told him something of his new-found freedom in Christ.

"The Lord be praised," the kindly Tyrannus responded, "What miracles His Holy Spirit performs when we are obedient. Your story will be of incalculable value to us all, especially to those among us who are still slaves externally, as many still are. You will be glad to know, however, that some of us who own slaves have given them secret letters of manumission. Most of them have continued to share in our *familias*, though a few have returned to their old homes because of close family ties. Nevertheless, your witness concerning the gift of true freedom is one that all of us need. To be enslaved to our sinful nature is to suffer the most grievous of bonds. I know, because for years I struggled for the freedom of love and peace of mind I did not yet possess, though I was what would be called a wealthy man."

"Tyrannus," Onesimus exclaimed, "your words give me more of the courage that I surely need to face my old master Philemon. I have no idea how he will respond, but I must risk it, for I have stolen from him and betrayed my dearest friend and brother, his son Archippus. I must make whatever amends I can for my wrong."

Early the next morning Onesimus and Tychicus joined in

worship with the church in the Hall of Tyrannus. Tychicus spoke first, telling with thankfulness the good news of Paul's tremendous ministry as a prisoner in Rome. He told of the praetorian guards such as Plutonius and Janus as well as of the distinguished Lady Pompania, of their new lives as followers of Christ. Then he read a few of the most challenging selections from the letter he carried to the church at Colossae. When he finished, murmurs of praise and thanksgiving were heard from the hundred or more persons assembled in the hall. They were all Christians, or on their way as catechumens. Tyrannus had thought it wise not to encourage those who knew little or nothing of the Christian faith to be present. He was especially concerned that Onesimus's witness not be twisted and misused or through some unhappy circumstance reach Colossae ahead of him.

Tyrannus introduced Onesimus as "one of our own, a member of Philemon's familia from Colossae. During his year in Rome, about which I will ask him to tell you, he has had a remarkable entrance into the new life in Christ with a freedom that is the most priceless gift anyone can accept. I know you will receive him even as Paul did and pray for him as he and Tychicus go on their journey tomorrow back to his home in Colossae."

Onesimus arose with his feelings barely under control and a prayer under his breath, "Lord, I can do all things, even this, in Your strength." He gave his witness and told his story with a quiet, rich voice that was heard throughout the hall.

"So I stand before you," he concluded, "a slave of Christ and yet a son, your brother, your partner in the gospel. I am ready to go to Colossae and do what I can to make amends, to accept whatever he, as my master under the external law, proposes to do with me, and to give the best of my mind and heart, my body and strength, in all the time ahead to serve Christ and share His glory. For He alone is our hope and our joy. He is our peace and our freedom. May the grace of God our Father and the love of his Son Jesus Christ and the fellowship of His Holy Spirit be with you all. Amen."

The little group of Christians sat almost breathless to hear

every word from Onesimus. Many of them as slaves knew just
how he had felt when he ran away. All of them could share in the
joy and victory which this handsome young Phrygian proclaimed. As he came to his conclusion, they joined in with a
resounding "Amen" that shook the hall. Again and again they
said "Alleluia! Amen!" Then they stood and began to sing one of
the new songs which expressed their joy and thanks, and
Onesimus joined in with them.

When the little church finished singing, the elder Tyrannus,
now called "bishop," baptized the catechumens who were ready
for the great moment of affirmation as each was declared in
union with Christ as members of His body.

Then another bishop visiting from the church in Smyrna was
invited to assist Tyrannus as he uncovered the table and broke
the bread and lifted the cup. They prepared to join with the
community of faith in the holiest, most joyful moment of all.

The first Eucharist Onesimus had celebrated after his baptism was still vivid in his mind. It had been the day before he left
Rome. The bread had been broken by Paul and a piece of it
given to him. As he ate and drank from the chalice of wine, the
words of Jesus in the Upper Room had come alive in him: "This
bread is my body which is broken for you. . . This cup is my
blood which is shed for you. . . Take this in remembrance of
me." It was an awesome moment, Onesimus recalled, as he took
the bread and the cup with faith that the living Christ was now
within him. He shared the broken body and the sprinkled blood
*re*presented now *for him.*

Tyrannus himself broke the bread and placed a piece into
Onesimus's trembling hands held open to receive it. Onesimus,
for a moment, had a vision of the time when his own body would
be broken. When the wine was passed, he drank from the
chalice with sure knowledge that his own blood would someday
be spilled because of this love, given him by the Lord of life.
Strangely, he was free of any fear. Like Paul, he now wanted
only to know Christ and the power of His resurrection, even if it
meant sharing His sufferings and bearing His cross. The sufferings might come within the next few days or they might be

delayed, but Onesimus was sure they would come. He remembered the words accredited to the apostle John, whom the other disciples called "the beloved disciple." "Perfect love casts out fear."

---20

Next morning, the provisions for their journey were tied behind their horses' saddles, horses Tyrannus had generously provided. With the solicitous good-byes of the Ephesian Christians ringing in their ears, they mounted and began the seemingly interminable last leg of the journey to Colossae.

Onesimus and Tychicus talked about many things, especially the remarkable unity that seemed to rule the church both in Rome and in Ephesus. Tychicus was a good leader, Onesimus decided. He was glad Paul had sent this brother to carry the letter to the Colossians and to serve as ambassador to Philemon on his behalf. With all their talk, Onesimus still drank in the lovely Meander River lined with trees and the hillsides covered with spring flowers. It was a good time to travel in Ionia.

On the second night they camped at the identical spot where, five years before, Onesimus had been so humiliated. He described it all to Tychicus, and as he did he was surprised how little of the old *animus** was left within him.

By the next afternoon, they had left the Meander and were following the Lycus River. Just as the sun went down, they entered the gates of Colossae. The city was built on a flat plateau with three sides formed by a sharp cliff. The River Lycus ran at the bottom of the cliff on the northeast corner. Here they crossed the river on the travertine bridge Onesimus

---

*Animosity.

remembered so well. At last they rode through the gates and into the courtyard of Philemon's magnificent grounds. They stopped their horses just at the entrance.

"Stay here for just a short while, Tychicus," Onesimus requested. "I want to meet with Archippus first, tell him my story briefly, and let him lead us into the presence of Philemon." Tychicus agreed, but by this time several of the slaves had recognized Onesimus and had come out to greet him. Several asked the questions all were bursting to have answered. Onesimus reassured them that all was well.

"You will hear the whole story after a little while. Right now, all I ask is that you take my friend Tychicus who has accompanied me from Rome and has been so kind to me—take him and our horses as quietly as possible into the stable and wait until I return. Say nothing to any of the others."

The slaves, knowing the enormity of the risk he was taking, silently agreed. Onesimus turned to walk rapidly toward the part of the house where he knew Archippus was most likely to be found. He opened the door into the hallway leading to his friend's room and saw that the hallway was vacant. Without hesitation he walked to the door of the room and knocked. With heart pounding, he waited. The door opened, and for a few moments Archippus looked into the face of his father's slave, the young man he had once called his friend and brother, the man who then had drugged his wine, robbed him in his sleep, and rebelled against his bondage. Suddenly he took his friend in his arms, as quietly Onesimus murmured, "Forgive me, Archippus, my true friend and brother. It was an evil, a dastardly betrayal of your trust and friendship. Forgive me."

"I have forgiven you, Onesimus. That morning when I awoke and saw what had happened, I admit being angry at first. But before I left the room, I knelt to pray for forgiveness for breaking the first law our Lord taught us: 'Love your brother as you do yourself . . . forgive as you have been forgiven.' That morning I forgave you, and I have been praying for your return whole and well ever since."

They entered the room and shut the door. Onesimus's pent-up feelings were poured out with a quick description of his sufferings and loneliness in Rome, his meeting with Paul, his life in the church at Rome, his acceptance of new life in Christ, and the letter Paul had written after Onesimus told him of his decision to return to make restitution and to begin his life, forgiving even as he hoped he, too, would be forgiven.

"Thanks to our Lord!" Archippus exclaimed. "I admire you, Onesimus. I am not sure I could have come off as well. That must have been a terrifying experience for you in Rome. I want to hear more about your coming to Christ."

"But now, dear Archippus," Onesimus spoke with quiet awareness of the seriousness of the next few minutes, "the real test comes as far as you and I and Philemon are concerned. What do you think your father will say?"

"That I cannot foretell, Onesimus. One thing I know—Father has mellowed since you were here. I will say my father is in a much better mood to forgive than he was a year ago. When he first heard of your betrayal of our trust, he was so angry we were afraid he would make himself ill. We have not spoken of you since, so I cannot predict how he will act. I know he has high reverence for Paul, and his letter, together with Tychicus' presence, will be of great help. All I can say is I admire your courage and conviction more than words can say! I know as a Christian you must be willing to make amends. You have no other choice. So, let us go and meet Father, knowing our Lord is with us."

Reverently, they paused and grasped hands for a moment and stood in silent prayer. Then they walked out through the hallway to the stables. Here Onesimus introduced Tychicus, whom Archippus greeted with words of deep appreciation for his accompanying Onesimus.

"The pleasure is mine," Tychicus answered. "We, who were in the church in Rome, have all been singularly blessed by your young friend's honesty and clarity of thought. He is going to make a great addition to the church."

"Let us go now," Archippus suggested. "To all of you members of this familia," he said, addressing the small number of slaves gathered in the twilight near the stables, "I hope we will have some good news shortly for you concerning our brother Onesimus. First we must go and meet with my father. We will call you as soon as we can; hopefully so that we may all celebrate. Will you keep this matter to yourselves for the time being and remember to pray for us? Your master is a kind and gentle man who takes his Christian faith seriously. Let us expect the best and hope together in our Lord."

The three turned and made their way to the central part of the house. Onesimus's heart was pounding furiously, but his mind was calm and his faith serene. They knocked on the door where Philemon and Apphia would now be preparing for the evening meal. A young slave girl, whom Onesimus could not remember, opened the door and led them into the inner court where there was still light enough to see without a lamp.

Philemon was sitting, reading aloud from a parchment. Apphia was sitting near, listening. When Philemon looked up and saw Onesimus approaching, he stood up hastily, his face white. Before he could say a word, Onesimus was on his knees before him.

"Forgive me, Master, for my betrayal of your trust. In the name of our Lord Jesus Christ, whom both of us love and serve, I ask your forgiveness. I plead no justification for my thievery and deceit.

"Before you decide what you are to do with me, I ask only one thing: Our brother Paul, with whom I have lived for nearly six months, has written a letter to you. He sent it with me in the care of one of his most trusted helpers, Tychicus, whom I present to you. Paul and our fellow Christians in the church at Rome paid our passage out of their own funds. They were so lovingly gentle and compassionate toward me that through their love I have found the forgiveness of God for my rebellion, and through His grace I have been given an inner freedom that is more priceless than all else."

As Onesimus spoke, Philemon's face changed from his first look of shocked consternation. The little group looking on noted a loosening of the tightened jaws and the slow removal of the frown on his forehead. He walked over, placed his hands on Onesimus's shoulder, and helped him to his feet. "Son, first let me read Paul's letter. Then I will talk with you."

Warmly, he greeted Tychicus. "I have heard of you from John Mark and others who knew you in Cyprus and Rome. You are heartily welcome. This has been one of the greatest trials of my life as a Christian. I was truly disappointed and hurt by Onesimus, for I had come to love him."

"Philemon, as one brother to another," Tychicus responded, "I can understand just how difficult it has been. I, too, had a great injustice done to me, and it was not easy to forgive."

Onesimus pulled from his inner tunic the precious letter that Paul had sent to Philemon. As he handed it to him, Onesimus said with husky voice, "Master, I did not realize my wrongs hurt you so much, wrongs in which I felt justified. I sorrow deeply over the pain they have caused you. Your willing spirit makes me love you regardless of what your decision may be concerning my future."

Philemon's face was serious as he called for a lamp. The dusk had fallen rapidly, and he wanted to see clearly what his beloved brother Paul had written to him. To this man he owed his salvation, his life of joy and hope, and the love that had made such a difference in his personal family as well as with his familia of slaves. After the light was brought in, he opened the single sheet of papyrus on which the letter was written. All in the room watched as he began to read slowly and carefully.

They watched his face soften as he read. Quiet expressions of joy and satisfaction came from his lips. Onesimus observed him with mingled affection and thankfulness. Once Philemon looked up and, seeing the expression on Onesimus's face, he almost rose, but with a quick, "Praise to You, O Lord!" he returned to read the remainder.

Just at this moment, Onesimus was conscious that Helen had entered the room and was watching breathlessly. Onesimus turned toward her. Their eyes met, and he felt his face burn; his whole body tightened.

Philemon finished the letter, laid it on the table, rose and walked the few steps between him and Onesimus. Putting one hand on each of Onesimus's shoulders, he said, "Son Onesimus, *I* also am your father. You are no longer my slave but, as I, a slave to Christ. You are so much more than a slave to me, you are my dear brother—yes, even my *son!*" Saying this, he embraced the one who had betrayed him.

"Come here, Apphia, and meet our son and brother. Archippus, your brother whom you have loved so long! And Helen, come, take the hand of this our son who was lost and is found, who was dead and is alive again."

Tychicus was overwhelmed with joy as he watched the tender scene that followed, as each one came and took both of Onesimus's hands in theirs: Apphia, diffidently but with sincerity; Archippus with an elation that he had never known; and lastly Helen. Timidly, but with winsome affection, she spoke as she held his hands, "Onesimus, I have never ceased to pray for you, to believe in you. I am so glad you have found the love of Christ and that you have come back to us."

Her few words were worth a thousand to Onesimus as they all stood in a circle, Philemon inviting Tychicus to join them. They stood together in prayer to the Father before whom all were sons, daughters, brothers, and sisters.

"Tychicus, as Paul's and our Lord's minister to us, will you say in words what all our hearts and minds are trying to express?"

The words came simply with deep meaning as Tychicus spoke their common prayer: "O Mighty Lord, ruler of heaven and earth, our friend and Savior, You have guided us by Your presence into the very reality of the kingdom of heaven itself. As You did on the cross, You have taken the worst evil and hurt and turned it into the best compassion and healing forgiveness any of us has ever known. We praise You! We bless You! We exalt Your name, O Father, Son, and Holy Spirit. And in Your presence, we now dedicate ourselves to live in this *koinonia*, where each one bears the burdens of the other and forgives even as we are forgiven. We thank You Father that in Your kingdom there is no question of Greek and Jew, circumcised or uncircumcised, barbarian, Scythian, freeman, slave; but You, O Christ, are all and in all.

"Enable us from this time on, even as now You have helped us, to put on the garments that suit God's chosen people, His own, His beloved: compassion, kindness, humility, gentleness, patience. May we continue to be forebearing with one another and forgiving; where any of us has cause for complaint, to forgive as the Lord forgives us. To crown all, we accept Your love to bind all together and complete the whole. For Your peace, O Christ, is the arbiter in our hearts; to this peace we accept Your call as members of a single body. Accept our gratitude and from this time forth, as we sing and make melody in our hearts to the Lord, whatever we are doing, whether we speak or act, let us do everything in the name of the Lord Jesus, giving thanks to God the Father through Him."

And all in the room said "Amen" and embraced with joy. The household was called together and told the story. Afterwards Alcestia, taking her son in her arms, kissed him as a mother whose prayers have been answered and whose joy made complete.

"I knew you would come back, Onesimus," she said, with tears glistening on her cheeks, "but sometimes I confess it was hard to believe. Helen has been of great help to me, and so have Apphia and Archippus. This is a dear family indeed to which the Lord has called us." She walked over to Philemon her master and with great dignity said, "Philemon, my brother and my master, I have loved you in the Lord and respected you all these days. I know how this has hurt you, and I have prayed for you that your faith would not fail. My prayers have been answered for us all. If only my husband, Aristarchus, could have seen this."

Philemon responded with noble gentleness. "Alcestia, my sister and my friend, you have encouraged us all. Your presence has been a blessing. It is no wonder that with such a mother your son has come through these trials and found the liberty with which Christ has set us free. But now," the old master said, "let us rejoice! How better to celebrate the return of the prodigal son than to have our evening meal a feast of joy indeed."

He invited Alcestia to stay and eat with Onesimus and Tychicus and his family. As they reclined around the well-laden table, Philemon opened the dinner conversation after the giving of thanks.

"Onesimus, you are too useful in the Lord to remain my slave. Since you have been given sonship in our eternal Father's family, I can do no less than make you my adopted son. In the morning I will write a letter of manumission, declaring to all that you are henceforth a freedman, no longer a slave of Philemon. I am glad to know that you consider yourself now, as Paul does, a prisoner and slave of Christ—so should we all. I believe you should be free in Christ to serve Brother Paul. Perhaps the time will come when you can return and serve all our brother and sister Christians in Ionia, for I am sure you have much to give to us."

Nearly wordless, Onesimus said simply, "Master Philemon, this is so much more than I had dared to ask or expect. I can assure you that nothing would give me more happiness."

When the meal was over, the slaves and all the familia assembled in the large court. In the light of the torches, Philemon asked Onesimus to tell the story of his experiences and how he came to enjoy the freedom in Christ that had made such a change in his life. The evening ended with Philemon's reading of the "Hymn to Love" which he had copied from the letter of Paul to the Corinthian church. It was more beautiful now than Onesimus remembered. Then Philemon led in a simple evening prayer, thanking God for this blessed day.

$\mathcal{T}$he morning broke fair and cool with Onesimus awake and ready for another momentous day. The newly enlarged family met for breakfast in the small dining room. Philemon asked Onesimus to give the prayer of thanksgiving before the meal. He responded with his first spoken prayer in this new relationship.

"Gracious Lord, to You we give our thanks on this most beautiful day. Your redeeming love has broken all our chains, and we are supremely thankful for the new freedom to love each other even as we are loved. We praise You for the providence, mysterious yet real, by which we have been reunited in peace and joy. Lead us now as we begin a new day to begin also a life for the sake of Christ who loved us and gave Himself for us. Amen."

After breakfast Philemon invited everyone into the library. They were seated—Philemon at the end of the large reading table where Onesimus and Helen had sat for many hours. He beckoned to Onesimus, Helen, and Apphia to sit on his right hand and Tychicus, Archippus, and Alcestia on his left.

"Now, *amenuensis* of the apostle Paul, will you write your own letter of manumission? Archippus, you have some parchment. Give one sheet to Onesimus and the pen and ink that is in front of you. Let us proceed."

The members of the entire family were smiling as Onesimus took the parchment and the pen, looking up thankfully, waiting for the dictation.

"TO ALL WHOM IT MAY CONCERN: Be it known that on this day, the twenty-fifth day of August, I, Philemon of Colossae, a citizen of Rome and of the province of Ephesus, do hereby set free one slave, Onesimus by name. He is four cubits* tall, with brown eyes and dark brown hair, with no blemish on his face, but with several scars on his back."

Philemon stopped his dictation, saying, "Forgive me, but Archippus tells me he has seen these scars which, I must sadly admit, were made by my own hand. They may be needed for further identification should your state as a freedman ever be questioned.

"From this hour on, Onesimus is a freedman," and he added with obvious exhilaration, "and even more important is now adopted as my own son. Receive him well, as you would receive me." He paused, "Now let me sign with my own hand." He took the parchment and the pen and wrote his signature: PHILE-MON. "Now, Archippus, you, Helen, and Apphia may sign as witnesses."

The work was done. Freedom was his. Onesimus was glad, but he admitted that, as thankful as he was for this letter of manumission and with no slighting of its importance, his true freedom came when he became "a new creation in Christ Jesus." As he gave his witness, their eyes again were filled with tears of gratitude and understanding. Onesimus was free!

The remainder of the week was spent making plans for Onesimus's return journey to Rome, including several tender hours spent with Helen. Again they sat together in the library. It was all so natural, and now there were no outside barriers between them. They sat side by side talking about the future. Philemon and his familia understood and left them alone. Finally Onesimus was able to embrace her and pour out his love and deep-felt need for her without fear of reprisal. Helen also was able to confess her love freely. Their time was all too brief.

"As soon as possible, let us be married," he said with earnestness, "if your father agrees."

"I believe he will. I have scarcely slept for thinking of you

---

*About six feet.

these past months," Helen responded. "Whenever Father tried to discuss my betrothal to someone else, I would become so upset I could not eat. Eventually I told him of my love for you. He did not want to hear of it then, but now I think he is ready."

"I will approach him when we're alone, tonight if possible," Onesimus said, adding, "As much as both of us want to be together, we must wait to be married until I return. If something happens to me, it will be much better for your future if you are not left a widow. Do you agree?"

She paused a moment and answered pensively, "Yes, my Onesimus, you are right. But it is so difficult to wait!"

The dinner bell was ringing. With a hug and a brief prayer of thanks for each other, they walked together into the dining room where the others in the family were waiting.

When the meal was over, Onesimus asked to see Philemon privately. "I want to ask the hand of your daughter in marriage," he said with a hushed voice. "We would like your permission to marry when I return from the journey."

"So, you are not only my son, but you are now taking my daughter," Philemon said jokingly, but with great affection. "I give you both my blessing and pray that you, Onesimus, will have a safe return. I know the home you make together will be most blessed. As they embraced, Onesimus knew he now belonged not only to the household of God, but to the love and care of this man and his family.

Onesimus's departure was delayed until after the first day of the week. Philemon wanted all of his fellow Christians in Colossae not only to hear the reading of the very special letter Paul had written to them but also the announcement of the engagement of his daughter and new son. Philemon presided as elder over the Colossian church. As he entered this morning with Tychicus, the congregation arose and responded to Philemon's greeting, "The Lord be with you."

They answered heartily, "And with your spirit."

Word had been passed to all the Christians in Colossae so that everyone waited expectantly for the great experience in store. After a simple prayer of invocation which presented their little church to the Lord and asked for His blessing, Philemon asked Alcestia to sing a hymn she had written after the happy events of their first night and day with Onesimus and Tychicus.

"This song," Philemon explained, "Alcestia has written to celebrate the return of her son Onesimus who was lost and in despair but, now through the ministry of the apostle Paul, Doctor Luke, and the church in Rome, has found what her hymn calls 'loving freedom.' Indeed, there is no other kind."

Alcestia had written several songs that were already in use in their worship, and now she sang with her whole heart and spirit, playing her own accompaniment on the harp.

> Lord of all your great creation,
> You who made us to be free,
> Praise to you for love you give us,
> Breaking chains of hate and greed,
> Bonds of love that can't be broken.
>
> Glory be, Eternal Father,
> Son of Love in Jesus living,
> Now, O Christ, your Spirit giving!
> Lord of all your great creation
> Praise to you for loving freedom!

"And now," Philemon continued, "it is most appropriate that we should ask our friend from Cyprus, one of Paul's most trusted helpers who has accompanied Onesimus back home, to read the letter our father in the gospel, Paul, has written specifically to us.

Tychicus took out the precious scroll of papyrus and began to read. Onesimus listened carefully to the apostle's words:

It is now my happiness to suffer for you. This is my way of helping to complete, in my poor human flesh, the full tale of Christ's afflictions still to be endured, for the sake of his body which is the church.

"To be happy to suffer for others. . ." Onesimus knew he would remember these words as, inevitably, suffering would come to him if he continued in the pathway of Christian discipleship. He could not imagine himself ever departing from the Way.

When the service of worship was over and dinner was out of the way, Onesimus and Helen spent the last afternoon they would have together for a long time. He would remember those hours with exquisite tenderness and gratitude during the long months of separation ahead.

The two of them walked hand in hand to the bridge over the River Lycus. As they watched the waterfall, Onesimus shared with Helen the night two years earlier when he had stood in this same spot and resolved to be free no matter what the cost. Then he turned to his wife-to-be and, holding her hands in his, said, "I could not bear the thought of remaining here, knowing that you would become another man's wife. I considered it impossible that we could ever be married. How good God is to give you to me! I can still hardly believe it."

Impulsively, Helen threw her arms around his neck. Then, taking his hands again, she looked into his eyes and said, "I love you so much, Onesimus. During these many months I have repeated often what the Lord said, 'That which is impossible with men is possible with God.' While you are away, I will continue to remember this, trusting Him to bring you back safely."

With tears running down her cheeks, she looked up at Onesimus, unable to speak. He brushed her tears away and kissed her tenderly. Without a word, they walked back to the house, content with the knowledge that their love for each other was God's gift and they were under His care.

Later, Onesimus and Tychicus went over the details of their journey with Archippus and Philemon. Philemon insisted that they take some of his best silk and woolen cloths as gifts to the elders of the churches at Laodicea and Hierapolis, and to Tyrannus and Joanna in Ephesus, and then to the other churches in Asia whom Tychicus would visit after seeing Onesimus safe aboard a ship going back to Rome.

On the following morning, affectionate and difficult good-byes were said to the entire familia. Philemon embraced Onesimus warmly. "Please remember, you are to return here as part of our family. I will pray for you, Son, that you keep this freedom that both of us have found." Onesimus promised to carry out his mission and return.

As he held his mother close to him, she whispered words that would strengthen him in all that was to come: "Son, remember that nothing, nothing can separate us from the love that is in Jesus Christ our Lord."

His parting with Helen was most difficult of all. Unashamedly he wept as she did when they embraced.

Mounting his horse, he waved to all, and he and Tychicus, pulling a donkey laden with the gifts Philemon had sent, rode back down the road which had once evoked bitter memories. The smell of the oleander and the wild roses in bloom filled the air with fragrance. The peace and joy of the Lord filled their hearts, even as reluctantly they rode along the River Lycus toward the unknown future.

Part Six

Triumphant Tragedy – Paul's Martyrdom

22

*T*he docks at Ostia were alive with the excitement of the entrance of *The Diana* in the harbor. Any large sailing vessel from such a faraway port as Ephesus, laden with rich cargo brought by long camel caravans from the East, provided a fascinating spectacle for merchants and the merely curious. The ship slid easily up to the dock, and the gangplank was down in a matter of minutes.

The journey of Onesimus and Tychicus from Colossae had gone well, as had their visit with the Ephesian church. Tyrannus and Joanna with the other Christians had rejoiced over Onesimus's manumission from slavery as well as his betrothal to Helen. Now, as Onesimus watched the preparations for landing, he reflected on the news that the apostle Peter was planning to journey to Rome from Jerusalem as soon as possible to strengthen the faith of the disciples and to be of encouragement to Paul. Tychicus had explained how Paul and Peter had differed at first over the ministry to the Gentiles, but how Paul had helped convince Peter that the gospel of Christ was for all persons, Jews and Gentiles alike. Now the ex-fisherman was coming to Rome to join in ministering to the Gentile Christians who made up a large part of the church there. Onesimus was excited as he thought of the courage of this once fickle braggart Simon who had denied Jesus but whom Tychicus described now as a strong leader worthy of the name Jesus had given him: Peter the Rock! *What an unexpected privilege I will have,* Onesimus thought, *to be able to know another great apostle. I need to find some of Peter's faith, too.*

From the deck Onesimus watched several scenes of affectionate reunion between members of families long separated. He was searching among the waiting crowd to see if by any good providence one or more of the Christians from Rome would be there to meet him. If they were, it would be due to something more than chance, for he knew that Nereus, Junia, Doctor Luke, and his other dear friends would likely seek to discover the arrival of any ship from Ephesus on which he might be returning. He felt sure someone would be there.

He almost shouted his joy when he saw the strong, weather-beaten face of Nereus standing out among the crowd. Without waiting to see who might be with him, Onesimus ran for the gangplank as the last passengers were leaving. Quickly he made his way to Nereus who was standing at the edge of the crowd. The two embraced with exclamations of thanksgiving. "Onesimus, my son, you did return!" Nereus cried. "I can see by your looks that all is well. The Lord be praised!"

"Yes, Nereus, these weeks have been more deeply satisfying and truly remarkable than anything I had ever dreamed possible. I am a *free* man, with the full forgiveness of Philemon and Archippus and the love and prayers of all the family of Christ in Colossae and Ephesus. Best of all, Philemon gladly gave Helen and me permission to marry upon my return."

"I am glad to hear the good news. I assure you we all have been waiting eagerly for your arrival."

"What faith you have!" Onesimus cried, almost bursting with gratitude as he realized how many prayers had been lifted up for him during the long weeks. Then the principal object of his concern came to mind as he asked, "But how is Brother Paul?"

Nereus was silent for a moment; a look of sadness came over his face.

"Onesimus, things have not gone well with Paul nor with the Christian *communitas* since you left. Soon after you sailed, the order came direct from Nero to Burrhus, captain of the praetorian guard, to remove Paul from his rented house. He has been put in the darkest and most galling of all our prisons, the Mammertine. He is permitted to have little or no company and is suffering from the damp stinking mud and dung in a foul room in which only a rough cot is placed. Were it not for the praetorian guards who belong to the church, I am afraid he would be dead by now. Plutonius and Janus have been assigned by Burrhus to guard him, though even they are not now permitted to be with him, except as they bring him the small amounts of food and drink allowed.

"The difficulty is, the Mammertine Prison is not under the direct control of Burrhus. It was only by his skillful maneuvering and some substantial payments that Paul's life barely continues to exist. Brutus, the officer in charge of the prison, for years has taken delight in making life miserable for his victims." His voice was choked and his eyes moist as he talked.

Only then Onesimus became aware of Nereus's companion, a boy of twelve years who, as his Uncle Nereus recounted the trials of the apostle Paul, listened sympathetically, almost in tears. The boy was Hermas, a nephew of Nereus, whom Onesimus had met several times at Christian gatherings.

Onesimus fell on his knees and clasped the young lad around the waist.

"Hermas, it is good to see you, but do not be so sad. Remember how Paul said to us continually, 'Rejoice in the Lord always; in everything give thanks.' Would he not say to us, 'Trust in the Lord. For all things fit into a pattern for good to those who love Him and accept the call of His purpose'?"

Onesimus spoke these words to comfort not only Hermas but also himself. Did he or did he not believe these words? Nereus affirmed his convictions that Paul would stand the test, as would Onesimus and all who had partaken of the sacrament of the presence of *Christus Victor*.

The three walked from the docks toward the horses which Lady Pompania had insisted Nereus take for the trip. Before they began the journey, Nereus suggested they stop at the inn where Onesimus remembered so vividly buying some bread and cheese on that first journey to Rome a little over a year earlier.

As they mounted their horses and started up the Appian Way toward Rome, he told Hermas and Nereus the story of his fright as he first walked this famous highway, how he had escaped to the bushes in fear of being caught, and then entered Rome at night. Hermas was interested and full of questions. By now he was excited and eager to talk. Onesimus learned much about what had happened while he was away, with Nereus providing the basic facts and Hermas giving the more colorful details.

Paul's case had been deferred time and time again. He had appealed to Caesar, but Caesar and his profligate friends, Otho and Tigellinus, were too busy with parties, buffoonery, and evening trips in disguise on the streets of Rome to deal with a Jewish case, even if the defendant were a Roman citizen. He and his conscienceless companions found sadistic pleasure in roaming through the Valabrum and other streets late at night. In the absence of police or adequate lights, they could terrify and insult groups of citizens returning home.

Hermas and Nereus described the unbelievably low state into which their Emperor had fallen. Otho and Tigellinus were vying for Nero's favor by outdoing each other in giving expensive and ornate banquets with every kind of food and wine, including the tongues of nightingales and the brains of peacocks and African flamingoes. Nereus told how their orgies of sexual perversion mixed with the comic opera of Nero drunkenly reading his poor poetry to the mock acclaim of his subjects had become topics of conversation in all of Rome.

With the Emperor occupied in such cruel diversions and with the help of Otho's wife, Poppae, a beautiful Jewess who had set out to woo and win Nero's affection, Paul's Jewish accusers at last were able to get their way.

Paul's privileged position when he first came to Rome had been largely due to the influence of Lady Pompania and the help of a splendid group of fair-minded Jews, some of the richest and most influential citizens of Rome. Though they did not accept Jesus as the Messiah, they believed Him to be a prophet and wanted to have nothing to do with the persecution of His followers. For nearly two years Paul had been allowed comparative freedom in the house guarded by the praetorians. But the influence of Paul's benefactors had come to an end.

"The tragic part is that our Emperor is a boy, and a *bad* boy at that," Nereus exclaimed.

"Yes," Hermas interrupted, "he enjoys doing monkey tricks, such as hiding in the curtains at the top of the stage in the theatre, frightening the actors out of their wits, and throwing sticks and stones at people's heads."

"The worst part, of course," Nereus went on, "is his being so completely under the influence of vicious persons such as Otho and Tigellinus. They have weaned him almost completely away from the counsel of his old teacher Seneca. Nero still uses Seneca to write his speeches, but he will not listen now even to Lady Pompania's quiet urging. He still has respect for her but refuses to grant her requests."

"This means," Onesimus summed up the situation sadly, "Paul must pay the price for our Emperor's folly. What a tragic twist, when the ultimate folly of the hedonistic philosophy of 'pleasure while you can get it' has to be shown at the expense of one of the kindest and most loving men on earth."

Entering Rome through the main gate, they rode their horses directly to the house of Pompania. She met them at the inner gate and embraced Onesimus with tears of happiness, as though he were her own son returning from a difficult and dangerous journey.

"So you are back with us! Praise to our great Lord, whose grace is greater than our sins and beyond all our highest dreams," she exclaimed as she led them into the atrium after directing her servants to care for the horses.

"Now tell me the whole story." She sat with eyes alight, eagerly drinking in all Onesimus said as he told of his remarkable experience with Philemon and his family. When he came to the story of his relationship with Helen, she clapped her hands with enthusiasm.

"Set free to love and be loved!" she exclaimed. "May our Lord lead you during the difficult days ahead and bring you back to Helen and your mother and family. In the meantime, we will all be your family. You can stay here or with your first-found friends in Rome, Nereus and Junia. I know your coming will be a great help to Paul, if we can find some way to get the prison officer, Brutus, to let you visit him at least an hour or so each

day. I know Paul has numerous notes and letters he wishes to
write to the various churches and to his friends in so many
places. What a priceless gift Philemon has given, not only your
personal freedom but your opportunity to serve Paul in his time
of greatest need."

Onesimus impulsively went over to her chair and took her
hand in his as he responded with warm affection, "How can I
ever thank you, my dear mother in Christ—for you are just that
to me. I will be glad to stay here or go with Nereus. It may be
better to live with him and Junia, for their house is much nearer
to the prison; but I shall visit with you as often as I can and bring
you news from Paul. Your offer to help me get in to see Paul is
too generous. I know you can work through Burrhus and his
guards as soon as possible to secure the permission required."

Hermas and Nereus were sitting with them in the atrium,
and Onesimus noticed with amusement how Hermas's eyes
were roving over the magnificent room with its graceful statues
and potted flowers arranged artistically around a worship
center with a rough wooden cross. Pompania had noticed him
too, and now she arose and led him to the cross.

"Yes, Hermas," she explained, "this is to remind me and my
household and all who come here for worship that the cross of
our Lord is a symbol of victory and joy as well as agony and
suffering. Of course," she said, turning to Onesimus, "this cross
is removed when visitors other than Christians are expected."
She sighed. "I am afraid the time is coming soon when everyone
of us will pay a great price to identify ourselves as Christians."
Speaking again to Hermas she said kindly, "You must come to
see me sometime, and I will tell you the story of these statues
and pictures."

"We had better go now, Onesimus," Nereus said, thanking
Pompania for the horses and all her help. "Junia will be wonder-
ing what happened to me. You can get a good rest, and perhaps
by tomorrow the Lady Pompania will have secured permission
for you to visit with Paul."

Onesimus had brought only two small bags with extra clothes
and a few choice pieces of Philemon's finest silks and woolen

cloth. He opened one of the bags and took out a beautiful silk piece which Philemon and Apphia had specifically asked be given to Pompania. It was an exquisitely woven purple, more than enough for at least one dress. They left after Pompania had offered a prayer of thanksgiving and of intercession for Paul and for Onesimus in his ministry to him.

Junia was waiting anxiously and embraced Onesimus fondly. "Our prayers were answered, Onesimus," she exulted. "Nothing could make me happier right now than your coming unless it could be the release of Paul. But come in and wash, for I have prepared dinner for you. Hermas, we will be happy for you to join us."

But Hermas was tired and anxious to tell his own family and the other Christians the good news of Onesimus's return. He shook hands admiringly with Onesimus and thanked Nereus and Junia and started off on the run for home.

"That's a fine lad," Nereus murmured. "We lost our son when he was about his age, and Hermas is helping take his place."

After a good meal and more conversation, Onesimus found himself in the same room where he had spent his first night outside the Subura. Recollections of all that had happened filled him with indescribable peace and joy. *This must be the peace that is beyond the world's understanding*, he said to himself. Falling on his knees he offered himself anew in thankfulness to be used by the Lord to do all he could for Paul and the people whose love meant so very much to him.

Next morning a messenger came from Pompania telling him that she had arranged for him to be met at the prison by Janus at eleven. He could have just one hour with Paul. After a good breakfast and prayers Onesimus put on his cloak, for the cold wind of late fall was blowing. He went out into the street and walked rapidly several minutes before arriving at the prison called Mammertine.

The prison was a bare, gray stone building lacking the usual architectural ornaments of other state buildings. Its walls, blackened by the polluted air of the city, had not been cleaned in

several generations. Onesimus climbed the steps to the iron
door before which stood two soldiers with their helmets,
swords, and shields. He walked up to them and with as cheer-
ful a greeting as he could manage, introduced himself as
Onesimus, a friend of Burrhus, captain of the praetorian guard.
He showed a short letter from Burrhus to Brutus the chief
officer of the prison, asking for the privilege for Onesimus to be
permitted an hour each day with a certain prisoner named Paul
of Tarsus, a citizen of Rome, now awaiting trial before the
Emperor.

The two soldiers evidently had been informed of his coming.
Without a word they opened the huge iron door and called to
Janus, who was sitting at the entrance to Paul's cell where he
had been stationed at Burrhus's request. Janus walked rapidly
over and, with stoical face, bowed and invited Onesimus to
come with him. The two soldiers closed the door and resumed
their position outside.

"Onesimus, how good to have you here with us, free and
well," Janus said in low but elated voice. "All of us who love
Brother Paul are sick at heart to see him suffer so. We are doing
all we can for him, but that is not much. Clearly, the Emperor
has decided to make an end of him. His enemies have the upper
hand, and there is nothing anyone can do. But be careful—I
must not be seen too friendly to you."

Noting the papyri, pen, and ink Onesimus had brought, he
added, "How blessed your coming is, not only because of Paul's
love for you but because he had had little or no way to communicate with the Christians and the churches."

With his large brass key, Janus turned the lock in the door
built into the floor. The key grated in the rusty lock and, with
his powerful hands, he slowly lifted the heavy wooden door
back on its hinges. Onesimus could see little in the dark hole
beneath, except a small ladder reaching to the floor of what
appeared to be a small round room. In the dim light coming from
the open door and a narrow slit in the wall, Onesimus saw with
swelling heart the outline of a man seated on a hard cot near to

the outside wall. "Brother Paul," Janus whispered, "I have brought you Onesimus as I promised."

From the depths of the darkened cell, Paul's weakened voice responded with gratitude, "Thanks to you, Janus—and to Captain Burrhus and all who have made this possible. Welcome, Onesimus! How glorious are the works of our Lord! How good it is to see you. I have prayed for you often."

"You had better climb down the ladder now, Onesimus," Janus warned, "for I must quickly lock the door behind you. No doubt we are being observed. I will warn you when your hour together is almost over."

The ladder was loosely hung from the entrance of the open door. Onesimus, with shaky hands, descended slowly; when his feet reached the bottom they sank deeply into the filthy, mud-covered floor. His nostrils were offended by the reeking smells of the dark pit. The mud was the result of water seepage mixed with urine and human offal. Here it was that Paul was existing day and night. No wonder he had become ill and physically weak.

As the door closed above him, Onesimus moved toward the bent figure on the cot. After a short but fervent embrace in which he could feel the bony, shrunken body of his friend and teacher, he stepped back a little. With his eyes more accustomed to the semi-darkness, he saw the haggard, bearded face of this man to whom he owed his new life and freedom. Paul's hair was shaggy, his back stooped, his cheeks hollow, but though still diseased his eyes shone with the same light Onesimus had seen on that first day in the Agora at Ephesus.

"My son, I knew you would return with the full forgiveness of our brother Philemon." Paul's voice was alive and vibrant with the same joy which had first won Onesimus's admiration. "Praise to the Lord Jesus Christ who in all things turns even the evil that hurts us into instruments of His good will. I am still a prisoner—no longer in chains, unless you call this dungeon chains—but I am a prisoner of Christ and shall always be. I know not what hour or day my life will be called to pay the price of devotion to Christ, but I am ready. Until that time comes, I will be comforted and blessed by the continuing presence of our Christ and, so Janus informs me, by an hour each day that I may spend with you. What great comfort the Lord of all comfort has given me—not only by your coming, but by your readiness to do what I requested of Philemon. You can help me write some letters to some of our dear friends in several of the churches. But there will be time for that later. Now I want to hear of your journey and what must have been a glorious time in the house of Philemon."

Onesimus sat by Paul's side on the cot and at Paul's suggestion found he could thus lift his feet from the cold, stinking mud. "Here, let me pour a little of this clear water from the bucket supplied by my two friendly guards to wash off your feet!"

Onesimus gratefully pulled off his sandals and washed his feet as Paul poured the water sparingly over them.

"This is the only bit of cleanliness I have been allowed," he explained, "but I am grateful for it and for the small bit of lime Janus and Plutonius slip in to me. Now, let's hear your story."

Onesimus gave the account as quickly and yet with as much care as possible, in order not to miss the kind of details he knew Paul would enjoy. As he talked, he saw the sallow face lighten and the old glow return, until it seemed to Onesimus that more light came from the apostle's face than from the narrow window above them. As he described Philemon's response to Paul's personal letter and his forgiveness as he embraced his runaway slave, Paul exclaimed, "Love never fails, when it is the love given to us by God in Christ. Surely His Holy Spirit's gift of *agape*-love is the most priceless and powerful force on earth! The Lord Jesus Christ is indeed the Ruler of all things, for in Him all the fullness of the Godhead dwells."

Paul was particularly pleased with Onesimus's description of their first worship together as a familia back in Colossae and of the response to his letter. As Onesimus progressed in his story, including the welcome from the Christians in Ephesus, Paul responded with even more fervent expressions of joy. Onesimus took much of their first hour together giving the account of his experiences, for Paul would not let him skip any of the more important details. He drank in the words as a starving man would drink pure water. His spirit was revived, and when Onesimus concluded Paul thanked him, saying, "Now that you have finished your story, let me tell mine." Onesimus thought he would probably recount the sufferings and insults that had been dealt out to him. Instead Paul was filled with delight as he told of the numbers added to the Roman church. He related how courageous they had been in the face of rising opposition and threats of persecution.

"From the word I receive from Janus and Plutonius, I am told that any time now an all-out attack on the Christians is expected. As for me, I awaken each morning from the gracious sleep the Lord gives me, not knowing whether I will be summoned that morning or the next."

"This is a horrible experience for you, Brother Paul," Onesimus spoke sympathetically.

"From the human point of view, yes," Paul responded. "I'll admit I despise this stench and darkness and, most of all, the separation from friends and fellow Christians in the church. But I give thanks to the Lord who is nearer now and more gracious than I could ever have known when surrounded by friends and loved ones. I have found again that when I am weakest even then I am strong; for my strength is made perfect in weakness. Over and over I have found His grace is sufficient for me, as it will be for you and for all who submit to Him in love and trust. I am learning increasingly the great secret of finding resources within me for these trying days.

"There are times," and here Paul's voice faded and for a few moments there was only the vast silence of the dark prison, ". . . there are times when I am lifted out of this human flesh and raised to the third heaven where I share an unspeakable communion with Him who is ever near . . . I cannot describe it . . . but again and again I have found that I have strength for anything—even the worst that human bodies and minds can endure—through Him who gives me power."

Onesimus sat under the spell of this man's great spirit. Who

but the mighty God of heaven and earth could give him this kind
of victory? He vowed silently that whatever came to him, he
would never forget this testimony of the unseen reality of the
Love that created and rules all things.

"Your time is almost up, Onesimus," Paul spoke matter-of-
factly, "but since you brought some papyri and writing materi-
als, I will dictate a brief note to the people at Iconium, where
once I was beaten and almost killed. A few loyal Christians
found me and nursed me back to life. I went back a few months
later and found the church prospering. Now I hear they are
suffering under another tyrannical governor readily influenced
by our enemies. I would encourage them by a short letter to be
sent by Epaphras. He has been in Spain, but is back now and
ready to return to visit some of the churches that are in
trouble."

Paul's letter to the church at Iconium was a brief pastoral
epistle which Onesimus transcribed as best he could in the
semi-darkness. It covered only one length of papyri. Later on
that night in his room he made a copy to keep for his own use. It
was a masterful description of the armor which God provides
faithful Christians.

Just as he finished writing, the trap door above them opened
and Janus—speaking loudly so the other guards would hear,
said, "All right! Time's up down there!" Onesimus hastily bade
Paul good-bye with a promise to return as soon as Burrhus
could arrange it. With his papyri folded, he stepped out on the
muddy floor with a grimace he hoped Paul could not see and
climbed the ladder to the outside.

Janus led him to the small fountain of water just within the
entrance. Here he washed his feet. Janus then, with a whisper
of encouragement, opened the door and Onesimus was let
outside the prison.

As he walked back to Nereus and Junia's house, he was
thankful for the fresh air and his freedom from the fetid prison.
His disgust with the prison cell only filled him with greater
admiration for Paul's remarkable spirit of faith and joy.

23

*T*hat evening at supper Nereus disclosed that all the Christians were meeting in a newly discovered cave just outside the walls of Rome.

"Several of our younger men have been exploring the many caves near the city for days," explained Nereus. "We realize we must no longer go to Lady Pompania's house for worship. The danger is too great for her and for us. We have talked about using one of these subterranean caves for some time, because almost all Romans are too superstitious to enter one. They are supposed to be the dwelling place of evil spirits, but since we do not believe in the dominion of evil spirits, we are not afraid. Here we may hear the ministry of the Word and celebrate the Eucharist without fear. Tonight we are to be led from several places in the city to the one cavern chosen as largest and most suitable as a place for worship. Someday we may have to seek refuge in these caves."

Only a few persons at a time were to proceed to the appointed place. Nereus, Junia, and Onesimus were joined by several others as they stood by a designated statue on Capitoline Hill. A young man greeted them quietly and told them to follow him in groups of only two or three together. The others could come but at a safe distance.

After passing through the city gate, they walked about fifteen minutes into a valley near the southern walls. Here in a clump of trees they found an entrance into a cavern lighted by torches placed along the damp walls. Climbing down some clay steps and walking through the cave for a few minutes, they came to a large circular room filled with Christians, some of whom were well-known to Onesimus. His friends, including Pompania, welcomed him warmly. Nereus then led him to the center of the room and introduced him to a tall, thin man whom they addressed as "Elder Linus." His face was kind, and he was dressed in the humble garments of a tradesman.

Linus smiled, took both of Onesimus's hands in his and said, "Welcome home, Onesimus! We have heard of your return and of your visit with Paul today. We will be waiting for any word you can bring us not only from Paul but also from the churches in Ephesus and Colossae. We regret the stern necessity of such a meeting place, but we know the times of testing are upon us, as Paul and as Jesus Himself warned us they would come."

"Thank you for your kind welcome, Elder Linus. I have had some blessed, though trying experiences today with the apostle whom we all love. I will be happy to share his witness with you."

"Before we begin the Holy Eucharist," Linus said, motioning to a handsome young man standing near, "I want you to get acquainted with John Mark, who has recently come from Jerusalem with the good word that the apostle Simon Peter is to arrive very soon. John Mark, this is Onesimus of whom you have heard so much. I am sure you have much in common."

Turning to Onesimus, Linus explained, "John Mark is the son of the good woman in whose house Jesus and His twelve disciples observed the last supper together before His betrayal and arrest. He has been a constant companion of Peter and from him and other disciples who knew Jesus in the flesh he has gathered many inspiring stories of the acts of Jesus and some of his teachings. He is to share some of these precious accounts with us tonight."

Linus made his way to the front of the cave-room and asked for silence. Onesimus felt again, even in the cold dampness, the quickening glow of the *koinonia* which had meant so much to him. Linus moved to the wall, where between two large candles a rough wooden cross was hung from the ceiling. The cross was made of fir with the horizontal arms slightly shorter than the vertical. With a smile of thankfulness, he began the service:

"The Lord be with you!"

The people responded, "And with your spirit."

"Brothers and sisters in the family of our heavenly Father," he continued, "on this first time together in this unusual place, where we and those who come after us are likely to meet for worship and fellowship for some time to come, let us begin by offering our thanks for the unspeakable grace of our Lord Jesus Christ. He has called us to accept our places as God's people, as children of the light in this dark world."

Lifting up his hands, his face, and his voice, he prayed one of the simplest, most moving prayers Onesimus had ever heard. He understood why, in the absence of Paul, Linus had been chosen as their elder and overseer. His prayer began with praise to God the Father of all humankind who "in these later days has revealed Himself and His love for His children through the gift of His Son, Jesus the Christ—the One sent of God who is our Lord and Savior."

He thanked God for the presence of the Holy Spirit and of the eternal Son who lived and was crucified, dead, buried, and rose again on the third day, and especially that His presence among them was so real and powerful even in this day when they were on the verge of trials and sufferings greater than any had known before.

He expressed their confidence that "by the power of Your Spirit who dwells with us we shall be strengthened in His glorious might to meet whatever comes" with courage and even with "the joy of the Lord."

Onesimus entered whole-heartedly into the prayer, recognizing Paul's own words. As Linus mentioned "the joy of the Lord," Onesimus could not help but see the joy on Paul's face as he sat on the cot in the stinking prison cell. *Ample power to meet whatever comes with fortitude, patience, and joy,* he observed to himself.

Linus continued in special thanks for all that the coming of the apostle Paul had meant, and for the many new believers who had joined their fellowship, some who were to share with them that night for the first time the bread and the cup of the Holy Eucharist.

He led them in the confession of their sins, and Onesimus marveled that Linus knew what was in his own heart: his

doubts and fears for himself and his dear ones, his bitter
resentment of the mistreatment of Paul, his lack of faith at
times in the reality of the love of God.

After each confession, the people responded with the genuine
plea, *"Kyrie eleison*—Lord have mercy, Christ have mercy!"
Onesimus noted that for himself the cry was not a begging but
an accepting declaration of this amazing mercy of Christ. And
so it must be for others, for he saw the light break on their faces
as they joined in the prayer.

Linus then gave the prayer of pardon and forgiveness, which
ended with all singing one of the new songs of thankful acceptance. Onesimus had never heard it before, but it fully expressed
and released his feelings.

"John Mark is here," Linus announced. "He will read from his
newly collected writings about the life and acts of Jesus,
gathered from his talks with Peter and the other disciples who
knew Jesus personally."

Mark was of slight but straight stature and had blond hair
and hazel eyes. He came forward with a small scroll, unrolled it,
and began to read the account of the last supper their Lord had
shared with his disciples in the upper room of his own mother's
house in Jerusalem.

" 'And as they were eating, he took bread, and blessed and
broke it, and gave it to them, and said, "Take, this is my body."
And he took a cup, and when he had given thanks he gave it to
them and they all drank of it. And he said, "This is my blood of
the covenant which is poured out for many." ' "

When Mark finishing reading, he reminded those who were
standing in the eerie light of the candles in their first meeting in
the cavern, that this same Lord was with them now and was
sorrowful, because even among them were those who would
betray Him and His church as Judas had.

"But let us be glad," he concluded, "that so many of us by His
grace will be faithful through the days ahead. Let us take this
cup and this bread not only in memory of the One who was
faithful even to the death for us; but who through God's Holy

Spirit is present now to forgive and make whole, to strengthen and heal every one of our lives."

Then they exchanged together the kiss of peace. John Mark invited those who were prepared to partake of the holy meal to come forward. "You who are ready to love and forgive even as you are forgiven and to follow our Lord to whatever services and sacrifices He may call you, come and receive the bread and the wine, even as by faith you accept the loving presence and strength of the risen One who speaks through these creatures of our common life."

Onesimus, with rapid pulse walked up with Nereus and Pompania to receive the bread and the cup.

"The body of our Lord broken for you. The blood of our Lord shed for you," Linus said. "The one whose body was broken and blood was shed is alive and victorious," Onesimus affirmed. "He won the victory over sin, sorrow, pain, and death. Therefore the word *eucharist** is right. What greater joy than to take this bread and this cup." Onesimus stood with his whole being suffused with the power of the moment. His faith was renewed. He believed he could face the trials whatever they were.

After they had all been served, they sang a joyful song of hope, expressing their confidence that as God was in Christ with victory over evil, suffering, and death, so He was with them.

After the hymn, Linus introduced Onesimus as a young man who had a story to tell that would bring gladness not only to all who remembered him from his earlier visit, but also to those who were still slaves. "He will tell us of the only true freedom," Linus declared.

Onesimus told his story simply but with thankfulness and concluded with his experience with Paul. "Today, through the help of some of you, I was granted the privilege of visiting with Paul in the Mammertine Prison. The hour I spent with him in

---

*Thanksgiving

that foulest and most feared of all prisons was one of the most inspiring hours of my life."

Onesimus described in detail the arrangements of the prison room with its filth and stench, and the help Janus was to Paul. The courageous soldier was present with them in their *koinonia*. Onesimus thanked him for all of the Christians.

"I wish you could have seen the light on Paul's face," Onesimus continued. "I wish you could have heard his testimony of joyful faith. Just seeing him in that fetid place waiting for the executioner to come any morning and hearing his strong and vibrant witness is for me the unanswerable evidence that our Christ is still ruling. His power is greater than all 'the principalities and powers, the world rulers of this present darkness, and the spiritual hosts of wickedness.' "

He then described Paul's short letter to the church at Iconium, where a new persecution had broken out. "I have brought along a copy of a beautiful analogy Paul included in his letter. He suggested I bring it to you as his message of hope and as the way to keep strong in the Lord by taking on the whole armor of God."

It was just what the little group of Christians needed. As he read, he looked at their faces in the light of the flickering torches and knew the parable was speaking to them. When he had finished, there was a light of new determination in many eyes. It was a night they would need to remember in their own times of testing.

24

everal days passed before Onesimus was permitted to make his second visit to the prison, and he noticed immediately a growing weakness in Paul, affecting most obviously his voice. But with a consummate courage only a person of great faith could understand, he dictated letter after letter to his young *amenuensis*. Though oftentimes he had to stop to rest for a minute or so, the fires burned inextinguishably as he sent word to those whom he had loved and ministered to in several places around the Mediterranean world. He knew it was his last chance, and he must give his best thoughts in the hope that his letters would be read not only by those to whom they were sent but in many other churches as well.

The longest letters he wrote were to his son in the gospel, Timothy, whom he loved as he would have a son. Onesimus, who now was able to visit the prison weekly, was moved several times to tears as he recorded the precious sayings of this man whose life's blood was being poured out as a libation of love and thankfulness to his Lord.

Timothy was still in Greece, helping to keep the faith burning in the churches where Paul had enjoyed such remarkable fruitfulness in his effort. Even in Corinth, where there had been severe divisions after Paul left and to whom, while he was at Ephesus, he had written what he called "the harsh letter," there was now a new unity and spirit of *agape* love. The beautiful "Hymn to Love" which had first captivated Onesimus in Colossae was becoming the model for Christian living. Many did not live up to it, true; but more and more the "fruits of the Spirit," as Paul had described them in his letter to the Galatians, were ripening in the people called Christians.

Nevertheless, as the churches grew in number and influence, there were new dangers, and Paul instructed Timothy in the kinds of leaders and the training necessary. For instance, in one of the letters, Paul gave specific instructions concerning the character and work of the bishops—a word he used interchangeably with *presbyter* or *elder* to describe the pastors who were shepherds of the flock making up the church. Sometimes he addressed Timothy personally with winsome and wise exhortations. At other times he wrote as though Timothy were to use his words to set up standards and qualifications for leaders of the churches.

In one letter he wrote, "Our bishop must be above reproach,

faithful to his one wife, sober, temperate, courteous, hospitable, and a good teacher; he must not be given to drink, or a brawler, but of a forebearing disposition, avoiding quarrels, and no lover of money."

At other times he pointed his words directly to the people where certain disputes and quarrels were disrupting the life of the church. He reminded Timothy in his first letter of the time when he started for Greece and had asked him to remain in Ephesus. There he was to counsel certain leaders who had become more interested in "studying those interminable myths and genealogies, which issue in mere speculation and cannot make known God's plan for us, which works through faith."

Paul dictated fiercely yet convincingly:

> The aim and object of this command is the love which springs from a clean heart, from a good conscience, and from faith that is genuine. Through falling short of these, some people have gone astray into a wilderness of words.

In a second letter to the young Christians, Paul described those who "preserve the outward form of religion, but are a standing denial of its reality." Obviously, already there were those who went along with the new Christian movement without submerging themselves deeply enough into its meaning and power. Some of the sentences that moved Onesimus most were Paul's injunction to Timothy

> to stir into flame the gift of God which is within you through the laying on of my hands. For the spirit that God gave us is no craven spirit, but one to inspire strength, love, and self-discipline. So never be ashamed . . . of me his prisoner, but take your share of suffering for the sake of the Gospel, in the strength that comes from God.

Paul sank back on the cot for a few minutes with closed eyes. Onesimus waited breathlessly until he rose with dramatic intensity to say the choice words which he and many others would cherish throughout the years.

> He has broken the power of death and brought life and immortality

to light through the Gospel. Of this Gospel I, by his appointment, am herald, apostle, and teacher. That is the reason for my present plight; but I am not ashamed of it, because I know who it is in whom I have trusted, and am confident of his power to keep safe what he has put into my charge, until the great Day.

The dictation had exhausted him, and Onesimus waited silently until Plutonius came to rescue him from the stench of the prison—stench which Onesimus had come to ignore as he breathed in the fragrance of the beautiful life slowly being extinguished in the dank darkness of Paul's cell.

The next day was to be Onesimus's last visit, though he did not know it at the time. Paul was unusually bright, almost feverish, with his desire to conclude his letter to Timothy. Without more than a brief greeting, he asked Onesimus to sit and write.

"Now, therefore, my son," Paul began, "be strengthened by the grace of God which is ours in Christ Jesus. . . Take your share of hardship, like a good soldier of Christ Jesus, like an athlete who keeps the training rules. . . Remember Jesus Christ who is risen from the dead. This is the theme of the gospel, in whose service I suffer hardship, even to the point of being locked up like a criminal; but the word of God is not locked up. . . Here are words you may trust:

> If we died with him, we shall live with him;
> If we endure, we shall reign with him.
> If we deny him, he will deny us.
> If we are faithless, he keeps faith, for he cannot deny himself.

Later on Onesimus would read this familiar creed with new understanding, as the very words that meant the difference between his own despair and hope. Paul continued with some practical instructions to Timothy and the people of the churches. Then remembering the past, he reminded Timothy how he had followed his mentor's teaching and manner of life,

> my resolution, my faith, patience, and spirit of love, and my fortitude under persecutions and sufferings—all that I went through at

Antioch, at Iconium, at Lystra, all the persecutions I endured; and the Lord rescued me out of them all.

Paul reflected on news he had heard from the churches. There were so many who wanted to take the *fruit* of the gospel without the *roots*, and without paying the price. They were willing to follow any teacher who could "tickle their ears . . . but you, my son, are to keep calm and rational at all times; face trouble, work hard to spread the gospel, and do all the duties of your calling."

Paul's voice trailed off into silence as he fell back exhausted on the cot. For a few minutes Onesimus feared for Paul's life. He knew his master did not want to die in the cell but to give his last witness before the Roman court—if possible, before Caesar himself.

Then Paul stirred and sat up. A faraway look was in his eyes as he spoke the words softly: words that were to be his final declaration of faith, the summary of his life and ministry:

As for me, already my life is being poured out on the altar, and the hour for my departure is upon me. I have run the great race, I have finished the course, I have kept faith. And now the prize awaits me, the garland of righteousness which the Lord, the all-just Judge, will award me on that great Day.

His words were now coming in short gasps, but characteristically he did not stop with himself. ". . . and it is not for me alone, but for all who have set their hearts on His coming."

He ceased speaking and rested a few minutes, then concluded the letter with simple greetings to Prisca and Aquila and the house of Onesiphorus. "Greetings from Eubulus, Pudens, Linus, and Claudia, and from all the brotherhood here. The Lord be with your spirit. Grace be with you all!"

He was utterly exhausted, but he was able to grip Onesimus's hand and whisper a blessing.

As Janus helped Onesimus climb the ladder and wash his feet at the fountain, he said quietly, "I think tomorrow morning is the time."

"It is not any too soon," Onesimus responded. "I don't think he could last another day. I am glad that his end can come, God willing, somewhere so that his last witness can be heard by his persecutors."

"I have an order to lead him to his execution at the eleventh hour in the morning. Burrhus has asked Plutonius to join me in taking him into the execution chamber. Nero has decided to be there 'just for fun,' together with Tigellinus and Nero's new wife, Poppae, who is said to be with child. They say it is she who has most strongly urged Nero to end the life of our brother and apostle.

"If you will come at a few minutes before eleven, I will see that you have a chance to say farewell and to receive his blessing, as Plutonius and I hope to do. Though we would give our lives to deliver him from death, we will consider it our highest honor to lead him to the great experience which Nero and Poppae could never even suspect—the hour of his triumphant admission into the resurrected life with our Master. I will report to you the glorious entrance Paul will enjoy and how he gives his final message to the infamous court of Nero."

Noting the sorrow on Onesimus's face, he hastened to remind him, "Do not forget Paul's words to the Philippians which you wrote for him a few months ago, 'Rejoice in the Lord and again I say rejoice! In everything give thanks. . . .' I am sure he wishes you and all his brothers and sisters in Christ to celebrate his going to be with the Lord. Good-bye and good cheer, my friend and brother, Onesimus."

Onesimus was moved by such a remarkable expression of faith in this rough praetorianus. As he walked back to the house of Nereus, he remembered how Paul had written to the Corinthians of the difficulty he had in deciding whether it was better to be present in the body and temporarily separated from the Lord, or present with the Lord and absent from this earthly body. "But either way, we make it our purpose to be acceptable to Him."

Tears streamed down Onesimus's cheeks as he walked down the street. They were tears not only of sadness but of joy, for he knew that Paul rather than Seneca—and the best of the philosophers—was right: "For me to live is Christ, and to die is gain." Death is not an end (as they described it) to all of life with its suffering and its joy, but rather a new beginning—a life eternal.

When he told the sad news to Nereus and Junia that afternoon, Nereus responded with a heavy sigh. "What a loss to all of us and to the church," he said, but then he brightened.

"Since Poppae rather than Pompania now has the influence over Nero and Paul has suffered so long in that horrible Mammertine hell with no chance of escape, I am glad that his time has come." His practical mind saw what must be done that evening. "We must get word to every Christian in Rome to join us in the cavern meeting place. We must pray for Paul, and whatever happens be ready for a celebration of his victory tomorrow. Lady Pompania tells me she has arranged with Burrhus, if and when the time comes, to be given the privilege of caring for his body."

At dusk, they were all gathered by the light of the torches in the large round room, already sacred to them from the many times of high worship. Their faces were solemn as they heard Onesimus's account of his morning's experience with Paul and Janus. At the request of Linus, Onesimus had been giving reports to the assembled church as often as they were able to meet. Over the weeks he had brought to them most of the letters Paul had dictated, and the people had listened in awed silence to hear some of the most inspiring words ever written. Tonight Onesimus concluded his readings with Paul's last letter to Timothy. Onesimus described the weakness and the recurring fires of strength that had enabled Paul to make his final moving declaration of faith. Most of those who now heard his account were in tears. When he concluded he suggested that Linus lead them in a prayer of thanksgiving and intercession for Paul. Never had Onesimus remembered the little group of Christians—now grown to around three hundred—so bound together in a spirit of intense love and concern.

When Linus concluded, he announced that a place had been

found outside the walls in a heavy clump of trees off from the main road to Ostia where Paul's physical body would be interred if the execution took place. He invited Onesiphorus, Eubulus, Pudens, Epuenatus, Ampliatus, Urban and Aristobulus, the seven leaders of the smaller groups into which the Roman church was now associated, to be present and share with him and with Onesimus, Lady Pompania, and the two praetorian guards, Janus and Plutonius, in a service of thanksgiving and praise for Paul's life and ministry as they buried his fleshly remains.

"Any larger number would be too dangerous," he explained. "With our knowledge of the influences on Nero, there is little hope for Paul's life being saved for us in the flesh. But they cannot take away his person or his influence. His great life and ministry will go on in us and throughout all ages in the world as well as in our Father's 'other rooms.' Nothing can stop the gospel he preaches and the risen Lord for whom he will be laying down his life!"

Then the whole company sang with strong joyful voices a hymn of the Resurrection, expressing their faith and hope in Christ and His gift of eternal life. With exchanges of affectionate assurance the little group of Christians left the cavern and went home to wait.

On the fateful morning Onesimus arose early for prayer and reading. He had copied portions of Paul's letters to the church at Corinth, and now he read with reverence and thankfulness the words he once would have mocked:

If it is for this life only that Christ has given us hope, we of all men are most to be pitied. But the truth is, Christ was raised to life. . . .

And we ourselves—why do we face these dangers hour by hour? Every day I die: I swear it by my pride in you, my brothers. . . . If, as the saying is, I "fought with wild beasts" at Ephesus, what have I gained by it? If the dead are never raised to life, "let us eat and drink, for tomorrow we die."

Onesimus realized with thankfulness that Paul's view of

death was one with his view of life. Both were part of each other, death being a continuation on a different level and not the end. If one knew life "in Christ," he or she would possess "eternal life" as a gift before the physical fact of death. How meaningful Paul's words sounded as Onesimus read them aloud:

> The sting of death is sin, and sin gains its power from the law; but, God be praised, he gives us the victory through our Lord Jesus Christ. Therefore, my beloved brothers, stand firm and immovable and work for the Lord always, work without limit, since you know that in the Lord your labour cannot be lost.

Onesimus realized the time was approaching when Paul would win this last earthly victory over death. "His work and influence, his labor and love can never be lost or wasted," he said aloud. One more paragraph stirred Onesimus deeply. It was from the joyful letter Paul had written on hearing of the new unity in the church at Corinth as the bitter divisions were healed:

> Hard-pressed on every side, we are never hemmed in; bewildered, we are never at our wit's end; hunted, we are never abandoned to our fate; struck down, we are not left to die. Wherever we go we carry death with us in our body, the death that Jesus died, that in this body also life may reveal itself, the life that Jesus lives. . . . Though our outward humanity is in decay, yet day by day we are inwardly renewed. Our troubles are slight and short-lived; and their outcome an eternal glory which outweighs them far.

Onesimus wiped the tears from his face, put on his cloak, and went down the stairs with a deeper calmness. He, too, would walk and live and die by this the noblest faith of all. Nereus was waiting to walk with him almost to the prison. Junia embraced them both as Onesimus comforted her with the words used so often by Paul, "Remember, Junia, for Paul 'to live is Christ and to die is gain;' let it be so for us, also."

The day was dark, cold, and dreary. They walked in silence for a few minutes as the wind whipped their cloaks and the cruel facts of human brutality and selfishness tore at their minds.

"Nero can have his way with the little, worn, wasted body of Paul, which bears so clearly the marks of our Lord," Onesimus exclaimed, "but he cannot mar that spirit which is his and shall never be taken away from him."

"Thank you for your confidence, Onesimus," Nereus responded. "On a day like this, it is hard to believe that the tender heart that broke that black day when Jesus was crucified on the cross is truly ruling this evil old world!"

"Indeed, it is difficult," Onesimus responded. "Such faith cannot be humanly created. It can be passed on from one to another as Paul has passed it on through the grace of God's Holy Spirit to us. How thankful I am that I can see Paul once more and receive his blessing. I wish you could go with me, Nereus; but, for the good of all, Pompania has decided she should not add to the scene at the prison. Captain Burrhus thinks that since I have been visiting Paul regularly nothing will be hurt by my coming a few minutes before the time. But thank you for walking thus far with me."

With an affectionate clasp of hands, Nereus turned and walked back and Onesimus went on up the prison steps. The guard, recognizing him, opened the heavy doors and there stood both Janus and Plutonius.

"The time is come," Plutonius whispered. "I will go in and bring out our friend Paul. They say his trial will be only a mockery—a time of jesting and buffoonery when Nero expects to have some fun and Paul's enemies can have their day. Poppae appears to have the upper hand. But Christ will win the victory!"

With this, he and Janus lifted the heavy door to Paul's cell. Janus had told Paul the night before what to expect. Both Onesimus and Janus now listened as Paul greeted Plutonius.

"The Lord be with you, my son! The time has come to give my last witness of His great power and love. I am ready."

Plutonius said softly, "Thank God for your faith, Brother Paul. You are stronger than we who come unwillingly to carry you to your death." As he picked up the frail body in his arms, he said tenderly, "It is *you* who carry us!"

Onesimus ignored the tears that came unbidden from his eyes and waited with Janus as Plutonius climbed the stairs with his frail burden. Once out, he passed Paul's wasted form to Janus while he carefully washed the stench and filth from his feet and sandals.

Seeing his young *amenuensis* standing with Janus as they emerged, Paul spoke with tender affection, "My dear son Onesimus, one thing I want to say since Janus tells me you cannot accompany me to my execution: Remember, if God be for us, who can be against us? For God who spared not His only Son but freely offered Him up for us all, will He not with Him freely give us all things? You recall these and other words I wrote to the Romans in that letter penned before I ever came to Rome. I reaffirm my conviction now. Please share it with all our Christian family:

> What can separate us from the love of Christ? Can affliction or hardship? Can persecution, hunger, nakedness, peril, or the sword? . . . overwhelming victory is ours through him who loved us. . . . For I am convinced that there is nothing in death or life, . . . in the world as it is or the world as it shall be, . . . nothing in all creation that can separate us from the love of God in Christ Jesus our Lord.

Onesimus walked over and took hold of Paul's withered hands as he said these words softly and yet with a flash of the old fire. When Paul finished, seeing the regular prison guard motioning from the door with growing irritation, Paul placed his hands on Onesimus's head and said firmly, "The Lord is leading you, my dear Onesimus, and will make you greatly useful in the years to come. In the name of the Father, the Son, and the Holy Spirit, take my blessings and love with you also. Farewell until we meet again."

With those words Janus carried him out through the open prison door, but not before Janus had whispered to Onesimus, "Plutonius and I will meet you at the appointed place near dusk."

Onesimus thanked the two guards at the door for their kindness, but the only response was a grim insolence in their faces. They were obviously jealous of the praetorian guards who had been asked to deliver their prisoner. Onesimus stood and watched as Paul was placed tenderly on a litter in a large cart used for the purpose of transporting prisoners. As the horses moved the cart forward, Onesimus saw Paul's hand, raised again in his final blessing, and a smile on his haggard face. Onesimus's eyes were again brimming with tears as he watched the cart turn the corner and move out of sight.

25

*O*nesimus turned and walked the other way almost blindly, not knowing where he was going. It would be several hours before he would meet Janus and Plutonius with the remains of Paul's earthly body.

To Onesimus the foundations of his whole existence seemed to shake. The cobblestones beneath his feet were reeling. He steadied himself against a wall. With Paul's words in his ears, "in all things the overwhelming victory is ours through Him who loved us," he walked and walked trying to find something he could hold on to—something more even than that blessed man's words of hope and promise.

What kind of overwhelming victory is this? he asked himself. *To be incarcerated in a stinking prison for six months and now to go before a spoiled boy emperor, whose vanity and cruelty will be poured out on his blessed head. To have that head chopped off by the headsman's as to the shouts of the blood-crazed Nero and his court–it does not make sense."*

Onesimus found himself again judging the value of experiences by seen and observable evidences. But Paul had said, "The seen is transient, but the unseen is eternal." He had chosen to believe Paul, and he had found freedom. He wanted to believe now, but his stubborn reason—part of "the pride of the old man" as Paul would put it—filled his mind with desolation and turmoil.

Sorrowfully he wandered down the streets, unmindful of route or direction. His mind could not leave the tragedy he had witnessed. Some time elapsed before he realized he had made his way to one of the principal streets of the Subura. Suddenly, he ran head-on into a young woman dressed in a colorful crimson chiton.

"Well, by all the gods, as I live and breathe," she said looking him squarely in the face, "if it isn't our handsome Adonis of the soft heart, Onesimus! What on earth are you doing here?"

Onesimus was startled. He awakened to the situation and responded calmly, realizing that he was face to face with his first friend—and his first enemy—from the Subura.

"I am walking along this street. What about you?"

Marcia laughed. "The same old Onesimus. I am surprised you would even speak to me."

"Marcia, I am not the 'same old Onesimus.' I am a different person from that night when you watched Nicia kick me down the stairs, caring nothing for my well-being. Many things have happened to me since then."

"What in the name of Jupiter do you mean?" For the moment Marcia was awed by the confidence and strength of Onesimus's words.

"I mean that from the worst thing that has ever happened to me and the most unjust has come the greatest, most remarkable experiences of my life. I have found the Way, the Truth, the Life, as the Christians say. I am free in body and mind."

He paused, realizing that again Marcia was doing him another good turn, though unintentionally. For the moment he had gone back to his stance of faith from which new life and joy and the only true freedom had come. He was distracted from the tragedy now taking place in the life of the man who had helped him win his victory of faith.

"Marcia, I have a story to tell you."

Marcia stood as in shock. Something remarkable had happened to this handsome young Adonis, as she called him. There was strength and nobility in his bearing as he spoke these mystifying words that gripped her.

"You sound so strange, so different! What has happened to you? It is unusual indeed for one treated so unjustly to be so forgiving of the one doing the injustice."

"Come and I will tell you the difference. I have forgiven you and only want to tell you why." She acquiesced and followed him into an inn, where they sat at a table in a quiet corner.

"First, I am interested to know what happened to you and Nicia with all the money and jewels you took from me."

Marcia responded with a brief account of the way she and Nicia had bought a small shop not far away. There they sold perfumes, toilet equipment, and other luxuries and necessities used by both men and women, and they operated an even more lucrative business in their regular profession.

"We have made enough profit," she exclaimed proudly as she recalled his aversion to their "regular profession," "that we are thinking of leaving this business of selling our bodies to others, but," shrugging her shoulders, "that may not be so easy. Now, about yourself."

Onesimus began by telling her of his bitterness and desolation after losing his money, his hunger and desperation, and his visit to the Christian home of Nereus and Junia and the meeting with Paul. It was a fascinating story to Marcia, for she had a few friends who had joined this mysterious movement called *Christian*. It had intrigued her, but she had never been willing to listen before. It all sounded too elusive and dangerous.

She sat with open mind as one whom she had wronged told the story of his friendship with Paul and of his conversion to Christ. When he came to his courageous return to his old owner and the dramatic meeting in Philemon's house, she held her breath until she heard the remarkable outcome. She realized that here was something new indeed. If Philemon could forgive Onesimus for his crimes, adopt him as his son, grant him the hand of his daughter Helen, and send him back well-equipped to minister to Paul—this was a miracle. She said as much to Onesimus, "I have never in my fondest dreams imagined such a story. To see your faith and hear your words, I realize that it must be true."

"Indeed it is," Onesimus stated emphatically, "and when you have met some of these spirited Christians who are facing unbelievable persecution, you will surely be convinced that this is not mere superstition. No, Marcia, this is the deepest truth of all the universe. In our Lord Jesus Christ, whose earthly life John Mark is telling to our *communitas* whenever we meet, you will find the story of the mighty Son of God who has taken to Himself our human flesh and lived and died to reveal that He is God and that his *agape* for us has overcome the evil one."

"So you have at last found an answer to the question you asked several times that day of the gladiatorial combat: 'Is it better to suffer unjustly than to do injustice?' You would say 'yes.' But look! Your very faith is being denied this moment as your wonderful leader, Paul, is being executed. What is so good about that?"

Her question stopped Onesimus for a few moments. This was his own unspoken doubt. But now that he had told his story and could see the whole picture of Paul and his life in its entirety, he recalled the words of Paul which he had vowed never to forget, "All things fit into a pattern for good to those who love the Lord and accept the call of His purpose."

"It is true, Marcia. I know it is true. It has happened to me! All things, even the worst things, including what you and Nicia did to me and my own rebellion and wrong, have turned out for the best, because I have accepted the grace of our Lord. So we will find this to be true in what is happening to Paul now: like his Master's death on a cross, Paul's martyrdom will be like a mighty fire to light the flames of love and hope in millions of lives through the centuries. As he wrote to the Philippians through my own hands, 'All this has helped rather than hindered the gospel!'

"The body may be killed, but Christ's truth and love continue still. His kingdom rules forever! As Jesus is alive, so Paul is alive and shall never die! This is our hope, and no Aristotelian evidence can deny it. It cannot be proved or disproved by logic or any visible proof. The evidence is in the resurrected life which we live."

Marcia was deeply touched. "Onesimus, I want Nicia to hear your story and to meet some of your fellow Christians."

Onesimus agreed and invited both of them to the home of Nereus and Junia the next day. "I am sure Nereus and Junia will welcome you as they did me." He gave her directions to the house. "If you desire you may become a member of those who seek to understand our faith, and if you so choose you may join the catechumens, as we called the seekers after truth in Christ. May I thank you and Nicia for kicking me down the stairs to my freedom!" he said with a smile as they parted.

Onesimus hurried now to the house where Nereus, Junia, Lady Pompania, Linus, and the leaders of the seven groups of Christians in Rome were gathered. Burrhus had told Lady Pompania it would be better to wait until near dusk before attempting the burial, but the Christians were anxious to hear what news they could from Onesimus.

"It was my most difficult and yet wonderful experience," Onesimus said as he sat down. "You would have been as proud as I was at the calm joy that radiated from the haggard face and the poor sick eyes of Brother Paul."

"Please eat at least a little," Junia implored. "You look so tired and you have so much yet to do."

"All right, Junia, just for you," Onesimus replied as he took some fresh fruit. "You also would have been proud of Janus and Plutonius." They nodded as he told them Plutonius's words as he lifted Paul out of his stinking cell. " 'You are stronger than we who carry you to your death; but it is you who carry us.' "

Onesimus then related every detail of his experience, to the last wave of the hand and smile from Paul as he lay in the cart.

"I knew it would be this way!" Lady Pompania exclaimed. "I am glad you received his blessing, and through you all of us will receive it," she added. "I cannot wait to hear of Paul's triumphant meeting with that poor wicked boy, Nero, who calls himself 'Emperor and Lord of all the earth.' "

"Since we have the time, I have another surprising story to

tell you," Onesimus began. The group was gathered in the atrium around the charcoal burner for warmth. They were again eager to listen as Onesimus told of his great sorrow and struggle with doubt arising not only from his human loss but from his previous Aristotelian training. "I had been taught since boyhood that 'seeing is believing.' Now I have discovered that 'believing is seeing,' when one believes the unseen realities of the love of Christ." He told the amazing story of his confrontation with Marcia and how she had shocked him back to a stronger grip on his faith.

"Your experience is so true," Lady Pompania put in. "I, too, have found that when I am nearest to losing my faith the best defense is to go out and proclaim Christ to another. Now you may have won to our faith these two old enemies, and perhaps now they may become your friends. How true Jesus' saying is that love for our enemies is the only way to deal with them. 'Unless you forgive, you will not be forgiven.' When we do forgive, the door to the other's soul may be opened."

All of them agreed to share their love and faith with Marcia and Nicia and to welcome them into their fellowship if they were open at all to the Way. With new insight Onesimus realized the power of their faith—it broke down dividing walls of hostility and separation of every kind. No wonder it spread so fast.

26

The sun had set. The winds had quieted. The last touch of winter had shrivelled the new green leaves of early March that had promised an early spring. The little group shivered as they waited in the clearing at the center of the thicket just outside the walls of Rome. The temperature had fallen, and they were all trying to keep warm. No one spoke.

Then they heard it—in the distance the sound of a carriage and two horsemen. They waited in silence. As the carriage appeared, they recognized on the front seat two of Pompania's most trusted servants, Horatius and Appho. The two horsemen were Janus and Plutonius. The little group gathered around the carriage as the two praetorian guards dismounted and were embraced by Linus and Onesimus. As if in answer to the unspoken question of all, Janus broke the silence.

"Yes, he is dead, but as we say of our Lord, he is alive forever more!"

"Alleluia!" all responded.

"At the assembly we will want you to tell the story of his last hour, but before we lay in the earth his physical remains tell us briefly what happened." Linus made the simple request. Janus and Plutonius with terse sentences told the story of the mock trial.

They had driven the cart up to the palace where Nero held court with his new wife and a few of his henchmen. Janus described what happened next.

"The apostle Paul was too weak to walk, so we carried him on the litter. As we entered the palace, he quietly gave his blessing to each of us and asked us to pray for him and to share with you his last witness. This we promised. It was a sorry spectacle—certainly nothing resembling the dignity of a Roman court."

Plutonius described the scene: Poppae and Tigellinus seated on either side of the fat little Emperor, who was hardly awake from the revels of the night before. His eyes were almost hidden by the purpling flesh, indicating the extent of his overindulgence. "He could hardly sit up," Plutonius continued, "but when we came in he asked Poppae to prop him up with pillows so he could watch the wasted body and haggard face of Paul sitting in the trial chair before him. I was standing by Paul to keep him from falling.

" 'Ha! So this is the great apostle Paul who has been stirring up so much trouble in Corinth and Ephesus and Jerusalem,' Nero mocked. 'And now he would do all he can to stir up all of Rome!'

" 'Sir,' Paul answered, 'it is my calling to bring peace where there is division and love where there is hate. If there is trouble, it is not of my own doing.'

" 'Well now,' Nero growled, 'this is a pretty story, but from what your accusers have told me, you are a farce. Certainly, you have given me more trouble than any of my prisoners. Your followers have bothered me too much for me to be merciful to one who has been so seriously accused of wrongdoing.' Then, as Poppae whispered in his ear, he exclaimed, 'All right, let's hear what your accusers say.'

"The guards at the door ushered in two Jews from Rome—an event made possible because they were friends of Poppae. She smiled and nodded, and they bowed towards her and the Emperor.

" 'What have you to say to our noble Emperor?' Tigellinus asked as they approached. 'What are your accusations against this prisoner?'

"The Jewish leaders gave the same old charges: Paul had incited riots in various places, destroying the business of certain merchants in Ephesus and Corinth and other Roman cities, and had disturbed the peace in Jerusalem."

" 'Enough, enough!' cried Nero. 'It is clear he is guilty. Look at his shabby appearance; yet he dares stare at us with such bold spirit.' Looking at Paul, he challenged him directly. 'Let us hear from you,' he snarled. 'Since you are a citizen of Rome and have appealed to Caesar, what do you have to say to these charges?'

"Paul leaned forward and answered quietly but with a firm voice, 'Sir, I have but one aim in life: to be herald, apostle, and teacher of the gospel of Christ Jesus. Brought up by humble parents in the village of Nazareth in the province of Galilee, He revealed the very fullness of the mighty God and Father, the creator of all. He was crucified at the instigation of some of these very Jewish leaders, because He put the law of love above all the many laws that burdened the people. He was dead and buried, but on the third day He rose from the dead by the power of God, for it was impossible that He should be held by the bars of death. And He is now risen and present, ruling all things. All of us alike will meet either His judgment or His mercy, according to our choice.'

"The Emperor's face was livid with fury. 'I did not ask you for an address. What a fool to speak of one's rising from the dead or of some God who rules the universe! *I* am ruler, you driveling idiot. . .' Overcome by his own anger, he almost fainted from exhaustion. A cup of wine was held by Poppae to his lips as she whispered in his ear, and then he croaked, 'Bring the ax. This man's folly has gone on long enough. . . love, resurrection, the ruler of this universe! Ridiculous!' Then followed a string of curses until he fell back, unable to say more. The block was brought in and placed within a few yards of his golden throne, and a strong soldier with bulging muscles followed holding a sharp ax. When the block was in place, Burrhus, the chief of the praetorian guard, motioned to Janus and to me. The three of us exchanged looks which, if Nero could have seen them, would have given him apoplexy. Janus and I picked up the frail form and laid the weary head upon the block as tenderly as possible. We breathed a blessing which none but Paul could hear."

"And under his breath he whispered to us, 'the grace and peace of our Lord will keep you. Farewell till we meet again,' " Janus added.

"Now Nero pulled himself up on his throne. 'We will see who is the ruler! Let the ax decide who has the power and the glory.' At that moment the executioner stepped up and with one quick blow severed Paul's head from his body. Nero cried out with approval, his face flushed with sadistic enjoyment as he watched Paul's blood flow."

"At Burrhus's command," Janus continued, "Plutonius and I picked up the broken body and severed head. We took the pieces out of the room and put them in the box of sandalwood Lady Pompania had provided. Her two servants Horatius and Appho carried the box to the carriage, and then we made our way here.

"The world would call it a horrible experience, but to the three of us who knew and loved him and believed in his Lord as our Lord it was a triumphant entrance into the kingdom of heaven."

The little group stood in the darkness and listened with deep feeling. When Janus and Plutonius finished, different ones expressed their confidence in quiet joy: "Alleluia!" "The Lord Christ reigns, and His kingdom shall never end!" "Amen!"

The two guards with the help of Pompania's servants went to the carriage and gently lifted out the sandalwood box containing Paul's physical remains. Onesimus and Linus, as pre-arranged, walked before them to the open grave dug that morning. With some cords underneath each end, the box was let down, and as the guards and the other men helped throw shovels of clean earth onto the box, Linus repeated some of the best known of Paul's writings:

"Love never fails, never ends . . . Faith, hope, and love last on and on, but the greatest of these is love."

"For me to live is Christ, to die is gain."

"The sting of death is sin, and the strength of sin is the law, but thanks be to God who gives us the victory through our Lord Jesus Christ."

At Pompania's request Onesimus stepped forward to give Paul's own final valedictory:

I have run the great race, I have finished the course, I have kept faith; And now the prize awaits me, the garland of righteousness, which the Lord, the all-just Judge, will award me on that great Day; and it is not for me alone, but for all who have their hearts set on his coming appearance.

As the grave was covered and a secret marker inserted at the head with the dead leaves scattered over the top, they stood around in silence. Darkness had fallen, but as they grasped each other's hands in a circle around the grave, they all looked up. Paul was not in the grave. He was with the Lord.

With one accord they sang the doxology and prayed together the prayer their Lord had taught them and that Paul had said included all the prayers anyone need pray. Then they left the spot for their homes, each one knowing that the apostle's prayers were still with them.

Before dawn the next morning Christians from all over Rome were entering the secret doors to their cavern meeting place. There were two openings located on a secluded spot not far from the road outside the walls. One was from an unpretentious house with a trap door in the basement opening into the cavern. The other was in a large clump of olive and other fruit trees where a fruit storage building contained a passageway to the other end of the cavern.

As Onesimus looked over the faces of the faithful, so many of whom he knew personally, he realized the diversity of followers Christ had in Rome. Here were slaves and artisans, rich and poor, plebians and patricians, "saints in Caesar's household" as Paul had described some of them.

Janus and Plutonius stood next to him as Elder Linus signaled for silence. First, at his suggestion, a joyful hymn of the resurrection was sung. Then came prayers of thanksgiving with fervent "amens" from the entire company as Linus thanked the Lord for the great privilege they had experienced in Paul's presence, teaching, encouragement, and inspiration. Onesimus realized that a good part of those present had known and shared personally with Paul. Many were believers through his direct or indirect influence. He knew how great their loss, because he knew his own feelings of sorrow—how much he would miss the daily visits to the prison. But he sensed their faith, and as they sang a second hymn, he joined with all his heart and voice:

> Christ the Lord is risen.
> Every mind and heart rejoice!
> Alleluia! Alleluia!
> Death is conquered. Life eternal given!
> Alleluia! Alleluia!
> God is love and rules all things
> We shall love as He loved us!
> Alleluia! Amen!

"Now, my dear brothers and sisters in Christ," Linus announced, "we continue our celebration of the victory won by our beloved apostle Paul, as we hear from the three persons who have been with him often during these last few weeks." Linus then introduced Onesimus, Janus, and Plutonius. Each one told as simply and clearly as possible the experiences of the previous day, giving full weight to the witness Paul had given before the court of Nero.

Onesimus concluded with the words Paul had expressly asked him to communicate to the church, ending with the immortal lines, "If God be for us, who can be against us?. . . Nothing can separate us from the love of Christ. . . neither life nor death. . . In spite of all, overwhelming victory is ours through Him who loved us."

As Onesimus spoke these words, he made a new affirmation of his own faith. He recalled the battle with black doubt over these very words the day before and his providential meeting with Marcia. *I must continue to proclaim the holy faith as often as possible,* he thought as he sat down, *or else I could all too easily lose it.*

Janus was now speaking. His sentences were short. His affection for Paul and the clarity of his understanding of what had happened were evident. Plutonius added only a few words but closed by thanking Lady Pompania for preparing the sweet-smelling sandalwood box in which the mutilated body of their leader had been interred. He also thanked all who had assisted in digging the grave and, though they had all wanted to be present, he thanked them for staying away from the departure from the prison and the burial the night before. Then Plutonius added with deep feeling, "I wish each of you could have seen the love on his tired and strained face and the flash in those black eyes when he responded to Nero's jibes. By the grace of the Lord, I pray that I may have some of his courage and strength when my time of testing comes."

—Part Seven—
The Road to Prison and Release

$\mathcal{W}$ith the kindly encouragement of Nereus and Junia, Onesimus spent the next few days resting from the exhausting experiences through which he had passed. He slept late, read some of the favorite passages from the manuscripts he had copied from Paul's letters, and walked out by the River Tiber to the place where he had made the decision that sent him to his freedom.

Several times he went with John Mark or with Nereus outside the walls to visit the spot where Paul's earthly body was buried—not that any of them felt he was any closer to them there, but the silence of the area, broken only by the whisper of the wind, was comforting. He did not again experience the doubt that had plagued him on that difficult day when he said good-bye to Paul, but everything that had happened left him numb and tired, as if suspended between one mighty event and another yet to come.

The most helpful influence was his experience with fellow Christians in common worship and *koinonia*. And, as on the black hour after parting with Paul when his faith was so shaken, by the opportunity of sharing his gospel with Marcia and Nicia and finding these his once-hated enemies becoming true friends. They had come for the evening meal on the first day after Paul's execution. Nicia was very reserved at first when Onesimus met him at the door. Shamefaced and apologetic, he took Onesimus's outstretched hand as he said, "This is something I never in a thousand years would have believed possible, Onesimus. But if you are foolish enough to forgive two who have done you so much harm, to thank us for it, and to invite us to a meal, I believe we are foolish enough to come and see what the game is."

"No game at all," Onesimus laughed, "rather a happy fact. I

forgave you for what you have done, because I have been
forgiven for all of my wrongs. It took me a long while to accept
this kind of pardon; but I have seen and experienced so much of
it, I know there is no greater fact in life. But come in and let's
have something to eat. Talk will keep, but Junia's dinner will
get cold if we don't get to it soon."

They entered the house, were introduced to Nereus and
Junia, and in a few minutes were reclining at Junia's well-laden
table. Before beginning their meal, Nereus suggested, "After
this day and its difficult but beautiful experiences, we as
Christians have so much for which to be thankful. We cannot
eat with you our new friends until we have expressed our
heartfelt thanks."

With this explanation the simple, hardworking artisan lifted
a prayer of thanksgiving for the food they shared, for the
comfort and strength of their *communitas* as Christians, and
for the hope and courage the Lord Christ had given them. It
was a deeply moving prayer for Onesimus, and he felt it must be
so for his guests.

When the prayer was ended, Nereus said, "We are thankful, Marcia and Nicia, that you have accepted Onesimus's
invitation to eat with us tonight, for we too have experienced
what he means when he says there is no greater gift on earth
than forgiving love. So as we eat, I think you would profit much
by hearing something of his story and of the happenings of the
last two days."

Onesimus began his story where Marcia and Nicia had known
him last—bleeding and heartbroken at the foot of their stairs.
By the time he reached his meeting with Paul, Junia interrupted, "My son, if you don't eat a few bites now and then you
won't be strong enough to tell all your story."

Onesimus ate for a few minutes, and then continued. Marcia
and Nicia both were entranced by his description of Paul, of
their conversation concerning true freedom, of the slow growth
of Onesimus's understanding, and of his growing ability to
believe in the reality of the love of Christ and the nature of
God's kingdom. When he described his moment of faith in

Christ and the flood of peace and joy that overwhelmed him, they could see it was no sudden impulse.

When he completed the story of his decision to return to Philemon, regardless of the cost, Nicia whistled, "What a risk that was, a gamble with your life. And I thought you were weak and cowardly!"

"Yes, it was a high risk, Nicia. As far as being weak and cowardly, so are we all when we try to live by high moral ideals without the proper resources. I was living by the law, as Paul would have put it, but 'what the law could not do in that it was weak, God did by sending His own Son in the flesh.' You were not concerned with the law, so you could do whatever the situation required to save yourself without bothering over matters of conscience.

"It was my deep sense of security in the love of Christ that gave me the courage and the will to go back and face my wrongdoing, even though I had justified it by the wrongdoing of my master Philemon. When I no longer attempted to save my own freedom, to force what I wanted from life at whatever cost, I found that life was given to me; and the very freedom for which I yearned was mine as a gift!"

Nicia and Marcia were obviously perplexed by this paradoxical statement.

"It sounds crazy to me," Nicia exclaimed, "this 'good news', as you call it, of 'losing to find'; but go on with your story. We'll have to talk and think about this a great deal more. It surely has done something for you."

Onesimus went on to recount the events in Philemon's house, his shared announcement with Helen of their love (Onesimus wanted Marcia especially to understand this), Philemon's granting him freedom and sending him back to minister to Paul. Then the story of the last few days and Paul's triumphant spirit at the mock trial in Nero's court before his execution.

"What a man!" Nicia exclaimed. "*There* is a story of bravery and courage such as I have never heard."

"Yes," responded Onesimus, "but Paul himself would have said that his strength was made perfect in weakness, 'For the grace of Christ is sufficient for me. When I am weak, then am I strong.' "

"This is something I cannot understand," Nicia murmured. "All my life I have been taught the only way to be strong is to grit one's teeth and take what he can get, 'doing unjustly rather than being the recipient of injustice,' to quote your philosopher. I desire very much to hear more about this Jesus of Nazareth and His remarkable teachings, His life and death, and certainly His resurrection. Like you were once, Onesimus, I am bothered by this incredible declaration which you say is the basis of your life and faith. How about you, Marcia? Would you want to join with the new group of learners—what is it you call them?" he asked Nereus.

"Catechumens," said Nereus. "There is a new group meeting in Lady Pompania's house every Wednesday night." He told them about Pompania and gave directions to her home.

With this exchange, they parted company for the night. The two expressed their gratitude for "this amazing display of what you call Christian love."

"If this is an illustration of what Christian faith does for people like us, we want to learn more about it," Marcia affirmed.

"It is wonderful to be loved by such people as Nereus and Junia," Onesimus exclaimed, "but even more wonderful to believe that there is at the center of all things an eternal heavenly Father who accepts and delights in you and in giving you 'power for anything' you are called on to do. This is the greatest joy and peace on earth."

As they left the house, Marcia requested, "Please pray to your loving Father—as you call God—that Nicia and I may find the freedom and love that all of you have found."

Onesimus went to his room with his heart singing. "If these two hardened minds can be softened and opened by the Holy Spirit, there is indeed hope for the world."

28

"*T*he apostle Peter is coming." The news circulated quickly through the Christian grapevine in Rome. Doctor Luke, through his connection with the shipping companies, had found the name, date, and approximate hour of the ship's arrival. Onesimus and Nereus, accompanied by Linus, Hermas, Doctor Luke, John Mark, and even Nicia, set out early one morning to walk the Appian Way to Ostia. Lady Pompania decided it would be too risky to send horses and a carriage. Already she had heard that Nero's experience with Paul had made him fanatical in his hatred of the Christians.

Onesimus recalled Paul's words about the gospel being "either a fragrance from life to life or a stench from death to death." For Nero, it was the latter. Burrhus informed Pompania that Nero had even gone so far as to appoint Tigellinus as director of the campaign to "root out these evil *Chrestians.*"* He gave orders to jail them and, if they did not recant the faith, to punish them as he saw fit.

"This means," Lady Pompania said grimly, "many of us will be in prison soon, and if I know Tigellinus, some will be used for sport in the gladiatorial exhibitions at the Colosseum. Burrhus has confirmed palace gossip, that Nero is cool to him and Tigellinus is seeking to poison the Emperor's mind about Burrhus's loyalty. He thinks his time will come quickly. The apostle Peter is coming none too soon. How greatly our beloved *communitas* needs him!"

The long walk to Ostia was bracing. It was a clear, cool day. As they went along, John Mark and Doctor Luke took turns telling Nicia some of the stories of the life of Jesus. They

*"Chrestian" signifies the common pronunciation of "Christian" in Rome at this time.

stopped by the wayside to eat the good lunch provided by Junia. By the middle of the afternoon, they were standing with the crowd by the docks waiting for the first sight of the ship from which the apostle Peter would be disembarking.

They waited for over an hour before the white sails of the vessel were seen shining against the late afternoon sun. Onesimus was excited. He had heard so much about Peter. John Mark had told many stories of the man known first as Simon son of John and then, through the influence of Jesus, as Peter (*Petras*, the Rock).

As the ship moved slowly up to the dock, Onesimus saw a tall, heavyset man with a bushy beard and a thick, unruly mass of dark brown hair covering his large head. When the gangplank was lowered, he watched as this man, whom he knew from Mark's description must be the apostle Peter, shook hands with several of his fellow voyagers and then made his way down the plank. Mark had seen him too, and with a glad cry, he called them all to follow. They made their way through the waiting crowd to the place where Peter stood looking for them.

Peter and John Mark embraced affectionately. John Mark's eyes were shining as he introduced his friends, the leaders of the little church in Rome. Peter took the hand of each in both of his own and warmly acknowledged their welcome. Onesimus felt the apostle's hands must be nearly twice the size of his own and marveled at their strength and roughness, remembering that for years he had been a successful fisherman on the Sea of Galilee.

Linus gave the official greeting: "Welcome to Italy and to Rome, Brother Peter! We have been looking for your coming and are thankful for your safe journey and your good health." And then in a lower voice, "You have come to us in troubled times, when your strong faith and exhortation are greatly needed by us all."

The apostle answered in his deep rich voice and with gladness, "Many thanks for your welcome, Brother Linus, and for all of you who come to meet me. I am sure you will teach me many things, but I want to be of any help I can to your growing church. I have heard of its depth of fellowship and love and look forward indeed to sharing with you, even in what you say are difficult days."

They had moved apart from the crowd to the farthest side of the dock, but Linus, fearing Tigellinus's spies, warned them to break up and return in small groups to Rome. John Mark, Doctor Luke, Onesimus, and he would accompany Peter. The rest would follow at some distance with no more than four or five walking together. Carrying a torch, Linus led the way as Peter and the others began their journey through the dusk.

During the long walk in the darkness, Onesimus could sense the greatness of this big fisherman, now leader of the Christians. It came out in his concern for the welfare of everyone, and the questions he asked about Paul. "Bless the Lord who again has revealed Himself in the loving victory of Brother Paul!" he cried in thanks, as Onesimus described the apostle's last few weeks in prison and his execution.

The time passed quickly as they shared together news of the other churches and spoke of the coming tests. Linus explained the situation with Nero and described something of the fierce fanatical hatred of Poppae Augusta.

"There are, of course, many Jews even among the most wealthy and influential who are as horrified at the coming persecution as we are," Linus hastened to say. "But they now have lost their influence with Nero, and we may expect the worst."

It was sometime past midnight when the little party of five arrived at the house of Lady Pompania. In the darkness they were safer than in the daytime, and they wanted this strong woman who had meant so much to the Christians to meet Simon Peter. Extinguishing the torch, they walked into the spacious grounds where Linus was met by Pompania's trusted helpers, Horatius and Appho. The two immediately took them to the house through the back way. Pompania had been waiting. By the light of the lamp, her animation was obvious as she took the apostle Peter's big hands in hers.

"O thank you, Brother Peter, for your coming! We have

waited so long, and since Paul has been separated from us we have needed the inspiration and hope you can give us. We know the great risks you are taking. It will not be easy to hide your identity from the soldiers sent out at Nero's command to find and imprison every Christian in Rome."

Peter responded with warmth and without affectation, humbly acknowledging his gratitude for their love and admitting his own limitations in giving them the help they needed.

"But I will stand by you and visit with any of our people who need encouragement. If our Lord can use me in this way, it will be only a small thing compared to what He has done for me."

"What happened today, Lady Pompania?" Linus asked with concern.

Pompania shook her head sorrowfully. "Tigellinus's men have been almost everywhere in the city. Evidently, there must have been informers, because at least fifty Christians we know have been thrown into prison. Burrhus, who a few weeks ago could have helped, is now under serious suspicion and is expecting his own execution at any time. I will go tomorrow to talk with Poppae. She welcomes my visits because she is lonely and says she feels that I care for her personally and not for what I can get from her. Possibly I may be able to help, though I doubt it. She is bitter against the Christians and that bitterness continues to feed the fires in Nero's sadistic mind. So, Brother Peter, you see that your coming is just in time. May God lead us all as we seek to give our witness and support to each other during our days of testing."

The hour was late and, after a hopeful prayer by the apostle, they left Pompania's house. Peter went with John Mark, Doctor Luke with Linus, and Onesimus returned to the house of Nereus. As he walked into the night alone, Onesimus thanked the mighty God and Father who, through His Spirit in this great-hearted Simon Peter, would minister to His children in their need.

Word quickly passed to all the Christians in Rome, including those who had already spent a night in prison, that the apostle

Peter had arrived. The word was a breath of fresh hope to all of them, especially to the new Christians. They had all heard from John Mark and Doctor Luke the inspiring and very human stories of Simon Peter's experiences with Jesus—how he had been overwhelmed by the strange fascination of Jesus' presence. They knew of the healing of Peter's wife's mother, how he had been mystified by Jesus' announcement of the necessity to go to Jerusalem, how Peter had had the nerve to rebuke Jesus by implying that the cross of suffering was no place for God's beloved Son, and of Jesus' rebuke in return. The part of the story that stirred them most was the account by Doctor Luke of the way Jesus, on trial for His life had turned and looked at Peter, who had just denied knowing the Lord for the third time. Following Peter's realization of what he had done, he had gone out and wept bitterly. For three days he had mourned his failure. But Jesus had forgiven him and set him free to become Peter the Rock. Simon Peter was one of the first to meet Jesus after His resurrection, according to the apostle John.

Then there was the wonderful story of Peter's meeting with Jesus by the lake—so unexpected, so gracious, as Jesus said no word of condemnation. Putting His hands on Peter's big shoulders Jesus had asked simply, "Simon, son of John, do you love Me?" Three times he had asked it; and when Peter answered with a broken heart, "Yes, Lord, You know I love You," Jesus had replied, "Tend my lambs. Feed my sheep." Now Simon Peter, the rock of strength and faithfulness, was in Rome doing just that—feeding and caring for the young lambs, the tender sheep whose faith was frail and easily shaken but who were enduring the horrible brutality and demonic hatred of Nero.

Early the next morning Onesimus hurried to the house of Linus, where the leaders of the churches in Rome had joined Doctor Luke and John Mark to make plans with the apostle concerning his ministry to the Christian community. Peter was finishing his breakfast as the last of the council arrived. After greeting each one, the apostle offered a prayer of thankfulness for his safe arrival and the kindness of these his fellow Christians. He closed with a petition for wisdom and strength to know how best to inspire and encourage them. Then he stood to his full height and declared his firm intention to visit all of the imprisoned Christians. Linus, joined by the others in the council, warned him of the danger.

"Tigellinus, no doubt, will be informed of your presence in Rome, if he doesn't know of it already. He will consider you a prime target and will use you as an example to frighten the other Christians into renouncing their faith."

But the apostle replied "I denied our Lord three times that black night of His trial. Now, on this my first day in Rome, I am not going to run like a coward from the evil minions of a crazy boy emperor, no matter how great the danger to me. I must carry out the command my Lord gave to me on that last day by the seashore when He said, 'Feed my sheep.' I intend to do so."

Linus, speaking for the others, expressed their deep appreciation of the apostle's fearless love. "But, Brother Peter," he pleaded, "we have an obligation to several hundred other Christians who will be coming this evening into our secret worship center in the cavern outside the city walls. Surely all our people need you."

Peter saw the point and agreed to wait until the following day to visit the more dangerous prisons. Today he would be shown the way by Onesimus to one of the safer *ergastulums*, where the chief keeper, Patroculus, was known to be a Christian. How Patroculus had escaped detection was a miracle of confidences kept.

"There are twenty-three Christians in his prison, and you may be able to visit with them today without word getting immediately to Tigellinus," Linus explained. "Tomorrow we will attempt to get you into some of the other prisons. Lady Pompania will use her influence to help us."

After an hour of sharing together concerning the state of the churches in other parts of the empire and hearing more of the plight of the Christians in Rome, Peter indicated his desire to begin his visitation. Onesimus had spent many exciting days in Rome already, but the hours he spent with Peter were like medicine to his soul. When they arrived at the *ergastulum,* as the prisons for ordinary criminals were called, he knocked at the door of the chief officer in command. Patroculus himself opened the door and, seeing who his guests were, dismissed his lieutenant, invited them in, and shut the door.

Without waiting for an introduction, he said with a mixture of awe and cordiality, "So you are Simon Peter! I have looked forward to your coming, though I probably know better than anyone the danger you are in. The stories of your life with Jesus during His earthly ministry have inspired us all. I have learned much from your example already. You can be sure I will do all I can to help you now as you seek to bring courage to these our brothers and sisters in the faith. I assure you their conditions in this prison are filthy and disgusting beyond anything you can imagine. I, myself, may be there with them before too long. However, at present I am not suspected, and as long as I am able I am at your service. I was in this position before I became a Christian and now believe I can best serve my Lord here for as long as He needs me."

Peter responded with an expression of gratitude as Patroculus led the way into a dimly lighted hall, on each side of which were two large crowded rooms enclosed by iron bars. In these rooms dozens of criminals in filthy rags and with matted hair were sitting or standing next to the new prisoners, there because of the faith. Having been in prison only a day and night, they were still much cleaner than their companions. Onesimus recognized several of them and greeted them by name. Then he spoke to all of them, "I have brought you a very dear friend of whom you have heard so much."

They crowded as close to the bars as possible while their hardened cell mates looked on with indifference. The latter were thieves or other criminals who had been in the foul *ergastulum* so long they had given up hope, knowing their only escape would be a trip to fight with the lions in the Colosseum. Roman justice under Caesar Nero would not have been recognized by that name in the former days of Rome's grandeur.

None of these lowly prisoners were considered worthy of even a minor judge's attention. To be consigned here was almost a sentence of death itself.

Peter, speaking in his low resonant voice, greeted them in the name of Christ. (Patroculus had brought the two guards to the other end of the prison where they could not hear what was being said. He had warned Peter that, at best, he could spend only a very few minutes with them.)

"Grace and peace to you in fullest measure who are suffering for Christ's sake," Peter began. "Praise be the God and Father of our Lord Jesus Christ, who in His mercy has given us new birth into a living hope by the resurrection of Jesus Christ from the dead! This is your gift by His surpassing love, dear brothers and sisters. I call upon you to look to Him who is present with you. The inheritance to which you are born is one that nothing can destroy or spoil or wither. This is cause for great joy, even though now you smart for a little while under trials of many kinds. Even as gold that is tried in the fire, so your faith is more precious as it stands the test.

"Remember you are going through this for our Lord Jesus Christ, who is the true King of Kings. You have not seen Him, as I have, yet you love Him and, trusting Him now without seeing Him, you will be filled with an unutterable and exalted joy. This is the joy that our Lord possessed even as He faced what you are now facing. The price of this joy and confidence, this power to love even those who hate and hurt you, is paid in His precious blood. Through Him, you have confidence in God, who raised Him from the dead and gave Him an immeasurable glory. I saw His glory. I have experienced His love. I know He is here with you. I give you my blessings and pray for your victory—a victory the world can neither see nor understand. Grace and peace to each of you who is in Christ!"

Onesimus listened and watched the faces of the faithful young Christians. He observed there were also two or three middle-aged persons. Each of their faces was transfused with a strange glow of expectancy as they listened to the rich, low voice of the man they knew had been personally with their Lord. Some of them were crying softly. Onesimus could imagine their terror during the long dark night, shut up in this foul prison, men and women together, criminals, robbers, and demented persons. Now he watched as new light shone on their faces—it was this "living hope" Peter proclaimed to them.

When Peter finished, he crossed his huge arms, and they understood he was making the sign of the cross. Then he lifted up his hands and blessed them.

By this time Patroculus had returned and hastily took the two out through the door. "We made that all right," he smiled grimly. Then he explained more of what Peter had heard of the wild tales of the evils purported to be practiced by Christians which Tigellinus and Poppae had capitalized upon in securing Nero's edict.

"The strange part," Patroculus commented, "is that so many of the common people, including these felons, are ready to believe it. This is one reason they have to a large extent withdrawn from the Christian prisoners and stay in another part of their common cell. They are really afraid of our brave young Christians, especially since they are seemingly devoid of the frenzy of fear which they themselves felt on first being imprisoned. Brother Peter, there are two more wings to this prison. Do you want to go there also?"

He did, of course, and the same experiences were repeated in the other parts of the prison. Before leaving, Peter thanked Patroculus and told him he would return as often as he could. "Let us pray that some new compassion will touch the heart of Nero, and these dear friends of ours may be saved," he said as he shook hands. "Patroculus, seeing the obvious change that has taken place in you and knowing what has happened to me, even Nero's mind and heart could be changed."

Patroculus agreed, but added realistically, "It is possible— all things are possible to our God—but remember He did not take His own beloved Son from the cross."

Peter nodded and added as they left through the open door of the prison office, "But no Nero or any other power in the heights or the depths can rob us of His presence and the gift of eternal life. Good-bye, Patroculus, until I see you again."

After leaving Peter at Linus's home, Onesimus went back to his room. He had several hours alone before leaving for the cavern meeting. The first thing he did was write as much as he could remember of Peter's message to the Christians in prison. He had been inspired by hearing his words three times that day and wanted to put them down so that they could be transmitted to as many of the churches as possible. He rightly understood how valuable they would be to others who must go through the tests and trials of a pagan world threatened by a twisted understanding of the loving truth of the gospel. After writing what he could remember, he took a clean sheet of papyrus and wrote another letter to Helen, Philemon, and the dear familia back in Colossae. He wanted to report the events of the past few days and let them know that he was still safe and well.

--- *29*

After a nourishing meal, Onesimus, Nereus, and Junia made their way to the meeting place in the cavern. Though there were at least sixty fewer than usual—ten more Christians had been ferreted out by Tigellinus's spies and cast into another dirty, fear-filled prison—the room seemed as crowded as ever. One of the deacons explained to Onesimus that a new group of catechumens was ready to be welcomed, baptized, and to receive their first communion at the hands of the apostle Peter.

The singing that night was more beautiful and meaningful than ever, Onesimus thought. Several gifted poets and musicians had become Christians and were using their talents to write some joyful songs which lifted the spirits and expressed the faith better than any mere spoken words could do. The prayers were genuinely entered into by the entire group, and the Lord's Prayer, or the prayer Jesus taught, was lifted in full voice by everyone present:

"Our Father . . . Your Kingdom come, Your will be done on
   earth as in heaven
Give us this day our bread for today;
Forgive us our sins as we forgive those who sin against us.
Save us in the time of trial, and deliver us from evil."

As the words resounded through the cavern, Onesimus was conscious of the presence that sanctified the place in which they were gathered. He found himself again conqueror over his own human doubts and fears, and he knew that even without Peter this bread of life would sustain them.

"Simon Peter's presence is the added miracle of grace we all so desperately need at this time," Onesimus whispered to John Mark, who stood near him. John Mark's face was filled with admiration of his father in the gospel, and he answered with an enthusiastic, "Thank the Lord for his coming."

After a brief welcome, Elder Linus presented Peter to the assembly. Simon Peter arose and greeted them in his strong, full voice: "The Lord be with you!" and they responded with the same strong feeling, "And with you also, Brother Peter!"

He began a message which included some of the things he had said to the ones in prison that day, but going on he addressed them with words that were to be classic in Christian history as one of the most significant descriptions of the church:

Through Christ Jesus you have come to trust in God who raised him from the dead and gave him glory, and so your faith and hope are fixed on God. Now that by obedience to the truth you have purified your souls until you feel sincere affection towards your brother Christians, love one another whole-heartedly with all your strength. You have been born anew, not of mortal parentage but of immortal, through the living and enduring word of God.

And then he quoted from Isaiah,

> "All mortals are like grass;
> all their splendour like the flower of the field;
> the grass withers, the flower falls;
> but the word of the Lord endures for evermore."

> And this "word" is the word of the Gospel preached to you. . . . But
> you are a chosen race, a royal priesthood, a dedicated nation, and a
> people claimed by God for his own, to proclaim the triumphs of him
> who has called you out of darkness into his marvellous light.

Lowering his voice and holding out his arms with great compassion, he said, with all the bigness of his faith and love, words that were comforting to this little group of Christians who faced some of the most cruel and heartless sufferings any people would ever face:

> My dear friends, do not be bewildered by the fiery ordeal that is
> upon you, as though it were something extraordinary. . . . If
> Christ's name is flung in your teeth as an insult, count yourselves
> happy, because then that glorious Spirit which is the Spirit of God is
> resting upon you. . . . And the God of all grace, who called you into
> his eternal glory with Christ, will himself, after your brief suffering,
> restore, establish, and strengthen you on a firm foundation. He
> holds dominion for ever and ever. Amen.

With one voice the people shouted, "Amen! Alleluia! Maranatha!"*

The Holy Supper that night was a time of unusual joy, a feast of spiritual hope and courage. Onesimus took the body and blood of Christ with thankfulness, sure that he could, by the grace of the ever-present Christ, fulfill his mission at whatever cost. Seeds of a living and abiding faith were planted that night, and the fruit when it was harvested would feed humankind.

Several weeks passed with more "seeds" sown by the inspired apostle and by those who worked with him. He visited the prisons and remained safe through the influence of Pom-

---

*Even so, come Lord Jesus!

pania and some of the sympathetic Jews. His messages in the early morning worship hours in the cavern were personal and profoundly relevant to the people's needs. Onesimus accompanied Peter on several of his visits to the prisons and found more and more memorable sentences to copy on his papyri at night.

On the first evening of Peter's message to the people and the admission of the new catechumens, Onesimus was grateful to see Marcia and Nicia both included. He had told Peter of his experience with them before he brought them up to introduce him to them. "Their appearance and attitude are changed in so many ways," Onesimus had said to him. "They are becoming 'new persons' in Christ. Gone is the arrogant hardness they had when I first knew them. In its place is a new strength and vitality from which they are able to smile and laugh from inner security."

Onesimus had been to their apartment several times to help them understand the faith; each time he left them he marveled at their enlightened hearts and vivacity. Now, Peter said to them prophetically, "Though you have treated Onesimus unjustly in the past, you will have opportunity in the coming days to do something for him that will more than repay for any hurt you gave him in the days of bondage to your pride."

"We will surely be looking for such an opportunity, Brother Peter," Nicia responded, "though we cannot imagine what it will be. He has done more for us already than we could ever do for him. Though our physical lives are more insecure than before, our hearts and minds are at peace. We are able truly to enjoy life in freedom from the fears and hatreds that plagued us before. We were both shocked and skeptical when Onesimus first talked to us after his return, but now we know! We who were once slaves are now indeed free—free, if the need comes," he spoke these words with deep seriousness, "to die for Him who died for us."

As Nicia finished, Simon Peter said seriously, "The grace of God is always undeserved and unearned, but thank God for His power to laugh and find joy. How much more interesting life is

when we are seeking to fulfill our purpose as sons and
daughters in the family of God than when we are only trying to
save ourselves. To be able to forget ourselves in the loving
service of others in His Spirit is to live!"

The next day Onesimus went to Nicia and Marcia's apartment in the Subura for supper. They spoke of Peter and his
visits to the prisoners and of the growing menace to anyone
suspected of being a Christian. Peter himself had narrowly
escaped arrest on several of his prison visits.

"It is only a question of time," Onesimus declared, "before he
is captured. Tigellinus knows he is here and how much his visits
to the prisons are doing to increase morale, despite his cruel
punishments. Lady Pompania is close to the Empress Poppae
and can be trusted to talk with her without danger of betrayal
on the one hand or the quest for some favor from the Emperor
on the other. As she seeks to help this poor maddened woman,
whose hold on Nero is so strong but whose inner life is so beset
with fears and guilts, Pompania has discovered that Nero,
spurred on by Tigellinus, is determined to root out what he has
been persuaded is a dangerous movement. But the remarkable
bravery of the Christians in prison, before the lions, and in the
other tests in the Colosseum spectacles has shocked the
superstitious young Emperor. 'Why,' he asks, 'are they not
afraid of anything, not even torture or death?' "

Marcia and Nicia had gone with some of their Subura friends
to one of these gladiatorial combats and related now to
Onesimus what they had seen with their own eyes. "It was
really a horrible scene, the kind once we would have enjoyed,"
Marcia said as she described the different events in which the
punishment of the Christians was featured. "In one game
several of these beautiful young believers were pushed into the
arena to be pawed over, bitten, and killed by lions prepared by
several days without food. In other events the prisoners were
forced to face wild dogs and bears. But contrary to the usual
terrified response of ordinary criminals, our fellow believers
demonstrated an unheard of bravery."

"Yes, they were superb souls whose faces showed courage

even as the lions and other animals tore at them," Nicia added. "Never before in our visits to the Colosseum had we seen such bravery. Onesimus, do you recall the young couple, Petronius and Acte, whom we all admired greatly for their sincerity in the last group of catechumens to be received at the Eucharist? They were among the first to be thrown to the lions the day we were there. I wish you could have seen them standing there arm in arm in the open arena as the lions were released and rushed in to attack them! Both of them had on their faces what only could be called a heavenly smile. It certainly was not like the grimaces of fear on the part of the usual victims. These two remained together holding hands until one of the hungry lions tore off Petronius's arm. But our Lord, as Peter promised, gave him the power to stand the test. Even as he saw another lion take the lovely face of Acte in his mouth and crush her to death, there was no cry of fear or bitterness."

"I am sure this lack of hatred," Onesimus said, "this unconquerable love, along with fearless courage, has frightened Nero and Poppae. Pompania says Poppae is almost beside herself. However, instead of discouraging Nero, Poppae seems to be more intent on pushing him to the limit until these strange people whom they have come to fear are extinguished. Pompania is saddened beyond words, for she has used every bit of logic and persuasion she knows to convince Poppae of the innocence of the Christians. She feels she soon may have to declare openly to Poppae that she is a Christian and hope that her witness will bring a reversal of the Augusta's insane fears and hatred for our people. If she fails, as well she might, she too may pay the supreme price."

"Onesimus," Nicia spoke with deep feeling, "that day when we were crying 'habet' with the crowds in the Colosseum while you were reacting with horror, how little did we know the hardness of our own hearts. If you feel yourself unworthy of the grace of our Lord who saved you from your spiritual bondage, how much less worthy Marcia and I are of His goodness!"

"Remember Peter's words when you first met him, Nicia," Onesimus remonstrated. "None of us deserve to be accepted, loved, or forgiven. This is the miracle of our new life in Christ. Remember also that our time may come soon. Can you, can I take it and give their kind of witness? I ask myself that many times, as I know you have."

"My only answer to this question," Marcia said humbly, "is that 'I am ready for anything through Him who gives me power.' These are among the first words I can remember which you said Paul had taught you, Onesimus. It was true of him; it was true for Petronius and Acte, and it will be true for us."

Onesimus turned to look at her with affectionate pride. His *agape*-love for these two had become one of his most prized joys.

30

*S*uddenly all three noticed a rosy glow coming in through the window. Rushing over they saw what looked like the whole eastern part of the city on fire. They opened the door and could hear the popping, crackling roar of a fire that was literally devouring the section of the city where many of the plebian homes were located. Then they looked to the west, and to their horror they realized that that side of the Subura was also burning. They ran down into the street and were met by a frantic, hysterical mob of denizens from the human sewer. People were carrying clothes or a few possessions and running in terrified fright from the fire devouring their living and working places.

The fire was only a *millare* away, Onesimus estimated as he pulled Marcia and Nicia back into their dwelling.

The three were aghast at the situation.

"What shall we do?" Marcia cried. They had been preparing themselves for prison or the lions, but this was completely unexpected.

"Come with me," Onesimus responded. "Get a few clothes, not too many to burden yourself unnecessarily, and we will go to Nereus and Junia's house where I have some scrolls of papyri I must save."

Hurriedly Marcia and Nicia grabbed a few of their belongings and rushed out into the street to join the throngs fleeing the fire. Onesimus knew the shortest route, which brought them out on the Palatine Hill where some of the richest villas were located. After a few minutes of running, they stopped for breath. "What monstrous demon could be responsible for this?" Nicia asked as they leaned against a tree, their faces lighted by the fires on either side of them.

"These fires are not accidental," Onesimus rejoined, "and there is only one person I know powerful and sadistic enough to have set so many of them all at once." Marcia and Nicia nodded in comprehension. They continued at a slower pace until they noted signs of fire to the north also. Without a word they began to run again and were soon across the Caelian Hills and on the northern slope where Onesimus's temporary home was located. To their relief, Nereus and Junia were still there, but with serious faces. The fire to the north was growing brighter. It was sure to envelop their house if it were not extinguished, and Rome's fire-fighting equipment was notoriously poor.

"Thank God, all three of you have come," Junia exclaimed. "I wonder what Linus and his guests are doing?"

"They had better do what we are going to do," answered Nereus, "head for our subterranean meeting place outside the walls. It may be the only safe spot except for places such as Lady Pompania's estate on the hill. Nicia, you know where Linus lives, do you not?" Nicia nodded assent. "Run as fast as you can and see that Peter, Doctor Luke, and John Mark, as well as Linus, get out of the city as quickly as possible. The best route will be to follow the path we have used so often. Hopefully it is not yet cut off by the fires on the east and the west. That may give us only a half hour at most the way the fires look from here. We will meet you there, by the help of our Lord, within the hour."

Nicia gripped their hands and started running in the direction of Linus's house. Nereus and Junia were getting a few clothes together and Onesimus ran up the stairs to get his precious scrolls and the money Philemon had given him. Putting these and an extra tunic into a bag, he came down the stairs, and the four set out for the caverns. Their path was lighted by the raging fires seemingly on all sides. It led through the streets lined with marble state buildings and onto the main road leading to the southern gates. The road was already filled with all kinds of frightened Romans—plebians, patricians, the poor, the rich—the fire was impartial.

Staying close together, they soon found themselves outside the walls and into the shaded byways they knew so well, leading to the entrance to the cavern in the olive grove. As they drew nearer, they met numerous other Christians going the same way. Their greetings were warm but sorrowful. Most of them knew their houses and places of work were going up in flames. Few words were said until they were safely in the entrance to the welcome coolness of their sacred *caverna*.

Once within the huge room where so many precious meetings for worship had been held, they began to greet each other and seek out other loved ones. Onesimus, Marcia, Nereus, and Junia were immensely relieved to see the animated face of Nicia coming toward them. As if answering their unasked question, he said, "Yes, we are all here safely. Thank God you made it! What a catastrophe to the people of Rome! What a devilish fiend to have set such fires to burn a whole city!"

Nicia led them to the place where the apostle Peter and Linus were preparing to call the meeting to order. Though the room was only half-filled, it was evident a great many of the Christians who still were not imprisoned were present. Hopefully, more would come. When the call for silence was sounded, Linus rose. After the usual greeting—which was more meaningful than ever—he began.

"My dear brothers and sisters in the family of God our Father, by the mercy of our Lord, we are safe from this terrible fire, which obviously has been planned. Let us thank God, but let us also spend the next few minutes in prayer for the people of Rome, for those of our *communitas* who are still imprisoned—many of whom are perishing in the flames—and even for the evil one whose cruel plans have brought this holocaust upon this great city. Let us pray for those of the church who are safe, we hope, because their homes are on hills and who have means of protection from the fire. We will have their support and help in securing food by which we may exist until the fires are over. I am going to ask our bishop, the apostle Peter, to lead us in prayer. His presence and ministry have meant so much to us all, especially to the prisoners and victims of Nero's torture."

The apostle had spoken many times of "faith that stands the test being much more precious than gold tried in the fire." Now he thanked God that so many had stood the test and remembered those who had perished physically but whose persons were now in the presence of the resurrected Christ. He closed with a declaration of the faith he had used so often in ministering to the imprisoned brothers and sisters of the faith. "The inheritance to which we are born is one that *nothing* can destroy or spoil or wither—not even this fire!"

The musicians among them led in several doxological songs that filled the hearts of these homeless and bereaved persons with exaltation—the paradox of their faith. They sang the words Jesus Himself had said, "Blessed are you when you are hungry, poor, persecuted, for the kingdom of heaven is yours!"

That night most of the Christians who had escaped the fire were very sure their homes and possessions had been destroyed, and many were distraught by the absence of members of their family and friends. But in thankfulness they curled up on the earthen floor of the cavern, using their bundles of clothes for pillows and, after the blessing and benediction of the apostle Peter, tried to sleep. Onesimus joined with Peter, Linus, Doctor Luke, and others in seeking to comfort those who continued to cry softly because of their losses or uncertainties concerning their dear ones. At last, about the first hour of the morning, all were asleep.

Early the next morning they were awakened by Lady Pompania and several of the wealthier Christians whose homes were out of reach of the fire. These more fortunate now entered the cavern with their servants laden with food and blankets. Among them were some of the plebian Christians in areas of the city yet untouched by the fire, also bearing their offerings for the needs of their fellow Christians.

"What a heartening sight!" Doctor Luke said to Peter and the little group around him. "Does this not remind you, Brother Peter, of the first few months after Pentecost in Jerusalem? I am writing an account of the beginnings of the church, and one of the most important sentences I have written describes how 'they met constantly to hear the apostles teach, and to share the common life, to break bread and to pray.' These words describe us now, for we have the opportunity not only to 'have all things in common' but also to share an unusually long amount of time in worship and in hearing you teach."

"Yes," said Peter with animation. "Those also were days of persecution and hardship. Just as Jesus said, the more it costs to hold to our Christian faith, the more likely we are to understand and appreciate its depth of meaning and the victory of our risen Lord." Sensing the great spirit of gratitude which filled the hearts of the people, Linus called them together to thank not only those who brought the food, but to give Peter the chance to express their thankfulness to God.

Onesimus's memory was etched deeply with the experiences of that morning and the hours that followed. After a brief meeting, the leaders agreed that it would be unwise to attempt to enter the city, which from all reports was still in flames. Linus advised the homeless Christians accordingly, adding: "Those of your families and friends who escaped the fire will find you here in the cavern," a promise that was fulfilled as a number of other victims joined them. The stories were terrifying, indeed.

The worst part was the actual deployment of soldiers in some parts of the city to prevent anyone from putting out the fires. This was the final evidence that Nero himself must be behind the burning of Rome. He had been quoted as saying—and his words were repeated a thousand times that day—"A burning city is beautiful when upon its ruins a more beautiful city is built!"

Some of the Christians described seeing soldiers from the legion actually setting more fires in the highly inflammable poorer sections of the city. And others had heard the fierce laughter coming from the legion camps on the Palatine Hill. The soldiers were celebrating like boys at a bonfire. Their laughter and shouting were encouraged by extra large portions of wine. One of the Christians who had journeyed from Antium, near Nero's summer resort, the day after the fire began, reported that Nero held a great banquet on the night the fire began, at which he read with bravado one of his own poems comparing the burning of Rome to the burning of Troy.

"This is just what Nero would have done," Pompania observed. "He has a fabulous vanity that makes him want to recreate everything that has been created—whether it be the writings of Virgil or Horace or even Homer. He thinks he can outdo them. Most likely he thinks he can build a great city. Now that we know he ordered the fires himself, even letting his own palace and many of the temples with their treasures of art and valuable manuscripts be destroyed, we know just how insane he is."

"The tragic part," observed Doctor Luke, "is that thousands of the poorest and most helpless are the ones who have died or have lost all their possessions."

For five days the fire raged, a blazing inferno turning the sky red even in the daytime. Onesimus with Marcia, Nicia, and Nereus had gone to the entrance of the city and watched with awe the terrifying spectacle. When the fire seemed to die down, it was started again, until every one of seven sections of Rome were destroyed. The roads streamed with the terrified poor, weeping pitifully, carrying the few remnants of their meager possessions with no place to go. The Caelian and the Palatine sections, of course, were untouched. Here most of the patricians, senators, and wealthy merchants lived, their houses built of stone in the center of spacious grounds with plenty of water. Fortunately, among these were a few Christians whose generosity made possible the survival of the homeless fellow believers in the cavern.

Nearly a week passed before anyone ventured into the city. During this time the shocked and sorrowing Christians had an unparalleled opportunity to hear from the apostle Peter and Doctor Luke the stories of the life and teachings of their Lord and Master. Onesimus noticed how carefully both Doctor Luke and John Mark recorded the stories as they were told. Sometimes Doctor Luke would tell a story or describe the teachings of Jesus which he had heard from the lips of Mary, the mother of Jesus, Mary Magdala, or the other Mary, or from other disciples. It was he who told them the story of the two who met the Lord on the Emmaus road after the resurrection. They did not recognize him until "he was known to them in the breaking of the bread."

The days were a veritable school for all the Christians. Lady Pompania and the others whose homes were spared from the fire came daily to join in the great *koinonia*. They brought food and drink for their brothers and sisters and returned home with food for the spirit, so amply provided by this remarkable gathering of Christian leaders. Many times Onesimus thought that this privilege was as valuable as his hours with the apostle Paul. Learning so much more about the life and teachings of Jesus would give him a foundation of strength and understanding on which he could build his own life and ministry. *If only Helen could be here to share in it—and Archippus—and all of my family in Colossae!*

"This is another marvelous illustration," Onesimus confided to Peter, "of Paul's conviction that 'all things fit into a pattern for good to those who love God and accept the call of His purpose.' Even the worst turns into the best for those who, like a little child, are willing to trust where they cannot see."

"Indeed so," Peter answered. "This is what our Lord meant when He said 'those who lose their lives shall find them' and 'a seed cannot bear fruit except it fall to the ground and die.'

Surely the blood of these our Christian brothers and sisters who have paid the supreme price is the seed of Christ's body, the church."

He was speaking not only of those who perished in the flames, including at least forty who were in prisons that were destroyed by fire. He was speaking also of the increasing number who were being thrown to the lions and would pay the price of martyrdom within the next few weeks.

On the morning of the fifth day as the church council was meeting to decide what could be done to help, the whole assembly was surprised and delighted to see the strong, friendly face of Janus the praetorianus. Neither he nor Plutonius nor their captain Burrhus had been able to visit them since the fires started because of the pressures upon them as Nero's bodyguards. They had been with him in Antium until his return to Rome the day before. As Janus was greeted by Peter and the other leaders, the distraught people pressed around the little circle waiting to hear the news.

"We're so glad to see you," Linus said with evident relief. "Perhaps you can give us some insight into what has happened and what we may expect when we return to Rome."

Janus turned to speak to the assembled *communitas*, upon whose faces were written the suffering and pain of these days of uncertainty: "Dear brothers and sisters in the family of our heavenly Father, you can know just how much we as members of the praetorian guard who share your faith have agonized with you. You know that three of the prisons in which many of our numbers were held have been destroyed by the fire, and that many of your loved ones and our fellow Christians perished in the flames—how many we do not know. But seeing such a large number of you present here in this sacred place, I believe not as many have been lost as we first thought likely. Praise to our Lord for that, and for the wonderful week of fellowship and teaching you have had here with Brother Peter and Doctor Luke.

"Now I must tell you some good news and then some very evil news. Caesar Nero has announced provisions for financial aid to those 'loyal citizens' of Rome who desire to rebuild their homes or places of business. Undoubtedly, he is expecting to build a new and better Rome, including his own palace, which as you have heard he permitted to burn.

"Upon his return to Rome, Nero discovered what all of you have known, that the vast majority of the citizens of Rome believe he ordered and Tigellinus planned this holocaust. The people are bitter and threatening revenge. Since it was so obviously planned, Nero knows that his own position is most insecure unless he can blame the burning on someone else. Considering the ill repute in which our little group of Christians is held by the people, due to the many lies told on us, he has announced officially that his officers found sufficient evidence to prove that it was the 'evil and brutal Chrestians' who set the fires. The idea was suggested by the Empress Poppae and enthusiastically spread by Tigellinus.

"I regret to warn all of you that when you return to Rome, as obviously you must, you are in great danger of discovery and arrest. Some of you may be able to secure financial aid from the Court officers without revealing your identity as Christians. I have the names of a few officers who are Christians or at least in sympathy with us. However, I do not know for sure about some of them. The fear for their own lives may make many of them cowardly. I know you will want to return and try to rebuild your homes, just as I would. But you must know that now that we are proclaimed the criminals responsible for burning Rome, we will be subject to even more merciless persecution.

"The time may come soon," here his voice was husky with emotion, "when Captain Burrhus will be removed from office and forced to pay the price with Paul and the others who have gone before. So may you and I. But as our beloved apostle Peter has told us, let us 'hold to our living hope by the resurrection of Jesus Christ from the dead' knowing that 'we have an inheritance that nothing can destroy or spoil or wither.' Let us face our future with faith and hope that in the Holy Spirit gives us joy and courage."

The people said "amen," and Linus stood to announce that he

would post the list of Court officers thought to be friendly so that each one could make his own decision.

"The risk must be taken," he said. "We will take it by faith, knowing that some of us will be arrested and tortured to death. Before we break up, let us ask the apostle Simon Peter to lead us in prayer."

The air was tense as Peter rose, but as his strong voice resounded through the cavern, the Christians joined hands and their faces relaxed, and once again, a spirit of hope and joy pervaded them. The one who prayed had once denied his Lord, but now he was a tower of strength. In his reflected strength they would go to meet whatever lay ahead.

Onesimus stood between Junia and Marcia with Nereus and Nicia on either side. The moment was like a precious bit of *kairos** in which the whole assembly was caught up in a unity of the Spirit believing that the Lord, *Christus Victor,* was indeed with each of them.

31

n the days that followed, Onesimus walked through the burned-out city with pain and unbelief in his heart. The smell of roasted flesh now putrefying in the hot summer air filled his nostrils. Cries of sorrow and despair rang in his ears. He shared the unbelievable sights with the plebians and poor returning to Rome to start again, poking through the rubble, finding parts of the charred bodies of loved ones, or more often only ashes. He accompanied Nereus and Junia and was inspired as he witnessed their inspection of the ruins of their house, free

---

*The Greek word for "time," indicating quality rather than *chronos,* meaning quantity or length.

of the despair so visible all around them. Nereus even cried out in thankfulness when he found some of his tools by which he could resume his skilled trade. There would be plenty of demand for bronze utensils and ornaments.

Lady Pompania had personally invited them to find temporary living quarters in her large villa. When they arrived they found fifteen others who shared her hospitality, including Marcia and Nicia. Though their home and shop were ruined, they were eager to begin anew.

The believers were especially glad to learn that Linus's house, being on higher ground than most of the houses in his section, had been preserved, though it had been looted of many choice possessions. Peter was invited to continue his stay with him. With the help of some of the younger Christians, Linus was able to make his home livable. He was a widower, with grown children who had families of their own. One of these families had perished in the fire; the other had escaped and now with two small children shared the house of the father and grandfather.

The apostle Peter had been of great comfort not only to Linus and his remaining family but to many other Christians whose losses were heartbreaking. Since Peter had asked John Mark to visit the church in Cyprus, he had reluctantly departed from Rome. Onesimus was invited again to attend Peter as he visited the Christians; Onesimus continually marveled at the big man's capacity to counsel and encourage the despondent and sorrowing.

On the morning of the tenth day after the fire, as Onesimus arrived at Linus's house, he found Peter engaged in conversation with Linus and three group leaders, Onesiphorus, Pudens, and Ampliatus. They welcomed Onesimus, and Linus communicated Peter's determination to visit the Christians in the two remaining prisons and the new prison Tigellinus had set up. A temporary structure had been erected in the burned-out marketplace of one of the poorer sections destroyed by the fire. The building was more like a cattle shed than a prison and within a few days was filled with nearly one hundred Christians. Since most of the Christians were among the plebians, most of them had suffered the loss of their houses and small places of business. Hence they were among the first persons to apply for the aid made available either as loans from the rich patricians or as outright gifts from Nero. Everyone who applied, even to the officers whose names were on the list suggested by Janus as sympathetic to the Christians, were asked the required question, "Are you a member of the sect called Chrestians?"

Many of them, when asked the question, would confess their faith in Christ. Then, unless the officer was himself a Christian, or was very prejudiced in their favor, those confessing Christ were immediately turned over to the *sparteoli* and sent to the new *ergastulum*. Here they lived in indescribable conditions of filth, amidst the stench of their own excretions—a wholesale version of the Mammertine Prison.

Linus and his group leaders could understand the apostle's deep concern for these Christians who were willing to go to their deaths rather than deny their Lord. But they still did not want him needlessly to expose himself. After Onesimus arrived, Peter declared with deep feeling his obligation to go and encourage these new prisoners, no matter the danger to himself.

"I denied my Lord three times that black night!" he said over and over again, "and I will not, I *will* not do it again. Last night in a dream I saw myself running away. In my dream I justified myself by declaring that my ministry to the church is too important to endanger my life." Here he could not continue. His huge shoulders shook with uncontrollable sobs, as he stopped speaking for a full minute. Onesimus and the others were deeply moved to see their respected friend so grieved.

"I awakened in a cold sweat. Realizing it was only a dream, I got on my knees and prayed, 'Lord, I will not deny You again! You will not have to be crucified for me again. Once is enough.' And I prayed for strength and courage to meet whatever comes today and tomorrow and however long I live."

Onesimus, Linus, and the three deacons looked at each other

and nodded agreement. "Dear Brother Peter," Linus spoke for them all, "we understand and admire your determination. I am sure it is our own selfish need for your presence and encouragement that has led us to plead with you not to risk your life. But I can see how you believe you would be denying your Lord again if you do not seek to bring courage and strength to these who have also refused to deny the Lord."

"Surely, Brother Peter," Onesiphorus, the most perceptive of the group observed, "our Lord must have a special place in heaven for His *martyrs.** Who can tell how valuable will be the witness of this valiant hundred who are now awaiting your coming? Whatever you can do to encourage them may be in His sight the greatest gift you can give, for your witness may be the best means our Lord has to help us all to be true to our faith."

"We will be praying for you," added Pudens, and Ampliatus and the others agreed.

Then Onesimus, having made the most difficult decision of his life, spoke quietly but firmly: "Brother Peter, with your permission, I will go with you, whatever the cost. I, who once might have died as a runaway slave, am willing and ready now to die as a slave of Christ, if my witness is needed."

Peter arose, put his brawny arm around Onesimus's shoulders and said tenderly, "Son, if this is your desire, you will not be denied your request. You have been of much comfort and help to me in the weeks that I have known you. Come, let us be on our way." After a brief prayer by Linus, Peter and his young companion walked out into the street.

At the same time there came a new report from Caesar Nero's private quarters. At Nero's bidding, Burrhus, chief captain of Caesar's choice praetorian guard, entered Nero's chambers accompanied by Rufus Faenus, the first lieutenant, and two other praetorians, one of whom was Plutonius. As they made their way into the interior of Nero's palace, Burrhus

---

*The Greek word for "witnesses."

whispered to Plutonius, "This is my last chance to witness for our Lord. Nero is to challenge me I am sure."

Nero had just awakened from a drunken sleep in his luxurious bedroom. The four praetorians came to attention before his couch. Nero lifted his fat little body up on his elbows and said with disgust, "So, Burrhus, the captain of my famous praetorian guards, many times I have asked you to serve me and you have done well, or I would have replaced you. Now I have one question to ask." Nero shouted in his fury, "Why have you not captured the big fool Chrestian, Simon Peter?"

His exertion caused him to pant, but he continued in lower voice, growling, "It is well known that even before the fire he was the strength of this evil sect who call themselves 'Chrestians.' I have been informed by one of your own guards," he looked significantly at Rufus Faenus, "that several times before the fire this man Simon Peter visited the prisons where these vile Chrestians are confined. You were given instructions, were you not, to bring him in—one of the most important orders I ever gave you?" He waited, breathing heavily as Burrhus answered quietly but firmly.

"Yes, Caesar, you did give that order and I understood it."

"Why then did you let him escape? Are you too a Chrestian?" he screamed, then fell back exhausted.

"Yes, Caesar, I too am a Christian," Burrhus continued with a strong, calm voice. "Jesus Christ is my Lord. I will serve Him and Him only."

Nero looked up in astonishment. He had suspected Burrhus's relationship with the hated sect, but this open confession without a trace of fear shook the dissipated Nero as few things ever had. He had loved Burrhus and depended on him, not only for his safety but for his counsel. As Burrhus continued, Nero stared unbelievingly.

"I have served you as long as I am able. Do with me as you will, but I refuse to protect any longer a sadistic murderer, liar, lecher, and traitor to his people. I love the Nero that you were, but I can no longer serve the Nero you have become."

By this time Nero had risen from the couch, spluttering, his face purple with anger. At last he found his voice, "You . . . you . . . you dog! You foul traitor, betraying your Caesar in favor of this Christus!" With a flick of his hand he motioned to Rufus Faenus.

"Take this vile wretch and cut off his head. Tigellinus is now the chief captain of my praetorian guard and you, Rufus Faenus, are now the head centurion. Take him out of my sight." He then fell back on his pillows with a groan.

"I was never so proud of my captain as I was in that hour," Plutonius said as he told the story later to all the Christians assembled in the worship hall of the cavern.

"Since Nero had not challenged me, there was nothing for me to do but follow Rufus and Paulus as they seized Burrhus by the arms, still quiet and unresisting, and led him out. What a blessed witness he was! As disgusted as I was with Rufus for his treachery, I accompanied them without a word to the execution hall, where evidently Rufus had warned the executioner to be present. There on the same block where our dear brother Paul's head was severed, I placed the head of my beloved captain. Still unresisting, he whispered to me, "My blessings on you, son. Give my witness to our friends. Peace!" I struggled hard to keep the tears from my cheeks as the executioner lowered the ax and Burrhus was released to be with Christ."

Plutonius continued the story with difficulty: "Evidently, I went through the horrible hour without revealing my feelings, for Rufus then ordered Paulus and me to take Burrhus's body out to the cemetery where the praetorians are buried. Though Rufus was willing to betray his former captain, he admired him enough that he wanted his body placed with his former comrades-in-arms."

When Plutonius finished he broke down and wept. It was all that Linus could do by his counsel and prayers to release him from the sense of guilt he bore. Plutonius felt guilty, as did many others, for being free and unharmed while his brothers and sisters were being killed for their witness. He felt guilty, even though when the persecutions began the question had been discussed fully and the Christian community had decided that none of them should become voluntary martyrs. They should witness to their identity as Christians only when challenged, "otherwise there will be no Christians to carry on the witness among the living!"

32

As the apostle Peter and Onesimus made their way through the burned-out streets to the new makeshift prison, they did not know of the change in leadership of the praetorian guard. But, as Onesimus looked back on that day, he realized that even if they had known, it would not have made any difference. Simon Peter was not running away again and neither was Onesimus.

Through the help of Lady Pompania and Burrhus, they had been told the name and something of the character of the officer in charge of the *ergastulum* called "The Cattle Shed." His name was Volusius. He was known to be a tough, sadistic brute of a man who enjoyed presiding over the suffering of others.

"We may not have as easy a time with him as we did with the other prison officers," Peter warned, "but we do have a letter from Burrhus, which even Volusius will respect."

Peter was right in both surmises. Volusius read the letter and grouchily opened the door to the Cattle Shed. The letter, introducing the two as agents of Caesar, declared that they were visiting the prison to investigate the character and kind of persons imprisoned. As the door closed behind them, they did not suspect that Volusius called immediately to a trusted representative of Tigellinus, who had been hiding near the prison entrance to spot anyone with the resemblance of the huge man named Peter. When Volusius showed the letter to the agent and described the two visitors, the man hesitated only a moment.

"There is something wrong with that letter, for undoubtedly this big man is the Simon Peter we are looking for. Let me take it to Tigellinus."

By the time the apostle and Onesimus entered the stinking shed where the dirty band of Christian martyrs welcomed them with joy, Tigellinus had sent word to the new captain, Rufus, and four praetorians were on their way to the prison.

Thus Peter and Onesimus had but fifteen minutes to do their blessed work of encouragement. The apostle gave a short message of hope and began to offer up a prayer of thankful trust and intercession for these who in a short time would suffer untold physical agony as the price of their witness. Suddenly the door to the prison burst open and an angry Volusius, accompanied by the guards, confronted Simon Peter and Onesimus.

"Are you not Simon Peter, leader of the sect called Chrestians?" Volusius asked threateningly.

"I am Simon Peter, a humble apostle of the Lord Jesus Christ," Peter answered without a tremor in his booming voice. "what would you do with me?"

"You are under arrest as a traitor and a criminal who led your people in the burning of the city of Rome!" Volusius answered.

"I am not a traitor to anyone, not even Caesar, and certainly, neither I nor any of my people had anything to do with the burning of Rome. Many of our own group were among those who were killed or who suffered the most from the fire." Peter spoke with indignation and without fear.

"You lie," shouted the prison keeper. "Take this liar and his companion away," he said to the praetorians. He turned to Onesimus.

"Are you not also one of these Chrestians?"

"I am, by the grace of God. Jesus Christ is my Lord and I have none other," Onesimus answered.

Without a word the four praetorians came forward and tied the two Christian's hands behind them. Peter and Onesimus offered no resistance. As Janus, who had still never been challenged, completed tying Onesimus's hands, he whispered into his ear, "Thank God for your witness!"

The imprisoned Christians began to cry out their love and appreciation as Peter and Onesimus were led out the door. As they were placed in a horse-drawn cart, Onesimus heard them singing the familiar chant of the doxology. He realized that only a Christian could understand praise at such a time!

Onesimus looked at Simon Peter. The big apostle's uplifted face was suffused with ecstasy as he prayed aloud, "Lord, you are with me. I did not fail You. Thank You for giving us the courage to be Your witness. Strengthen us in the days ahead. Amen." Onesimus thought that the memory of that face would always be one of his most precious possessions!

"What am I doing?" he stopped suddenly. "I, too, am a prisoner for the Lord. I, too, will die and discover for myself the mystery of the Father's other rooms."

"Well, Son," Peter was addressing him after a brief period as both were occupied with their own thoughts, "the hour has come. I am proud of your courage. I am thankful for the presence of our Lord. Do you not feel Him near you?"

"I can not see him with my eyes," Onesimus replied truthfully, "but I do sense His presence. I am thankful to be at your side at this momentous hour. Pray for me that my faith may not fail in the supreme test soon to come."

"That I will, my son," the big man answered, "and you pray for me that my last hours on earth will be worthy of the love of Jesus, who forgave me and asked me on that beautiful morning by the lake so long ago, 'Simon, do you love me? . . . if you do, feed my sheep.' This I have been trying to do with all my heart."

"You have, Brother Peter, you have!" Onesimus exclaimed. "How thankful all of us are who have been with you in the prisons and in the cavern. You have fed us at His holy table. Now we will trust others likewise to feed His sheep."

"Son, I am getting old, but you are young. It is a pity that you cannot use that brilliant mind to bear witness in a different way than this. I am going to pray for your deliverance from this hour."

Onesimus was deeply touched by Peter's words. "If it is our Father's will for me to be delivered, I will seek to feed the sheep as faithfully as you have. If not, I will gladly join you as we meet the Lord face to face!"

---*33*

arcia and Nicia had gone through the terrifying days with a surprising sense of wonder and inner peace. Lady Pompania had given them the hospitality of living temporarily in one of her rooms and taking their meals at her bountiful table. She even offered to loan them enough money to reopen their small shop. To be thus included in a circle of such kindness was altogether unbelievable: "grace from God through the Lord Jesus Christ" as Nicia described it to Marcia.

One day at lunch a runner came to tell the shocking news of Burrhus's deposition and beheading by Nero, and on the same morning the arrest and imprisonment of Simon Peter and Onesimus in one of the small prisons near the praetorian guard headquarters. The runner was a Christian, a friend of Pompania's household who worked in the palace of Caesar. As he finished his story, the Christians around Pompania's table sat stunned for a few moments. They quickly realized what a major catastrophe this was for the entire Christian community in Rome. Then some began to weep, including Marcia. Various expressions of appreciation were made for what Burrhus had done for them all and for the invaluable witness he, Peter, and Onesimus had given.

"It is only a question of days or hours before our beloved brother Simon Peter meets his Lord again, face to face," Lady

Pompania said quietly. "Let us rejoice with him that he goes this time having been faithful even to the last.

"What a great witness he will give! I will find out when and how the translation is to take place. Nero thinks he can stop the influence of this mighty apostle. What he does not know is that when Simon Peter is tortured and killed, he will set into motion a power for good, a light of love that can never be extinguished!" she said prophetically. "While we will miss Peter's presence, this seems to be one of our Lord's appointed hours. But Onesimus? How tragic that his life and ministry should thus be ended!"

"It shall not be, dear Lady Pompania," Nicia spoke up. "I cannot see our Lord's permitting Onesimus to die now. I for one am going to do something to secure his release."

"But what can you do?" they all asked at once.

"Do you recall the name of the new captain of the praetorian guard? He is Rufus Faenus. I have good reason to believe that I can influence him to let Onesimus go free. I cannot guarantee it, but the least I can do is to try."

"But what if you fail and Rufus puts you in prison?" Marcia asked anxiously.

"If I fail, I fail. Of what value is my life, if knowing the possibility of setting free such a useful living witness as Onesimus, I seek to save my life instead? No, like Onesimus, I too could have been killed as a runaway slave. It would be an honor to suffer death as a slave of Christ. But I am realistic in my hope of freeing Onesimus. Marcia and I owe him our faith and our life with you in the beloved *koinonia* in Christ. Simon Peter prophesied when he first met us that I would return the gift to Onesimus in some wonderful way. Perhaps this is it. Anyway I shall try. Only pray for me the wisdom and skill to do what is required."

With thankfulness mixed with deep concern, they promised as they watched him leave for the fateful visit with Rufus Faenus.

Rufus Faenus was sitting in the official chair of the captain of the famed praetorian guard. Though Tigellinus was officially chief of the praetorians, he had asked Rufus Faenus to take over the day by day management of the guard as his subcaptain and permitted him to use Burrhus's old office.

Rufus's spirits were high as he neared the close of his first day's work in his new position. His plot with Nero had succeeded. Burrhus had been deposed and executed on the same morning, and Rufus had salved his conscience by seeing that he was buried in the praetorianus cemetery. Simon Peter had been captured and was now incarcerated in the prison reserved for Nero's political prisoners. Rufus's salary was tripled and to crown it all, he was now, next to Tigellinus, at the top.

"Who knows, one day fortune may decree that I shall be Caesar!" He said it out loud as he savored his victory. At that moment he heard a knock on the door, and his first lieutenant entered.

"Sir, one of your friends, as he calls himself, insists on seeing you. He calls himself Nicia and says you will remember him well."

Rufus started with pleasure. Indeed he did remember Nicia. In fact, he had been seeking him for several weeks. Could it be that this young man who had given him so much pleasure was coming to celebrate with him his new position?

"Of course, I remember Nicia. He is a good friend. Show him in!"

When Nicia entered, Rufus advanced to meet him. As the door closed behind him, Rufus noticed that Nicia was as handsome as ever, but somehow different.

"How wonderful of you, my dear Nicia, to come to see me on this the greatest day of my life," he exulted as he put his arm around his former friend and lover. "Sit down and let me tell you all that has happened, though doubtless you have heard most of it already." He showed Nicia to a seat next to his official chair.

"Yes, I have heard of it, Rufus, and that is the reason I have come to see you."

"How kind of you to give me this pleasure," Rufus continued.

"As your longtime friend, I am glad for any truly good thing that comes to you," Nicia responded. "Perhaps my coming may enable you to do a good turn for me and a person who saved my life and the life of my sister, Marcia."

"Of course, of course," Rufus said spiritedly, "I will be happy to do anything I can for one who has given me so many hours of pleasure as the handsome Nicia."

"First, I must be frank with you. I am no longer in the profession to which you have alluded. I am unable to resume the kind of relationship we once had."

Rufus was mystified.

"This is indeed a disappointment, Nicia. But you are still my friend, and I will still do anything I can within reason to help you."

"I hoped this would be true. I trusted our friendship enough to risk my life in coming today. The truth is, I am now a Christian. I have discovered the meaning and joy to life that I always sought but never found."

Rufus heard the word "Christian" with a start. His smile turned into a frown, but he listened as Nicia continued.

"You remember those long conversations you and I shared after we had spent ourselves, talking about the emptiness and futility of life? We shared our thoughts about the Epicurean and Stoic philosophies. You, as well as I, were always hungry for more light, more hope, more assurance of the meaning and purpose of life. And generally, we gave up and decided to live by the moment and find all the pleasure we could, living with as much honor as we could afford."

As Nicia continued, talking of the faith, Rufus was at first repelled and then attracted to the story of his former lover. "This must be an unusually great experience," he said with a mixture of curiosity and disgust, "or an intelligent man like you would not be risking his life to tell it to the chief of Caesar's guard. Either, my dear friend, you are a fool, or else you have found something better than I have ever imagined."

"Exactly!" Nicia proceeded quickly, sensing that he may have reached the 'inner man,' as Paul would have described it.

"I have sense enough to know, Rufus, that my own life is at stake in this conversation; but with all my heart I also believe that your life—indeed your whole future of joy and hope—is at stake, as well as the life of my friend and fellow ex-slave."

"Hmm . . . your talk is convincing, Nicia. You have always been better at philosophy than I. . ."

"I am not talking primarily as a philosopher now, Rufus," Nicia interrupted. "There is indeed a Christian philosophy—or maybe I should say there are Christian philosophers. But I am bearing witness to a new life, 'the Way, the Truth and the Life,' as hundreds of these noble Christians in Rome, many of whom I have come to know and to love, have experienced it. It is called 'the Way' by many thousands all over the Roman world. What the philosophers Plato, Socrates, Heraclitus, and other great thinkers talked about in their more optimistic hours, Jesus Himself lived and promised to those who follow Him. We have realized His promise."

"So now, out with it," Rufus interrupted. "What is your request concerning the friend whom you say saved yours and Marcia's life?"

Nicia took a deep breath. The conversation had come much farther and gone deeper than he had really expected. With a silent prayer of thanks, he presented his request.

"The young man's name is Onesimus. We first met him as a runaway slave from Colossae—a Phrygian just as Marcia and I. We took him into our group and offered to start him in our profession, for he is one of the most attractive young men I ever met. But as desperate as he was to find a livelihood in the Subura, he refused on philosophical principles to become a *scortum.** No, he was not yet a Christian. He had run away from a Christian master because he had accused Christians of talking one way and acting another. His refusal to join us angered Marcia and me and the others in our little party. So we drugged his wine and robbed him of everything he possessed.

---

*Male prostitute.

He left us and evidently nearly starved to death, being unwilling either to join us or to become a criminal in order to make a living. Then he found the apostle Paul, one of the great leaders of the Christian faith, at that time a house prisoner of Nero under the care of two members of your praetorian guard."

"Yes, I remember this Jew, Paul, and the good reports brought back about him by Janus and Plutonius, two of our men," Rufus observed quietly. Nicia's story was making a deep impression on this strong, ambitious man. Nicia marveled at the revelation of the two natures of the man and wondered which one would win.

"Through Paul's kindness and Onesimus's service to him in writing several of his letters to the churches, Onesimus became a Christian, and in what he calls 'the only true freedom' insisted on returning to his master in Colossae, regardless of what might happen to him."

"By Jupiter!" Rufus exclaimed. "To do that he must have been either bewitched or truly have found something of great value."

"Yes! And the remarkable part of the story is yet to come; His master Philemon forgave him, set him free from his physical slavery, promised him the hand of his daughter, and sent him back to serve Paul in prison. He has been here in Rome before and after Paul's execution. And when the apostle Simon Peter was arrested by your men and imprisoned this morning Onesimus was with him also. Onesimus is now locked up in your praetorian prison."

"I see now, friend Nicia," Rufus said sardonically. "You are asking me to set this Onesimus free. Of course, there is nothing I can do for Simon Peter, even if I wanted to," he mused. "He is marked for execution sometime tomorrow, for Nero has placed the blame on him and all the Chrestians for this terrible fire . . . but I will say no more about that." He withdrew carefully from what could have been dangerous talk. "However, this Onesimus intrigues me. I would like to meet him and listen to the two of you tell about your faith in this *Christus*, whom you say is 'the Way, the Truth and the Life.' "

He continued, thinking out loud. "I have never heard of Onesimus before, neither has anyone high up in Nero's court. So one Christian more or less would not make much difference. Oh, I know what I will do!" and here he spoke with enthusiasm, "I will ask Janus and Plutonius, who guarded Paul and who obviously know Onesimus, to go to the prison and tell the guard that Onesimus is wanted for questioning. They will bring him here and I will have a chance at least to meet and talk with him for a brief time. Perhaps then, I will decide to release him or," he said with a frown, "send him back to prison and death with the other fools who call themselves Chrestians."

"Captain Rufus," Nicia spoke crisply and to the point, "if you do that I will ask you to put me in your prison too."

"Ah, my handsome friend," Rufus laughed, "I was testing you. And you stood the test."

He clapped his hands, and the door opened as a tall praetorianus stood at attention.

"Crispus, command Janus and Plutonius to come here immediately."

Crispus saluted and obeyed. The door closed, as Nicia's mind raced and his thanks overflowed. *This is too good to be true,* he thought, *but the Lord works in mysterious ways. Perhaps Rufus is not as unreachable as I feared.*

"Friend Rufus," he spoke out loud, "I want to thank you for listening to me. A smaller man would have shut his mind. I honestly admire you, not for some of the things you did today—though here I will let God be your judge; but for the seeker of goodness that you can be. I know you will never regret your kindness to me and one of the most noble young men I know."

At this point, the door opened and Janus and Plutonius walked in and stood at attention. Seeing Nicia, there was a moment of uncertainty. Nicia knew they were asking themselves whether this was the beginning of the end for them and Nicia. Their concern was relieved as Rufus returned the salute and invited them to be seated.

"Fellow praetorians," their captain spoke tersely and to the point, "you are two men whom I utterly trust. You have the reputation of honesty and integrity among all our guard, and I believe you will not betray me. For this reason I have chosen you for a pleasant task. I can see by your faces that you know my friend Nicia. You know another young man whose name is Onesimus. Nicia has told me his story, and I am interested in talking with him. He may have something to say to me that will be valuable. Go immediately and tell the prison guard that the Captain desires to question Onesimus. Do not say anything to Simon Peter; there is nothing we can do for him."

"Captain Rufus," Janus spoke with emotion, "you cannot know how much this order means to us. We have come to know Onesimus over the past two years and consider him one of the bravest, most intelligent, and honorable men we have ever met. We know the risk you are taking, but we will take it with you; and you can be sure that our lips are sealed. We thank you from our hearts."

With these grateful words to their new captain, whose other acts that day they despised, the two guards hastened to carry out this joyful order.

Onesimus had spent his first day in prison. He and Peter both bore bruises and cuts from the vicious kicks given them while they were being thrown into the cell. But it was a cleaner and more comfortable prison by far than either the Mammertine or the Cattle Shed. *Here,* Onesimus thought with a touch of bitterness, *is where my father spent his last night.*

He and Peter had been placed in a cell together, and they spent the day sharing their concerns, praying, and waiting in silence. They were just finished with their meager evening meal, when a key turned in the lock, the door opened, and they were amazed to see the two praetorians whom they loved. Realizing that they were accompanied by the prison guard, both Peter and Onesimus were careful not to respond as their hearts dictated. Janus spoke officiously.

"Onesimus, you are to accompany us to the Captain of the Praetorian Guard for questioning."

Onesimus was puzzled, turning to Peter. "I do not know what this means, but I do not want to leave you, Brother Peter."

"Peter is to stay here. Our order has only to do with you. Come!"

Onesimus embraced the big apostle with deep emotion. There were no words to express his feelings. Peter smiled and spoke cheerfully, "God's ways are not our ways, Brother Onesimus. We must accept His will. Go with these guards and the Lord will guard your heart and mind in all that is ahead. You know the prayer I have been praying for you. I will believe it is being answered. Grace and peace go with you."

With these parting words in his ears and with a backward look of affection, Onesimus left the cell and accompanied the two old friends outside the prison.

Once outside, Onesimus walked between the two guards, his hands tied behind him. Janus, standing erect as he walked and looking straight ahead, described in low tones the happening in their new captain's headquarters: "Plutonius and I do not know what it all means, but we have high hopes that Nicia has broken through to the heart of our captain. We have admired his bravery, but we know he is out for himself and willing to do almost anything for advancement. Burrhus appreciated his ability as a praetorianus or he would not have had him as first lieutenant; but, he also knew of his egotistical ambitions."

"Yes," Plutonius put in, "Burrhus was too trusting. What a terrible day this has been for all of us who love him! He was indeed a great and good man—a true Christian. But don't fool yourself. Rufus has a very thick shell about him. If Nicia did break through, it is truly a miracle of grace. Don't count on too much until you have seen just how much Nicia's witness has done to open his heart. I hope you may help him to see the light of the gospel and repent of his dastardly betrayal."

"Whatever happens," Onesimus responded fervently, "I want you two to know how highly I admire you and your witness in this most difficult spot. Please pray for me and I will pray for you, that whatever comes we may be faithful."

They had arrived at the door of the captain's headquarters.

With a silent prayer the guards waited until it opened and led Onesimus into the presence of Rufus.

"Captain Rufus, this is Onesimus, the friend of whom I have been speaking," Nicia said warmly. To Onesimus and the two soldiers' surprise, Rufus commanded Janus to untie Onesimus's hands. Then Rufus slowly walked over and took both of his hands, looking with great curiosity and obvious admiration at the tall young man with the strong face and fearless eyes.

"Onesimus. I have heard much about you."

Then turning to Janus and Plutonius, he dismissed them.

"It is a pleasure to tell you, Onesimus, that as far as my responsibility goes you are free again, as free as when your old master gave you your freedom back in Colossae. You have the courage to live by your convictions, and I admire that above all things."

For the next hour, he sat as one entranced by the story Onesimus told of the reasons for his faith in Christ. Onesimus began with the simple story of the life, death, and resurrection of Jesus and of his once cynical view of this good news.

"But how do you know?" Rufus insisted.

"I asked that same question for many months. I wanted the kind of proof that would have satisfied an Aristotle; but I have discovered that such proof is lacking for most of the truly important realities of our lives, such as the faithfulness of a friend or the love of our mothers. The evidence is in the living."

Onesimus continued to proclaim to him as plainly as he could the way he had come to faith, "the only true freedom" as he described it.

Suddenly Rufus jumped up, remembering that he must be present as the new head of the praetorian guard at the Emperor's banquet, being given, he said, "to celebrate the capture of the evil genius of the Chrestians, the 'Big Apostle,' Simon Peter.

"You have almost persuaded me to seek for faith in your 'Lord Jesus Christ,' as you call Him, though I confess I find difficulty in calling anyone Lord except Caesar. Perhaps this is the reason Caesar Nero considers you Chrestians such a threat to him and to his empire. I also consider that your story, though hard to believe, is the most attractive and hopeful possibility I have ever heard. I respect and love Nicia. I believe in your integrity and honor. Perhaps someday I will consider again the 'good news' you are telling; but now I must be present at my first official function. I shall stand next to Tigellinus at Nero's right hand as captain of his famous praetorian guard." Here he stood erect, his voice filled with pride.

"Nicia, take care of Onesimus and yourself. I don't want to be forced to see you boiled in oil, or burned at the stake, or crucified, or thrown to the lions as so many of your fellow Christians will be. When I have a time of more leisure, I will send Janus or Plutonius to find you. In the meantime, this is our secret, known only to them and to us. Onesimus, good luck with your future. It should be bright and happy if Tigellinus's spies do not find you again."

34

*O*nesimus and Nicia walked out into the streets of the Palatine Hill, hardly able to believe what they had experienced. Both were quiet for a few minutes. Then the dam of their pent-up feelings burst as they stepped onto the porch of one of the many temples, so they could not be observed. They embraced with expressions of thankfulness, and yet of concern. Sitting down on the stone steps, Onesimus was the first to speak.

"My dear Nicia, how can I ever repay you for the miraculous way in which you saved my life? I am sure there is no one else but you who could have secured my release. You did it at the risk of your life, but your witness reached the heart of this unscrupulous man who today has done so much evil. For him to have responded as he did even though he knows you will not return to your old relationship with him is . . . well . . . truly unbelievable."

Nicia stopped the torrent of words. "Brother, who owes what to whom? I will never, never be able to repay the debt I owe you. But from your own teaching, why should we worry about that? We are both saved by the free grace of God. We cannot deserve that nor even the love of our friends. So let us be glad and thankful."

Onesimus, with his head in his hands, agreed and was quiet for a minute as obviously he struggled within himself.

"Nicia, is it wrong for me to take my freedom, when our brother Peter is still in prison waiting to be tortured and put to death? I am burdened with this question. I . . . I just don't know the answer."

"I may not be as good a philosopher as you, brother, but I know the answer. It would be wrong if you did *not* accept this freedom that God in His providence has given to you again. You are needed in Ionia, in Colossae, and in Ephesus to encourage the saints. The persecution we have experienced here is but a sample of that which will come in all the Roman Empire. Who can do more than you to multiply the witness of the apostles Paul and Peter, of these hundreds of noble Christians who are to give their witness as martyrs during these black days? You must accept your calling of God and go back to Colossae to Philemon—and to Helen—and to the people who desperately need your witness. Do you not see how plainly this is your calling?"

Feeling better, Onesimus accompanied Nicia to Lady Pompania's house.

Onesimus's reunion with his friends in the Christian family was ecstatic. Nicia recounted briefly the opportunity he and then Onesimus had been given to share their faith and experience with Rufus Faenus.

"He was much more open and responsive than I could have ever expected," Nicia exclaimed. "Your prayers and the ever-present grace of our Lord made my task easy. I know that all of us are heartsick over his betrayal of our dear brother Burrhus and his part in the imprisonment of Peter, but forgiving love is still Christ's greatest gift to us all. 'Love never fails!' as the apostle Paul was so fond of saying. Sometimes it may seem to fail, but surely the love of Christ was alive today."

"It took a miracle of that love to enable you, Nicia, to forgive this cruel man in such a way that Rufus opened his heart and released me," Onesimus reflected.

"Let us praise God from whom all such blessings flow!" Lady Pompania cried. "Onesimus, now that you are free, surely it is a sign that our Lord needs you for his ministry back in Ionia."

"That is just what Simon Peter said to me as I left him in the praetorian prison. 'You know the prayer I have been praying for you,' he said, 'I believe it is being answered.' Immediately after our arrest, as we rode in the prison cart, he had assured me that he believed I would be freed to return as a witness to the churches in Ionia, and to this end he would be praying. I have shared with Nicia my feelings of guilt at having left him, and now at leaving all of you. But I have no other choice than to believe you and Peter must be right. By your kindness, generosity, and understanding love, I will take the next ship sailing to Ephesus."

All who were present breathed an audible sigh of relief, saying as one, "Thank God you are free! We will help you in your passage."

"Thank you, my very dear brothers and sisters in Christ. But I shall go with a heavy heart. Nicia tells me that tomorrow Nero plans to make a public spectacle of our beloved apostle Simon Peter as he is tortured and put to death. And all that noble hundred in the Cattle Shed will be martyred as well."

That night he packed up his few belongings, including the parchments he had collected of Paul's and Peter's teachings. He looked forward to his return home, but he paused to pray for those who would never return.

Two days passed before a ship sailed from Ostia to Ephesus. During those two days, the little Christian *communitas* passed through the severest trial of its brief history. Onesimus was able to see with his own eyes part of this horrible brutality and suffering—horrible, that is, to the tender hearts of those who loved the apostle Peter and the brave one hundred who died.

Early on Onesimus's last morning in Rome, he attended the worship with the remnants of the Christian *communitas* in the cavern. As he looked out over the haggard, yet still hopeful faces, he knew that over half their original number either had been killed or were awaiting death in the prisons. *Nero should be proud of his minions*, Onesimus thought. *Tigellinus and Rufus are thorough with their job!*

He missed Doctor Luke, who had left Rome soon after the fire at the urging of Peter and the other Christian leaders. *First John Mark was sent to Cyprus, then Doctor Luke to Corinth, and soon I will be in Ionia*, thought Onesimus. *This very day will be Simon Peter's last—and I will not be there to share in his pain and suffering or in his triumphant departure.* Onesimus felt a constriction of his heart, a heaviness that could not be shaken.

He was brought up with a start by the words Linus was saying, for they spoke directly to the grief and feelings of despair that were gripping his heart: "I know how you are tempted to despair," Linus was saying. "But to those of us who believe in the ressurected Lord who promised us, 'Because I live you shall live also', this is not a day of tragedy, but of victory for all those who have been chosen to be his faithful martyrs. Let us rejoice in their triumphant entrance into all that God has prepared for them!

"This afternoon our beloved apostle Peter will meet his Lord again face to face. He has sent word by Janus and Plutonius begging us to be of good cheer and asking for us to pray for him on his last day. Will you join me as we offer up our love and prayers to the Good Shepherd of us all? Let us pray for our brother Simon Peter and for all the others, among whom are some of our own dearest ones."

The assembled congregation knelt together as Linus led in the prayer of thanksgiving and intercession. Onesimus, his heart bursting with sorrow mixed with only a faint sense of hope, looked out on their upturned faces. He would never forget the sublimity of their faith, etched on every line of their brave but sorrowing countenances. But even then it was difficult for him to feel the joy many who faced the test possessed.

My faith is still not strong enough, he confessed to himself.

After the prayers and the celebration of the Eucharist, Onesimus was on the brink of tears as the good Linus announced to the *koinonia* that Onesimus was taking passage that evening from Ostia for Ionia and his home in Colossae. All of the *communitas* knew Onesimus either personally or by the story of his bravery and effectiveness as Paul's *amenuensis* and then Peter's companion.

"Several of you may have something to say to this brilliant and loving young man who has such a tremendous witness to give to his own people back in Colossae and in the other churches of Ionia," Linus suggested.

Onesimus could not keep back the tears but wept unashamedly as Nereus, Junia, Nicia, Marcia, Lady Pompania, and lastly Janus and Plutonius arose to speak their love and appreciation for him. When they had finished, Onesimus rose to give his farewell.

"Dear brothers and sisters in Christ, you will understand the difficulty I have to put in words and to say my thoughts in this hour. I have seen such bravery, such faith, such Christ-like love in you. You have given me so much more than I could ever repay. But for the grace of God who pours out on us through the Holy Spirit more than we can ever deserve, I could not have been anything even resembling the kind of person you describe." Onesimus took a moment to regain his composure and then began to speak with assurance.

"I have seen the greatness of human love and courage, the nobility of the human spirit when transfigured by the Spirit of our living Christ. How could I ever doubt the reality of those unseen truths upon which you are daily, hourly risking your lives and that even this afternoon our honored and beloved apostle Peter will experience—the victorious triumph of fearless martyrs for our Lord.

"In spite of all this brutality and suffering let us remember the words of the apostle Paul, 'these things will not hinder but rather help the furtherance of the gospel of our Lord.' I pray that each of you will be found faithful, and that the witness of our Christian brothers and sisters will be so glorious that many will be awakened to the reality of the love of God as revealed in Christ. For as Brother Peter has said, 'He has destroyed death and brought life and immortality to light through the gospel.' Of this gospel you and I are appointed heralds, teachers, and witnesses. May the grace of our mighty God and Father, the love of our Lord Jesus Christ, and the fellowship and support of the Holy Spirit be with you all now and evermore. Amen."

The whole congregation said "Amen!" and the sound resounded through the cavern. They all crowded around to embrace Onesimus or shake his hand in a heart-opening time when the tender love of the *koinonia* was at its very best.

Soon the assembled Christians dispersed to their work, though many were brave enough to melt into the huge crowd that was even then making standing room only in the Colosseum. There, according to the royal announcement, Simon Peter was to be crucified. Word had come through Janus and Plutonius that he had told the prison guard of his one request, "If they are to crucify me, I ask only that you nail me to the cross with my head downward, no matter the pain; for I am unworthy to die as my Lord died!"

With this heart-numbing news, Onesimus set out for Ostia with only Nereus, Nicia, and Marcia by his side. They traveled in Lady Pompania's carriage, driven by Lucus, her most trusted servant. Nicia told them of the news Janus and Plutonius had shared with him of Nero's plans for the night after the execution of Simon Peter.

"Some fifty crosses are being prepared and holes dug around Nero's garden. The crosses are similar but smaller than the huge cross that will be used in the spectacle of Simon Peter's agony this afternoon. Large pots of oil are being heated. Fifty of the prisoners are to be nailed to these crosses, which then will be lifted in place. The oil will be thrown on their heads and down their bodies and set on fire."

"Could anything be more horrible than that?" Marcia exclaimed, her face covered with her hands.

"Nothing, dear Marcia," her brother continued, "for they are going to keep these bodies burning as long as there is anything left to burn. The citizens of Rome are invited to walk through the garden to see the 'delightful suffering,' as Nero put it in his announcement, 'of these cruel Chrestians who are responsible for burning your homes and many of your loved ones to their death. They will be repaid for their evil by being burned on crosses.' "

The four friends were silent as they imagined the agony through which their fellow Christians were to go.

When they arrived at Ostia, Onesimus bought his passage and said farewell with a whispered prayer for each as they embraced. He walked up the gangplank and, looking back, waved to them as they stood tearfully watching the departure of one who was as dear to them as their closest brother. As the ship pulled away from the harbor, Onesimus reflected that the apostle Peter was at that time being welcomed by his Lord; "that is, if our faith is the truth!" He knew he would still have doubts and that they would be most severe when he was alone.

As Ostia receded into the distance, Onesimus realized that it was the end of a precious but costly era in his life and the beginning of a new one. Would he be as faithful as these brave Roman Christians? Would he be as wise and loving as his beloved friends and brothers, Paul and Peter? For this he prayed with all his heart.

—Part Eight—
Homecoming

35

When Onesimus awakened, it was night on the Mediterranean, with only the dusky pink of the sunset behind the ship. He walked over to the rail and looked at the water rushing in the wake of the trim sailing vessel.

"So it is with our lives," he thought out loud, "we pass through the waters and they close in behind us, leaving not a trace of our passage." Suddenly he realized that he had lapsed back into the mood of an Epicurean. The memories of the past few weeks flashed through his mind, filling him with an unbearable disgust and repulsion. Waves of doubt washed over him, the same nagging doubts he had experienced the day Paul was executed. Onesimus's faith was being engulfed by something deep within that rebelled at the whole human tragedy: the horrors of pain and suffering, the anguish of so many noble innocents, and the overpowering evil of Nero and his followers. He struggled against the onslaught of his doubts like a tired swimmer battling too many huge waves. He heard his voice crying out, "All thy waves and thy billows have gone over me!" Then he went on to shout the remainder of the psalm that had sounded so beautiful when Onesiphorus read it at the beginning of the worship in the cavern that morning:

> "By day the Lord commands His loyal love;
> And at night His song is with me,
>   a prayer to the God of my life.
> Why are you downcast O my soul,
>   and why are you dismayed within me?
> Hope in God: for I shall again praise Him,
>   my help and my God."

The words were lost in the wind and the disappearing wake of the ship. He had felt such hope and assurance that morning, but now the words seemed useless.

He thought of the fifty young Christians being burned on their crosses in Nero's gardens at that moment.

"What price love and goodness?" he asked the wind and the sea. "How could an intelligent person with any reason at all possibly believe that in these events Christ is the victor? Won't Nero's power, motivated by satanic lust and pride, win this battle?"

He remembered the upturned faces of the Christians that morning in the cavern as they sang and prayed; he thought of the courage of Simon Peter as he met his death on the cross he had once so feared. He could still see the newfound joy and hope in the faces of Marcia and Nicia, and the influence of these brave spirits returned to strengthen him as he stood at the ship's rail. Now he wished he had Luke or Peter or Nereus to talk to. He remembered again how he had recoverd his faith the day Paul died, as he walked blindly into the Subura and providentially ran into Marcia. At least, he had *believed* it was more than an accident. As he shared with her what had happened to him, his faith had returned. Summing it all up as the wind and the spray rushed over him, he spoke aloud words he knew were honest concerning the status of his faith.

"Yes, Christ has set me free from guilt and shame and meaninglessness, but I still have to struggle with my doubts concerning the ultimate victory of the love of Christ. I *want* to believe it. I *will* to believe it. But the doubt is still there! For these child-like Christians awaiting death in Rome, the line between the seen and the unseen is so very thin; they are filled with vivid assurance and unquenchable hope! But I—I have only a little faith!"

He was startled by the voice of someone standing near him. "Son, that is what faith is," the strong voice rose above the sounds of the sea, "the assurance of things hoped for, the conviction of things not seen."

Onesimus turned to see the weatherbeaten face of one of the

ship's officers. Evidently he had been standing there listening to Onesimus's soliloquy.

"I am sorry if I surprised you, young man," the sailor said warmly as he put his hand on Onesimus's shoulder. "I am Publius, the ship's mate. I also am a Christian and have been as disturbed as you have by the news of the persecutions in Rome. I heard the gruesome story while our ship was tied up at the docks in Ostia."

Onesimus, relieved, took his outstretched hand.

"Thank the Lord you are here, Brother Publius. You can see how much I need to talk with someone like you."

The mate graciously invited Onesimus to his quarters. Here, protected from the elements, they spent the next two hours sharing their experiences. Onesimus told his story from beginning to end, describing in detail the bittersweet last days in Rome.

"Praise to our Lord, who in all things works for our good— even in this!" the officer's voice was vibrant with exaltation.

"How can you believe that?" Onesimus blurted out of his own mind's agony. "Fifty beautiful Christians sprayed with hot tar and burned slowly to death on their crosses! The noble apostle Peter crucified with his head downward and the loving apostle Paul the victim of Nero's axe! How could any good come out of that?"

"In the same way that our Lord's humiliation and cruel sufferings have opened the eyes of thousands to the love of the mighty Father of us all," Publius answered with deep conviction. "I say to you, Onesimus, the power of those crude crosses will have more influence in the years to come than all of the Neros, Herods, and Pilates who think they have the last word!"

The confidence in his voice and in his eyes calmed the turbulence within his young companion.

"Thank you, Publius, thank you, thank you! Surely the Lord sent you to me this evening. I am ashamed of my doubting, but you have cleared the fog from my eyes. I can and I do believe it! Pray God I always will!"

During the remaining days of an otherwise uneventful voyage, Onesimus spent every hour available with the big-hearted Publius. He learned of the man's own trials after his conversion in Caesarea-Philippi. From a roistering sailor covering up his insecurities by drinking and fighting, he had grown into a strong, happy man whose love made him the confidant of many a sailor who had lost his life's compass in the dark. A year and a few months before he met Onesimus he had returned home after a long voyage to find his wife and four children mutilated and killed by minions of a bitter Roman governor who had set out to eliminate the Christians. Onesimus could see the price Publius had paid.

"When I first heard what had happened, I was ready to take on the whole Roman Army," he reminisced. "I, too, lost my faith. I hated and vowed revenge. My friends in the Christian *communitas* knew I was in need of help, just as you were the other night. They brought me, cursing and raving in my anger and grief, to the house where Phillip the evangelist was staying. Gently and firmly, he let me talk and then taught me what Jesus meant when he said, 'Love your enemies.' I was rebellious at first, but as he described Jesus' words on His cross, forgiving the soldiers who nailed Him there, I began to listen. Phillip said he was not a follower of Jesus at the time and was standing with the mob as Jesus died.

"I recall Phillip's words as he described what this did for him: When the tough centurion, moved by the amazing love of Jesus, cried, 'Surely this man was the Son of God,' he, too, was deeply touched. Suddenly he knew that only One who could call God 'Father' and forgive in an hour like that could be the Victor in life, even though He died."

Publius described how Phillip had walked as one in a dream for several days until he sought and found some of Jesus' disciples. They had helped him to believe, and he was able to share in one of the resurrection appearances of the risen Lord.

"As Phillip told me of his experience of the forgiving love of Jesus, I knew that this was the reality for which I had been looking—the power of love that would enable me to accept and forgive the cruel persons who had killed my dear wife and children. No, I don't like it. I hate the evil within them, the pride and vanity that made them do it, but I have forgiven them. And I believe that His love in the end will conquer!"

"I see it now," Onesimus said with a new humility. "Phillip's love came from the love of Jesus even on the cross. He shared this love with you in your sorrow, and now you are giving the same love to me. Surely there is nothing higher or more to be desired than to know the love of Christ which passes all knowledge."

The ship was pulling into the harbor at Ephesus. An affectionate good-bye was said to Publius as Onesimus walked off the ship and headed toward home and loved ones. Through the remarkable faith of this rough seaman, he had received a renewed confidence in his own ability to meet whatever tests for his faith lay ahead.

His welcome back to the little church in Ephesus and to his family and friends in Colossae was joyous, in spite of the sad news he brought concerning the sufferings of their fellow Christians in Rome. He was given the honor of telling the story and bringing his own message of hope and love both to the church in Ephesus and in Colossae. His experiences with Paul, Peter, Luke, John Mark, and the others in Rome were even more significant as he read portions of the letters he had copied from the two apostles' words and from the notes he had taken of the stories Peter and Luke told of the life of their Lord before and during His trial, crucifixion, and resurrection.

The church in Ephesus did not want to let him go until he had read all the letters. But Onesimus was eager to see Helen, his mother, and the other members of his adopted family. The vision of Helen's face and their last embrace had come to him again and again in his loneliness, especially at night, as he traveled eastward in his berth on the long journey home. With a promise to return and spend several days with the Ephesian church, he told them good-bye and left for Colossae on a horse loaned him by Tyrannus.

As he rode through the gate of Philemon's domain, a shout went up and all the familia rushed out and surrounded him. Archippus embraced him first, then Philemon, his mother, and Apphia. And finally he saw Helen, as he had dreamed so often, in a white silk chiton with a purple chalmys, coming toward him. Everyone was quiet and reverent as he took her in his arms and they walked slowly into the house. The tender moments that followed were a healing balm to the pain of their long separation.

After the worship service early the next morning, in which Onesimus gave several readings from Paul, Peter, and Luke, the family of Philemon met in the atrium to consider the plans for the coming weeks and to hear more of Onesimus's story. He had spent several hours the night before sharing the witness of the Christians in Rome and describing his experiences with the apostles Paul and Peter. But his family was eager for more. After two hours of questions and answers, Philemon stood and said what Onesimus long had wanted to hear, "Onesimus, my son, you have made good use of your freedom. Now you are home at last. We are thankful for your growing faith and for the rich experiences which you will be sharing with us and the other Christians in Ionia in the months to come. We have talked about it at length before you arrived, and we want you to be free to travel and share with the churches as much as you are able. At the same time, I want you to be a partner with Archippus and me in our business of dyeing and selling our fine woolens and silks. We will furnish you with a horse and expenses from our business for your travels—this is only a part of what we owe to the Lord who has made us fellow citizens of His kingdom."

Onesimus responded with gratitude as he accepted their offer.

"The least I can do—after all our Lord has done for me and after all you have done in making possible these months with two of the greatest of His apostles—the least I can do is to share their witness. I will give as much time as possible to sharing the burdens of the business and will try to take my part of the load."

"One last thing, Onesimus." Philemon spoke with a warm

smile as he looked toward Helen, "every one of us knows that you and Helen have been waiting these many months for the fulfillment of your promises to each other, promises made before you parted. Whenever you are ready, we will invite Bishop Papias of the church at Hierapolis, to help us celebrate your marriage."

Helen's lighted face left no doubt as to her feelings, and Onesimus found himself blushing with pleasure.

At twilight they sat in the garden or in the library with only a candle to light their long delayed companionship. Every day he spent at least an hour alone with Helen. They shared thoughts and feelings that often were too deep for words. He was amazed that she understood so well his doubts after Paul's death and his ravaging experiences during the Neronian horrors. He shared with her some of the more delicate and difficult times which he could not tell the others. The hours together were always too short, though the anticipation of their rapidly approaching marriage made the days too long.

Much of his time each day he spent familiarizing himself again with the business of which he was now a partner. He spent hours with Archippus, who made most of the major decisions. Together they went over the books with the new clerk of accounts, Theseus, an intelligent young Greek from Athens whom Philemon had freed because of his honest, open, warm spirit and his superb intelligence. Onesimus remembered him as a boy of eighteen who had been specially tutored by the aged Polectus before his death.

"Recognizing his abilities, father and I have given him special attention since you were away. He has mastered our bookkeeping and the special skills needed in our business."

"I am thankful that Philemon has kept his word in regard to freeing some of the slaves," Onesimus spoke with an enthusiasm which Archippus could well understand.

"Together he and I have sought to find the most worthy and receptive of the slaves in order to give them special attention and training. When we found them trustworthy, we have been happy to set them free."

"You sound as if it has been a good experience."

"Certainly it has. Most of them have chosen to remain with our familia as free men and women, receiving wages that enable them to enjoy a sense of dignity and a certain measure of independence. For instance, they can choose their own clothing and on their days off can visit friends and, on occasion, take several days for a journey to Ephesus. Since Laodicea is so near they can leave early in the morning and spend several hours in the warm waters of the spa."

"How in the world could exslaves be permitted in these exclusive resorts?" Onesimus exclaimed. "I thought only the rich and affluent are seen in such places."

"Father has a way," Archippus laughed. "It happens the owner of one of the best spas is a Christian and sympathetic with what we are doing. So, for a reasonable fee, any member of our familia is admitted. Only one thing Father expects, and he is rather firm here. They must be humble about their freedom and careful not to boast, either to those who are still slaves or to their friends elsewhere."

"This could be a bit dangerous, don't you think?"

"Look at the man talking now!" Archippus joked. "A former slave who ran away at the risk of his life, now speaking about the dangers of freeing other slaves!"

Onesimus smiled broadly, "I'll take my medicine—I deserved that! But have you found this system of wages for freed slaves profitable enough to make it a policy of our business?"

"The persons who are freed and remain in the familia work harder, are happier and more dependable than those who are still slaves. We have seen enough to know that the costs in the long run are less than the old way of forcing as much work as you can out of persons who hate being slaves, even as you did. It works, Onesimus, it works!" Archippus clapped his adopted brother affectionately on the shoulder. "Christ's way of loving respect for others works!"

"It is the only way that will work," Onesimus responded with conviction. "Perhaps we may be able to give a slow push to the arrival of that time when most of the slaves in this sad old empire are free!"

"Now you are dreaming."

"Perhaps so, but I remember Paul's prayer in writing to the Romans: 'May the God of all hope so fill you with all joy and peace by your faith in Him, so that through the power of the Holy Spirit there will be no bounds to your hope.' "

"Before you get your head too far in the clouds, let me tell you that there are any number of our slaves who are so jealous and resentful and whose spirits are so bad we dare not set them free. I don't know how long we can continue part slave and part free, but that's the story." Archippus shook his head.

Onesimus was depressed as he listened.

"There are some who are unwilling to pay the price for freedom."

"It is difficult in this system of slavery for us to set ourselves up as judges as to who is and who is not ready for physical freedom. One thing I would say in general: those who cannot be freed externally are generally the ones who are unwilling to open their minds and hearts to the Spirit of our Lord."

"Where the Spirit of the Lord is, there is liberty." Onesimus again found himself quoting the apostle Paul. "I suppose there are those who have learned how to deceive, to pretend a faith and a spirit they do not have in order to be freed?"

"I'm afraid so," Archippus sighed, "and that is the agonizing heartbreak of our position. You remember Leslia?"

Onesimus blushed.

"Her wiles were not only for you but also for our young Theseus. For a while we were afraid she would either break his heart or force us to set her free. Fortunately, Theseus awakened one day to see that he was being used. When he told her he would see her no more, she was so indignant at what she called his 'prudery' that she asked father to sell her to some other master where she would not be subject to 'your crazy religion'!"

"Your father is a wise good man, Archippus. I am sure he

took her at her word. I just hope she will find herself before she hurts too many others."

The day for the marriage arrived. For two weeks the best seamstresses in the familia had been preparing the bridal gown. The day before, the well-loved Papias, bishop of the church of Hierapolis, arrived. He spent several hours conversing with Onesimus and then with the bride and groom together. He was so moved over hearing the reports of Onesimus's stay in Rome, he almost forgot to inquire concerning the couple's attitudes toward each other.

Papias, a middle-aged man, was a former jeweler who, like Philemon, had been converted to the Christian faith after listening to Paul in the Agora at Ephesus. With an unusually keen mind, he had spent much time learning all he could from Paul during his stay in Ephesus. This, combined with his ability to speak with great power, made his leadership and influence known throughout Ionia. He was a man of intense convictions. He owned a thriving business in the manufacture and sale of gold and silver vessels and ornaments and had a large familia of slaves. Through the influence of his friend, Philemon, he also had begun the practice of freeing those slaves he thought capable of using their freedom wisely. His wife, the mother of his two sons, had died. His sons were old enough to share the business responsibilities, leaving him free to spend much of his time as overseer of the growing flock of believers. Several of these had also found their new life of faith in Christ through the apostle Paul. Among them, Papias stood high as their friend and counselor and soon was acknowledged to be their shepherd.

Having studied as a youth in the gymnasium at Pergamos, Papias was well-versed in the philosophers. With his winsome and attractive personality, he was already one of the city's civic and social leaders. When he became a Christian, it was only natural that some of the other leaders of Hierapolis should become interested and several had been baptized as members of the church that met in Papias's house. He was of good repute among all the people.

Knowing of this, Onesimus was thankful for an opportunity to talk with Papias. Part of the time that afternoon they spent making plans for Onesimus's itinerary through the several churches of Asia.

"You are greatly needed in Ionia at this time, my dear Onesimus," Papias said with enthusiasm. "Your witness to the terrifying, yet heartening, events in Rome and your relationship with Paul and Peter and Doctor Luke, plus what I have heard of your Spirit-filled ability to share your experiences so effectively—all equip you to do for your fellow Christians in our Ionian churches what we need so greatly. We know that our time of testing is coming; it has already begun in Philadelphia and Smyrna, where the leaders of the synagogue have direct connections with the Jewish leaders in Rome and Jerusalem. Wild tales about the gross evils practiced by the Christians have been spread here as well as in Rome. We need your witness."

"I will be most happy to give as much time as is needed," Onesimus replied simply. "Philemon and Archippus have agreed that I should be absent from our business to visit and preach in the churches. Though I hasten to say, I feel most unworthy to represent such great men as Paul and Peter, I will do the best I can."

"Having listened to you this afternoon and hearing from the Ephesian Christians how powerful your witness is, I am sure you will be of great service to our Lord and to the people in our churches. But don't forget, young man, you have some very important obligations as a husband to the lovely Helen."

"Thank you for your trust in me and your concern for our marriage, Brother Papias. Your coming is a signal honor to us all, especially to Helen and to me."

That evening the family met at dinner with Papias at the center of the table next to the bride and groom. The wedding feast would be the next evening when all the friends and members of the familia were invited. This evening was a private dinner enriched by Papias's presence and the happy thoughts of tomorrow's events. The planning and preparation for both of these meals had been made by Alcestia, who now sat at dinner with her eyes glistening with the joy of a mother whose prayers had been answered. Though she was also now a free woman, she had chosen to remain and to preside over the preparation and service of the food for her newly adopted family as well as for the familia of slaves.

That night in the new room built for him and for Helen, Onesimus slept alone—what time he did sleep. His thoughts were full of memories and of thankfulness but also of prayers for his own constancy. He knew the vagaries of his own mind and heart. He did not want to hurt or betray the innocent, trusting love of Helen or the confidence shown in him by Philemon, Papias, and the Christian leaders. His renewed experience of faith on board ship under the inspiration of the rough seaman, Publius, had done something for him.

"Surely, Lord," he prayed as he lay looking at the stars through the window, "You know what is in me. You know how difficult the struggle with my doubts. I will trust You for the days to come. 'I can do all things through You who strengthen me.' "

At length he went to sleep with a deep sense of peace and well-being.

36

The marriage between Helen and Onesimus was celebrated first at a simple worship service held in the garden at the fifth hour of the afternoon. Papias, clad in a long, white silk tunic with a purple belt around his waist, stood in the center under an arch covered with green vines, to which were fastened hundreds of red roses and white lilies cut from the gardens of several of Philemon's friends. All of the familia were present, washed, perfumed, and in their best clothes. The members of the church of Colossae sat together on wooden benches. Also present by invitation were numerous other citizens of the city, waiting with some curiosity to see a "Christian wedding." The common practice among both Jewish and Gentile families was to celebrate a wedding primarily at the wedding banquet; a "worship service" such as this was a new experience.

Before Papias entered, musicians had presented a concert of traditional Greek wedding music, and they continued to play as Apphia and Alcestia entered, followed by Archippus and Onesimus from one side and Helen and Philemon from the other. Helen's wedding dress was a masterpiece of simplicity and beauty. Her face was radiant. The music stopped as she and Onesimus stood together before the bishop, with the others grouped on each side.

The silence was broken by a harpist beginning the accompaniment of the beautiful hymn to love and freedom Alcestia had sung at the first worship service after Onesimus was set free. At the request both of Onesimus and Helen, she lifted her voice rich with emotion:

> Lord of all Your great creation,
> You who made us to be free,
> Praise to You for love You give us,
> Breaking chains of hate and greed,
> Bonds of love that can't be broken.
>
> Bind us as Your chosen people
> Meeting each one's deepest needs
> Peace of Yours when wrong would hurt us—
> We forgive as we're forgiven.
> You who loved us in our bondage
> Bore our wounds upon the cross
> Now we praise with joyful language!

Papias began a brief homily that stirred the deepest feelings in Onesimus and Helen and in the others who loved them. He recounted the story that the apostle John had told of the

wedding in Cana of Galilee, in which Jesus had blessed the
marriage and shared in the festivities.

"Let us be thankful for the presence of the living Christ who
through the Holy Spirit blesses you, Onesimus and Helen, as
you become one in the sacred bonds of the love He has given
you."

Then to Onesimus's great joy he read the beautiful "Hymn to
Love," which had become such a valued part of their spiritual
treasures.

"Let this gift of *agape* love now be the foundation of your life
together," Papias concluded, as he joined their hands together
and asked them to kneel. He placed his hands on their heads
and, lifting his voice, said with great power, "May the eternal
Father make you to be one together as husband and wife so that
you may be united in the love of our Lord Jesus Christ, sharing
your joys and sorrows, your pains and happiness in the communion of the Holy Spirit. What God has united let no one
divide. Rise, Onesimus and Helen, and stand before our Lord,
your family and friends. You are now one in Him whose you are
and whom you serve. Amen!"

As Onesimus and Helen rose from their knees and turned
first to embrace each other and then the members of their
family, the Christians stood and burst into singing, "Praise God
from whom all blessings flow. . . ."

It was a high moment in their lives as tears mingled with
laughter and the blessings of those who had such happy reasons
to be thankful. Even the unbelievers were moved by the drama
of the scene, though the prayer to "the Father" and to "our
Lord Jesus Christ," asking for the "communion of the Holy
Spirit" sounded strange to their ears. As friends of Philemon's
family, they joined in the delightful gaity of the hour.

On the other side of the garden, a large tent had been set up
under which the wedding banquet was being prepared. Since
early morning Creto and his helpers had been roasting the
meat, cooking the vegetables, and setting out the fruits and
pastries for the great feast. At the sixth hour in the afternoon,
the musicians began to play festive music as the family and

guests gathered around two huge tables. The tables were long enough to include all of the familia except those who were serving the dinner.

Those who were not Christians were surprised that freed men and women and slaves sat together, but Archippus passed the word that they were invited at Onesimus's request. The guests had heard the story of Onesimus's experience as a runaway slave and Philemon's forgiveness and manumission. Though some of them disapproved in general of the idea of freeing slaves, they had respect for Philemon and, with some whispering among themselves, decided to accept the situation without protest. Privately, several of them agreed this was a dangerous practice that could threaten their whole economy. These Christians would need to be watched.

The climactic moment of the wedding banquet came after the simple and touching "Thanks to our Lord Jesus Christ" was offered by Philemon—another practice strange to the unbelievers. Then he stood to speak.

"As the father of the bride and the adopted father of the groom, it is my great happiness to present to them the golden goblet from which they are to drink together for the first time as husband and wife. I do so with praise to our Lord who in all things is working for good for those who love Him and accept His purpose. I am grateful beyond words for the priceless gift of the Father of us all in sending His own Son that we might have this kind of true freedom to love and to serve each other. Onesimus and Helen, I give you this cup. As you drink together from it, may you also drink from the Water of Life so that you will never thirst. From the home which you are beginning, may there be a well of water springing up for many others unto eternal life!"

Onesimus and Helen grasped the cup together, and while everyone else held their breath, they lifted the large goblet to their lips and drank from it. A cheer went up from the assembled family and guests, the Christians all saying, "Praise the Lord." With high spirits and much laughter, the banquet continued. To Onesimus the whole day had seemed a dream.

Papias began talking with him concerning his coming to Hierapolis. Onesimus responded, "I promised the Ephesian Christians to return as soon as possible. Helen and I plan to take the first of our days of married life together and journey to Ephesus. After we return home, I will come to Hierapolis and share my story, as I will be happy to do for all the other churches in Asia."

"Helen, you had better make the most of these days together," Papias said laughing. "I am sure your husband is going to be traveling for some time to come." Then he spoke seriously, "It is a providence of our Lord to have you with us, Onesimus. I also have received word from the church at Antioch inviting you to come. But do not neglect the lovely Helen."

"You can be sure, Bishop Papias, I will never do that. She can accompany me some of the time, but I plan to spend as much time as possible here with Philemon and Archippus assisting in our business."

When the banquet was over and the guests had gone, the little family met in the atrium for evening prayers. It was a rich time of fellowship together, of shared thanks and intercessions for the new family begun.

When the little meeting ended and they were left alone, Onesimus embraced Helen tenderly. With their arms around each other, they walked down to their old trysting place, the bridge over the Lycus River.

As they stood in silence looking down at the waterfall where the two underground streams came together, both knew that in the same way their lives were now united and would flow together to a limitless future, in spite of barriers and difficult straits. Onesimus drew his bride closer and whispered, "It seems our separation was a thousand years ago . . . God is so good to us . . . Oh, my beautiful Helen . . . !"

Helen turned and, caressing his face, lifted her lips to his and kissed him tenderly. Then, holding his face between her two soft hands, she looked into his eyes adoringly. "Oh, Onesimus, I have dreamed and prayed and waited for this hour . . . You are my dearest one . . . how could I have lived without you!"

He drew her to him and a long passionate kiss declared the beginning of their journey together. Words were out of place as they walked back to their new home. They knew with conviction that nothing, not even death, could separate them from the love of Christ and from each other.

Epilogue

Tradition tells us that for the next thirty years, Onesimus served with the apostle John who is now called not only the bishop of Ephesus but the bishop of Ionia. Thus John was spiritual leader over all of what today is called Asia Minor. As the beloved apostle grew older and weaker, Onesimus grew stronger and wiser.

John died as a very old man of ninety-five or more years. Onesimus at the age of fifty-five was chosen by the people in the church at Ephesus as their bishop, succeeding the beloved apostle.

A fascinating story remains of Onesimus's later life. It has yet to be imagined how his faith was severely tested again and again by the earthquake destroying Colossae in 64 A.D., taking most of his family; by the Christian gnostics whose heresies were so appealing to his philosophic mind and yet so divisive in the church; and by the continuing persecutions under the emperors who succeeded Nero. The story also includes Onesimus as one of those who listened, with the other disciples, to the aged apostle John as he told of the life, teachings, death, and resurrection of Jesus Christ.

As bishop of Ephesus, Onesimus was peculiarly equipped through his own growth in faith to enable his flock to be strong and fearless in the second wave of persecutions after Nero. As Eusebius's Chronicle declares,

The Emperor Domitian was the first to proclaim himself Lord and

God . . . Domitian was the second after Nero to persecute the Christians.

Then followed the third wave of persecutions under the Emperor Trajan. In 117 A.D. the Roman Governor in Antioch, according to Pliny, arrested Ignatius, bishop of Antioch. Chained to ten soldiers, he was taken overland through Cilicia and Asia Minor to Rome where he was killed. On his way he was permitted to stop at Laodicea, Philadelphia, and finally Smyrna. Here he was met by the famed Polycarp and delegates from the neighboring churches of Ephesus, Magnesia, and Tralia. Among the leaders present was Onesimus, bishop of Ephesus.

Writing afterward to the church in Ephesus, Ignatius describes the modest, quiet but strong character of Onesimus:

> I received the welcome of your congregation in the presence of Onesimus, your bishop in this world, a man whose love is beyond words. My prayer is that you should love him in the spirit of Jesus Christ and all be like him. Blessed is He who let you have such a bishop.

Thus, one who once was determined to be his own master instead became a slave of Christ—perhaps that he might learn to govern with compassion the people of God under his charge in Ephesus. The words of Paul and John would remain his anthem, with Helen joining him:

> Stand fast in the freedom with which Christ has set you free. . . And above all, love one another, for God is love.

Chronology of the life of Onesimus

With Approximate Dates

		Roman Emperor	Onesimus's Age
Birth of Onesimus	33 A.D.		
Sold as slave to Philemon	50 A.D.	Claudius (41-57)	17
First trip to Ephesus	56 A.D.	Nero (57-68)	23
Escape to Rome	April 60 A.D.	"	27
With the apostle Paul	June 60 A.D.	"	27
Return to Colossae	August 61 A.D.	"	28
Return to Rome	October 61 A.D.	"	28
Execution of the apostle Paul	March 62 A.D.	"	29
Burning of Rome and Execution of Simon Peter	May 62 A.D.	"	29
Return to Colossae and Marriage to Helen	June 62 A.D.	"	29
Earthquake destroying Colossae	October 64 A.D.	"	31
Return to Ephesus as assistant to the apostle John	65 A.D.	"	32
Sharing in writing of the Gospel of John	90 A.D.	Domitian (81-96)	57
Death of the apostle John	92 A.D.	"	59
Onesimus as bishop of Ephesus	92-117 A.D.	Nerva (96-98)	59
Collection of Paul's Writings	107 A.D.	"	74
Visit with Ignatius in Smyrna on his way to execution in Rome	117 A.D.	Trajan	84
Death of Onesimus	117 A.D.	"	84

About the Author

The details and background of *Escape from Ephesus* are authentic. First published in 1980 and titled *Onesimus*, Lance Webb brings to this, his first historical novel, an enthusiasm and scholarship brimming with color and life.

Webb spent nineteen years researching early Christian history and tradition, as well as studying Greek and Roman history, customs, philosophy, mythology, art, and architecture.

He personally visited the historical sites of ancient Colossae, Hierapolis, Laodicea, Ephesus, Smyrna, and Pergamos, as well as Rome, Athens, Corinth, and other Greek cities. To gain a local perspective, Webb employed a taxi and hired a Turkish ranger as guide.

Webb received his B.A. from McMurry College, Abilene, Texas; B.D. from Perkins School of Theology, Dallas; M.A. from Southern Methodist University, Dallas; and has done extensive post-graduate work spanning a thirty-year period at Union School of Theology, New York City. He has eight honorary doctorates. He is the author of numerous books, including *Conquering the Seven Deadly Sins*, *Disciplines for Life in the Age of Aquarius*, *God's Surprises*, *Make Love Grow*, and *On the Edge of the Absurd*.

The story of Onesimus was written in order to "recreate in our imaginations the indomitable spirit of the early Christians" and to "deal adequately with the powerful Christian movement of the last half of the first century."

Webb lives in Dallas, Texas.